# THE LAST VICTIM

Kali's eyes were riveted on the sketch the clerk had brought in. It showed a young woman with curly, shoulder-length hair; apple cheeks; and wide set eyes.

"Who's that?" she asked, trying for offhand indifference and failing.

Michelle Parker seemed not to notice. "That's what we'd like to know. Her body was found a couple of weeks ago."

*Body.* "She's dead? How did she die?"

"Asphyxiation. She was dumped in a wash in East Country. Looks like she'd been dead a couple of weeks, maybe longer."

Kalie's mouth was dry. She forced herself to swallow. "You must know *something* about her."

"Best guess is she was in her late teens or early twenties."

*Breathe,* Kali reminded herself. *Keep calm and don't give anything away until you've had time to think this through.*

When Kali got to the main lobby, she slipped into the women's room, where she splashed cold water on her face and rinsed out her mouth. It couldn't be, she told herself. The similarity was too striking to be a coincidence. The young woman in the sketch who'd been so brutally murdered had to be Olivia's friend—the redhead on the right in John's mysterious photo . . .

Books by Jonnie Jacobs

Kali O'Brien Novels of Legal Suspense

SHADOW OF DOUBT

EVIDENCE OF GUILT

MOTION TO DISMISS

WITNESS FOR THE DEFENSE

COLD JUSTICE

INTENT TO HARM

THE NEXT VICTIM

The Kate Austen Mysteries

MURDER AMONG NEIGHBORS

MURDER AMONG FRIENDS

MURDER AMONG US

MURDER AMONG STRANGERS

THE ONLY SUSPECT

Published by Kensington Publishing Corporation

# THE NEXT VICTIM

## JONNIE JACOBS

**PINNACLE BOOKS**
**KENSINGTON PUBLISHING CORP.**
www.kensingtonbooks.com

PINNACLE BOOKS are published by

Kensington Publishing Corp.
850 Third Avenue
New York, NY 10022

All Kensington titles, imprints, and distributed lines are available at special quantity discounts for bulk purchases for sales promotions, premiums, fund-raising, educational, or institutional use. Special book excerpts or customized printings can also be created to fit specific needs. For details, write or phone the office of the Kensington special sales manager: Kensington Publishing Corp., 850 Third Avenue, New York, NY 10022, attn: Special Sales Department; phone 1-800-221-2647.

ISBN-13: 978-0-7860-1668-6
ISBN-10: 0-7860-1668-X

First Printing: June 2008

10  9  8  7  6  5  4  3  2  1

Printed in the United States of America

*For Rod, Matthew, and David*

*With Special thanks to*
*Camille, Peggy, and Rita*

# CHAPTER 1

The call came a little after two in the morning and pulled Erling from a particularly pleasant dream. As a homicide detective with the Pima County Sheriff's Department, he was used to being awakened at odd hours, but engaging his brain was always a struggle. He remained blurry eyed, clinging to the remnants of sleep, until the dispatcher read off the address of the crime scene—one that was painfully etched in Erling's memory.

Instantly, he was fully alert.

His pulse quickened and an involuntary cry escaped from his lips, waking Deena, who had long ago learned to sleep through the intrusion of middle-of-the-night calls. She shot him an inquiring look, which he pretended not to see.

"Sorry, honey," he said. "I've got to go."

"What is it?"

"Just work."

"Figures." Deena sighed and rolled over, turning her back to him.

A shaft of moonlight illuminated her form and Erling took a moment to study the familiar curves of her body, the splash of auburn hair streaked with gray. There were times he could still see in her the playful and sexy woman he'd married twenty years earlier. What he saw more often, though, or rather felt, was an aloofness tinged with reproach. It had been that way for four years—since their eleven-year-old son, Danny, had died in a skateboarding accident. Erling could never decide whether the tragedy had caused the problems in their marriage or simply exacerbated existing ones he'd been blind to at the time.

Erling headed for the bathroom, where he showered quickly before pulling on slacks and a collared knit shirt. Before leaving the house he gently shook Deena.

"Don't forget, Mindy needs to be up by seven in order to study for her sociology test." At eighteen, their daughter still had trouble getting out of bed on her own.

"I'll make sure she's up."

He kissed Deena on the cheek. "Have a good day."

"I'd tell you the same but I guess a dead body kind of precludes that."

Especially given the address, Erling thought, with an ache in his gut.


There was no mistaking that the large, tile-roofed house on Canyon View Drive was a crime scene. Half a dozen patrol cars were parked in front. The coroner's van and mobile crime tech unit sat in the driveway. Yellow police tape cordoned off the house entrance and part of the yard. Already, a news helicopter was circling overhead.

As he passed under the tape and through the front door, Erling felt a tremor of longing and sadness. *Please*, he whispered silently, *don't let it be her.*

Inside, the evidence of carnage was everywhere. A blue hand-blown glass vase had been knocked from the library table, one of the floor lamps had been overturned, and the rocking chair lay on its side. Bits of flesh and brain matter were splattered against the cherry cabinets. Dark, sticky blood pooled on the terra-cotta tile floor. Erling had trouble breathing.

Across the room, he could see a female form crumpled against the wall. Olive-toned skin. Wavy black hair, long enough to fall below the shoulders. Erling felt a surge of relief. Definitely not Sloane.

"Other one's over there," the uniformed officer told him, pointing in the direction of the fieldstone fireplace. An image flashed in Erling's mind: Sloane in front of a blazing fire, facing him and slowly unbuttoning her blue silk blouse. *Don't think about it,* he told himself. *Stay cool and don't think.*

"It's pretty awful," the uniform warned. "I couldn't do more than take a peek myself."

Erling glanced over and saw a woman's leg and sandaled foot protruding from behind the sofa. Female also, but fair. He didn't recognize the shoes but that didn't mean anything. He hadn't seen Sloane in five months.

He said a silent prayer as he moved closer. The body was sprawled on the floor, arms and legs akimbo, the face largely blown away. Erling's gut rumbled and churned.

*It might not be her. No way to know for sure without a formal ID.*

But in his heart, he knew. The curve of the neck, the mole on her shoulder, the jade and silver ring on her right hand. Swallowing hard against the bile that threatened to rise in his throat, he crammed his shaking hands into his jacket pockets, hoping no one would notice, and closed his mind to the memories.

Erling experienced a familiar tug of anger and sadness at the senseless loss of life. The feelings came with the job, he supposed. Only this time the mantle of professional distance failed him. This wasn't just another victim; this was a woman he'd held and kissed, and laughed and loved with. This was Sloane.

Michelle Parker, his partner of six months—a younger detective with the tenacity of a bulldog—had been talking to the responding officers when he had arrived. Now, notebook still in hand, she crossed from the wall of windows in the living room to join Erling by the kitchen archway.

Michelle brushed a wisp of chestnut brown hair from her forehead. "What a way to start the day, huh?"

"It's what we do," he snapped. His chest was so tight he could barely breathe.

Michelle's face registered surprise at the curt response. A moment of hollow silence followed while she regarded him thoughtfully. "Some of us do it in better humor than others," she said finally.

The sudden, if subtle, hint of tension in the air jolted him like the snap of a rubber band against his skin. *Get a grip, Shafer. You want the whole damn world to know?*

"So, what've we got?" he asked, more hospitably.

Michelle glanced at her notebook. "Call came in just after midnight. A neighbor noticed the lights had been on all day and the morning paper hadn't been picked up. She called the house and when no one answered came over and rang the bell. Then she went around the side and peeked in the window. She saw a body on the floor and called nine-one-one."

"Do we have an ID on the victims?"

"Nothing positive. Best guess is that the older one is Sloane Winslow. This is her home."

*Older one.* Erling cringed. Sloane was only forty-one, two years younger than himself, and much too lovely to be called *older*.

"Her maiden name was Logan." Michelle paused. "As in Logan Foods."

When he didn't respond right away, she added, "The grocery chain."

Erling whistled softly. It bought him a moment's time. "You know anything about the family?"

"I didn't even know it was a family business until the neighbor filled me in. Do you?"

The moment of truth.

Or not.

Erling knew he should remove himself from the investigation. He had personal connections to one of the victims. Emotional connections. Big-time emotional connections. Department policy dictated he step aside and let someone else handle it.

But he couldn't do that. Not without explaining. Word would get around. Eventually it would get back to Deena. His stomach clenched. He couldn't. He simply couldn't take that chance. Not after Danny.

Besides, he wanted to personally nail the creep who'd done this. He needed to do it—for Sloane even more than for himself.

Michelle gave him that curious look again. She was still waiting for an answer.

"Only what I read in the papers," Erling said. The lie burned his tongue. Maybe, just maybe, they'd find the killer and wrap this up quickly.

"So, tell me."

"The grandfather started the business right here in Tucson. Sloane Winslow and her brother, Reed Logan, have controlling interest, though it's Reed who actually runs the company. Winslow lived in L.A. with her husband. It wasn't until she divorced and returned to Tucson a few years ago that she got involved in the business at all."

"Local gentry, local money." Michelle frowned. "I guess this one's going to be in the headlines."

"Afraid so." They looked at one another and Erling voiced what they were both thinking. "The lieutenant will put our feet to the fire if we don't hand him a suspect in short order."

"Can we do that?"

"You tell me. How's it look?"

Michelle flipped to a different page in her notebook. "Crawford's here from the medical examiner's office. His initial estimate is that they've been dead twenty-four to thirty-six hours. Both were shot at close range. The older woman in the head. The younger one in the chest and right leg. Weapon appears to be a shotgun."

Again Erling felt the tightness in his chest. Sloane moved with grace. A woman completely comfortable in her own skin. He couldn't imagine the terror she must have felt when she saw the gun in the killer's hands. His mind flashed to a vision of Sloane trying frantically to fend off the inevitable. For a moment, he couldn't breathe. Then he shook his thoughts clear.

"We have the weapon?" he asked.

"No." Michelle paused and glanced around the room. "Looks like they put up a fight, doesn't it? But even with two of them, they'd be no match for a sleazeball with a gun."

Erling grunted agreement. "Any ID on the second victim?" he asked, moving in to take a closer look. She appeared to be in her late teens or early twenties. The *older woman* comment made sense to him now.

"The neighbor who called it in is a regular verbal fountain. Says there was a young woman living here with Winslow. Olivia Perez is the name. She was a student at the university."

"A relative?" Last Erling knew, Sloane had been living alone.

"A boarder, I think."

"A boarder?"

"I know, it doesn't make a lot of sense. The Logans must be loaded."

Certainly not in need of taking in boarders. "What do we have in the way of trace evidence?" Erling sent a silent prayer to the heavens for a dumb perp. One who'd left fingerprints and fibers, maybe even his driver's license.

"We won't know until the techs have finished going over the place. But there's an old guy a couple of houses down who gave us the description of a car he saw out front Tuesday night. A silver Porsche with a broken taillight. If Crawford's right about the time of death, that would put the car here near the time of the murders."

An eyewitness wasn't as good as a dumb perp, but Erling would take it. At least a Porsche wasn't your average, run-of-the-mill kind of car. "Did the old guy see anyone?"

"He thinks the driver was male but can't say for sure."

"What about other neighbors?"

"Nothing so far. The houses are pretty far apart and private."

That was one of the things Sloane had liked about living in this part of Tucson. It wasn't as affluent as some of the newer gated communities, but the houses were all set on large lots, many of them an acre or more, and the neighborhood landscaping had matured to the point where plantings provided a screen. They'd made love one night out in the yard under the black, star-speckled sky. Erling remembered the soft breeze that grazed their skin, the lilac scent of Sloane's hair, and the rough texture of the nubby blanket beneath them.

The crime scene photographer reached into his equipment bag. "I'm about done here unless there's something in particular you want."

"You get both stills and movies?" Erling asked. His voice was gruff with the invasion of memories.

"Right. And I checked with Crawford about shots of the vics."

"When do you think you'll be able to get us prints?"

"Later today good enough?"

"That the best you can do?" Erling asked.

The photographer capped his camera. "Afraid so."

"I guess it's good enough, then." He turned to Michelle. "Anyone notified next of kin yet?"

"Boskin and Dutton are on their way to the brother's. Maybe he can give us more on the girl."

"Let's hope so."

Independently, Michelle and Erling walked the crime scene, taking their own measurements, making their own sketches. Erling pulled out his palm-sized digital camera and shot the room from a dozen angles. The crime scene photographers did a terrific job, but he liked to have his own pictures, too, because they sometimes jogged his memory and filled in the details of his sketches.

"What's your take?" Erling asked as they worked. "First impression."

Michelle rocked back on her heels and frowned. She was wearing dark, form-fitting slacks and a cream-colored silk shirt that draped softly over the swell of her breasts—her standard uniform for the job, even when she was called out in the middle of the night.

He'd initially resisted being partnered with her because he'd considered her a lightweight, or worse. But Erling had come to see that despite the eye-catching body and head of soft, brown curls, she was as earnest and intense as anyone he'd worked with before. A little too intense sometimes.

"I'd say there's a good chance the killer was someone Winslow was familiar with," Michelle replied. "Either that or she was comfortable enough with what she saw that she had no qualms about letting him in. There's no sign of forced entry, and both victims were dressed in street clothes, so it's not like they were rousted from bed in the middle of the night. The lights are on, and there's an open bottle of brandy on the counter."

Had she been entertaining a new lover? Erling wondered. But the girl, Olivia, was in the house. He doubted Sloane would bring a man home under that circumstance.

Michelle gestured toward Sloane's body. "Looks like the killer went for her first, and while she was trying to fend him off, the younger woman surprised them. He got Mrs. Winslow in the head, probably standing close to her. The girl . . . my guess is that the autopsy will show she was hit from farther away."

"Not bad for someone who's only worked a couple of homicides," Erling said. Michelle had worked vice in Phoenix before moving to Tucson and signing on as a detective with the sheriff's department.

She acknowledged the compliment with a slight twist of her head. "Doesn't mean it's right."

"No, it doesn't, and it's good to remember that."

"You get locked into a mind-set too soon," she said, parroting one of Erling's favorite adages, "and you'll miss the important stuff."

"Guess I've hammered that one home."

"You might say that." This time there was the faintest hint of a smile. "Shall we check the rest of the house?"

Erling took a deep breath to still the pounding in his chest. Sloane's house. Sloane's things. Rooms charged with bittersweet memories. He wasn't sure he could manage it.

Finally he nodded. "Now's as good a time as any."

A canvass of the home was standard procedure for detectives in instances like this. The techs processed the actual crime scene, but careful inspection of a victim's personal possessions revealed a lot about his or her life. Some of it interesting, most of it dull and irrelevant to the murder. Sometimes, though, they got lucky. A receipt, a phone number, a photo, some small tidbit that would eventually lead them to the killer.

But normally the detective and the victim were strangers.

Erling and Michelle spent the next forty minutes going through dressers, files, desk drawers, wastebaskets, and medicine cabinets. He was half afraid he'd find something that marked his own previous presence in the house, and equally fearful of discovering that Sloane had obliterated his memory. He almost smiled when he found the copper and bronze pendant he'd bought her for Christmas last year laid out on the velvet lining of her jewelry drawer.

"Looks like she was a stylish woman," Michelle said at one point.

Erling shrugged. "I wouldn't know about that."

He paused at a familiar sight on Sloane's bureau: a framed picture of Sloane and her brother, Reed, taken during a family barbecue. Her fair skin was virtually unlined, her blue-green eyes sparkling with humor. And often, Erling recalled, with mischief. He felt an ache in his gut, a longing somewhere deep inside him that was less about her death than his own loss.

It had been a brief affair, six months and fourteen days, to be exact. Over since early May. Him like a panting mongrel around a pedigreed bitch in heat. Her words, but they resonated as much as they stung. His behavior was nothing to be proud of. Erling had known that even then. Still, he'd wanted to hate her for ending it. There were times he'd come close. But he'd certainly never wished her dead.

By the time he and Michelle finished their canvass of the house, the sun was just rising over the hills near Sabino Canyon. Morning was Erling's favorite time of day. Blue, cloudless sky, wide and open, the air soft, just beginning to build to the blinding heat of day.

Leaving the house, he saw that the media were already out in force. A cameraman from one of the local news channels shoved a camera in Erling's face. His cohort held a mic.

"Detective Shafer," the reporter shouted, "what can you tell us? We understand there's been a homicide inside. Two victims. Was one of them Sloane Logan Winslow?"

"We're not prepared to make a statement at this time," Erling barked.

He could only hope Boskin and his partner would be able to notify Sloane's family before they learned about her death live on television. Erling figured the murders would be the lead story on the morning news.

# CHAPTER 2

John O'Brien pulled his Porsche GT3 into the Logan
Foods garage and parked in his reserved space, nosing the
bumper up to the sign that read EXECUTIVE VICE PRESIDENT.
The left side of his jaw was still numb from his morning visit
to the dentist. He checked in the rearview mirror for drool,
then brushed an errant speck of amalgam from his cheek before pulling his briefcase and jacket from the passenger seat.

With a flicker of irritation, he noted that Reed Logan's
slot was empty. John had raced from the dentist's to be in
time for their one o'clock conference call with Goldman
Sachs, and Reed wasn't even back from lunch. Not surprising really, given Reed's propensity for being late, but irksome all the same. At least A. J. Nash, their chief counsel,
would be on hand for the call and probably better prepped
than anyone else there.

Skirting the main entrance to the building, John took the
private, side doorway that led directly to the executive offices, thus saving himself a pro forma smile and cheery good
morning to the layers of receptionists and clerical staff sta-
tioned along the public approaches. As he neared his office,
he saw his secretary, Alicia, of the long scarlet nails, huddled
at her desk with Reed's secretary, whose knockout body
made the state of her nails irrelevant. The two women were

clutching wads of tissue and dabbing at their eyes. The latest boyfriend fiasco, John decided. There was at least one a month.

"Oh, Mr. O'Brien," Alicia wailed. "I'm so glad you're here."

Perhaps not a boyfriend problem, after all. A mishap at one of the stores maybe? That would explain Reed's absence. John felt a knot of tension form in his chest. Things were dicey enough for him already with the board of directors.

"I told you I'd be late," John offered, in case Reed or A.J. had been ranting about his absence.

"You haven't heard?"

"Heard what?"

"About Mrs. Winslow. It's been on the news."

"Sloane? What about her?"

Alicia choked back a sob. "She's dead."

John's mind reeled. It took a moment for the words to register.

"Murdered," Alicia explained.

Reed's secretary chimed in but John heard none of what she said. Heard nothing but the pounding of his own pulse in his ears. He gripped the edge of the desk to steady himself.

Sloane, dead. Jesus.

Suddenly, he realized that the women had stopped talking and were looking at him strangely. "Are you okay, Mr. O'Brien?" Alicia asked. "Maybe you should sit down."

"I'm fine." He swallowed. "Just in shock, is all."

"We all are."

"How did it happen?" he asked.

"She was at home. They think it happened sometime Tuesday night. Mr. Logan had to identify her"—Alicia's eyes welled with tears—"her remains. She was shot in the head."

"Tuesday night?"

Reed's secretary nodded. "Mr. Logan called from home to tell us. He won't be coming in today."

"No, of course not." John felt as though the floor at his

feet had given way. Mumbling something about canceling the conference call, he bolted for his private office, where he tumbled into his chair, then stared blankly at the wall in front of him.

Sloane was dead.

She'd been so alive when he'd left her that night—hot-headed and impatient as usual. A veritable tornado of edicts and complaints. How could she be dead?

His mind flashed on an image of Sloane at fifteen. His freshman year at USC, John had gone home with Reed for Thanksgiving. Fraternity brothers, roommates, both so full of themselves their heads were the size of weather balloons.

And Sloane hadn't been the least impressed. "Strut and show," she'd told her brother. "You're a moron and so's your friend."

She'd been a beauty in the making even then, despite the thick glasses, a mouthful of braces, and the perpetual scowl. John could see her, hip jutted to the side, arms crossed, railing against the evils of capitalism and narrow-minded people, which in Sloane's adolescent mind encompassed ninety-nine percent of the country.

By eighteen she'd shed the glasses and the braces, and much of the attitude. And John had learned she never scowled in bed.

She'd more than scowled at him Tuesday, however. He cringed at the memory of their angry exchange. Their *last* exchange, he realized with horror.

*"Go rot in hell, Sloane."*

*She'd regarded him with her ocean-green eyes and lifted her chin ever so slightly. "Easy for you to say now. But that doesn't change what is. The real question is, just how much of a bastard are you?"*

John pressed his palms against his eyes and tried not to think about the bombshell that had precipitated their argument. She'd been wrong about him. He wasn't going to run away this time.

He sat up straight and glanced at the time. Top of the hour. He flipped on the radio and waited through an excruciating five minutes of national news and weather before the newscaster got to the local headlines.

*"Police are confirming the murder of Sloane Logan Winslow and a second woman at the Winslow home in the Tucson foothills sometime Tuesday night. Mrs. Winslow was the vice-chairman of Logan Foods, a family-owned grocery chain with stores throughout the Southwest, and along with her brother, Reed Logan, held a controlling interest in the company. The identity of the second victim has not yet been released. The police have several leads but have named no suspects to date. With neighbors understandably nervous, police are cautioning vigilance, though they believe the attack may not have been random."*

That was it. The newscaster moved on to other matters.

John was numb. He knew he should go to Reed and offer condolences, but first he needed to get a handle on his own emotions. Shock, disbelief, sorrow—they roiled and churned inside him.

And in the corner of his mind, something else. At first it was just a spark, come and gone before it really registered. Then, like a wildfire fueled by high winds, it consumed him.

His name was bound to come up.

He experienced a flutter of uneasiness in his stomach.

Should he call Kali? His hotshot younger sister was a lawyer in California now. They could hardly be called close, but she wouldn't turn her back on him. Still, he hated for her to think he'd gotten in touch only because he needed help.

And he didn't need help. Not yet.

Finally, he buzzed Alicia and told her he was going to see Reed.

Reed's wife, Linette, answered John's knock on the door of their sprawling Mediterranean-style home.

"Am I intruding?" John asked. "I just heard about Sloane."

"No. I think it would do Reed good to see you." Linette

Logan stepped back, inviting John into the cool interior. She was in her early thirties, a dozen years younger than her husband, with a delicate face and a sleek cap of coal-black hair. Despite what must have been a difficult morning, she looked as though she'd taken time with her appearance. Her cotton shirt and khaki capris were fresh and crisp, the navy belt, earrings, and sandals well coordinated. Her lipstick was fresh, pink and glossy.

"How's he holding up?" John asked. He supposed he should offer Linette some sort of condolence, but truth was, he doubted she really cared that Sloane was dead. She'd never struck him as caring about anyone but herself.

She made a so-so gesture with her hands. "I don't think it's really sunk in yet. Come on," she said, leading the way. "He's out back. Staining the gazebo."

"Staining the gazebo?"

"Don't ask. I think it's his way of coping."

They stepped into the yard and John was taken, as he always was, by the sweeping vistas and the lushness of the landscaping. An English country garden transported to the Arizona desert.

Reed was on his knees furiously slopping stain on the floorboards with a wide paintbrush. His thinning blond hair was plastered against his forehead and the back of his shirt was wet with perspiration.

"Honey," Linette said, "John's here." She paused uncertainly. "I'll leave you two alone. Holler if you need anything." Then she retreated to the house.

Reed rocked back on his heels, wiping his brow with his freckled forearm. His long face showed streaks of the pigmented stain that never made it onto the deck. "It's too damn hot to be working outside."

"Yeah, it is." John cleared his throat. "I just heard the news. I was at the dentist's this morning. I still can't believe it."

"You and me both," Reed replied gruffly. "It's fucking incomprehensible." Despite his protests about the heat, Reed dipped his brush into the can and continued working.

John felt helpless. "I don't know what to say."

"You're here. That says a lot in itself. I mean that."

"Do you know what happened?"

"All I know is some cop showed up here at the crack of dawn this morning. Told me Sloane had been murdered. Her and another woman, whom I suspect was Olivia Perez, the girl who cleaned for Sloane. I had to go down and identify Sloane's body." Reed tossed the brush angrily against the corner post and stood up. His tall, angular frame seemed suddenly frail. "It was awful," he said. "Worse than you can imagine."

What John imagined was bad enough. He felt a tremor. "Why did it happen? Do they have any idea? The radio made it sound like it wasn't part of a burglary."

Reed shook his head and shrugged at the same time. "They haven't shared much with me. A Detective Shafer came by a little bit ago and asked more questions. Was she romantically involved with anyone? Who might have reason to want her dead? Did she do drugs? Was she into anything kinky? That kind of crap. Wouldn't tell me a damn thing except to say he was sorry for my loss. Like that's supposed to make me feel better."

"I imagine at this point they don't know a whole lot themselves."

Reed sighed, wiping his hands on his pants. "No, I suppose not. Although there was apparently a neighbor who saw a car he didn't recognize parked at the house that evening."

"That's something, I guess." John felt a disquieting flutter in his gut.

"They asked about the business, too," Reed said hesitantly. He was silent a moment. "I had to tell them Sloane wanted you gone. They were bound to hear about it sooner or later."

"It's hardly a secret that we had different visions for the company's growth," John said. Sloane had been outspoken in her lobbying to get him removed, and he knew the cops would see motive written in neon letters. That only fueled the uneasiness churning inside him.

"Still, I didn't like having to tell them."

John nodded. "We may have been like oil and water, but deep down I loved her like a sister."

"Not always like a sister," Reed pointed out with what, under other circumstances, would have been a laugh. "Come on, let's move inside, where it's cool."

They settled in the rear-facing family room, and Reed pulled two icy bottles of beer from the wet bar. "Sometimes I wish things had worked out between you two," he said. "You'd have made a hell of a better brother-in-law than the smartass she married."

"We were young," John offered lamely. Although it was more complicated than that, of course. More complicated than either of them had understood at the time.

"Ha. You were stupid. Screwing her best friend behind her back. Geez, I still can't believe you did that."

John held up his hands in mock surrender. "I was a cad. I admit it. Sloane deserved better." And she sure as hell didn't deserve to be murdered.

"Remember how she used to go off on tangents?" Reed chuckled. "There was that vegan period, and then the phase where she wouldn't buy anything that wasn't used, recycled, or day old."

"Don't forget her crusade to save some damn endangered mouse." John started to laugh, then caught himself. "God, I can't believe it."

Reed nodded glumly, staring at his beer. "She could be a pain in the butt sometimes. Especially after she moved back to Tucson and decided to get involved in the company. But she was still family. Siblings are funny like that. You can argue till you're blue in the face, but there's always a bond."

"Maybe in your case." John and his sisters didn't fight. They hardly even talked. Well, he and Sabrina talked or, rather, she talked and he listened, getting a word in edgewise when he could. But he and Kali might as well live on different planets. Kali was a lot like Sloane, now that he thought about it. Both of them controlling and critical. Smart and attractive women, good women really, as long as your paths didn't cross too often. Or maybe the fault was within him. They'd both pointed that out often enough.

It didn't used to bother him, but as he'd gotten older he'd come to regret not having closer family ties. He just didn't know how to bridge the distance, or if, at this point, it was even possible.

"With you, too," Reed insisted. "If you needed them, they'd be there."

John hoped Reed was right. He might just be approaching an honest-to-God test of the theory.

"Sloane told me the two of you were going to have dinner Tuesday night," Reed said.

So the cops would know about that, too. "It wasn't a big deal," John said. "We went out after work. I was home by ten." After he'd stormed out of the restaurant in anger. John felt that flutter in his belly again. There was sure to be someone who'd witnessed their argument.

"Funny, you guys having dinner." Reed started to grin; then his face crumpled. "Ah, shit, John. All the times I wished she'd just go away, and now she has. Forever."

Reed leaned forward, forearms on his knees. His shoulders trembled. "I appreciate your coming by but I need to be alone right now."

"Sure." John was never comfortable with physical displays but he felt like something was called for, so he gripped Reed's upper arm briefly. "Let me know if there's anything I can do."

In the car, John closed his eyes and sighed. Then he pulled out his cell phone and called his sister Kali. It had been much too long since he'd talked to her. Besides, he knew it was only a matter of time before he'd need her help.

# CHAPTER 3

Kali O'Brien awoke to sunlight so bright and intense it was blinding, even with her eyes shut. She rolled onto her side, used the top of her sleeping bag as a shield, and gingerly opened one eye. Then she smiled at the beauty of the morning. The sun was just rising over the mountain peaks, illuminating the dew on the meadow and transforming the muted grays of dawn into full color. The crisp morning air was fresh and scented with pine. All around her, the birds welcomed the day with song.

She leaned over and shook Bryce's shoulder.

"Huh? What?" He opened his eyes, then quickly squeezed them shut. "Geez, turn off the light."

"It's the sun, silly. It's morning."

Bryce grunted and glanced at this watch. "Barely. And it's freezing."

He was right about the temperature. Kali's breath came out in puffs of steam. At 7,500 feet, the late September nights and mornings were chilly even when the days weren't.

"Did you sleep well?" Bryce asked.

"Like a log. How about you?"

"Ditto. And I'm not finished." He offered a half smile, then rolled over and buried his head under his pillow.

Kali gave thought to tickling him awake, which she'd

likely have done if they'd been inside in the comfort of a bed instead of outdoors wrapped in separate bags. In truth, she wasn't eager to brave the nippy air herself.

Three days into this vacation and she was still trying to figure out if she was enjoying herself. A friend of Bryce's had offered them use of his rustic, one-room cabin at the edge of the Desolation Wilderness in the California Sierra. She'd been skeptical. No electricity, no running water, no plumbing, no beds—it hadn't sounded like much of a vacation. And no way was she a fan of desolate. But Bryce had been so eager, regaling her with stories of Boy Scout camping trips from his youth, that she'd relented. She wasn't exactly a novice to the out-of-doors, after all. And in the wake of her last big trial and subsequent brush with death, she was desperately in need of time away.

They'd arrived late Wednesday afternoon and Kali had fallen in love with the place immediately. It was far from desolate. Pine forests, meadows, streams, a jewel of a lake. No motorboats or Jet Skis, only the quiet of canoes, kayaks, and tiny sailboats. The lake and surrounding cabins sat in a basin at the foot of a mountain range whose granite peaks were still dotted, albeit sparsely, with snow. She'd discovered the lack of electricity was a small price to pay for such natural beauty, and that a bucket of well water went a long way.

It wasn't the surroundings that gave her pause, but Bryce himself. Kali's idea of a vacation was having time to unwind. Give her a swimsuit, a body of swimmable water, sunshine, and a good book, and she was in hog heaven. Bryce, it turned out, didn't know the meaning of the word *relax*. He'd morphed into a camp director the minute they'd arrived and hadn't taken a break since. So far, Kali had managed only one quick dip in the lake and two chapters of the mystery novel she'd been saving especially for a stretch of time when she could devour it.

She was discovering a whole new side to the man, and it didn't always sit well with her. She'd known from the beginning that they were different. A homicide detective and a defense attorney. A broad-shouldered hunk with a reputedly well-worn "little black book," and a slender brunette who didn't know how to trust. A man who was sometimes a bit too brash, who lived a smidgen too close to the edge, and a hard-nosed woman who'd been told more than once that she was rigid and relentless. But the chemistry had been strong enough to overcome the differences. For the most part, it still was, though Kali would have gladly traded a few steamy kisses for an hour or two of lollygagging on the sandy beach.

Moreover, Bryce's skills as a woodsman weren't quite what he remembered. The wood fire that had smoked them out of the cabin the first evening was definite proof.

Kali felt Bryce stir. He rolled toward her and snaked an arm out of his sleeping bag. But instead of tickling her, as she expected, he pulled her close and kissed the end of her nose.

"This is the life, isn't it?" he said.

"I have to admit it's pretty nice."

She snuggled in the warmth of their impromptu nest, envisioning the day before them. An easy morning walk around the lake, maybe a glass of wine with lunch, and a leisurely afternoon of sunshine and relaxation at the water's edge.

"How about hiking to one of the upper lakes today?" Bryce asked.

"I thought we were going to take it easy."

"Sure, after we get back. It's only about four miles in."

"And four miles back," she pointed out.

"We should still be back by noon."

Inwardly, Kali groaned. But a morning hike would allow her to enjoy her lunchtime wine with impunity. And four miles Kali could do in her sleep. She covered nearly that distance on her regular morning walk at home. "Okay," she agreed. "Sounds like a plan."

"Bring your cell phone, if you want," Bryce advised. "The pass is only another mile or so beyond the lake. There should be reception near the summit, not to mention a fantastic view."

"Good idea." The inability to make and receive calls was the only real drawback to the place. Even with her associate,

Jared, covering for her at the office, and her neighbor Margot keeping an eye on the house and her dog, it made Kali nervous to be out of touch. "Are you going to call in, too?"

"Not me." He grinned. "Vacation means getting away from all that."


Four miles scrambling over granite with a thousand-foot rise in elevation was nothing like four miles on the paved streets of Berkeley. And counting the times they'd missed the trail and taken a wrong turn, they'd gone far more than four miles by the time they reached the upper lake. By then it was already noon, and Kali had given up her fantasy of lunch on the deck and an afternoon swim. She agreed to press on to the summit, because having come this far, she wanted to make her calls.

The trail to the top was steep and hot, an endless succession of rocky switchbacks. But she reached the summit before Bryce did and was rewarded with an impressive, panoramic vista. A succession of Sierra lakes fanned out below her to the west, and to the east, a gently sloping trail meandered through a mountain meadow before disappearing in a steep descent into the next valley. She let her eyes feast on the beauty of it all while she breathed deeply to catch her breath.

"What took you so long?" she joshed when Bryce appeared some two minutes later, still huffing with the exertion of the ascent.

"Watch it, lady. You take a nosedive off a ledge way out here, and no one's going to know what happened." He stripped the pack from his shoulders and offered her some water.

Kali felt exhilarated by the strenuous climb and proud of herself for having done it. Her spoiled afternoon plans were only a minor irritation. She handed back the water bottle, took out her cell phone, and made several calls while Bryce explored the rocky outcroppings around them.

"Anything important?" he asked when she was finished.

"Jared seems to be holding down the fort just fine at the

office, and Margot says Loretta misses me, but I know she's just saying that to make me feel better."

"Dogs are very loyal," Bryce pointed out.

"Oh, Loretta's loyal, but she also recognizes a sweet deal when she's got it."

"No urgent messages, then?"

"Nope. My hairdresser called to change an appointment, the stockbroker who's been trying to get my business wants to schedule a meeting, and my brother called."

"John? Did you call him back?"

Kali shook her head. "We haven't talked in months. Waiting a few more days isn't going to matter. We won't have anything to say to one another, anyway."

"Then why'd he call?"

"Who knows? Sabrina probably browbeat him into it." Her sister lived under the misguided notion that she could orchestrate everyone's life.

Bryce offered Kali more water, then capped the bottle without taking any for himself.

"Aren't you thirsty?"

He shrugged. "We're getting low."

Another miscalculation. Like the amount of time it would take them to get to the lake, and the missed forks in the trail.

"Should I be getting worried?" she asked.

"We could make it back with no water if we needed to. It won't be nearly as hard as the hike in. It's just that I underestimated."

Kali knew Bryce was embarrassed and her heart went out to him. Befuddled and vulnerable was sexy in a man who was used to calling the shots.

"We'll ration what's left, then," she told him. "But we should share equally."

"I want you to have it, Kali. You've been a good sport about this."

"Hey, I'm having fun."

Surprisingly, she was.

"When am I going to get to meet your family?" Bryce asked as they headed back down the steep path.

"You want to?" Bryce would have less in common with her siblings than she did.

"Of course I want to."

What did it say about their relationship, Kali wondered, that he was interested in meeting her brother and sister when she'd never once thought of introducing him? For that matter, what did it say about her own relationship with them?

"There are three of you, right?"

She nodded. "John's the oldest. He was already away at college when my mother died." Her mother's suicide Kali's freshman year in high school had been a defining point in her life, yet John had barely acknowledged it. She'd since come to realize that avoidance was his way of coping with the loss, but at the time she'd felt he'd abandoned her.

"You've mentioned before what a tough time that was for you."

"Yeah, it was." Kali's foot slipped on a sandy patch of steep granite and she staggered to catch her balance. She slowed her pace a bit. "John and I weren't particularly close growing up. I was the pesky baby sister he didn't want to be bothered with."

"And it hasn't gotten any better?"

She shrugged. "Mostly, I don't think about him much, and I doubt he thinks about me. But when we're together, we get along okay."

Bryce crossed a fallen log bridging a creek bed, then turned to offer Kali a hand. She'd nearly fallen off on their way up.

"John's lived all over the world," she said when she reached solid ground again. "He's been involved in some questionable business practices—and habits. He went through rehab once for addiction to painkillers. But he's done all right for himself. Made a small fortune at one point, then lost most of it when the market went south."

"He's in Tucson now?"

Kali nodded. "Working for a fraternity brother whose family owns a chain of grocery stores."

"Your sister's in Arizona, too, isn't she?"

"Scottsdale. She's a lot more like John than I am, and she keeps trying to make us all one big, happy family."

"Nothing wrong with that." Bryce sounded almost wistful. From the little he'd told her, his family made hers look like the Brady Bunch.

"Except that Sabrina wears blinders when it comes to reality," Kali explained. "She keeps trying to make things fit her fantasy." Kali was pretty sure her sister nagged at John as much as she did at Kali.

Only Kali wouldn't have expected John to give in. Usually, she was the one who reached out—with mixed results. Still he *had* called. It was, she decided, an interesting new twist to their relationship.

# CHAPTER 4

After a string of late nights, Erling arrived home Monday evening in time for dinner. Sandwiches actually, but at least they were all three eating together, seated at the round pine table in the kitchen. Deena had set out red-checkered place mats and matching cloth napkins.

"You should have told me you'd be home," she said, reaching her well-tanned arm across the table for the pepper. "I'd have made a real meal."

"I didn't know myself until the last minute." But he should have called, Erling realized now. Deena continually complained that she never knew when to expect him. "Besides, I love tuna salad sandwiches."

She made a face like "yeah, sure." "Anyway, we're honored you could make it home."

Erling was working on a response when she held up a palm. "Wait, I didn't mean that the way it sounded." She smiled at him warmly with dimpled cheeks, then covered his hand with her own. Her fingers were stubby, the nails unadorned except for streaks of indelible yellow marker that must have been part of the day's classroom project. As a first-grade teacher, Deena had a signature style that often involved splashes of primary colors, or grime.

"I honestly wasn't being facetious," she told Erling. "We've missed you. Haven't we, Mindy?"

"Geez, Mom. It's not like he's been on a trip or anything. He's come home at night." Mindy shot a sideways glance at the readout on her cell phone, momentarily distracted. Then she frowned. "Hasn't he?"

Deena brushed the air with her hand. "Can't you put that away, honey? In fact, turn it off. We're eating dinner."

Mindy moved the phone closer to her plate, but she didn't turn it off. Erling supposed he should jump in and say something stern, but in truth, the phone didn't bother him. If Mindy had friends calling her, all the better. In high school she'd had few enough of them.

"Of course he's come home," Deena continued, looking again at Erling. "But your dad's been putting in some very long days."

*Long and tough,* Erling thought.

Homicide investigations were inevitably demanding, but this one was taking a greater toll on him than most. Bad enough he was emotionally entangled with one of the victims. Worse, because of that, he was walking an ethical tightrope. By all rights he should have removed himself from the investigation. With every day that passed, he wondered if he'd made the right decision.

It was also a high-profile case, and the pressure to close it, intense. Tomorrow would make it a week since the murder occurred, and the lieutenant, eager for a break, was breathing down Erling's neck. The victims' families demanded constant updates. And with Sloane's family ties to the well-known Logan Foods, the press was having a heyday digging for dirt.

"Unfortunately, it's not over," Erling told his family.

"How's it going?" Deena asked.

Erling shrugged. This was one case he wasn't eager to talk about. "How was your day?"

Deena smiled. "Could have been better, could have been worse." She tucked a strand of silver-streaked hair behind her ear. "I heard on the radio you have a suspect."

"A person of interest," Erling corrected. Though John O'Brien certainly topped his unofficial list of potential suspects.

"An employee with Logan Foods, isn't he?"

Erling nodded. "An executive VP, and a friend of Reed Logan's from college."

"A longtime friend of Sloane Winslow's too, from what I hear. There was an interview on the radio today with her ex-husband. He said the suspect . . . the person of interest . . . was an old boyfriend of hers."

Hearing Sloane's name flow so casually from his wife's lips caused Erling's breath to catch in his throat. Or maybe it was the "old boyfriend" remark. Or "ex-husband." He had no right to be jealous of either man, but he was.

"Does their relationship have something to do with why he killed her?" Deena asked. "Were they still involved?"

"No, they weren't," Erling bristled. He swallowed a mouthful of sandwich and washed it down with water. "Why are you so interested, anyway? You usually don't like my talking about work. Especially over dinner."

"But this murder has been in the headlines. Everyone's talking about it. I'm interested."

Erling let his breath out slowly. The important thing was to act as if it was just another case. "O'Brien and Winslow have been butting heads over company policy. O'Brien was apparently pushing for greater profitability. Winslow wanted to focus on quality. Expand organic product lines, carry free-range poultry and grass-fed beef, that sort of thing."

Mindy slouched in her chair, her freckled face resting on one hand. "Seems like a stupid reason to kill someone," she huffed. "Like anyone really cares what their hamburger ate growing up."

"You may not," Deena scolded, "but some people do. And that's not really the issue. It's a power struggle about the direction of a business."

Mindy rolled her eyes. "Whatever."

"The rift was fairly deep," Erling explained. "Word is that

Mrs. Winslow was pressuring her brother and the other directors to get rid of O'Brien."

"They could do that?" Mindy had a finely tuned sense of what was fair. "For no reason?"

Erling nodded, but before he had a chance to explain the workings of corporate boards, Deena jumped in with another question.

"Anything that points to him actually having killed her?" she asked.

"They were known to have argued the night she was killed," Erling said, keeping the explanation brief. Discussing Sloane's murder with his wife was both terrifying and painful. "There's also a witness who puts a car similar to his at her house later that same night."

"What does John O'Brien say?"

"As little as possible."

Erling's dislike for the man went beyond what he usually felt for an uncooperative suspect. Maybe it was O'Brien's former brushes with the law—DUI and assault—though both charges had been dropped. Maybe because he'd been at odds with Sloane. Or it could simply have been the arrogance and raw good looks of a man blessed with the sort of movie-actor appeal Erling distrusted. And, as Sloane had once told him, John O'Brien had been her first real boyfriend. Her first lover. Whatever the reason, Erling's gut instinct was that O'Brien was guilty. And nothing he'd learned in the investigation had changed his mind.

"It's a shame about the girl." Deena turned to Mindy. "Did you know her?"

"It's a big school, Mom."

"Yes, you're right. I just thought since you're both sophomores . . . Anyway, it's a real tragedy. She worked for Sloane Winslow?" This last was directed to Erling.

He nodded as he poked an errant slice of tomato back into his sandwich. "General housekeeping and errands. In return, she got a place to live rent free. The girl was working to put herself through school."

"Unlike someone we know," Deena said pointedly with a glance in Mindy's direction.

Mindy had known since high school that if she wanted to live on campus, she had to earn the money herself. She hadn't, so she lived at home. She faulted her parents for being stingy; they accused her of being spoiled. Truth was, Erling was relieved that he could keep her close for a bit longer. Losing Danny had made him more protective than ever of his remaining child.

"So she had a job," Mindy replied haughtily. "Look what happened to her. She's dead. Is that what you want for me?"

"Of course not!" Deena barked, her face suddenly ashen. "It's a silly analogy."

Maybe it was silly, but Erling's initial reaction hadn't been all that different from Mindy's. A girl the same age as his daughter, a classmate in fact, killed for no reason other than that she was in the wrong place at the wrong time. Under different circumstances, it might have been Mindy. The thought squeezed his heart. Its grip had been especially painful during the autopsy.

Erling had never gotten comfortable with the acrid smell of formalin, the grating whir of saw blades on bone, the splaying open of a human being. For the most part, he'd learned to steel himself against the procedure by bottling his feelings until it was over. There were limits, however. He'd passed on Sloane's autopsy, claiming a schedule conflict, and sent Michelle instead. He knew that seeing Sloane's once warm and familiar flesh laid out on a steel table under harsh lighting would be more than he could bear. He'd attended Olivia Perez's autopsy, though. And the whole time, the refrain had played in his head: *This could have been Mindy.*

"Okay, so I'll get a job," Mindy muttered. "I'll move out. Will that satisfy you?"

"We're happy to have you live here," Deena said.

She looked to Erling for support, and he nodded just as his beeper went off. "You can stay as long as you'd like. You know that." He checked the readout and saw that it was Michelle. "Sorry," he told his family, "I've got to call in."

Deena frowned. "Surprise, surprise."

Erling went to the kitchen phone and punched in the number. Michelle picked up on the first ring. "We finally got our search warrant," she said. "But Jenkins is being a bear about it, as usual. The scope is more limited than we'd hoped."

Judge Jenkins, a former defense attorney, was a notorious guardian of citizens' Fourth Amendment rights. He drew his warrants narrowly and with a specificity that drove cops nuts.

"Lets hope we find something," Erling said. "Then we can go back and hit him with another affidavit." It was tricky, and to Erling's mind, needless dance, but at least everyone involved understood the moves.

"You want to serve it tonight or tomorrow morning?" Michelle asked.

Erling looked across the room at Deena, who was pointedly ignoring him.

*The only thing you care about is work. It's always the job first. Never your family. Never us.* Erling knew what she was thinking because she'd said it often enough. It wasn't true. Not true at all. He loved Mindy so much it hurt sometimes. His love for Deena was more complicated, but he *did* love her. And Danny was a hole in his heart big enough to drive a tank through.

But being a cop wasn't a job where you could punch out at five. He'd thought Deena understood that when she'd married him. Danny's death had changed a lot of things.

"Erling?" Michelle's voice cut through his thoughts.

"Let's hit him now," Erling said. "The sooner the better." He was eager to get the case wrapped up, and himself off the hot seat—both at home and at work.

"Shall I meet you there?" Michelle asked.

"You're at the station? I'll come by. I should be there in about thirty minutes."

"I've got Boskin and Dutton lined up to assist."

"Good. I don't expect trouble but you never know."

He returned to the dinner table long enough to brush Deena's cheek with a kiss, and to ruffle Mindy's golden brown hair. "I have to go out again. We've got a warrant to search the house of the man I was telling you about."

"Take care, Dad."

"I'll probably be in bed when you get home," Deena said flatly. "Try not to make too much noise."

# CHAPTER 5

Kali hauled her duffel and sleeping bags into her house in the Berkeley hills and dropped them on the tiled entry-hall floor, shaking loose a fine layer of dirt and plant matter. She removed her shoes before venturing farther onto the hardwood floor of the main rooms. She was far from being a fastidious housekeeper, but given the amount of dirt she'd accumulated in a week of outdoor living, she figured it was a wise move.

Parched and hungry after the three-plus-hour drive back to the Bay Area, she collected the week's accumulation of mail and padded in stocking feet to the kitchen.

The fridge was largely empty, as she knew it would be, but she found a half bottle of Diet Coke that had gone flat, poured herself a glass, and leaned back against the laminate counter. Her message machine light was blinking furiously, there was a small but steady stream of ants on the drain board, and the air inside the house was stale and smelled of the cabbage she'd cooked the night before heading for the mountains.

But it felt *wonderful* to be home.

With no one else around.

Despite her early misgivings about the vacation, Kali had ended up having a good time. And she'd truly enjoyed being with Bryce. He was kind and funny and generous, and there were moments she thought she might even love him. So it brought her up short to realize how pleased she was to be alone and back in her own space. In fact, she was so happy she was humming as she gave the mail a quick sort through.

She listened to her phone messages while wiping up the ants with a damp paper towel. John had called again, twice. And Sabrina had called on his behalf. "John's been trying to reach you," she'd announced. "Don't be such a jerk. Just call him."

He must want something from her, Kali decided. How typical. He could ignore her messages, rebuff her attempts to keep in touch, forget holidays and birthdays, but when there was something he needed, he'd hound her until she rolled over and played nice.

Well, he could just wait a bit longer.

Kali called her neighbor Margot and left a message that she was home, then headed for the shower. Twenty minutes later she was clean (or at least cleaner than she had been—mountain dirt, she discovered, had a way of imbedding itself in skin) and had just begun to unpack when Margot showed up at the door, springer spaniel in tow.

"I was on the other line when you called," Margot explained, waving an arm weighted with chunky metal bracelets. "Thought I'd just drop over on my way out since Loretta here has been pining for you all week."

"Not!" Kali snorted.

Margot shrugged. "She's got playmates at my house is all. It's nothing personal."

Loretta was half the size of Margot's wolfhounds and not nearly as well mannered, but she usually preferred their company to Kali's. To her credit, though, Loretta was now making a show of squirming at Kali's feet and wagging her stumpy tail.

Leaning down to scratch the dog's head, she asked Margot, "You want to come in?"

"Can't. I'm on a tight schedule. How was the wilderness adventure?"

"Good." Kali stood up. "Great, in fact."

"And the romantic escape angle?"

Kali hesitated. "Good."

"But not great?"

She was still sorting that one out. She grinned. "There were definitely some great moments."

"That's more than I can claim."

Given that Margot had been a man for the first thirty years of her life, her difficulty finding suitable companions didn't surprise Kali. In fact, Margot was still technically male. Not that Kali had any knowledge of this beyond Margot's often melodramatic grousing and grumbling. Margot was a friend—vivacious, impassioned, and with many fine qualities Kali wished she herself possessed—but there were details about her life Kali wasn't comfortable knowing, even if Margot was more than willing to supply them.

After Loretta's initial show of excitement, she settled into her spot near the window. Kali put in a load of laundry and watered the houseplants. She found a can of minestrone in the cupboard and heated it on the stove. Not much of a dinner, but she was too tired to go out to the store. Then she poured herself a glass of wine and settled in with the magazines and catalogues that had arrived while she was gone.

It was after ten by the time she remembered John. Was it too late to call? She didn't want to wake him but he *had* phoned twice. Well, too bad if he was in bed.

The phone rang four times before John picked up. "Huh?" he mumbled.

"John? It's Kali."

"Hey, Kali." The words were slurred, his voice more gravelly than usual.

"Were you asleep?"

"Huh? No, I'm just . . . just killing time." He made a sound something like a cross between a hiccup and a laugh. "I've been trying . . ." His voice faded off for a moment. "Trying to reach you. I need your help."

"Are you sure I didn't wake you?"

"Nah. Listen, we gotta talk. It's important." There was a shuffling sound in the background, the sound of another voice.

Drunk, not asleep, Kali guessed. And John either had company or was glued to the television. She was irritated. These were the last hours of her vacation and she didn't want to spend them dealing with an incoherent and self-indulgent brother. "Why don't you call me in the morning?"

"Wait, don't be like that. You gotta help me."

She hesitated. "What's up?"

"I can count on you, can't I?" His voice faded, and Kali thought maybe he'd fallen asleep.

"You there, John?"

"I'm just having a little trouble—"

"Focusing. Because you're drunk, right?"

"Hey, don't shoot the messenger." He laughed.

"I'll call you tomorrow," she said. "Try to be sober." She hung up. But not, she realized a moment later, before he'd hung up on her. *Well, screw him.*

She brushed her teeth and washed her face, half expecting the phone to ring. When it didn't, she crawled into bed, which felt particularly roomy after the close quarters of a sleeping bag. True, there was no glorious star-studded sky overhead, but the mattress was more forgiving than the thin foam pad had been, and there was a bathroom with a flush toilet and hot running water nearby. Kali fell asleep with the thought that she'd have made a terrible pioneer.

The next morning Kali sat at her office desk sipping the latte she'd picked up at Peet's on her way into work. Mail was stacked to one side, message slips to the other. In the middle was a commercial lease she was reviewing for a client who wanted to open a children's clothing store in north Berkeley. Her thoughts were far away, however, drifting between pleasant musings about Bryce and uncomfortable speculation about John.

One night of overindulgence didn't mean anything, Kali told herself. God knew she drank too much sometimes herself. If she hadn't been so tired last night, so desirous of a quiet evening with no one to think about but herself, if she hadn't put up with stuff like this from John before, she'd have shown more patience. A tiny niggle of guilt worked its way under her skin. She *should* have been more patient. There was clearly something on his mind.

But he'd hung up on her, she reminded herself. And he hadn't bothered to call back.

Jared knocked on her open door as he breezed into her office. He slid into one of the wood-frame chairs she used for clients, his long limbs splayed at odd angles around him. Jared Takahashi-Jackson got his height from his father, his delicate and handsome Asian features from his mother. He was smart, hardworking, and refreshingly willing to speak his mind, but he couldn't sit upright in a chair if his life depended on it.

"Glad you're back, boss. Just in time, too."

"For what?"

"Daryl Jensen got picked up again."

Kali groaned. "What for?"

"According to him, nothing. According to the cops, he was creating a public nuisance and threatening his soon-to-be ex."

"Can he make bail?"

"Not clear. I've got a deposition at ten and I was just trying to figure out how I could be in two places at once."

"I'll take care of Daryl. Any other fireworks?"

"Nope. It's been so quiet I'd occasionally check the phone to make sure it was working."

Kali was relieved to know she hadn't made herself unavailable during a crisis, but a quiet law office wasn't good either. Not when there were salaries and rent to be paid.

"Did you have a good time?" Jared asked.

"Yeah, I did."

"And you and Bryce are—"

"Still speaking," she said, eyeing him levelly.

"Whoa, that was terse. Am I going to get the longer version?"

Kali laughed. "You're not supposed to ask about your boss's sex life."

"What's the fun in that?" Jared swung one leg over the other. "You sure you don't mind heading downtown the minute you're back home?"

Mind, yes. But Daryl Jensen was a client, and clients paid the bills. "Not a problem," she said.

"You saved my butt again," Daryl told her. At his behest, they'd stopped at Taco Bell after leaving the jail. All six foot of him was now hunched over, elbows and forearms spread out on the plastic tabletop as though he were guarding his three tacos and two burritos from Kali's reach.

Kali nibbled at her own chicken taco, thinking longingly of the fresh salad she'd planned on picking up for lunch. "Your butt shouldn't need saving so often," she said.

"I didn't threaten her."

"She's hearing voices, you think?"

Daryl grinned, his teeth flashing white against his chocolate skin. "Might be. That bony-assed white woman's nuttier than a fruitcake."

"Then why'd you marry her?"

He glared at Kali in response, then went back to eating his burrito. Daryl Jensen had been a rising basketball star until an automobile with a drunk driver at the wheel had crossed the double line and shattered his left leg. Kali had handled the case and he had walked away, limped away actually, with a very nice settlement. Daryl was a decent man with a hot temper and bad judgment, but his postinjury indiscretions and scrapes with the law made him a consistent client.

"I'll agree Brandy isn't the most grounded person I've met," Kali admitted.

"She's a vampire. Only she sucks money, not blood."

"Still, you've got to watch yourself around her," Kali said. "Especially until the divorce is final."

"She's keeping me from seeing my son."

"We're going to get that straightened out. For now, the court has mandated a short visit every other weekend, so that's the way it's got to be. You're not going to win any points spitting in the face of the court."

Daryl polished off the rest of his meal and she drove him home. Not to the stunning redwood and glass house in the Oakland hills, which his wife had grabbed in the settlement, but to an older and far more plebeian condo downtown. It was several rungs below what he'd been used to.

"I fucking can't stand that woman," he muttered when Kali pulled up to the curb.

"You talking about Brandy?"

"She's Satan with tits."

"She's the mother of your boy. You two are going to be part of the same world for a long time, so you'd better figure out a way to be civil."

"Easy for you to say. Just wait till you've got a devil on your tail."

Kali was just pulling into the office parking lot when her phone rang. She picked up quickly, expecting John.

Instead it was her sister, Sabrina. "Where have you been?" Sabrina asked accusingly.

Her siblings seemed to expect her to be at their beck and call. If Kali hadn't just returned from a mellowing vacation, she'd have been annoyed right back. Instead, she responded with enthusiasm. "You won't believe it. I was camping."

Sabrina wasn't interested. "It's John," she said, her voice breaking.

"What about him?"

"He's . . . he's dead."

"Dead?" Kali stopped the car where she was. Thankfully no one else was coming or going in the lot. Sabrina's words pounded in her head. "What? That can't be. I just talked to him last night."

Only they hadn't really talked. Kali had brushed him off and hung up.

"There was an accident. That's all I know. I just got the call."

"An accident?" Kali wasn't thinking straight. Her brain had locked up. She couldn't think at all.

"They asked me to come in and take care of some paperwork." Sabrina's sobbing was muffled.

"My God. He's really dead?"

"I can't do it. Not alone. I really need you, Kali."

It took a moment for her to understand what Sabrina was suggesting. "You want me to fly to Tucson? Today? You're only a two-hour drive away."

"Please."

How could John be dead? Her only brother, gone.

"We can go in together," Sabrina said. "I'm not saying I won't go at all."

"I just got back from vacation." Feeling numb, Kali thought of the draft lease on her desk, Daryl's troubles, the clients whose work she'd already put off for her trip with Bryce. "Saturday," she offered. "I can come then. It's only a few days from now."

"This is our brother we're talking about, for Christ's sake. Your stupid job's more important than him?"

"Of course not, but—"

"Or me? What about me?"

"Sabrina, it'll be a signature and a—"

"You know I can't handle this kind of thing!" she shrieked. "Not by myself."

John was dead. Kali felt a burning in her throat, the sting of tears in her eyes. It finally hit her. He was really dead.

"Please, Kali." Sabrina's tone was imploring. "We need each other."

Her family. Sabrina was all she had left now. Jared could continue to cover at the office, and Margot would be happy to take Loretta again. Her brother was dead and her sister needed her. That was what mattered.

"Of course," Kali said. "Of course we should be together. I'll fly down right away. I'll let you know as soon as I've made a reservation."

*I'm sorry, John. I should have returned your phone calls sooner. I shouldn't have hung up on you. I'm so sorry.*

# CHAPTER 6

Erling had just gotten off the phone from talking with the lieutenant when Michelle signaled to him. "John O'Brien's sisters are here," she said.

"Sisters—plural?" He'd spoken over the phone with a sister living in Scottsdale, the only name he had.

"Two of them. I put them in the conference room."

Conference room was something of a euphemism, but the windowless space was an improvement over the two standard interrogation rooms, and it was often used by deputies for interviews and group meetings. It was larger, brighter, and generally cleaner.

"How do they seem?" he asked.

"Upset and confused. Pretty much what you'd expect."

Erling rose from his desk and grabbed his gray flannel sport coat from the back of the chair. "Might as well get this over with."

He hoped the sisters weren't the weepy, hysterical type. Displays of raw emotion made him uncomfortable. They reminded him painfully of his own despair following Danny's death. Besides, he was hoping the sisters would be clearheaded enough to shed some light on their brother's interactions with Sloane, maybe even offer up something of a confirmation that John O'Brien was capable of murder.

Erling followed Michelle down the hall to the conference room. The two women, looking somber, were seated side by side at the rectangular government-issue table.

Michelle made the introductions. Sabrina Ashford, with whom Erling had spoken over the phone, and Kali O'Brien, who'd flown in from California. The two women appeared to be about the same height, but Sabrina was a little heavier, and prettier in the conventional sense. Her hair was a warm shade of honey blond, a color, according to Deena, that came naturally to no woman past the age of twenty-five. Sabrina wore it short and soft around her face. Kali had a lean, athletic build, a mane of auburn curls and a strong handshake. Sabrina would turn heads when she first walked into a room, Erling thought, but Kali would be the one who lingered in people's memories.

"Can I get you a soda or some coffee?" he asked the women.

"No, thank you." Kali spoke without consulting her sister. "We'd like to know what happened."

Direct and to the point. A take-charge kind of woman. At least he wouldn't have to deal with hysterics, although he found her edginess slightly off-putting. He pulled out one of the plastic molded chairs at the table and sat down.

"I'm sorry about your brother."

"We both are," Michelle added kindly, taking a seat next to him. "We know this has got to be hard for you."

Sabrina bit her bottom lip, tried to hold back the tears but didn't succeed. She took a tissue from her purse and wiped her eyes, leaving a smudge of mascara. "Thank you."

Kali wasn't interested in sympathy. "What happened?" she asked again.

"He appears to have drowned," Erling told them.

Both women looked at him with surprise, and he realized that when he phoned Sabrina he hadn't given her the details of her brother's death.

"In his backyard swimming pool. His housekeeper found him yesterday morning. She called nine-one-one, but unfortunately it was too late."

"But he could swim," Sabrina protested.

"And the pool can't have been large," Kali added. "Do you think he might have had a heart attack?"

"It's possible. Or maybe he slipped and hit his head. We won't know for sure until after the autopsy this afternoon. He was dressed in shorts and a T-shirt, so best guess is that he fell in." Erling paused. "Preliminary tests show a high concentration of both alcohol and drugs in his system."

Sabrina looked as though she'd been struck. She glanced quickly at her sister, whose composed expression didn't change.

"We found a plastic baggie of Xanax on the bathroom counter," Erling continued.

At this, Kali's eyes widened. "A baggie?"

Erling nodded. "It's the way street drugs are often sold."

"We know your brother went through rehab at least once before," Michelle added.

"That was fast," Kali said. "I'm surprised you even thought to look into it."

Erling shrugged. They only knew about O'Brien's prior addiction because they'd pulled up his records in connection with their investigation of Sloane's homicide.

"We'll get a copy of the accident report?" Kali asked.

"That can be arranged if you'd like."

"We'll need to get contact information from you," Michelle added. "And there are some forms you'll need to fill out for release of the body."

Sabrina continued to wipe at her eyes, while Kali sat rigidly in her chair, forearms resting on the table.

Erling hesitated, then plunged on. "When was the last time either of you talked with your brother?"

"I saw him a couple of weeks ago," Sabrina said, wadding a tissue in her clenched fingers. "He came for dinner. And we had a brief phone conversation last weekend. Why?"

"What about you?" Erling asked Kali.

"I haven't actually talked with him in months, but he called last week while I was out of town."

"Did you speak with him?"

She took a moment before answering. "We never had a conversation, if that's what you mean. I called him back

Tuesday night when I returned from my trip, but he was . . . he couldn't talk right then. I told him I'd call him the next day, but before I could, Sabrina called me with the bad news."

Kali looked at her sister, then back to Erling. "Why is it relevant when I last talked to him? Is there something about the accident that—"

"No," Erling said. "Not about the accident. I'm wondering, though . . ." He tried to read their faces. Did they know John had been under scrutiny as a possible killer? "It's about the other matter," he said finally.

"What other matter?" The sisters spoke in unison. He could tell that neither of them had any idea.

There was no delicate way to break the news. "Your brother was our prime suspect in the recent shooting death of two women."

Kali appeared dumbfounded.

Sabrina paled. "Are you talking about Sloane Winslow?"

"Who?" Kali turned to her sister. "You knew about this?"

Erling repeated the question, mildly miffed that Kali had beaten him to it. "John told you he was a suspect?"

"Nothing like that," Sabrina said, growing agitated. Her hands fluttered to her neck and her voice sounded strained. "But I knew Sloane had been murdered." She glanced at Kali. "I heard it on the news. And John called and told me she'd died. But I never thought . . . I mean . . . I know John knew her and all . . . but—"

"What made you think John might be a suspect?" Kali asked Erling, cutting her sister off midsentence.

"His name surfaced almost immediately. He and Sloane Winslow were locked into a power struggle at work," Erling explained. "They were seen arguing the night of the murder. And a witness reported seeing a Porsche at the Winslow home the night of the crime. The description matches your brother's car."

"Did this witness see the driver? Get a license plate?"

Erling shook his head. "But the car he saw had a broken right taillight, as did your brother's."

Kali squared her shoulders. "That's it?"

"Your brother claimed he was home alone at ten o'clock Tuesday night last week, but we've got a gas station receipt that says he was out. There were shoe prints along the side of the Winslow house. Size and sole pattern matches a pair your brother had. John owned a twelve-gauge shotgun, same as the murder weapon. He had a box of Winchester number-four shot. And there was gunpowder residue on a shirt of his."

Sabrina shook her head in disbelief. "There must be some mistake. John wouldn't do something like that."

"I understand this might not sound like the brother you knew," Michelle said sympathetically, "but we have to look at facts."

Both sisters appeared dazed. But whereas Sabrina's emotions played out on the surface—a deep flush spread across her cheeks and tears welled in her eyes—Kali's appeared to be under tight control. Despite the set mouth and closed expression, Erling sensed that she was rattled.

"When will you be releasing John's body?" Kali asked.

"Later this afternoon." Erling wrote the number of the medical examiner's office on the back of his card and handed it to Kali. "You can call directly or have the mortuary call."

She nodded and put the card in her purse, then rose.

Sabrina's arms were wrapped across her chest; her shoulders trembled. She followed Kali in getting to her feet, but her movements were jerky and uncertain.

"I'm sorry," Michelle said again as they were leaving the room. "I know this has got to have been a shock." She followed the women to show them out.

When they'd gone, Erling closed his eyes and rubbed his temples. Part of him would have liked to see John O'Brien fry for murder. But another part of him—a bigger part—was relieved that the investigation could be wrapped up quickly without Erling's own involvement coming to light.

He wondered, not for the first time, if Sloane had told anyone about their affair.

# CHAPTER 7

Kali stomped up the stairs of the parking garage. Her stomach was churning and her pulse pounding in her ears. She felt as though she'd been tossed in the waves of a heavy storm and was still having trouble finding solid ground.

Could John truly have killed two women?

"Slow down, will you?" Sabrina, several paces behind, was gasping for breath. "Kali, please. We need to talk about this."

"What's to talk about? You heard the detectives."

"That John was a suspect in those murders, you mean?"

"Not just *a* suspect. Their *prime* suspect." The detective's words had been like a punch in Kali's gut. She was still feeling the pain.

"You don't honestly believe he did it, do you?"

"They didn't pick his name out of a hat, Sabrina. There are reasons they focused on him." Kali slowed to allow her sister to catch up.

"They can't prove it was him. There could be other explanations."

"But if you look at it all together—"

"John couldn't have done it," Sabrina protested. "He's not that kind of person."

*That kind of person.* As if all killers came from the same

mold. Kali had enough experience on both the defense and prosecution sides to know that wasn't so.

"He could have," Kali said. "You know as well as I do what a hothead he could be. Not to mention how damn self-centered."

Sabrina looked as though she'd been struck. "How can you say such things about your own brother? Especially now, when he's dead." She could barely choke out the words. Tears were streaming down her face.

"Because it's the truth," Kali told her. But she'd vented most of her anger and now felt a hollowness in its place. The notion of John as a murderer didn't sit any better with her than it did with Sabrina.

When they reached Sabrina's Ford Explorer, Kali asked, "You want me to drive?"

Sabrina wiped her eyes and handed Kali the keys. "You never gave him a chance," she said softly. "You think you're so much better than everyone else, you don't give anyone a chance."

"Oh, please." Kali opened the driver's-side door and climbed in.

*Never gave him a chance, indeed.* Kali was the youngest of the three. As a girl she'd idolized her older brother and longed for attention from him. But John couldn't be bothered. She was an annoyance he did his best to ignore unless it was to tease her or ridicule her in some way. To be fair, her parents shared some of the blame. In their minds, he could do no wrong.

When their mother died, Kali had looked in vain to John for the emotional support she didn't get from her father, who preferred staring at the television and downing liberal amounts of alcohol to consoling his daughters. Sabrina, with her multitude of friends and boyfriends, had found support elsewhere, but Kali had no one.

When their father died years later, John was again unavailable. He hadn't even come home for the funeral. Kali had tried for many years to build a relationship with John. She thought of the phone calls he never returned, the cards and notes he never acknowledged, the e-mails he ignored. John didn't have time for her; he was too busy looking out for John.

"He never gave a damn about anybody but himself," Kali said. "Even growing up."

"You think you were the only one who had a hard time in our family?" Sabrina shot back. "It wasn't easy for me, or for John, either. Especially John. He was the oldest, the only boy. Nothing he did was ever good enough."

"Could have fooled me."

"You know what your problem is?" Sabrina asked, slamming the passenger-side door. "You're inflexible. You expect everyone to be like you and do things your way."

"My problem? I thought we were talking about John." But Sabrina's words struck a chord. Several boyfriends, including Bryce, had told her the same thing.

"Don't you feel *anything*, Kali?"

She'd heard that before, too. "Of course," she countered angrily. "It's awful that John's dead. I feel wretched about it. And I'm sad and upset that he was a murder suspect. What do you think I am, anyway?"

"The Tin Man, maybe. Only *he* at least knew he didn't have a heart."

"That's so unfair—"

Sabrina seemed to have shocked even herself. "Oh, God. I'm sorry. I shouldn't have said that. It's just that I'm so . . . so mixed up, I guess. And it hurts so much."

Kali felt tears prick her own eyes. It did hurt, though she'd been trying to convince herself it didn't. She closed her eyes, hoping to stem the tide of sorrow. But it bubbled inside her, along with anger and guilt.

"I loved John," Sabrina said softly. "Even if I sometimes wanted to wring his neck." She paused. "Just like I love you."

Kali wiped her eye with the heel of her hand. "In spite of all the times you want to wring my neck?"

Sabrina managed a weak smile. "Yeah."

"I love you, too, you know." Kali didn't bother with the

qualifiers. They both knew how often she was exasperated with her sister.

"Yeah," Sabrina said. "I do know that."

For now, peace. If past experience was any guide, it wouldn't last forever. Maybe not even the rest of the day. But Kali was suddenly grateful for the chance to bury the tension, however temporarily. She realized, with a fresh pang of grief, that she'd never have that opportunity with her brother.

Kali started the engine. "You still want to stay at John's?" They'd decided on the phone that it made sense to stay there rather than a hotel, but now Kali wasn't sure it was such a good idea. Maybe it was too soon.

"We have to deal with the house at some point," Sabrina pointed out.

Kali nodded in agreement, though she was sure neither of them was up to doing anything about it tonight.

"And *not* staying there," Sabrina added, "that would be like . . . like avoiding John."

Not altogether a bad idea at the moment, Kali thought.

"I think he'd like it," Sabrina continued. "We're family. It feels right."

Kali remembered cleaning out the family home after her father's death, and the things she'd come to understand about both of her parents. Maybe by staying at John's she'd come to feel closer to him, too.

"Okay, tell me how to get there."


John's house, north of the city, was a Sante Fe–style stucco with a spectacular view of the Catalina Mountains. The red-orange sun reflecting on the mountains was the first thing Kali noticed when she stepped through the door. She set her purse and suitcase down in the entry and wandered through the main part of the house.

A large room of living and dining space with floor-to-ceiling windows opened onto the yard at the rear of the house. The floors were a mix of Spanish tile and random-plank maple. Combined with the natural log beams, a kiva-style fireplace, and neutral-tone plaster walls, the effect was lovely. It was a house that was both luxurious and comfortable, and not at all what Kali had expected. The furnishings, on the other hand, were exactly what she'd envisioned for John—basic. John's basics. The living room held nothing but a buttery-soft leather sectional, a glossy ebony-color coffee table, what looked to be a forty-inch plasma flat-screen television, and a state-of-the-art sound system. The dining table and chairs were sleek and modern and didn't, to Kali's eye, fit with the style of the house. The walls were bare. So were the kitchen counters except for a coffeemaker. The appliances, she noticed, were all upper end.

"Don't worry," Sabrina said, reading Kali's expression, "the bedrooms are furnished."

"It's too bad he did so little with it. It's a beautiful home."

"And a good investment. That was John's primary concern."

Sabrina made her way to the kitchen with the ease of someone in familiar space. She paused long enough to turn on the ceiling fan, even though Kali found the house chilly. Coming from the Bay Area, she wasn't used to air-conditioned interiors and always felt like she was walking into a refrigerator when she entered them.

They'd decided to stop for food on the way to John's. By unspoken accord, they'd ignored a large Logan Foods market, stopping instead at a Basha's, where they picked up corn chips, salsa, deli salads, and a roasted chicken. As well as vodka and wine. Although it was not yet five, Sabrina made herself a stiff drink.

*What the hell?* If there was ever a day that called for an early drink, this was it. Kali opened a bottle of wine and poured herself a glass.

"I can't believe he's really gone," Sabrina said, taking a long, slow sip of her vodka and tonic. "It's so . . . random. One minute he's alive, maybe watching television or walking around the house, and the next minute everything's changed."

Kali tried to envision their last phone call from John's perspective. It had been only hours before his death. "If only he'd had the sense not to mix pills and booze. You'd think he'd know better."

Sabrina nodded. "I thought he was past that. I mean, after the experience he had getting off pain medications and all. But"—she lifted her vodka tonic—"I guess I understand the appeal of escape, too."

"Being accused of murder would be something to escape from, all right." Had John already taken a bunch of pills when she'd called that night? Or was Kali's unwillingness to talk to him part of what pushed him over the edge? Suddenly, she felt the house closing in on her.

"Let's take our drinks outside," she said.

"Are you crazy? It must be ninety-five degrees out there."

Kali's own deck in the Bay Area was often shrouded in fog by evening, so the idea of a warm evening appealed to her. But she opened the patio door to a blast of air so hot and dry it was like stepping into an oven. Reluctantly, she joined Sabrina on the sectional in the living room.

"I told you it was too hot out there," Sabrina said, then added wistfully, "John was talking about having a misting system installed. We have one at home and it really helps."

Although it shouldn't have come as a surprise, Kali felt a pinch of envy that her siblings were closer to each other than to her. Sure, she talked to Sabrina every month or so, but she didn't really know much about the day-to-day activities of her sister's life. And her rare conversations with John were stiff and awkward. John and Sabrina were connected; she had been the odd one out.

"Did you and John see a lot of each other?" Kali asked.

Sabrina made a fluttering, so-so motion with her free hand. "Sometimes I'd drive down and we'd go to lunch. More often, he'd come for dinner or hang out and spend time with the kids."

*Uncle John.* Kali had never considered her brother in that light. She was struck once again by how out of touch she'd been.

"They adored him," Sabrina added. "Probably because he spoiled them rotten."

Her sister's three boys ranged in age from twelve to seventeen. Kali sent presents on birthdays and Christmas, and greeting cards on special holidays, but she saw them at most a couple of times a year.

"How are they doing?" Kali asked.

Sabrina brushed away tears. "I haven't told them yet. They'll be devastated."

Would they have felt the same if something had happened to her? Kali wondered. Maybe John wasn't as selfish as she'd imagined. "What did you and John talk about?"

Sabrina gave her a puzzled look. "Whatever came up. It's not like we sat around and debated theories of evolution or anything, if that's what you mean."

Kali wasn't sure what she'd meant except that she and John seemed never to have anything to say to one another. "What about the woman he's accused of murdering? You said he knew her. Did he ever talk to you about her?"

"Sloane? She's Reed Logan's sister."

"Oh, my God. I didn't know." Reed Logan had been John's friend at USC. Although Kali hadn't seen him in fifteen years, she'd seen a lot of him when she was in law school at Berkeley, and Reed and John were working together at a management consulting firm in San Francisco. "That's awful. Poor Reed."

Sabrina nodded. "He's lost two people close to him now."

"Had you met her?" Kali asked.

"Years ago, in L.A." Sabrina stared into space for a moment; then she tucked her legs under her and turned to Kali. "They dated, you know. John and Sloane. More than dated, actually."

"When was that?" Kali wondered if a lovers' quarrel could have led to murder.

"In college and after. They broke up for a while, but they were together again right before Peter and I got married. They must have split up again because John brought some other woman to the wedding. Do you remember? The one who clung to him like Saran Wrap. Sloane was off traveling through Europe, he said."

"Vaguely." What Kali remembered was that John and her father had both had too much to drink. They'd argued and ended up pummeling each other in the fountain outside the hotel.

"John told me at one point that Sloane was married and living in L.A. No children, I think. She was apparently very involved in charitable work."

"Society stuff?"

"Maybe. But she was also, like, save the dolphins, stop global warming, help the needy. And not at all interested in the family business. I learned all this after she returned to Tucson last year and started agitating to get John fired. He was really pissed. I mean, it was John who helped Reed turn the business around when it wasn't doing well after the senior Mr. Logan's death."

"She wanted him fired?" Was this what the detective had meant by "conflicts at work"?

"I know," Sabrina said, misunderstanding the source of Kali's dismay. "It's so unfair. John said Sloane didn't understand the difference between a business and a charity. He wished she'd just go back to saving the spotted whales or whatever, and leave the running of the company to him and Reed."

Corporate intrigue. A motive made in prosecutorial heaven. Kali's stomach clenched. "John benefited from Sloane's death, then?"

Sabrina shook her head. "Don't even go there, Kali. That's so . . . so—"

"So obvious."

"You're disgusting!" Sabrina shrieked. "How can you possibly think your own brother is a murderer?"

"You think most killers don't have families? Being somebody's brother doesn't make you a saint." Kali set her glass on the ebony-stained coffee table. "Sloane and John argued the night she was killed, remember? That's what it must have been about."

Sabrina put her hands over her ears. "Stop it! Stop right now."

"All I said was—"

"What's with you anyway?" Sabrina wailed. "I should think you'd be on his side."

Kali knew that being a suspect didn't mean you were guilty. She was a defense attorney, for God's sake. Yet here she was, buying into the detectives' case. Why? Maybe because the facts supported it. Or maybe it had something to do with never admitting to herself how much John's indifference had hurt. Or perhaps, suggested a tiny voice in her head, it was simply easier to blame John than look at her own faults.

Kali pushed the question from her head and stood up. "Come on, let's eat."

Though the coleslaw tasted of mayonnaise and the bean salad of oil and salt, the roasted chicken was surprisingly good. Kali went back for seconds while Sabrina pushed food around on her plate and polished off another vodka tonic.

Suddenly Sabrina rocked forward and pointed at the television, which she'd turned on when they sat down to eat. "Look," she sputtered, "it's John."

In split screen, their brother's face—a photograph Kali had never seen—appeared, along with that of a woman. Kali reached for the remote and turned up the volume.

"*. . . died sometime late Tuesday night. He drowned in the backyard swimming pool of his home. Sheriff's detectives had considered him the prime suspect in the recent double homicide of Logan Foods heiress Sloane Winslow and her housekeeper, Olivia Perez. Although there has been no official word on the status of that case, sources tell us that police are not actively pursuing other leads at this time.*"

"Good God," Sabrina wailed. "Now it's all over the news. Can they do that? Can't we sue them for defamation or something?"

"Sshhh." Kali wanted to get a good look at Sloane. The photo showed a smiling woman in her early forties. Her blond hair was just short of shoulder length and layered to frame her face. Her eyes were a deep blue-green, her teeth straight and white. There were freckles across her nose and fine lines around her eyes and mouth. Not a Hollywood beauty maybe, but Sloane Winslow was stunning in a timeless, wholesome way.

"You can't let them get away with this," Sabrina insisted. She stood up and began pacing between the sofa and the television.

"Get away with what? All the reporter said was—"

"If he was alive, you'd help him, wouldn't you? If for no other reason," Sabrina added sarcastically, "than because you're Ms. Big-Time Defense Attorney."

Sabrina's tone stung. "You've done okay for yourself," Kali said defensively.

"You're the big success, though." Sabrina stopped her pacing and planted herself near Kali. "You're the star."

Kali didn't think she lorded her achievements, such as they were, over her sister, or anyone else. And Sabrina certainly had many things Kali did not—a loving husband, kids, financial security, and a lifestyle that included exotic vacations and expensive jewelry.

But Sabrina was right about one thing: whatever her doubts, Kali would have stood by John and made sure he had a chance at the best defense possible.

He wasn't alive, though, and she'd turned her back on him when he'd needed her.

Never mind that he might have drowned regardless. Her own culpability lodged in her throat. Was that what made it so hard to admit that John might be innocent?

"He called me," Kali said after a moment.

"I know. You told the cops that." Sabrina plunked herself back down on the sofa and reached for her drink.

"Several times over the last few days. I was in the mountains where I couldn't pick up my messages." Not entirely true, she reminded herself. She'd received one message and ignored it. "When I finally reached him Tuesday night"— Kali's throat constricted at the memory of her own self-righteousness—"he said he needed my help."

Sabrina set her glass down with a loud clunk. "I thought you said you didn't talk to him, that he was busy or something."

"He was drunk." Kali paused. "I told him I'd call him in the morning."

"Oh, no." Sabrina started whimpering again. "How *could* you?"

"I didn't know he was going to die."

"Maybe if you'd taken the time to talk to him, he wouldn't have."

"What, I was going to stop him from drinking? From popping pills? It's not my fault he's dead." It really wasn't, she told herself. But guilt had a mind of its own.

Sabrina glared at her, then looked away. "Maybe not. But you never gave him a chance to tell his side of things. I'm sure he had an explanation for all that . . . that *evidence* the cops say they have. You owe him, Kali. You owe it to John to clear his name."

Kali felt the tug of something inside her. "What if he really did it?"

"He didn't."

"You don't know that, Sabrina. Not for sure."

She was silent for a moment. Her lower lip quivered. "Will you at least look into it?"

"There's nothing—"

"You're a lawyer. You know how to talk to cops and figure things out. *Please?*"

Kali would be in Tucson through the funeral anyway. That would give her time to get a better handle on things. She'd ask around, see what she could learn. Maybe she'd find some answers. If nothing else, she might be able to ease her own conscience.

"Okay," she agreed, "I'll look into it."

# CHAPTER 8

The next morning, Kali pushed through the wide double doors of Logan Foods's corporate headquarters into a carpeted lobby. The rosy-cheeked receptionist smiled. "Good morning," she chirped. "How can I help you?"

Kali had played this scene through in her head during the drive in, trying to come up with a plan. Would Reed Logan talk to her? Did he blame John for his sister's death? She assumed word of John's accident had reached at least the higher levels in the corporation, but she couldn't be certain. She hadn't settled on an approach that covered every contingency, so she said simply, "I'm John O'Brien's sister."

The young receptionist's smile faded. "Oh." She looked momentarily confused, then stammered, "I'm sorry. We're all in a state of shock. It's very sad what happened."

"Thank you." Kali wasn't sure what response was called for, but "thank you" covered a lot of ground. "I'd like to see Reed Logan, please."

"Mr. Logan isn't in today."

So much for planning. She tried to think who else might be able to talk to her about her brother, but she knew nothing about his position there other than his title. "How about my brother's secretary, then?"

"I'm, uh . . . I'll see if she's available. Why don't you have a seat?"

Kali sat down in one of the upholstered chairs while the receptionist picked up the phone and carried on a brief and muted conversation. A few minutes later the door to the inner offices opened. It wasn't a woman who greeted her, however, but a slender, sun-scrubbed man in his early fifties. He had a narrow, serious face and a full head of reddish brown hair. Frameless bifocals perched low on his nose.

He offered a hand. "I'm A. J. Nash, general counsel for Logan Foods."

"Kali O'Brien."

"I hope you won't mind if I ask to see some ID. The press has been hounding us this past week, so we have to be careful."

Kali showed him her driver's license and Nash offered a nod of condolence. "I'm so sorry for your loss. John was a great guy."

He escorted her to his office, which was smaller and more spartan than she expected, leading her to believe that much of the company's legal work was handled by outside counsel. Nash would be the point person, but not someone who wielded a great deal of power or influence.

"Please, have a seat. Would you like some coffee? It's actually a step above what you find in most offices."

"No, thank you."

Nash waited until Kali was seated, then settled himself and straightened some papers on his desk. Kali noticed a folded newspaper among them. This morning's edition, no doubt, which contained an account of John's death and a recap of the earlier murders. She and Sabrina had read it over breakfast.

"What can I do for you, Ms. O'Brien? Did you come for your brother's personal effects?"

"In part. My sister and I will have to settle his affairs. But I want information as well." She'd come to see Reed, but in many respects the attorney was actually a better choice. He wouldn't be as personally invested.

"Information about stock options, death benefits, and the like?" He reached for a file from the stack to his left.

Kali's mind hadn't even begun to deal with the minutiae of her brother's estate. She was still reeling from the shock of his death.

"That too," she said. "But what I really want is to know about Sloane Winslow's murder."

Nash sat back in his chair and pushed his glasses up the bridge of his nose. His expression was pained, but softer too. More human. It suited him better than the bland mask of corporate counsel.

He sighed. "It's been a terrible week for us. Terrible every way you look at it."

"You know the police considered my brother a suspect?"

Nash nodded. "The police spoke with a number of us and the local media have been on the story from the start."

"What was the general feeling here—that the police were right, or that they were way off track?"

Nash cleared his throat, looking uneasy. "Nobody *wanted* to believe it. John is . . . he was a likable guy. He got along well with people, myself included."

Kali nodded and waited for Nash to continue.

"We all knew John had a personal in with Reed, and to be honest, in the beginning it was a bit of a concern for those of us who'd been with the company for many years. But John never took advantage of their relationship. He was well liked and respected."

"Nobody wanted to believe it," Kali prompted, "but?"

"But as more and more evidence pointed in his direction . . ." Nash made a gesture of helplessness with his hands. "I assume the police have gone over their reasons with you?"

"In broad terms, yes. I understand that there was some tension between him and Sloane Winslow."

"Well, yes." Nash hesitated. Kali couldn't tell if it was simply because he was unwilling to speak ill of the dead, or if he held back for other reasons. "They had different visions for the company," he continued finally. "John and Reed were focused on maximizing profits with an eye toward being bought out by one of the larger chains. Sloane wanted to keep it in the family."

"Is it true she wanted to get rid of John?"

The hesitancy again. "She was lobbying to replace him," Nash said reluctantly.

In other words, the cops had been right. John had motive. At least in theory.

"How did Reed feel about it?" Kali asked.

"He was the one who brought John on board. I think he felt like he was caught in the middle."

"Did the police question him?" Sloane might have been trying to oust John, but Reed shared John's vision for the company—a vision that was now more secure with Sloane dead.

Nash again pushed his glasses higher on his nose. "They questioned all of us. Reed was never a suspect, if that's what you're getting at. He was at a business function the night Sloane was killed."

"Does *he* think John did it?"

"You'd have to ask him that. The official company position is that guilt or innocence is best left to the legal system."

Kali imagined that as general counsel, Nash had a hand in formulating that position. Not that she could fault him for it. It was a by-the-book response, one that she herself would recommend in a similar situation.

Nash checked his watch. "Is there anything else? I'm sorry to cut this short but I have a meeting in a few minutes."

"You mentioned options and insurance," Kali said. They hadn't been on her mind when she came in, but since she was here, she might as well gather what information she could.

"There's a company policy for one and a half times annual salary. You and your sister are the beneficiaries, though I have to warn you most of John's compensation came in the form of bonuses and options, not salary."

That John had listed her came as a surprise to Kali. No matter what the sum, she was oddly touched.

"It's with Global Mutual," Nash continued. "We've already notified them of John's death, so I imagine you'll be hearing from them soon. I'll have Alicia make sure you've got the necessary documents."

"Alicia?"

"John's secretary." Nash rose from his chair. "And as soon as we've had a chance to go through his office, we'll box up John's personal effects and get them to you. Where are you staying?"

"At John's. My sister and I both."

He nodded. "If there's any way I can help, please give me a call." He looked at her straight on, his eyes intense but warm. "I mean that."

Kali slipped the strap of her purse over her shoulder and headed for the door. "I appreciate your taking time to speak with me. I know you're busy. I can find my own way out."

Nash started to follow, but when his phone rang, he nodded a farewell in Kali's direction instead. "Your brother will be missed around here."

Kali brushed past an empty secretarial desk and started down the carpeted hallway she'd come in. But instead of continuing straight to the front exit, she took a left near the water fountain.

Waiting for the company to send John's things was well and good if all she was interested in was salvaging some commemorative letter opener or paperweight and stale packs of chewing gum. But Kali wanted a glimpse of the unsanitized John. She wanted to sit at his desk, to look through his drawers and papers, to get a feel for where, and maybe how, he spent his days. After so many years of keeping John at a safe distance, she now wanted to know everything about him.

And it couldn't hurt to talk to his secretary.

Passing a middle-aged woman carrying a stack of file folders, Kali did her best to appear lost. "Excuse me. I'm looking for Alicia. I must have taken a wrong turn somewhere."

"You sure did, honey." The woman pointed her down the

hall in the other direction. "Alicia's just past the stairwell, John O'Brien's office." This last was accompanied by a catch in the woman's voice.

Kali thanked her and headed back. Beyond the stairwell, the hallway fanned out into a sort of anteroom leading to two large offices. She passed first by Reed Logan's empty office, then came to the plaque that listed John's name. A Bridget Jones–plump young woman with long, scarlet nails and a cherubic face was engrossed in sorting the mail on her desk.

"Hi," Kali said. "Are you Alicia?"

The woman jumped and looked up. "Oh! I didn't hear you coming. Yes, I'm Alicia. Are you here to see Mr. O'Brien? He's"—she brushed the ash blond hair from her face, her expression sober—"he isn't available right now."

Kali pulled up a chair. "I know. I'm his sister, Kali O'Brien."

"Oh." Alicia appeared flustered, then distraught. "I didn't know you were coming in today."

"It was a spur-of-the-moment decision."

"I'm really sorry about what happened. If there's any way I can help . . ."

"Thank you. This must be a difficult time for you, too."

Alicia nodded and took a deep breath. "It is. He was a great boss. Demanding sometimes, but always fair. And if I messed up, he didn't yell or anything. Just told me to make it right."

"How long have you worked for John?"

"I started about a month after he did. That would be a little over three years now." She blinked back tears. "Sorry. Seems like all I've been dong lately is crying. First Mrs. Winslow, now your brother. And I'm a terrible crier. None of this dainty, Victorian stuff for me. My eyes get red, my nose runs, my face turns all blotchy." She fanned her face with her hand as if to stop the flow of tears. "I don't want to get started again."

"You knew Sloane Winslow, too?"

"Right." Alicia reached for a tissue. "We're a small group here. Everyone knows everyone else. And now two deaths . . ." She ran a hand along the edge of her desk, avoiding Kali's gaze. "I know what they're saying about your brother, but I don't believe it. Not for a minute."

"The police seem to think it's because Sloane was trying to get John fired."

"I know. And that part's true. At least according to the rumor mill. We all knew there were bad feelings between them, but I don't see John shooting her."

"What was Sloane like?"

Alicia bit her lower lip. "Let's just say she had opinions and she wasn't afraid to share them."

Kali offered a conspiratorial smile. "Difficult to get along with?"

"A bit, for those who worked with her directly"—Alicia returned the smile—"which thankfully wasn't me. But I don't think people actively disliked her. It's more like they were afraid of her. Always on their best behavior where she was concerned."

"Nobody with a specific grudge?" Kali asked. "Someone she reprimanded, or denied a raise to?"

"I can't think of anyone. She wasn't really involved in the day-to-day operations. She had an office here and all, and she was a director of the company, but there was no one she supervised or anything."

"Didn't she have a secretary?"

"She's had a couple of them." Alicia pressed her lips together. "I shouldn't really be talking bad about her, but truth is, she burned through them pretty fast. It doesn't make a lot of sense that one of them had anything to do with her death, though."

Maybe, Kali thought, though murder rarely made sense to anyone but the person committing the crime. She'd have to ask the detectives if they'd looked into the secretarial angle.

"One of the things that seems to have caught the cops' eye," Kali said, "was an argument John and Sloane had over dinner the night she was killed. You wouldn't have any idea what that was about, would you?"

Alicia shook her head. "I know Sloane was wired about something, though."

"Wired?"

"Tense. On edge. Short with everybody. It wouldn't surprise me if whatever they were talking about turned into an argument."

Except that in the cops' scenario John was the one who was angry. Angry enough to drive over to Sloane's house hours later and kill her.

"If John and Sloane didn't get along," Kali asked, "why were they having dinner?"

"Beats me." Alicia pursed her lips. "The dinner was actually a last-minute thing. Mrs. Winslow tried all morning to reach your brother but he was in a meeting. He called her back later that afternoon, and I heard him tell her to meet him for dinner at Jack's Bistro."

Another woman approached and greeted Alicia. "Sorry to interrupt. I'm going out for a latte. You want anything?"

"A mocha, double shot of espresso."

"With whipped cream?"

Alicia laughed. "You have to ask?" She turned to Kali. "Would you like something?"

"I'm fine, thanks."

When the other woman had gone, Kali said, "I'd like to gather a few of my brother's personal things, if that's okay."

"Sure." Alicia had obviously not been coached by the higher-ups. "The cops already took some stuff," she added.

"Do you know what?"

"Sorry, no. You want me to get you a box?"

"I'm not sure I'll need one. I'll let you know if I do."

Alone in John's office, Kali felt the palpable presence of a brother she'd hardly known. She sat in his chair, ran her hands over the glossy wood surface of his desktop, and tried to conjure up a mental picture of John the executive. All she could come up with were childhood images of a lanky, self-absorbed brother with a devilish grin, and a few memories of his last visit to the Bay Area two years ago. She'd been involved in a trial at the time but they'd managed a couple of nice dinners—one in San Francisco; one locally at Kali's favorite East Bay restaurant, Bay Wolf—and a hike up Mt. Tam on a windy day when the air was threaded with fog. They'd had a good time, Kali reminded herself. Maybe not a warm and fuzzy Hallmark visit, but a good one nonetheless.

And now John was dead. Whatever thoughts and sentiments they hadn't yet shared would remain locked away forever.

Kali shook herself free from the memories and started in on John's desk. She peered into all the drawers, read the notations on his calendar, even checked the underside of his blotter. She wasn't sure what she was looking for, but she figured the more she learned about her brother, the better.

Half an hour later she concluded her efforts had been futile. She'd found nothing about Sloane, nothing about the murders, and very little of a personal nature. She had no better understanding of her brother than she'd had before.

She gathered the few items she thought worth holding on to—John's framed college diploma, a leather-bound dictionary that had been a high school graduation gift from their parents, an abstract bronze sculpture that was on the credenza, and the extra sports jacket and pair of shoes he'd stashed behind the door, though the sentimental value of the last two items was debatable.

As she reached to turn out the light, the shoes and the dictionary slid from Kali's grasp and clattered to the floor. When she bent to retrieve them, a photograph fell from between the pages of the dictionary onto the carpet. Kali picked it up.

It was a standard four-by-six size. A glossy color print of three girls who looked to be in their mid to late teens. The girls were clowning for the camera, their heads close. The one on the left was dark and exotic looking, the one on the right, a flaming redhead. The girl in the center had light brown hair and a purplish bruise along the right side of her neck and jaw.

It was an upper-torso shot and the girls were dressed in bathing suits. All three had figures that would draw stares.

Alicia appeared at the doorway. "Everything okay in here?"

Kali slid the photo into her purse. "Sorry, I was trying to do too many things with too few hands."

"You sure you don't want a box?"

"No, I'm fine. Thanks." She gathered the fallen items in her arms and left.

As soon as she was back in the privacy of her car, Kali pulled out the photo and took another look. It was definitely a contemporary photo, not a relic from John's college days. She turned it over and saw an Epson watermark on the back. A digital snapshot printed at home. The sort of friends-and-family photo that filled albums in households across America. But these girls weren't family and they were too young to qualify as John's real friends. What's more, the photo wasn't in an album; it was hidden away between the pages of a dictionary in his office.

There was undoubtedly a simple explanation. Nonetheless, Kali found the discovery unsettling.

# CHAPTER 9

Kali's cell phone rang as she sat in the car.

"It's me," Sabrina said. She'd remained at John's house that morning to begin the arduous task of sorting through records and notifying people of his death.

"How's it going?" Kali asked.

"I'm making progress but it's tough. This is John's personal stuff, his handwriting, his *life*."

"I'll be able to help you this afternoon."

"Good," Sabrina said. "You can handle the phone calls, too."

"What phone calls?"

"Reporters."

She should have known that was coming. "What have you told them?"

"Nothing," Sabrina bristled. "Except I told the first one that we don't believe John killed anyone. After that, I gave up answering the phone."

"Good move. Another day or so and John's death will be old news."

"Not to us."

"No, not to us," Kali agreed. "I'm going to pay Detective Shafer another visit. Want to come along?"

"Not particularly. But come home after that, will you? Without my car, I'm stuck here. I can't even go shopping."

"Shopping?"

"For groceries." Sabrina sounded indignant, but Kali wasn't entirely sure that food had been on her mind initially. "What did Reed say?"

"He wasn't there. I was thinking we might try his home later this afternoon. It would be a good idea if you came along since you know him better."

"Yeah, okay."

"Look up the nearest rental car place," Kali suggested. "We'll stop there, too. It's probably best if we each have a car anyway."

"I still don't see why you won't use John's."

Kali wasn't sure she understood it either. In part, it was the Porsche thing—powerful, expensive cars made her nervous. But the fact that the car was John's added to her reluctance. She had more trouble articulating that reason, even to herself. She just didn't want to drive his Porsche.

"I'd just rather rent a car, okay?"

"Okay. Jeesh, you don't have to bite my head off."


Detective Shafer wasn't available, but his partner, Michelle Parker, was. That was fine by Kali. Parker was female and close to Kali's own age. Moreover, she'd struck Kali as a warm person as well as a competent cop. Kali had liked her in spite of the circumstances.

She met Kali at the intake counter and led her back to a room with half a dozen desks, most unoccupied right then. In the far corner, two men were conferring in front of a computer monitor.

"I appreciate your talking with me again, Detective Parker."

"Michelle, please. I just fixed myself some tea. Can I get you a cup?"

"No thanks, but you go ahead."

The detective took a seat at one of the desks and gestured to a chair for Kali. She picked up her mug, which was oversized and emblazoned with a large red pig in police uniform. "My sister's idea of humor," she said, with a wry smile.

"She doesn't approve of your job?"

"She thinks I'm nuts. No chance to wear good clothes for one thing. And the shoes"—Michelle lifted a foot in its sturdy thick-soled boot—"atrocious."

"Sounds a lot like my sister."

The detective sipped her tea. "Do the two of you get along?"

"Depends on the day," Kali said, with a laugh. "Sabrina's married with three kids. A stay-at-home mom who thinks criminal defense work is the same as being a criminal."

Michelle's brow creased. "That's what you do, criminal defense?"

"Among other things." Kali wasn't interested in discussing particulars of her legal practice with a detective whose views on the matter might not be all that different from Sabrina's.

The detective leaned back in her chair and cradled her mug. Yesterday her hair had been loose. Today, she'd pinned it back, accentuating the delicate planes of her face. "Are you of the camp that thinks cops bend the rules?" she asked.

"Sometimes they do," Kali told her. "But mostly I have great respect for them."

Michelle Parker grinned like she wasn't sure she believed it but she was willing to play along. "I think about going to law school sometimes."

"Not, I take it, to become a defense attorney."

They both laughed.

"So what can I do for you? Something about your brother? I'm afraid we don't have any new information."

"It's about Sloane Winslow's murder."

"Nothing new on that, either." The detective looked at her over the top of her mug. "Unless there's something you want to tell us?"

Kali shook her head. "It's just that my sister and I weren't thinking clearly yesterday. We didn't get all the facts."

"Detective Shafer laid it out pretty well, I thought."

"Only in broad brushstrokes. There was nothing conclusive that pointed to John."

Michelle set her mug on the desk. "What did you have in mind?"

Physical evidence, Kali thought. Something besides circumstantial innuendo, though she knew full well that you could build and win a case without it.

"What about John's gun?" Kali asked. "Were you able to tie it to the murders?"

"Not exactly."

"What do you mean, 'not exactly'?"

"A shotgun isn't like a handgun," Michelle explained. "We can't say with certainty which specific shotgun was used to commit a crime."

"I understand that."

"But his was the same gauge as used in the murders. And it had been recently cleaned and oiled."

From a defense standpoint Kali could think of any number of innocent explanations, but she knew that's not how the police would see it. "What did my brother say?"

"He told us he'd been target shooting."

"Sounds reasonable. That would also account for the powder residue you discovered on his clothing."

Michelle nodded. "Reasonable. And rather clever, really, if he actually went target shooting."

The perfect cover, in other words. Maybe they could show the gun had been fired recently, but there was no way they could prove it had been fired at Sloane Winslow.

Kali rubbed her bare arms to warm them. A hundred degrees outside, and now she wished she'd worn a sweater. How did anyone ever know how to dress around here?

"Were there other people you considered suspects besides my brother?"

"Suspects, no. But we did question a number of folks."

"Including the string of secretaries Sloane pissed off?"

Michelle gave her an amused smile. "Including them."

"And there was *nothing* that raised any red flags?"

"No, I can't say there was."

Not that the detective would tell her, even if she *was* female, close to Kali's age, and had a flaky sister. That kind of bonding only took you so far. "What makes you so sure it wasn't a random burglary?" Kali asked.

"Nothing was taken, for one thing. But more important, there was no sign of forced entry." Michelle leaned forward, forearms on her desk. She wore no jewelry except for a black sports watch. "I know it must be hard for you. We never want to believe the worst about people we're close to."

"Why didn't you arrest him if you were so sure he did it?"

"We were getting there. The DA wanted a few loose ends wrapped up first."

"So the investigation is closed?" Kali asked.

"Not officially. But, to be honest, we're not going to be working it as an active case anymore. If new evidence comes to light, sure we'll investigate. But we've got other crimes to deal with. Including, sadly, other murders."

And they could count this one as cleared without ever having to make the allegations stick. No need even to show probable cause, which would have been necessary if they'd arrested him. They could pin it on John and be done with it.

On the other hand, Kali knew police resources were limited. Cops worked crimes where their efforts would have the greatest effect. She couldn't really fault them for that.

"Speaking of which," Michelle said, getting out of her seat, "I need to get to an appointment with the DA on another matter. Why don't you walk me out and we can continue our conversation?"

Kali followed the detective into the hallway and down a single flight of stairs.

"What about the other victim?" she asked when they reached the ground floor. "A housekeeper, wasn't she?"

"Olivia Perez. She was a U of A student who got free rent in exchange for light housekeeping duties."

Kali had been picturing an older woman. An actual *housekeeper*, not a young woman with a full life before her. It shouldn't have made a difference, but it did. A new heaviness lodged in her heart.

"Kali, there's something . . ." Michelle paused before continuing. "I may be speaking out of turn, but you should know the Perez family is exploring the possibility of a wrongful death suit."

"What?"

The detective spread her hands in a gesture of acquiescence. "Olivia was only nineteen. She was the first person in
her family to go to college. I think they—"

"Want money," Kali said tersely. "That's the bottom line,
isn't it?"

Michelle Parker leveled her gaze. "I imagine what they
want is justice."

"God, I thought you'd never get here," Sabrina said when
Kali arrived back at John's half an hour later. "This is just so
depressing. I've gone through practically a whole box of tissues."

"I know what you're doing is hard." Kali was sympathetic, but she was also envious of the ease with which her
sister bared her emotions. The pain Kali felt stayed locked
inside like a knife in her gut. Tears would be a relief. "Why
don't we take a break and get some lunch?"

"Great. Crying must burn calories, because I'm starved."

Kali was thinking a quick deli sandwich, maybe even a
Subway if they could find one, but Sabrina had other ideas.
She took over the wheel and drove them to an upscale courtyard mall populated by jewelry stores, galleries, and restau-
rants with linen tablecloths. The place Sabrina had in mind
was a French cafe located toward the back, overlooking a
fountain.

"I ate here once with John," she said when they were
seated. Her eyes teared up again. "He brought me for my
birthday. It was one of his favorites."

"So that's why you chose it." Kali looked around at the el-
egantly understated interior and wondered if it was the food
or the ambiance that had appealed to John.

Sabrina nodded. "It seemed fitting."

"I guess it does." Kali wasn't in the mood for a leisurely
lunch, even in commemoration of John, but once they were
served, she had to admit the salad Nicoise looked delicious.

"What did you get done this morning?" Kali asked, spearing a piece of fresh tuna with her fork.

Sabrina looked up from her quiche Lorraine. "I pulled together a list of people from John's address book and started calling the ones I knew. I put a mark by those I've never heard of. We'll have to decide whether to contact them or let it ride. I found a copy of his will, too, and the name of the attorney who drafted it."

"Good work."

Sabrina fingered the rosebud vase on the table. "He left everything to us, you know."

"Both of us?" Kali could understand his naming Sabrina in the will, but she was surprised to find herself included as well.

"Of course," Sabrina said. "You didn't really think he'd leave you out, did you?"

"We've hardly seen one another over the years."

"You were his sister, for God's sake. Family. Who else would he leave stuff to?"

Families were funny, Kali thought. Simply by virtue of birth, you were inexorably linked. The bonds might be invisible, but they were powerful.

Sabrina's question was apparently rhetorical because she continued with barely a pause.

"And someone from the funeral home called back," Sabrina added. "We're set for Monday. I'll be back Sunday night with Peter and the kids, and I'll try to spend a few days here later in the week, as well."

Kali set her fork on the table. "Back?"

"I need to get home, Kali. We've already worked out what we're doing for the service, and the rest of it can wait a few days. I'm fine with whatever you decide about the household stuff. And if there's anything of John's you want—"

Kali exploded. "You stuck me with all the work after Dad died. You're not going to do it again."

"I've got kids to think about."

"Peter's there, isn't he? And *I* have a job!"

Sabrina slipped into a pout. "You don't have to yell."

"You're the one who twisted my arm about investigating the murder, and now you expect me to handle everything with John's death, too?"

"Well, if it's legal and financial, you know how I—"

"Like to pass the buck."

Sabrina inhaled sharply. "I worked hard this morning."

Kali conceded the point with a nod. She knew she was overreacting. Sabrina's kids did need their mother, especially at a time like this.

"It's just that I know I'll mess something up," Sabrina whimpered.

"I doubt it. And so what if you do? You think I never make mistakes?"

"This stuff's important, though. And I'm so upset about John I—"

"And I'm not upset? Is that what you're saying? You think because I don't sit around all the time sniveling, it doesn't affect me?" The volume of Kali's voice had risen and the couple seated next to them looked over.

"Okay, settle down." Sabrina fiddled with her fork.

They sat in silence a moment, until finally Kali spoke. "I'm sorry. I think we're both short-tempered because we're feeling so awful about John."

Sabrina nodded glumly. "I'm not trying to stick this all on you. Honestly. But I do need to go home."

Kali sighed. "I understand."

Sabrina grinned. "And I've never actually seen you make a mistake."

# CHAPTER 10

"It would have been nice if we could have done this when John was alive," Sabrina told Kali as they emerged from the restaurant into the heat of the afternoon. "All three of us."

Kali nodded. "It's been ages since we were together."

"Last time was six or seven years ago. Thanksgiving at the old house in Silver Creek. Dad was still alive, and you and I cooked."

"We roasted a turkey," Kali said, with a laugh. "As I recall, we bought everything else."

"The turkey's what it's all about anyway."

Kali couldn't have pulled the occasion out of memory on her own, but now the day came back to her in a string of vignettes. Her father half drunk before noon. Sabrina insisting they use their mother's china dishes, even though they had to be washed by hand. Sabrina's husband, Peter, withdrawn, as he often was at O'Brien gatherings.

"John and the boys were playing football out front," Kali recalled, with a chuckle. "They came to the table covered in grass stains and you were royally pissed at all of them."

"You don't know how hard it is to get young boys to dress up," Sabrina protested. "They were dirty before I even got a chance to get pictures." She was silent a moment as they crossed the parking lot. "You could have come to Scottsdale for holidays, you know. I invited you every year. John came."

"I know." Each year there'd been a reason why Kali had found it easier not to go. Now the three of them would never be together again.

Sabrina tossed her the keys. "You can drive. I'm stuffed."

Kali unlocked the doors. She started the engine and turned the air-conditioning on full blast, then waited for it to kick in before she pulled out of the parking lot.

"Why don't you give Reed a call?" Kali suggested. "Ask if this is a good time for us to come by."

"What should I say, exactly?"

"Ask if we can talk to him about what happened. He knew John better than anyone. Maybe he'll have some insights or other leads."

Sabrina pulled her cell phone from her purse. "You don't have the number by any chance?"

"Try information."

Not surprisingly, Reed Logan had an unlisted number.

"I know where he lives," Sabrina said, "and I've met his wife before. Let's just go there. It's in a gated community, so it's not like we'd be showing up at his door unannounced."


Half an hour later Sabrina was talking into the intercom at the entrance to Sunrise Estates, an exclusive enclave near Ventana Canyon. Reed was out, his wife informed them. Only when prodded did she add that he would probably be back soon.

"Would it be okay if we waited for him?" Sabrina asked, showing far more audacity than Kali would have been able to muster.

"I guess you could do that." Linette buzzed them through, and the wide gate opened.

Sabrina directed Kali along a looping road, past a succession of oversized houses on cactus-studded lots, and then up a long drive.

A petite, dark-haired woman with a husky, smoker's

voice greeted them at the door. She couldn't have been more than five two, with no curves to speak of, and big, brown eyes. Dressed in capris and a crop top, she looked to be in her late twenties or early thirties, a decade or so younger than Reed.

Sabrina introduced Kali to Linette Logan, then said, "We're really sorry about what happened to Sloane."

There was an awkward moment's pause while Linette seemed to be searching for the proper response. "Yes, well . . . it's all quite hard to believe, really." She shifted her weight onto one leg, regarded them for a moment, then lowered her gaze. "You must feel even worse about John."

Dead was dead, Kali thought. What did it matter that one death was the result of murder and the other accidental? Then it dawned on her that Linette was referring to John's alleged role in Sloane's murder. And she hadn't offered any additional comment attesting to his innocence.

The subtext of Linette's remark apparently eluded Sabrina, who murmured, "Thank you. It's truly incomprehensible."

"Well, Reed should be back any minute now." Linette led them to a family room at the back of the house facing a garden and redwood gazebo.

The room was light and spacious, with a terra-cotta-tiled floor and a beamed ceiling. The decor was heavily southwestern. A bit too thematic for Kali's taste, which tended to be more eclectic, although she had to admit the furnishings fit the house. Mostly she was impressed by the fact that the air-conditioning hadn't been cranked down to refrigerator levels.

"Were you and Sloane close?" Kali asked when they'd gotten seated. The furniture looked heavy and dark, and she was surprised when the chair turned out to be quite comfortable.

"Not really. We didn't have a lot in common." Linette paused for a half laugh. "Sloane was pretty assertive. Even Reed had trouble standing his ground with her sometimes."

"Assertive in what way?"

"We got along—don't get me wrong. Sloane could be warm and generous. But she was a force to be reckoned with." Linette swung her leg, her sandal slapping against her heel. "I mean, there she was, not involved in the business for years, then suddenly she takes it into her head to dictate the direction of the company. She started visiting the stores, talking to managers, and offering unsolicited advice. She thought she was helping, but in a lot of ways she was just creating more tension."

A garage door groaned open at the front of the house and Linette shot out of her seat. "That's Reed now. I'll tell him you're here."

She left and returned a moment later with her husband.

Kali hadn't seen Reed Logan in probably fifteen years. He was a little heavier than before and had a few more lines around his eyes and mouth, but the broad open face, square jaw, and pale Nordic coloring hadn't changed. She'd have recognized him anywhere.

He shook her hand warmly, gave Sabrina a hug, then collapsed onto the couch next to his wife. "I'm so sorry about John," he said, leaning forward, arms on his knees. "I hardly know what to say."

Sabrina nodded glumly. "I knew he drank, but I thought the . . . the pills were a thing of the past."

"He was going through a rough period." Reed dropped his head to his hands. "Jesus, it's all such a muddle."

Kali frowned. "A muddle how?"

Reed raised his head to look at them. His expression was pained. "You know the cops think John was responsible for Sloane's death?"

He directed the comment to both of them and they nodded in unison. Kali waited for him to continue, but instead, he wove his fingers together and let the words speak for themselves.

Sabrina looked confused. "You can't believe—"

But he clearly did. "You think they're right?" Kali asked.

Reed gave a labored sigh. "I don't know what to think, to tell you the truth. John was my best friend. Had been since freshman year in college. We could practically read each other's minds. And yet . . ." Another sigh.

"And yet, what?"

"I don't know. He seemed on edge about something. And he really freaked when the police started questioning him about Sloane."

"That's only natural," Kali said.

"He refused to talk to the cops until he'd talked to you," Linette added. "Not what you'd expect from someone who was innocent."

"Having counsel present is always wise," Kali said. "In fact, some attorneys advise clients not to talk to the cops at all." It was too easy to get tripped up, even if you were innocent. Intentions were misconstrued; details got twisted or didn't line up right; and before you knew it, your efforts to be helpful came back and bit you in the face.

"And then with his death . . ." Reed paused, looked down at his hands for a moment before again raising his gaze. "I've asked myself if it might not have been accidental. If maybe . . . I mean, coming when it did, it's crossed my mind that he did it on purpose."

"Took his own life, you mean?" Sabrina's voice was strident, her face suddenly flushed.

"I'm not saying I think that's what happened," Reed protested, "just that it's possible. Something was definitely weighing on him."

"But not necessarily guilt," Kali pointed out, rising to her brother's defense. Reed's words were like hot coals in her gut. If John killed himself, had she pushed him over the edge by refusing to talk to him? Kali felt ill; for a moment she couldn't breathe.

"It was just a thought. I probably shouldn't have said anything." Reed stared at his hands. "They were at loggerheads, you know. John and Sloane. John had his eye on the bottom line. But Sloane had other ideas."

"Where did *you* come down?" Kali asked.

"With John, mostly. Not that I was happy about some of the cuts we had to make, but the profit margin in the grocery business is thin enough as it is. I saw Sloane's side of it too, though. We're part of the neighborhoods we serve. Have been ever since my grandfather started this business sixty years ago. Honesty and quality, that's always been at the core of what we do."

"Bottom line," Linette interjected, "is that Sloane had voting rights and John didn't. And because she was a Logan, she had the directors' ears. She was a major thorn in John's side."

Sabrina's eyes narrowed and her mouth pulled tight. She turned to Reed, her voice quiet and controlled. "I would have thought you, of all people, would stand behind him."

"My sister was murdered. You think I'm happy about the fact that her killer may have been my best friend? It tears me up inside. But I'm not standing behind *anyone* who did that to her."

"That's the whole point," Sabrina said bleakly. "You're assuming the worst about John."

Reed dipped his head. "They're both dead. Does it really matter?"

"John couldn't have been the only potential suspect the police talked to," Kali prompted. "What about anyone Sloane was seeing? Or her ex-husband? Maybe someone with a grudge?"

"Her divorce was fairly amicable, especially considering what a jerk she married. Besides, the police cleared him almost immediately. He was attending some big conference at the time."

"What about the girl? Could there have been some conflict between them?"

"Olivia Perez? She lived with Sloane. Well, she had a room there. Supposedly in return for work she did."

"Olivia was another of Sloane's projects," Linette said.

"Her projects?" Kali asked.

Linette rolled her eyes. Her sister-in-law's *projects* were apparently something of a family joke. "Sloane adopted causes, and on occasion, people."

Reed explained. "She hooked up with Olivia through

an organization that matches disadvantaged students with members of the community who can offer housing in exchange for chores. Olivia did light housekeeping, ran errands and such, but she didn't work very hard. That's what Linette means. It wasn't so much that Sloane needed the help as that she wanted *to* help."

"How do the police know Olivia wasn't the intended victim?"

Reed shrugged. "I don't know why she would be. There's certainly no evidence to indicate that. She was a nice girl, good-looking in an exotic sort of way. Her father's an unemployed drunk, from what I understand—"

"That was Sloane's somewhat biased take on him," Linette interjected.

Reed ignored his wife's interruption. "But the mom's apparently a good influence. Works as a maid in one of the big hotels. There's an older brother, too. Had some trouble with the law at one point, but he seems to have turned himself around."

"Sloane arranged for him to work as a bagger at one of the stores," Linette said. "That's what I mean by *projects*."

Kali was beginning to get a feel for the kind of woman Sloane had been. She was also getting the idea that Linette wasn't one of her biggest fans.

"I understand why you don't want to believe John killed her," Reed said sympathetically. "Believe me, I wish it weren't true. But wishing doesn't change what is."

# CHAPTER 11

"Linette is such a snot," Sabrina grumbled, as she slammed the car door. She crossed her arms and pressed her head against the back of the seat. "I've never liked her. I'm sure she's the one who turned Reed against John."

Kali started the engine and turned the air-conditioning to high. "There's also evidence," she pointed out. "Reed can hardly ignore that."

"But they've been friends for years. I was sure he would tell us the cops had it all wrong."

"What Reed thinks isn't important," Kali told her. "It's what the police think that's the issue."

"And they think John killed her." Sabrina sighed and fell silent. After a moment, she added, "That's why you have to convince them they're wrong."

Assuming they actually were wrong. And that was something Kali needed to know for herself.

"I want to go by Sloane's," she said. "Do you want to come or would you prefer to drop me off at the rental car place and head back to John's?"

"The house where she was murdered?" Sabrina looked ill. "Why do you want to go there? That's ghoulish."

"It helps to get the lay of the land, to be able to visualize the crime, what witnesses might have seen, that sort of thing." It would be even more helpful, of course, if she could get inside the house. She might learn something about Sloane, as well. But it had been clear that asking Reed for a key wasn't an option.

Sabrina made a face. "You *want* to visualize the murders?"

"Not because I get a kick out of it," Kali snapped. She was hot and tired, and in the back of her mind, she was worried she'd only wind up convincing herself of John's guilt. "You were the one urging me to look into Sloane's murder. For that, I need information."

"Okay, okay. You don't have to get your knickers in a twist."

"So are you coming with me or not?"

"Yeah, sure. You're such great company, how could I pass up the opportunity for more sisterly bonding?"


Sloane Winslow lived in an older development in the foothills. The streets meandered in mazelike fashion and the houses were set far apart. They were less pretentious than some of the newer places higher up in the hills, but there was an air of established serenity about the area that appealed to Kali.

The driveway was circular and made of crushed rock. Kali pulled in and turned off the engine.

"This must be where John parked," she said. She realized she'd subconsciously bought into the official scenario and immediately corrected herself. "Where a car like John's was parked."

"Yeah, I guess so." Sabrina had apparently not caught Kali's slip.

"At night, it must be really dark out here." There were, Kali noted, no streetlights. Nor was there a house directly across the street. The roadway, also gravel, was divided by a median of natural scrub. She wondered how the witness had spotted the silver Porsche.

"It's dark everywhere in Tucson at night," Sabrina said. "Especially in the hills. It's because of the Kitt Peak Observatory. They don't want a lot of light making it difficult to see the stars."

Kali remembered sleeping under the open sky in the Sierra with Bryce only a few days earlier, the stars so bountiful they took your breath away. The memory seemed to belong to another life. She realized she hadn't called him since she'd arrived in Tucson.

"Let's take a look." Kali set the parking brake and they got out of the car.

"What are we looking for?" Sabrina shielded her eyes from the sun with a hand.

"Imagine you're the killer. What would you do?"

"Well, I wouldn't park my car in the driveway, for one thing."

"Good point." Kali tried the front door, just for the heck of it. Locked.

The gate on the right side of the house was open, and Kali pushed through. More crushed rock led past a cactus garden to the back of the house, where a patio and pool gave way to a vista of the city to the south and mountains to the east.

Large windows and French doors faced the yard. Kali pressed her nose to the glass, peered through the open spots in the blinds, but she wasn't able to see much. She tried the doors. Locked tight.

"You really want to get in?" Sabrina asked.

Kali shrugged, embarrassed to have been caught in the act. "I'd only be doing it to help John."

"Hey, I'm not judging." Sabrina wandered back to the side of the house and returned a moment later with a key.

"Where'd you get that?" Kali asked, incredulous.

"It was hidden in one of those fake rocks. I noticed it coming up the side of the house. I have the same thing at home." She tried the key in the door and the lock turned. "Ta-da."

As Sabrina pushed the door open, Kali had second thoughts.

"There might be an alarm system," she warned. They paused to listen. But the only sound to be heard was the high-pitched buzz of insects from the yard.

"Guess not," Sabrina said.

So much for security. Still, breaking and entering was a crime. One Kali had committed on previous occasions, true, but never without a degree of trepidation.

Sabrina was already inside. "Are you coming?" she called.

Their motives were honorable, Kali told herself, as she followed her sister into the sunny breakfast area. A vase of droopy asters sat in the center of a round wood table. The air was heavy and rank.

They crossed through the kitchen into the living area, where vestiges of violence presented a disquieting contrast to the cozy furnishings. Chalk marks and bits of masking tape left behind by the police. Shards of blue glass from a broken vase, an overturned lamp, an ivory-hued wall peppered with tiny holes. And blood. It had pooled on the tile floor, then dried, leaving a sticky, black residue. On the wall near the doorway was a dried streak of it, and above that, a smeared handprint.

"Oh, my God," Sabrina gasped. She pressed a balled fist against her mouth. "I don't think I'm up for this."

Kali felt the bile rise in her own throat. The sheer brutality of murder always shocked her. The thought that John might have had a hand in it was horrifying.

"You want to wait outside?" she asked. "I won't be long." In truth, she wanted to flee with her sister.

Sabrina nodded numbly and left the way they'd come in.

Kali made herself wander through the main rooms of the house, getting a sense of Sloane. Bold art, strong southwestern colors, and a sleek uncluttered style that she found inviting. Lots of books—fiction, history, art, cookbooks. A U-shaped kitchen with cherry cabinets and granite counters lined with upscale appliances.

Returning to the living area, Kali tried to visualize the scene as it would have been the night Sloane was killed.

From the police markings, it appeared she'd been in the living room, Olivia coming from the other wing. The killer must have been standing near where Kali was now.

Why had Sloane let him in? Or was it Olivia who'd done that? Was the face at the door someone they recognized?

John would be a familiar face. But not the only one, Kali reminded herself.

She moved on to the bedroom wing. The master bed and bath, again tastefully decorated in bold colors and furniture with clean lines. A guest room and an office. An oak file cabinet held too many files for Kali to examine in depth, but she glanced quickly through the folders—bills, bank statements, typical household records. Of course, the police had been here before her. No telling what they'd taken.

The answering machine light was blinking. Kali hit PLAY. Two messages: one from a telemarketer, the other letting Sloane know the print she'd taken in for framing was ready. Kali held the play key down longer, hoping she'd be able to pick up earlier messages, but they'd already been erased. She wondered what had been on the machine when the police had arrived.

She couldn't find an address book or a Rolodex, though she did find Sloane's cell phone, still plugged into its charger. She scrolled through the stored numbers and copied them onto a sheet of paper.

Then she retraced her steps through the main rooms of the house to the other end, where a door led to a separate guest wing with a studio bedroom, bath, and small kitchenette. Kali guessed it was the room Olivia Perez was using.

The bedroom walls were painted a soft peach. A wood-frame bed with a pin-striped comforter in subtle shades of green and rust was centered on one wall, a pine bureau next to it. On the opposite wall was a small desk with papers neatly stacked; no computer; and a low bookcase that held textbooks, school supplies, and a box of tissues. There were no posters on the walls, no dried flowers, stuffed animals, or other memorabilia tucked about. It was a functional room, warm and comfortable, but not personal in the way Kali would have expected a young woman's room to be.

On the desk, under a spiral notebook labeled SOC 251, Kali found a slim book of love poems with a soft, hand-tooled leather cover. On the inside flap was an inscription:

> *Olivia,*
> *There are hundreds of languages in the world,*
> *but a smile speaks them all. And yours speaks*
> *to me. Because of your smile, you make life*
> *more beautiful.*

The signature was an indecipherable scrawl ending in a loopy letter, maybe a *y* or *g,* in which the writer had drawn eyes and a mouth in smiley-face fashion.

Kali heard voices outside, near the front of the house, and froze. Was someone coming?

She quickly returned the book to its place under the sociology notebook, went back to the kitchen, and slipped out through the French doors.

She found Sabrina in the shade of the front porch talking to a pudgy woman in her midforties who was cradling a tiny white dog in her arms.

"Hey, Kali. This is Janet Fisher," Sabrina said. "And her dog Snowball. They live next door. Janet thought we were real estate agents."

"Just a guess. I might know someone who'd be interested in buying the place."

Kali looked to Sabrina for a clue. God knew what her sister had told the woman.

"I explained we were friends of the family," Sabrina said, with wide-eyed innocence.

"What they must be going through," Janet said, with a shake of her head. "You don't expect something terrible like this in a quiet neighborhood like ours. I know most everyone on this street and the next one over. We've never had a lick of trouble before this. Well, there was a string of auto thefts a couple of years ago. Being so close to the Mexican border and all, it's a problem."

"You weren't by any chance the one who spotted a car parked here the night of the murders, were you?" Kali asked her.

"No, that was Les Billings. He lives over there." Janet pointed to a house diagonally across the street.

From where they were standing, Kali could make out only the rooftop. "He could see the driveway from there?"

"He was coming home." Janet scratched Snowball behind the ears. "You have to drive down this side of the road to that break in the median in order to cross and get back to his place."

"Did *you* see anything?" Kali asked.

Janet shook her head. "Of course, with four kids, I've learned to block out a lot." The dog was squirming in her arms. She set him on the ground, with a warning to behave himself. "But I was the one who called the police," Janet continued, with an air of self-importance. "If the day hadn't been so hectic, I'd have noticed sooner. The police told me it wouldn't have made a difference, though. They were both already dead."

"Noticed what?" Sabrina asked.

"Little things. Like the newspaper wasn't picked up and the interior lights were on. I just *sensed* something was different. That's just the way I am. Observant, well, nosy according to my husband, but I like to know what's going on. They interviewed me on the evening news, you know."

A busybody, in other words. Kali could imagine Janet might be difficult to take in large doses, but for her purposes right then, the woman was ideal. "How well did you know Sloane Winslow?" Kali asked.

Janet took her time brushing loose stands of white dog hair from her shirt, loving the spotlight. "She moved in only a little over a year ago. But most of the folks on this street are older, and Sloane and I were close to the same age, so that gave us something in common."

Although Kali had never met Sloane, she had to imagine

that age might have been the only thing the two women had had in common. "What about her other friends?" she asked. "Did you know any of them?"

"Sloane pretty much kept to herself. Just recently that girl, Olivia, moved in. She was a quiet thing. You hardly knew she was there. And not very friendly, either. One of my sons is about the same age. We invited her to a party but she wasn't interested." Janet frowned. "Didn't you say you were part of Sloane's family?"

"Friends of the family," Sabrina said easily. "We've known her brother, Reed, for years."

Kali piped in, "He's devastated, of course. And he wants to make sure word of her death reaches the people she knew."

The frown softened to a look of understanding. "Of course. If Sloane mentioned names, it was only in passing." Janet paused, then continued conspiratorially. "Sloane *was* seeing someone for a while. It's been over for months, though."

"Really?" This was interesting. No one had mentioned that Sloane might have had an ex-lover as well as an ex-husband. Affairs of the heart were always worth looking at where motive was concerned. "What do you know about him?"

"She didn't talk about it much." Janet sounded miffed at not being in the loop. "I don't suppose it's important anyway. The police have a pretty good idea who did it, don't they?"

"There's some question whether they're right," Sabrina said emphatically.

"Oh, I hadn't heard that. I certainly hope they aren't thinking it was some random nut case. It's frightening enough as it is."

A young voice called out from the street. "Mom! Where have you been? I've been looking all over for you."

"I'm coming, Beck." Janet scooped up the dog, who'd been busily sniffing Kali's feet. "If there's any way I can help, tell the family to give me a call. Fisher. It's in the phone book."

When she'd gone, Kali held up the house key. "Show me where this goes, will you? Then let's go see if Les Billings is in."

* * *

The Billings house had the same type of circular gravel driveway as Sloane's, but the yard was landscaped with metal sculptures of desert animals instead of live plants. The door was answered by a skinny man in baggy Bermuda shorts and a short-sleeved shirt with what looked like mustard stains down the front. Kali guessed he was in his early sixties.

"You two look too pretty to be Jehovah's Witnesses," he said, with a twinkle in his eye.

Kali humored him with a chuckle. "Mr. Billings?"

"That's right."

"We'd like to talk to you about the car you saw the night Mrs. Winslow was killed."

"You're reporters?"

"I'm a lawyer," Kali replied, a nonanswer that sometimes worked.

Sabrina piped in with a cheery "And I'm her assistant."

"My older son's a lawyer. The other one," he said with a grin, "could be a perpetual client. What is it you want to know?"

"Can you walk us through what you told the police?" Kali asked.

"There isn't really much to tell."

"We'd like to hear what you observed."

Sabrina nodded. "It's important we hear it in your own words."

Kali shot her a silencing look, but Sabrina was busy batting her eyelashes and probably missed it.

"Well," Les Billings said, "I was coming home from a very long and boring evening with my brother and his wife when I saw a silver Porsche parked in Sloane Winslow's driveway. It was a car I'd not seen there before. It started up and pulled away just as I drove past, and I saw that one of the taillights was broken."

"Did you get a look at the driver?"

"Not a good look. My impression was of a male, but I couldn't swear to it."

Equivocating witness testimony might earn points for the defense in the courtroom, but unfortunately it wasn't going to help them now.

"What time was this?" Kali asked.

"About eleven."

"Did you see anyone else? Any other unusual cars on the street?"

Les Billings shook his head. "But I wasn't really looking, either. It's just that the Porsche caught my eye, especially starting up just as I drove past."

As Sabrina had remarked, it was a foolish killer who parked his car in plain view. Kali now added her own corollary: it was equally foolish to draw attention to yourself by fleeing the scene of the crime in front of a witness.

Kali had called John many things in her life, but foolish wasn't one of them.

# CHAPTER 12

Erling was finishing his report on an assault of an elderly woman outside a Walgreens store when Michelle Parker appeared at his desk. She slid a plastic-encased drawing across to him.

"We've got a sketch of our Jane Doe," she said, brushing the hair from her face, "but no match with any of the missing persons reports."

Erling closed his eyes briefly, taking a moment to center himself before looking down and finally putting a face to the young woman whose nude body had been discovered two weeks ago in a wash in East County.

The coroner had pegged the time of death as a couple of weeks earlier, but the combined effects of decomposition and animal scavenging made it difficult to be certain. His best guess was that she'd choked to death on her own vomit as a result of being bound and gagged.

He estimated her age to be between sixteen and twenty.

Erling took pride in never losing sight of the fact that murder victims were more than case files. They were people with hopes, dreams, and fears. With families and friends. In living and in dying, they touched many lives. Erling carried their stories in his mind and heart; they touched him, too.

And it was one of the reasons he liked working with Michelle. She felt the same.

Lately, though, he'd begun to wish he were more like his brethren who consciously distanced themselves from the crimes they were working. He'd about had his fill of perversity and death.

Erling took the black-and-white sketch from Michelle and pulled it closer. It showed a young woman with shoulder-length curls, round cheeks, and wide-set eyes. Neither homely nor beautiful, but attractive with the bloom of youth. She was more or less as he'd imagined, but seeing her likeness there on the page, as though she'd posed for a portrait at a local street fair, wrenched his heart. She was too young to have died at all, much less so tragically.

"Isabel says the mouth may not be right," Michelle told him. "She didn't have as much to work with as she'd have liked."

Isabel was the forensic artist who worked with the sheriff's department. She also taught criminology at the university. "So it's a good likeness," Erling asked, "but not perfect?"

"Right. With the identifying data of height, weight, and coloring, though, it ought to be close enough that someone will recognize her."

"Let's hope so," Erling said. He held on to the thought that somewhere this girl had family who loved her and were frantically trying to find her. He wanted that to be so, not because he wished them to suffer, but because the alternative, that no one cared about her, was worse.

Michelle reached for the sketch. "Too bad we don't have more to go on. "

"Yeah, even one little break would be nice." Nothing had turned up despite a thorough search of the area. And they'd yet to find anyone who saw the body being dumped. They didn't even have clothing or jewelry to trace.

"So we just sit on our hands and wait?" Michelle asked.

"If you've got any suggestions, feel free to share them."

She grinned at him. "When have I ever *not* shared my

suggestions?" It was something of a joke between them because Michelle was much more vocal than Erling.

He managed a feeble smile in return. He liked Michelle, and she was a good partner, but he wasn't in a joking mood.

"And I actually do have an idea," she said, more seriously. "Remember the tattoo on her back? It's an unusual design. If she's local, maybe we can track down the artist and get an ID that way."

Erling nodded, though he thought the prospects of success were slim. "Give it a try," he said.

"Oh, and one of John O'Brien's sisters came by again today. Kali. She's an attorney, it turns out. She had more questions about her brother's death, and also about Sloane Winslow's murder."

Erling felt his stomach knot. "What did you tell her?"

"About the murders, not a lot. It's technically still an open case, after all. About her brother, there wasn't much to add to what we gave her yesterday. When the coroner's report comes in, I'll make sure she gets a copy."

Michelle's response had been on target. Erling felt himself relax a little. "I imagine they're having a tough time of it."

"Right." She turned to go. "Have a good weekend. See you Monday, if not before."

That was also a joke. They'd see each other before Monday only if they got called in for another homicide. This time Erling didn't even attempt a smile.

"Monday it is," he growled.

Mindy was on the computer in her room when Erling stopped in to greet her. As always, and especially in the years since Danny's death, the sight of his daughter filled his heart with bittersweet love and pride. The loss of one child made the other child all the more precious. He regarded her quietly for a moment.

Mindy complained that her softly rounded face and small mouth made her unattractive. Jennifer Lopez, Britney Spears,

Paris Hilton—*they* were beautiful. Erling didn't see it that way at all, and it saddened him that Mindy couldn't appreciate her own unique and very real loveliness.

"Hi, sweetheart," he said.

"Hi, Daddy," she said, without taking her eyes from the computer screen. "How's the body business?"

"Better now that the weekend's here. How was your day?"

"I've got a huge paper due Monday, and a test the same day." She groaned. "Good-bye weekend."

"The professors just sprang both on you at the last minute, I suppose."

"Ha-ha. I can't spend *all* my time studying."

He blew her a kiss and closed the door behind him when he left. It seemed like only yesterday that she and Danny had raced to him for a hug when he returned from work each evening, then peppered him with the news of their day. Now Danny was gone forever and Erling was lucky if he got thirty seconds of Mindy's attention. He felt an ache in his chest that radiated deep into his soul.

Children weren't supposed to die. But growing up, he reminded himself, was part of the natural cycle. Mindy was a young woman now. Her life no longer centered on her family. Still, if he had the power, no question he'd turn the clock back and do it all again.

Deena was standing at the sink tearing lettuce for the salad. "Hi, honey," she said, tossing the greeting over her shoulder.

The second member of his family to greet him with her back turned. Not like the early days when she'd flown into his arms. "Can I help?"

"You can put a pot of water on for the pasta."

Erling gave her a peck on the cheek. "Were the gremlins good to you today?"

"The gremlins are fine. It's their parents that I sometimes have trouble with."

"What happened?"

"Just the usual 'my kid can do no wrong.'"

"We were probably just as obnoxious when our kids were young."

"We? How many parent-teacher conferences did you attend?" Her tone was teasing rather than bitter, but the words called up past arguments and Erling felt himself grow defensive. He'd been working, for Chrissake. Logging in long, hard hours to pay the rent and put food on the table. But he knew, too, that if that clock somehow got turned back, he'd do it differently this time.

Deena handed him the pasta pot and gave his butt a playful pinch. "Fill it about two-thirds full."

"I think I can manage that."

"And if you really want to be helpful, you could set the table."

Erling put the pot of water on to boil, then got out three woven straw placemats. What did it mean that Kali O'Brien had returned with questions about Sloane's murder? Nothing, he told himself. She was a grieving sister who'd just learned that her brother was a killer. Of course she'd have questions. Anyone would. Especially a lawyer.

And that was what concerned him. He didn't want her poking around trying to discredit his case. He didn't want her running to the media with cockeyed stories of *alternative killers*.

He just wanted the whole thing to go away.

Sloane was gone from him forever. In his mind he knew she'd been gone months ago, but his heart wasn't so rational, and in the ten days since her death he'd felt the pain of losing her all over again. The anger he felt toward John O'Brien boiled in his blood every day. He was glad the bastard had gotten sloshed and ended up at the bottom of his pool. It was no worse than he deserved.

But Erling's pain and anger were mingled with relief. So far his secret had escaped detection. As long as John O'Brien remained tagged as Sloane's killer, Erling's affair with Sloane would stay hidden. The last thing he needed now was a nosy relative looking to save her brother's reputation. A nosy *lawyer* relative.

"Honey?" Deena was at the stove, stirring the marinara sauce. "I forgot to tell you—your optometrist's office left a message confirming Monday's appointment. You need to call and let them know you'll be there."

"They'll have gone home by now." He hated the practice of confirming a confirmation, but it seemed to be standard these days.

"They've got voice mail."

Erling hit caller ID to return the call. Inadvertently he hit the up arrow, rather than the down arrow, taking him to the top of the list, twenty-five calls ago. And he felt as though someone had taken a sledgehammer to his chest.

Two days before she'd been killed, Sloane Winslow had called his home number.

Had she left a message that Deena had forgotten to tell him about? What if she'd spoken with Deena directly? He recalled Deena's curious interest in the case. Was that because she recognized the name?

Erling's pulse raced. Beads of perspiration formed at his temples. What had Sloane wanted? What did Deena know? And with a meddling lawyer in the picture, how likely was it that Sloane's phone records would come to light?

# CHAPTER 13

Kali placed a call to Sloane's ex-husband, whose number she'd copied from Sloane's cell phone, and left a message. Then she took her glass of wine out onto the shaded patio, where she watched the play of light from the setting sun reflected on the Catalina Mountains. The evening was warm but not unbearable as it had been the previous night. Or maybe she was simply getting acclimated.

The rugged beauty of the desert was impressive, but it didn't soothe her like vistas of the Sierra or even the expanse of the San Francisco Bay she could see from her own back deck. In the desert, Kali felt isolated and exposed. Especially out here where John lived. She knew there were houses around, but from where she sat now, none were visible. There was no hum of human activity in the background, either. No neighbors' voices, no car doors banging or dogs barking.

Despite the heat, Kali shivered and wished Sabrina were here.

Her gaze slid to the pool, which she'd been deliberately avoiding until now. How ironic that John had ended up drowning in a backyard pool. At their mother's insistence, all of the O'Briens had learned to swim at an early age, but none of them were serious swimmers. Sabrina had always preferred flirting on the sidelines and absolutely hated to get her hair wet. Kali liked to cool off in the water, and she'd some-times swim a lap or two, but she found anything more than that tedious. John was not big on exercise of any sort. Even with a pool of his own, she doubted he made much use of it.

She tried to picture how it might have happened. John coming out to enjoy the night, just as she had. Only it would have been much darker then, his balance and judgment impaired. Somehow he lost his balance or slipped and ended up face down in the water, too inebriated to save himself.

How could he have been so stupid? Booze and drugs—didn't he know better?

Anger choked back the tears that had begun to sting her eyes. But it wasn't just anger at John. As long as she was meting out blame, she had to look at herself, as well. Why had she cut him off during that last phone call? If she'd taken the time to listen to him, would he have felt the need to numb himself into a stupor?

Or to take his own life?

She bit her lip. No, she wasn't going there, no matter what Reed suggested. Not John. His death was a terrible, wasteful tragedy brought on by his own carelessness. But it was accidental. It had to be, or the burden of her guilt would be too great to bear.

Regret was difficult enough.

Kali was seized by the sudden desire to get a sense of the man others saw in John. She wasn't about to box up his be-longings without consulting Sabrina, but she could do a first cut and at the same time learn a little about her brother.

She wandered inside and poured herself another glass of wine, then looked around the kitchen. John favored high-quality cookware and appliances, no surprise there. His cup-boards were sparsely stocked but neat, his dishes and flatware simple but elegant. Not the sort of thing you picked up at Target. A bottom drawer held dish towels, including two that their mother had embroidered many years before. Kali remembered her sitting in front of the television every evening, sometimes embroidering, sometimes knitting, her hands never idle. John must have gotten them from Sabrina after she and Kali had cleaned out the family home following their father's death. They'd made a separate pile for John when they had divvied things up, but Kali hadn't paid much attention to what had gone in it. As usual, she'd stormed through the process of settling the estate without much thought to either of her siblings. Although, to be fair, neither of them had offered to help.

Moving on to the living room, she examined the CDs in the rack by the sound system. Jazz, country, and modern classics like Eric Clapton and Led Zeppelin. She wouldn't have pegged John as someone who listened to country, but their dad had been a big fan and maybe that had influenced John's taste. He had only a couple dozen DVDs: *Band of Brothers,* about World War II; three seasons of *The Shield;* and a small collection of what looked like porn movies. She wouldn't have pegged him for that, either.

She browsed the bookshelves in John's den—popular fiction, history, the classics, an economics text, and a few self-help books. She pulled a couple down at random to see if there were other photos tucked between the covers. There weren't.

But in one of the desk drawers, she did find a box of loose photos, mostly family pictures from their childhood. On top were more recent photos: Sabrina's family; holidays; and several of Kali, including one John had taken during his last visit when they'd climbed Mt. Tam. She'd been impatient with him that afternoon, telling him to wait for another time when the wind hadn't mussed her hair and she'd had a chance to put on lipstick. Now she'd give anything to go back and relive that moment, just to see her brother again.

The ring of her cell phone saved her from further self-recrimination. When she saw from the display that it was Bryce, she experienced a flutter of pleasure that was quickly quelled by uneasiness. She'd told Bryce only that John had died—not that he'd stumbled drunk into his own pool and drowned, nor that he was the prime suspect in a double homicide. And although it was foolish, Kali was hesitant about laying it all out now. She feared it might taint her by association. She hated that she felt that way—that she was betraying John by being embarrassed, and Bryce by not trusting him.

"Hi," she said into the phone, still breathless from the dash to dig it out of her purse.

"Hi, yourself." His voice was soft, like the caress of a summer's breeze, and she felt her skin tingle in spite of her nerves. "How are you holding up? You haven't called and I've been worried."

"I'm sorry. There's been so much going on." Although she *had* managed to call Jared to check on things at the office. What did that say? she wondered.

"What happened with John? Was it an auto accident?"

"He drowned," Kali said. "In his backyard pool."

"In the pool? Couldn't he swim?"

She closed her eyes, as if that would make the words less real. "Booze and Xanax. Too much of both."

"Oh, Kali, I'm sorry." Bryce seemed to be searching for something more to say. Offering condolences for an automobile accident was certainly a more straightforward matter.

"But that's only part of it," she blurted out. In for a dime, in for a dollar. "He was a murder suspect. In fact, the police were close to arresting him. I think that's probably why he was trying to reach me. And why he binged on drugs and alcohol."

A beat of silence, and then Bryce asked, "Who do they say he killed?"

"Two women." Kali filled him in on the details. "Sabrina isn't having any of it. She's sure the cops are wrong. But I think . . . I mean, I worry . . ." She took a breath. "What if he actually did it?"

"You think he could have?"

"I don't know. Part of me says *no way*. He's my brother, after all, even if he was sometimes a bit of a jerk. But there's evidence suggesting he did. And I know what a temper he had. I don't want to believe it, yet I can't rule it out."

"Jeez, you must be torn up inside."

The caring she heard in his tone brought tears to Kali's eyes. "I'm okay."

"No one would be okay in those circumstances."

"Well, maybe not okay, but I'm . . ." She wiped her cheek. "He tried to reach me. All that time we were in the mountains. Maybe if I'd returned his call sooner . . ."

"You want me to come out there?" Bryce asked.

"Here?" She was both surprised and touched. The emotionally supportive Bryce was new to her. But she wasn't sure she was ready to have him share the ugly parts of her life up close and personal. "That's sweet. There's really nothing for you to do, though."

"I could be there for you. That's something."

Touché. It hadn't even crossed her mind. "I'd like that," she told him. "I'm just not sure, what with the funeral and Sabrina being here and all. . . ."

"Sure. I understand." But his tone said he didn't.

Kali wondered what was wrong with her that she wasn't more eager to have him close.


With all that was on her mind, Kali worried she might have trouble sleeping, but the minute her head hit the pillow she was out like a light. She was still half asleep the next morning when she heard what sounded like the bang of a door closing in another part of the house. She shot awake.

"Sabrina?"

There was no answer.

Kali was sure she'd heard a sound. She swung herself out of bed. Her heart was racing. What now?

Confront the intruder head on, or hide here and hope he never found her? In either case, she didn't want to meet up with him wearing only her pink and white shorty pj's. She pawed through her suitcase for a skirt and sweater, which she threw on over the pajamas. If only she hadn't left her cell phone in the kitchen.

She looked around the sparsely furnished guest bedroom for some way to defend herself but came up empty-handed. Finally, she said a silent prayer and tiptoed to the hallway.

She thought she could hear someone breathing.

"I have a gun," she called out, hoping the lie wasn't blatantly transparent. "Whoever you are, get out now."

"Don't shoot! Please. I not know anyone home."

The voice was female, older, with a Spanish accent.

Mindful of a trick, Kali approached cautiously. A round-figured woman in her late fifties hovered near the coffee table in the living room. She held her hands over her graying head. "Please, no shoot."

"Who are you?" Kali demanded.

"Graciela. I work for Mr. John."

At the crack of dawn on Saturday morning? "Work for him, how?"

"Around the house." The woman was eyeing Kali's empty hands, no doubt looking for the gun.

"He passed away a few days ago," Kali told her.

"Sí. I find him." Graciela lowered her head and crossed herself before raising her hands again and giving Kali another skeptical look. "You police? Reporter?"

"I'm his sister, Kali."

"Oh, I am sad for you." Graciela started to reach a plump arm for Kali's hand, then pulled back uncertainly.

"Why are you here?" Kali asked. "And you can put your hands down."

Graciela looked embarrassed. She tucked her hands into the pockets of her blue cotton sweater. "I don't mean to cause trouble. I return something."

Kali waited silently.

"The day your brother die, it was a bad day. Very much happening. Many, many people, police"—she made a sweeping gesture with her arm—"and here," she said, placing a hand over her heart, "I feel bad."

"I can imagine it was confusing and upsetting for you," Kali said noncommittally.

"Sí. And when I finally leave, it's late. I am in a hurry. I take Mr. John's appointment book." She nodded toward a weekly calendar on the coffee table. "It was on the kitchen counter, near my bag. I no mean to. I am not thief."

"No, of course not." Kali had no idea, really, whether she

was or not, but the woman didn't look dangerous and that was all that mattered at the moment.

Graciela also had firsthand information about John. Kali wanted to pump her for what she could.

"Would you like some coffee?" Kali offered. "Or tea?"

"I make." Graciela hurried into the kitchen.

Kali followed. "I didn't mean for you to make it."

"Sit. I do it. Please."

Kali sat at the counter while Graciela bustled about the kitchen. Kali wanted to ask about finding John's body but couldn't decide the best way to raise the issue.

"It must have been horrible for you, finding John in the pool," she said finally.

Graciela nodded and again crossed herself. "The patio door was open. I think he outside. I begin work in here, in the kitchen. Much mess, like Mr. John make a sandwich and not clean up." She opened her hands, palms up.

That explained why the kitchen had been so neat when she and Sabrina had arrived, Kali thought. Graciela had just cleaned it.

Gracelia continued recounting the morning she'd found John's body. "I finish here in the kitchen, then scrub the bathroom. Still no Mr. John. I go outside, call his name. I think maybe he go to work and forget about the door." She paused, looking distraught.

"And then you saw him?"

"*Sí*. In the water, at the bottom."

"What did you do?"

Graciela started crying. "I no swim. I not help."

"No one's blaming you, Graciela. I'm just trying to understand what happened. There was nothing you could have done to save him."

"The doctor say that too." Still, she looked miserable.

Kali took the cup of coffee Graciela handed her. "Sit down," Kali said. "Please."

Graciela dropped into one of the empty chairs.

"Don't you want coffee, too?"

She shook her head, tucked her hands back into her pockets.

"How long had you worked for my brother?" Kali asked.

"Almost one year."

"What was he like to work for?"

"Mostly he is not here. He is at his job. When I see him, he is polite. Ask about my husband and children. Tell me thank you."

"Was he hard to please?"

Graciela shook her head. "Not like some clients. Mr. John could get himself into a temper, but never at me. I hear him on phone sometimes."

Kali was familiar with John's angry explosions, but it had been years since she'd experienced one.

"How did he seem the week or so before he died? Upset? Worried? Angry?"

"I talk to him only once. He is just leaving when I arrive. Hurry, like many times."

"Did you notice *anything* different?"

She thought for a moment. "He work more at his desk. Many papers there. Dirty dishes. Crumbs."

"At the computer, you mean?"

A nod. "Like he spend many, many hours."

A project for work? Something that involved his battle with Sloane Winslow? When she'd tried to check her own e-mail, Kali had discovered that John's computer was password protected, and she hadn't been able to get access. Not that whatever he'd been doing would tell them if he had really killed two women.

Graciela pulled her sweater across her broad middle. "Is it okay I go now?"

"Sure." Kali realized the woman had probably stayed and talked with her only because she was afraid not to. "Thank you for talking to me about my brother."

Graciela rose. "Thank you for not shooting me," she said softly.

"I didn't really have a gun," Kali told her. "I was scared because I heard someone in the house."

It took a moment, but Graciela laughed. "A trick. A good one."

* * *

The moment Graciela was out the door, Kali picked up the appointment book the housekeeper had returned and opened it to the week when Sloane and Olivia were murdered. A dental appointment was noted for Thursday morning, the day the bodies had been discovered. A coincidence, or had John planned that to allow himself a little breathing room? Kali hated that the thought even entered her head.

There was a golf game noted for Sunday, a "W. Clarke, 2:00" for the following Monday. On Tuesday, the evening of the murders, "7:00 Jack's Bistro w/S." John and Sloane had had dinner together, and had been arguing.

But hadn't John's secretary said it was a last-minute arrangement? Why was it noted on his home calendar?

Kali leafed through the weeks preceding and following, trying to get a feel for her brother's life, but nothing jumped out at her as telling, or even particularly interesting. She set the appointment book back down on the coffee table and considered her options.

The day was already too warm for a vigorous morning walk. She could continue with the paperwork Sabrina had begun or she could tackle packing up John's household possessions. They'd need to clean out his closets, his drawers. His kitchen and bathroom. The very thought of it was more than she could deal with.

Those chores would keep. More pressing was the matter of Sloane Winslow's murder, and the question of John's involvement. Or lack thereof.

News accounts of the crime would be a good place to start, but Kali was frustrated by lack of access to John's computer. She found it somewhat surprising the police hadn't seized the machine when they searched his house. Either they'd been granted only a very limited warrant or they'd messed up. But it didn't do her much good without a password.

She spent ten minutes again trying obvious password choices—his name, date of birth, address, favorite color and food. As she tried the last two she realized she didn't know John's preferences anymore. She doubted that black and hot fudge sundae still topped his lists of favorites as they had when he was a teenager.

Remembering that she'd passed a library not far from John's, Kali grabbed her purse and keys and headed there.

Accustomed to the small branch libraries in Berkeley and Oakland, Kali was pleasantly surprised by the large, modern branch near John's house. For five dollars she was able to obtain a guest library card that gave her access to the Internet. She settled in and began reading news coverage about the murders.

Most of the early stories were a rehash of what Kali already knew. The bodies of Sloane Winslow and Olivia Perez, who worked for Winslow and lived on the premises, had been found in Winslow's Foothill Estates home by a neighbor. The police were not releasing details except to confirm that both women had been shot and burglary did not appear to be a motive.

Kali clicked on later dates, following the developing story in sequential order and jotting down names of people she might be able to talk to. Friends of both women, the restaurant employee who'd seen John and Sloane arguing, Olivia's parents. She also made note of the reporter who'd covered the crime for the *Arizona Daily Star.*

Then she went back and began to click through the articles again, this time focusing on the photos and links to related stories. At the bottom of the second Web page, she found photos of the two victims. She stopped short as though she'd been punched in the gut.

She tried to enlarge the picture of Olivia but couldn't. She quickly clicked through other links, hunting for a larger photo, and finally found one. A high school graduation photo, from the looks of it. It showed a doe-eyed young woman with long, dark hair and a full mouth.

It had to be her imagination, Kali told herself. It would be easy to confuse one exotic-looking young woman with another.

But she knew she wasn't confused.

Olivia Perez was one of the girls in the photo she'd found hidden away inside John's office dictionary.

# CHAPTER 14

Kali stared at the photo of Olivia Perez for another minute, then logged off the computer. She felt ill. The cops had been ready to pin the murders on John because of his ties with Sloane. Here was another link. Olivia.

A link the police seemed to know nothing about.

What did it mean that her brother had tucked away a photo of the dead girl? If he'd wanted to hide the fact that he knew her, why not burn the picture or throw it away? If Kali wanted to learn the truth—to clear John's name—she needed to know more about Olivia.

The girl's parents seemed like the logical place to start. If they'd been aware of a connection between their daughter and John, they'd undoubtedly have shared the information with the police. Still, they might know something that would help Kali sort out the relationship.

She logged back onto the Internet, looked up the Perez family's address, and then went to MapQuest and printed out directions.

She drove back to John's, picked up the photo of the three girls, then headed down into the flatlands of central Tucson.

Luis and Angeles Perez lived in an L-shaped, two-story stucco apartment building. It wasn't fancy, but the landscaping was neat and the complex looked well maintained. Even though it was early on a Saturday afternoon, Kali saw no one about except for a little boy watching her from a first-floor window. Apparently the residents had better sense than to be out in the sweltering sun.

Kali waved to the boy, then climbed the stairs to the second floor.

She dreaded introducing herself to Olivia's parents. If they were planning to file a wrongful death suit against John's estate, as Michelle Parker had suggested, that meant they held John responsible for their daughter's death. As his sister, Kali would be unwelcome at best.

Once she found the correct unit, she took a calming breath and knocked on the door. She could hear the sound of a television action show in the background.

A male voice thundered, "Who's there?"

"It's about your daughter," Kali said.

Several moments passed without response. She thought maybe he hadn't heard her and knocked again just as the door opened. The man smelled of booze, sweat, and cheap aftershave. He was only slightly taller than she was, but thickly built with wide shoulders and a protruding gut. He wore a sleeveless undershirt, a "beater" in popular parlance, and jeans. Neither was particularly clean.

"Mr. Perez?"

"What do you want? You a reporter?" His voice held only the faintest trace of an accent.

She shook her head. "I'm John O'Brien's sister."

It took a moment for the name to register, and when it did, his face darkened. But rather than move in closer, as Kali had feared, he stepped back. "I don't got to talk to you," he said.

"No, you don't. But I wanted to tell you, first of all, how terribly sorry I am about Olivia's death. My heart goes out to both you and your wife."

"Yeah, it's terrible." He scratched his neck. "She's taking it hard, my wife."

"Is she home?" Kali tried to peer over his shoulder into the apartment. The drapes were drawn, so the light was murky, but she couldn't see signs that anyone else was inside.

"At work," he said.

Kali had hoped to catch them together. "I can only imagine how difficult it must be."

"I loved my daughter, no matter what people say."

"I'm sure you did," Kali offered. *What did people say?* was what she really wanted to ask.

Perez widened his stance. "I warned her 'bout trying to be what she wasn't." He shook his head. "Her and her big ideas, moving in with that rich lady, thinking she was somebody. If she hadn'a been there at the house . . ."

"It was her job," Kali pointed out. "I understand she was putting herself through school."

"Still, your brother got no reason to kill my Olivia."

Kali took a breath. "I'm not sure he killed either of them," she said evenly.

"It was on the news. They were looking at him. The cops said so."

"So you've spoken with them about the investigation?"

He spread his hands. "They said it was him."

Kali nodded. It wasn't a point worth arguing right then. "Do you think it's possible there was some connection between your daughter and my brother? Other than Sloane Winslow, I mean."

"What are you saying?" His voice was resonant with anger. "My daughter was a good girl."

"I wasn't trying to imply that she wasn't," Kali said hastily. "I just wondered if they'd met or something."

Perez dismissed the idea with a wave of his hand. "No matter, he had no reason to kill her."

Kali showed him the photograph. "Do you recognize either of these other girls?"

He frowned, puzzled. "You took this? You knew my Olivia?"

The question erased any doubt Kali had that Olivia was indeed the girl in the photo. "No, I never had the pleasure." She hoped he didn't press her about the origin of the photo. "What about the other girls? Do you know who they are?"

"More of her fancy friends from school probably." His tone was bitter. "Olivia wanted to get away. Thought she was too good for us."

"I'd like to know more about your daughter," Kali said. "I was hoping we could talk—"

"You got to talk to the attorney. Carmen Escobar. She told us not to talk to anyone but her 'bout what happened."

"Lawsuits are messy," Kali argued. "And costly. They—"

"Olivia was our baby. We got a right." He shut the door before Kali had time to press him further.


Back in her stifling car, Kali cranked the air conditioner up full force. So Michelle Parker had been right. The family had contacted an attorney. Or maybe Carmen Escobar was an ambulance chaser who had contacted them. In either case, the threat of a lawsuit did nothing to improve Kali's mood.

She debated contacting the attorney and tackling the problem head on, then decided her call might send the wrong message—that she and Sabrina were acknowledging John's guilt. Better to let Escobar make the first move. Maybe nothing would come of it, anyway.

Kali lifted her hair off her neck to let the cool air from the vents reach her skin. The photo troubled her. Three young women. Nothing strange in the abstract. So what if they were wearing skimpy bathing suits? That was the style these days. But context was everything. What was John doing with the photo in the first place? Why had he stashed it in what he presumably thought was a safe place? Now that Kali knew one of the women was Olivia Perez, the thought of the photo wrenched her gut.

Although she'd initially agreed to look into the murders to appease Sabrina, Kali had come to want answers for her own sake. Now she was beginning to wonder if she'd even been asking the right questions.

She scanned the list of names she'd jotted down in the library. One of the news accounts had quoted a high school friend of Olivia's, Melody Hughes. Since the two girls had

gone to school together, the family must live close by. Kali
drove around until she found a convenience store with a public phone and phone book, no small task in this day and age.
Then, armed with listings for Hughes and a map of the city she
picked up at the same store, she identified two possibilities
and called. The first listing was a miss. The man who picked up
knew nothing about Melody Hughes. But the second call
was a hit.

The phone was answered by what sounded like a teenage
boy.

"Is Melody around?" Kali asked.

"She's hardly ever here. Try her cell." He gave her the
number. Kali called and Melody answered on the third ring.
There was a clamor of conversation in the background.

"Hi," Kali said. She decided to skip the introduction if
she could get away with it. "I understand you were a friend
of Olivia Perez's."

"Who is this?"

So much for pulling the wool over the eyes of the younger
generation. "My name is Kali. I'm an attorney doing some
follow-up work on the murders."

"Okay, yeah. Olivia and I were friends."

"I'd really like to talk with you in person. I can meet you
wherever you'd like."

"I'm at work right now."

"When do you get off?" Kali asked.

"Well, I've got a break coming up in half an hour. Would
that be a good time?"

"Perfect."

"I'm a waitress at Applebee's." Melody reeled off the address.


Melody Hughes was slender and fair, with straight hair
pulled into a ponytail. To Kali's disappointment, Melody
wasn't one of the girls in the photograph.

"You wanted to talk to me?" Melody asked when they
met at the Applebee's entrance.

"Background questions for the most part. You want to go get an ice cream or something?" Kali had noticed a Dairy Queen across the parking lot. "Or maybe you're sick of food after serving it all day."

"No, ice cream sounds good. Actually," Melody added with a laugh, "anything that gets me out of this place sounds good."

In the ice cream shop they ordered small sundaes and found a table near the window.

"I'm sorry to bring up bad memories," Kali said. "I know how difficult it is to lose a friend."

Melody nodded, her eyes on her ice cream. "It's hard to believe she's really dead. Olivia was so . . . alive. 'Spunky' is what my mom used to say. I think she wishes I were a bit spunkier myself."

"Why do you say that?"

Melody laughed and held out her left hand. There was a very tiny diamond on her ring finger. "My mom thinks I'm selling myself short. Marco and I have been going together since eighth grade. He's in the military now, in Iraq, but we're getting married as soon as he gets back."

Silently, Kali agreed with the girl's mother. Nineteen seemed awfully young for marriage, but she offered her congratulations anyway, then said, "Tell me about Olivia."

"She was smart but she also worked hard. She knew what she wanted."

"Which was?"

"A different life than she had growing up. She wanted nice clothes, jewelry, a fancy car, travel. Excitement." Melody looked again at her left hand. "A rich husband."

Not the most admirable goals maybe, but Olivia certainly wasn't the only woman her age yearning for material goods and the easy life. "Did she get along with her family?"

A shrug. "Her mom's okay, I guess, but her dad's a scary guy. He can lose his temper for no reason, and he's always got to be right. He hasn't worked for years. Says he has a bad back but he never seemed that sick to me."

*I loved my daughter, no matter what people say.* Kali

wondered if this was what he meant. "Did he ever hurt Olivia?"

"Not physically. At least she never said anything about it. But he was mean to her. He'd ground her for no reason and take stuff away." Melody looked like she regretted ever raising the issue. "Her parents wanted her to get a full-time job and help support the family, but Olivia wanted to go to college. I know they argued over that. Her dad got really mad."

Melody took a bite of her sundae. "They told her to take some night classes at Pima, if she was so set on college, but Olivia wanted to go to the U of A. Her dad was furious she even applied. And when she got in, I think he saw that as a slap in the face."

"It's quite an accomplishment."

"Yeah, we were all like, wow, that's so great, and her dad about disowned her. He kicked her out of the house the day she turned eighteen."

"So she was on her own?"

Melody nodded. "Luckily she got financial aid at U of A. It's not like they just give you the money, though. They make you work for part of it and borrow most of it. Her freshman year she had a work-study job in the library that paid only five dollars an hour. That's less than I make." Melody sounded incredulous.

"It's not much," Kali agreed.

"That's what I mean about Olivia being determined. She was going to be paying off her student loans for years to come. Me, I wouldn't want that."

Kali knew about student debt. She'd only just paid off the last of her law school loans.

"Let me show you a photo," she said, reaching into her purse for the snapshot of Olivia and her two friends, and handed it to Melody. "Do you recognize any of these girls?"

Melody looked, then shook her head. "They weren't from high school. I didn't see much of Olivia after she started college. Our lives went in different directions." For a moment, Melody looked wistful. Maybe her "spunkiness" was just dormant rather than totally lacking.

"Have you met any of her friends from college?" Kali asked.

"A couple, but it's not like I know them or anything."

"Can you remember their names?"

Melody scowled in thought. "Joanna Sommers was one. She worked at the library with Olivia freshman year. And a guy named Randy."

"A boyfriend?"

"I don't think so, at least not when I met him. We were at the mall early last summer, and she ran into him. Really cute guy with a great bod. He was older than us, so maybe he wasn't even from college. When he left I asked Olivia if she was dating him, and she just laughed and changed the subject."

"Was she usually so secretive?"

Melody frowned. "Not when we were in school together. We talked about everything then. But after she went away to college, it was like she'd moved on and wasn't interested in me so much."

"When was the last time you talked to her?"

"Probably that time at the mall. She'd just moved in with Mrs. Winslow and she was feeling flush. She bought me lunch even."

"She was happy with the living arrangement, then?"

"Very. She was about as upbeat as I'd ever seen her."

"Did she ever mention the name John O'Brien?"

Melody blinked. "Isn't he the guy they say killed her?"

"That's one theory."

She looked pensive, shook her head. "No, Olivia never said anything to me about him. You think she knew him?"

"I don't know. That's what I'm trying to find out."

"I don't know why she would. That doesn't make sense."

No, it didn't. But there had to be a reason John had Olivia's photo hidden in the pages of his dictionary.

# CHAPTER 15

Kali devoted Saturday night to packing up John's clothes. She'd gotten through the whole bureau and half the closet when she was startled to hear the front door slam. She tensed. Pretending to have a gun had worked with Graciela. Could she pull it off again?

"It's me," Sabrina called out. "Anyone here?"

Kali felt herself relax. "I'm in John's room."

Sabrina's footsteps shuffled along the hallway to the bedroom. She dropped her tote in the corner.

"What are you doing back so soon?" Kali asked. "And where's the family?"

"They'll be down tomorrow."

"I didn't expect you until tomorrow morning."

"I'm not interfering with wild party plans, am I?"

Kali laughed as she inspected the ties she'd laid out flat in a cardboard box. "Hardly. In fact, I missed you. It was a little too quiet last night."

"You should have been at my house," Sabrina said. "It was far from quiet."

"The boys were being rambunctious again?"

She held up her hands. "Mostly. You want some help with that?"

"Yeah, but not tonight. I was about ready to quit anyway."

Kali folded down the top of the box and stacked it with the others in the corner. "You hungry? I had a toasted cheese sandwich for dinner. I could make you one."

"I grabbed a bite before I left Scottsdale. I could use a drink, though," Sabrina headed for the kitchen.

"Why'd you come back early?" Kali asked again. She felt bad about laying on the guilt earlier when Sabrina had announced she was going home. Her sister did have a family, after all.

Sabrina shrugged. "The kids are all out tonight anyway."

"And Peter?"

A half laugh. "He'll hardly know I'm gone."

"What does that mean?"

"Nothing," Sabrina answered tersely. "Forget I even mentioned it." She filled a sixteen-ounce measuring cup with ice, poured a hefty measure of vodka into the bottom, then added a splash of vermouth. As she stirred, she turned to Kali. "You want some?"

Kali gave passing thought to accepting, if only to save Sabrina from polishing off the whole thing. But she'd fallen prey to Sabrina's martinis in the past. "I think I'll stick with wine." She poured a glass from the open bottle of Zinfandel. "How are the kids handling the news of John's death?"

"Last night was pretty emotional. But the great thing about kids—well, the great thing and also the horrible thing—is that they're basically self-centered. If it doesn't affect them directly, they're quick to move on. That isn't to say they won't have some painful moments in the days and weeks ahead."

"You told them about the murder and John's alleged role?"

"Sort of." Sabrina joined Kali at the kitchen table. "I probably soft pedaled it a bit. I mean, we don't even know all the facts, right? And just because the cops had some crazy theory about John being the killer . . . there's no point upsetting the kids with that kind of talk."

When it came to kids, Kali didn't have the slightest notion what was right. But she thought not telling them the truth was probably a mistake.

Sabrina leaned back in her chair. "Damn fine martini if I do say so myself. Just what the doctor ordered." She turned to Kali. "Have you manage to dig up anything yet? Please tell me there's some good news."

"Just the opposite, I'm afraid."

Sabrina groaned. "What happened?"

"For starters, it looks like Olivia's family is moving on a wrongful death suit against John's estate."

"His . . . you mean the money he was giving us?"

Leave it to Sabrina to put a personal spin on things. In that regard she wasn't all that different from her kids. "Right," Kali said.

"Can they do that?"

"They can sue. To win, they'll have to prove John was responsible. But in a civil trial the burden of proof is much lower than in criminal court."

"How much lower?"

"Instead of a unanimous verdict, they only have to convince nine out of twelve jurors. And the jurors don't have to be convinced beyond a reasonable doubt, only that the preponderance of the evidence supports that conclusion."

Sabrina set her glass on the table. "In other words, it's a lot easier."

"Easier, yes. But they still have to prove their case."

"If they do, they'll get John's money?"

Kali nodded. "To the extent of the judgment." She was sure their claim would exceed John's estate, so the caveat didn't really matter. "A verdict in their favor will also cement John's guilt in the mind of the public." To Kali, that was almost worse.

"That's awful!" Sabrina cried.

"I'm hoping they never follow through. They may decide the odds of winning aren't worth the aggravation."

But Sabrina was apparently grappling with a different issue. "John promised he'd help," she lamented.

"Help?"

"With money. For college."

Kali frowned. Her sister led the pampered life of a suburban princess. What did she need John's help for? "John was going to foot the bill for the kids' college?"

"I said *help*. I didn't say he'd promised to pay the whole thing."

"Okay, *help*. What about you and Peter?"

Sabrina sighed, clenched her hands together. "Peter's business isn't doing well and we've got . . . some pretty big debts."

"So learn to budget like the rest of us." Kali didn't have a lot of sympathy for people who lived beyond their means.

"Gambling debts," Sabrina said hesitantly. "Peter's."

"Gambling?"

"I didn't even know about it until recently. When things started going badly at work, he spent a lot of time at the casino instead."

It was Sabrina's distraught tone more than the words themselves that made Kali take note.

"He lost money, a lot of it, then lost more trying to win it back. Our credit cards are maxed out, our savings are gone." She drew in a breath and looked away. "He even forged my signature and took out a second mortgage on the house. We've got nothing."

"Oh, Sabrina." Instinctively, Kali reached across the table and covered her sister's hands with her own. "I'm sorry."

"That's why I came back early," Sabrina said tearfully. "We had another big fight. And like I said, the kids were out anyway. There was no reason to stick around."

"How long has this been going on? Why didn't you say something before now?"

"I just found out about six weeks ago. And, well, it's embarrassing."

"But you told John."

"John wasn't like you," Sabrina snapped, pulling her hands free. "He wasn't so critical of everything I do."

"You think I'm critical of you?"

"Aren't you?" She got up and refilled her drink, ignoring Kali's empty glass. "You've always got all the answers. The perfect life."

"*I've* got the perfect life?" Kali couldn't believe what she was hearing. She had nothing to show for herself but a series of failed romances and a career that had taken a nosedive when the firm where she'd expected to make partner imploded. Sure, she'd been involved in some dramatic cases since then, but she was barely keeping her head above water financially.

"Don't you?"

"Hardly," Kali said. "And as for being critical, aren't you the one who's always telling me I need a *normal* job, a husband, and a family?"

"Did it ever dawn on you that I might be envious?"

"Of me?" The whole time they were growing up Sabrina had been the golden one. Cute and perky, whereas Kali was gangly and shy. Sabrina had inherited their mother's carefree disposition and sparkling good looks. She'd been daddy's little girl, high school homecoming queen, and the object of just about every boy's fancy. Conveniently helpless when there was work to be done, but otherwise the center of attention. She'd married Peter when she was twenty, choosing a "Mrs." over a B.A., and as far as Kali knew she'd never looked back.

"You're smart," Sabrina said between sniffles. "And successful. You've got a *life*."

That was an eye-opener. "Some life."

"At least it's *yours*. Without my husband and kids, I'm nobody."

"What about Peter?" Kali asked. "Is he . . . getting help with his addiction?"

"He joined Gamblers Anonymous and he promised me he's stopped, but I can't be sure he has. Even if he has, I don't see how we'll ever get out of debt." Sabrina twisted her hair into a knot at the back of her head, then let it fall loose. "Anyway, with Joey going off to college next year, John said he'd help out. Now you tell me that's up in the air."

Kali was still reeling with shock, not only at Sabrina's terrible predicament, but at seeing this side of her sister—one she'd never in her wildest dreams imagined. Once again,

Kali felt like an outsider in her own family. It was a damn unpleasant feeling.

"Do you think they'll win?" Sabrina asked quietly. "Olivia's parents?"

"I don't know. So far all I've learned is that Sloane Winslow was practically a saint. Olivia too. And the evidence seems to point to John."

Sabrina bit her lower lip. "Shit."

"There's something I need to show you." Kali went to her purse, pulled out the snapshot of the three girls, and showed it to Sabrina. "Do you recognize any of them?"

Sabrina shook her head, then gave Kali a puzzled look. "Who are they?"

"The one in the middle is Olivia Perez."

"The dead girl? Where'd you get it?"

"I found it in John's office yesterday. Hidden inside the dictionary our parents gave him for graduation. It seemed strange he'd have a photo of three young women, but I didn't think much about it. Today I learned that one of them was Olivia."

Sabrina's face paled. "Why would he have a photograph of Olivia?"

"I have no idea. I was hoping you'd recognize one of the others."

"How'd you figure out it was her?" Sabrina asked.

Kali told her about finding the Internet picture, and her subsequent conversations with the girl's father and friend from high school. "They confirmed that the girl in the photo is Olivia."

Sabrina dropped back down into her chair. "I can't believe this. John must have known her."

"He never mentioned Olivia, even if he didn't refer to her by name?"

"I'm sure he didn't." Sabrina put her head in her hands. "What do you think it means?"

"That there's a lot we don't know about both Sloane and Olivia. And about our brother."

# CHAPTER 16

Erling glanced at his wife, then again at both couches. He shrugged. "It's a toss-up."

The green couch was more comfortable, the tan one marginally better in terms of style. He didn't like either one as much as the couch they had now, but Deena had decided that it was "disreputable" and needed to be replaced. Erling was willing to concede that it was worn and stained, but it was perfectly serviceable. What's more, the couch had history. Purchased when Mindy was in kindergarten and Danny just a baby, it had stood them through more than a decade of slumber parties and holidays, all of which had undoubtedly contributed to the problem that brought them to Macy's furniture store this Sunday afternoon in search of a replacement.

"You don't have any preference at all?" Deena asked him.

"They're both nice."

She frowned. "I don't know. I can't say I love either one."

"Well, there's no rush, is there? I mean, we don't have to decide today, between these two."

"You're right. I guess I just want it done. I'm so tired of looking at that old thing we've got now." Deena sighed and took his hand. "Let's go. I appreciate your coming with me. It helps to have a second opinion."

"Even though I didn't really have one?"

She laughed and gave him a playful peck on the cheek. "You had one all right. It was 'What's wrong with the sofa we've got?'"

"I'm that easy to read?" Erling asked, as they got onto the escalator. He rested a hand on her shoulder, cheered by her good humor.

"Sometimes." She gave him an odd look. "But not always."

Erling felt his breath catch. Was it the look? The tone of her voice? Or maybe simply his guilty conscience? He couldn't tell if the remark had meaning beyond the obvious.

All weekend, ever since he'd seen Sloane Winslow's name and number in their caller ID list, Erling had been looking for signs that Deena knew more than she was letting on. He might as well have been trying to read tea leaves. The uncertainty was driving him crazy.

At times he thought about simply asking her, "Say, I saw that we had a call from Sloane Winslow a while back. Do you know what it was about?" Or "I was wondering, have you ever run across Sloane Winslow as part of your work with nonprofits?" These were questions Erling might well have asked if he hadn't been living a lie.

"I think Mindy may have met a guy," Deena announced as they crossed the hot asphalt of the parking lot.

"A guy?" He had the feeling she'd made an earlier comment he'd missed. "As in boyfriend?"

Mindy hadn't dated in high school. Hadn't had any male friends at all, as far as Erling knew. From the vantage point of a protective father, he'd been secretly pleased, though he knew Mindy hadn't seen it that way.

Deena nodded, clearly delighted. "Don't you dare say a word to her, though. You know how she is about not wanting us breathing down her neck."

"What makes you think she's got a boy . . . a guy?"

"Nothing I can put my finger on. More a feeling I've got. Little stuff, you know. Reading between the lines." She gave him a long look over the top of the car door before she climbed in. "Women's intuition. Some of us are pretty good at that."

Erling felt the burn of Deena's eyes all the way into the pit of his stomach. *Reading between the lines. Women's intuition.* Was she hinting at something about Sloane?

There he was again, trying to read tea leaves.

Erling was just pulling the car into the garage when Michelle Parker called on his cell.

"Don't worry, it's not another homicide," she told him straight off. When either of them called the other on off-hours, it was often because of a fresh murder. "I think I've found the tattoo artist who worked on our young Jane Doe. He's in the shop this afternoon so I'm going talk to him. Do you want to come along?"

Erling hesitated. The old conflict of family and job. Deena claimed to understand, but she also resented the time his work demanded. With Sloane's call to the house still rattling around in his head, he was feeling more than a little paranoid.

"Yeah," he said finally, turning off the engine and setting the brake. "Where are you?"

"It will be easier to meet me there." She gave him the address.

"More trouble?" Deena asked him when he'd pocketed the phone.

"We may have a lead on the identity of that dead girl."

"Good. It's sad no one has come looking for her."

"Yes, it is," Erling agreed. The database of missing persons had triggered a few hopeful leads, but nothing had panned out. "I won't be gone long."

"Don't worry. I've got stuff to get ready for the classroom anyway." She got out of the car and blew him a kiss. "Thanks again for going shopping with me."

"Any time."

She laughed. "Watch out. I might take you up on that."

* * *

The number of tattoo studios in the Tucson area was staggering to Erling, who'd grown up with the notion that only drunken sailors and hard-core criminals sported tattoos. He was aware that times had changed, but the widespread popularity of the fad left him scratching his head. For that reason, if none other, he was surprised that Michelle had actually been able to trace the tattoo to a specific artist. Although "artist" was perhaps a misnomer.

The address she'd given him was in a low-rent district a couple of miles from the university. Recognizing her car parked on the street, Erling pulled in behind.

"What do we know?" he asked when they were both out of their cars.

"Guy's name is Horse."

"As in 'neigh'?"

"Or smackhead," she said. "I talked to a buddy of his at another shop who said the design in question looked like one of Horse's. That delicate filigree stuff is apparently a specialty of his."

"Does he have a record?"

Michelle cocked her head. "You thinking he might be our killer?"

"I can see how it might happen. An attractive young woman comes in for a tattoo, the guy hits on her, she resists . . ." Erling stepped around a gluey wad of chewed gum on the sidewalk. "Just something we ought to keep in mind."

They entered the shop, sandwiched between a bar and a shoe repair place. The walls of the small anteroom were lined with drawings of tattoos—everything from monochromatic fire-breathing dragons and intricate geometric designs to colorful hearts and flowers.

No one was at the counter, but muffled conversation flowed from the back of the shop. "Be right there," a male voice called out. "I'm just finishing up with a customer."

A moment later a heavily tattooed man with a beefy face and shaved head appeared. Erling caught the flicker of wariness in the man's expression when he saw the two of them. It must have been obvious they weren't potential customers.

"What can I do for you?" the man asked.

"We're looking for Horse. Is that you?"

"To my friends."

Erling flashed his badge. "We're trying to identify a body. A young woman with a tattoo. We're hoping you can help."

"I talked to someone who thought it looked like your work," Michelle added.

Horse's eyes narrowed. "Hey, I'm licensed and I'm careful. I use only disposable needles and fresh ink. If there's a problem, it couldn'a been me."

"She was murdered," Michelle explained. "We just need help identifying her."

The edge of suspicion in Horse's expression eased some. "What's the tattoo look like?"

Erling showed him a close-up photo of the tattoo.

"Yeah," Horse said cautiously, "could be mine."

Michelle handed over the sketch of their Jane Doe. "This is an artist's rendering of the girl. Do you recognize her?"

"She's dead, you said?"

"Right. Do you recognize her?"

Horse ran a hand over his shiny head. "Yeah, I think so. Last spring sometime. Jesus, murdered?"

Erling nodded. "You know who she is?"

"I'm not sure I ever got her name."

Another man, slight, studious, and in his early twenties, emerged from the back room. His scrawny bicep was glazed with a layer of Vaseline covering what Erling assumed was a fresh tattoo.

"How are you feeling?" Horse inquired.

"Fine." The man admired his arm on his way out the door. "You do good work."

"Thanks," Horse replied. "Tell your friends." Then he turned back to Erling and Michelle. "I'd like to help you out, but I don't think I can. This is strictly a cash business. I don't take down personal information from customers. If I ever knew her name, I've forgotten it by now."

Erling had been afraid this might be the case. "Did she come in alone or with a friend?"

"You expect me to remember?"

"Try."

Horse sighed, thought a moment. "Alone, I think. Most women, they come with a friend, but not her."

"What else do you remember about her?" Michelle asked. "Where she grew up, went to school, anything. We're starting with practically nothing here."

Horse scratched his chin. Shook his head. "Sorry."

"How about what she was wearing?"

He snorted. "Do I look like someone who knows fashion?"

"We're not looking for labels," Erling said.

Another sigh. "Shorts and a T-shirt, probably. That's what the chicks usually wear." Horse sucked on his cheek; then his eyes flashed. "Yeah, it was a T-shirt. Pink. I remember because my girlfriend had just gotten into pink in a big way."

"Any lettering on it?" Michelle asked. "Or maybe a logo?"

"No, just plain. She brought a denim shirt, too. She wore that home instead of the T-shirt because it was looser. A fresh tattoo is like a wound, you know."

Erling knew how much even the smallest cut could hurt. He didn't want to think about what a tattoo must feel like.

"What about distinctive jewelry?" Michelle asked.

"Nothing that I remember. Like I said . . ." Horse frowned. "Wait," he said suddenly, with a snap of his fingers. "She was a dancer, I think. Really limber and graceful. We talked a bit while I was working on her. I can't remember what she said exactly, but that's what sticks in my mind. A dancer."

"What kind of dancer?"

"How the hell should I know? I didn't interview her, for Chrissakes. It was just meaningless conversation."

Erling tried again. "Professional dancer?"

Horse threw up his hands in a helpless gesture. "Maybe she wasn't even a dancer. It's just the impression I got, okay?"

"Okay," Erling said, retreating. "We appreciate your help." He handed Horse his card. "If you remember anything else, give us a call."

"Sure. Will do."

Outside the shop, Erling turned to Michelle. "What do you think? A young woman who liked to go clubbing or a real dancer?"

"From what Horse said, I'd guess it was more than a social pastime."

"Ballet?"

Michelle gave him the same look Deena sometimes did. Like whatever he'd said made no sense at all.

"I don't think so," Michelle said. "Not with a chest like she had. She wasn't built like a ballerina."

"There's a certain build?" He'd never thought about that before. The only ballet he'd ever seen was the *Nutcracker* he and Deena had taken Mindy and Danny to years ago. What stuck in his mind most vividly was a dancing bear.

Michelle ignored the question. "We ought to check with the musical theaters, dance troupes, bars, and nightclubs—"

"That's a lot of territory to cover," Erling pointed out. The dance angle seemed like a long shot to him, anyway.

"Yeah, but it's the only lead we've got."

Erling could hear the frustration in Michelle's voice. Finding the girl's identity was only the first step. There was no guarantee it would bring them any closer to finding her killer.

"We'll circulate the sketch," he said, "and pray we've got the winning numbers in the luck lottery."

He waited while Michelle fished her car keys from her purse. "What did you think of Horse?"

"As a suspect, you mean? I didn't see anything that set off alarm bells."

"Me either." Erling glanced back toward the shop and shook his head. "I don't get this tattoo craze. You see that nerdy little guy Horse had just finished with? Didn't seem like the type at all."

She grinned. "You're out of step with the times, Erling."

"So I've been told. Still, it makes . . ." He looked at her over the roof of her car. "What, don't tell me *you* have a tattoo?"

She smiled sweetly without answering and climbed into the car. She waved through the open window. "See you in the morning."

As Erling watched Michelle pull away, he felt the hot sun prickle his skin. He shook his head in befuddled amusement. Out of step with the times, indeed. Well, that was fine by him.

He unlocked the car as another postadolescent with tattoos strolled by. What about Mindy's new "guy"? Erling wondered. Did *he* have a tattoo?

It was one of those moments when Erling was reminded that being a parent was harder than being a cop.

# CHAPTER 17

Kali was making coffee Sunday morning when John's phone rang. Because Sabrina was still asleep, she grabbed it quickly.

A moment's hesitation on the other end; then a female voice asked, "Can I speak to John?"

"Who's calling?" Kali asked.

Another pause. "Susan."

Kali checked the incoming call display. Susan Harris. It wasn't a local area code. "What's it regarding?"

"Do I have the right number? John O'Brien?"

"Right."

A stretch of silence. "Are you his wife?"

"His sister."

"Oh, hi." The relief in Susan's voice was evident. "He said he wasn't married but you never know. Is he around?"

Oh, dear, Kali thought, as the pieces fell into place. Susan must be someone John had dated, someone who didn't know what had happened to him.

"I'm afraid there's some bad news," Kali said. "John died a few days ago."

"My God. What happened?"

Kali's throat tightened. Why did saying the words out

loud make them more real? "He drowned," she said softly. "In his swimming pool."

Her announcement was met with a moment of stunned silence. When Susan finally spoke, her voice broke. "How could that happen?"

"We don't know all the particulars yet." Kali decided not to mention the alcohol and drugs. She had no idea where Susan fit into John's life.

"I can't believe this. It's so, so . . . terrible." It sounded as if Susan was crying softly.

Kali gave her a moment before continuing. "If you don't mind my asking, what was your relationship with John?"

"We met a couple of months ago." Her voice broke again and she took a moment to collect herself. "I live in New York but I travel quite a bit on business. Tucson is part of my territory."

"You were dating, then?"

"We went out whenever I came to town. It wasn't anything serious. Not yet, anyway. But I think we . . . well, I was hoping it might be at some point. We really hit it off."

Kali had always seen John more as the dating type than one who would settle down in a long-term relationship, but there was clearly a lot about him she hadn't known.

"Did he ever mention me?" Susan asked after a moment. The hopeful tone of her voice made Kali cringe for her.

"We didn't talk much," Kali explained. She made a mental note to ask Sabrina when she woke up.

"I take it that's a 'no.'" Susan drew a quavery breath. "I thought things were going well between us. Then last time I was there, well, we'd planned to go out. He called at the last minute to cancel. A business meeting, he said."

"That happens."

"Yes, but I . . . I went to the restaurant anyway. I needed dinner, right? And Jack's Bistro was someplace I knew. We'd been there before."

Kali recognized the restaurant name from John's calendar. "You and John had planned to go to Jack's Bistro?"

"Right. It was one of his favorites." Susan paused. "I saw him there. With another woman."

"When was this?" Kali asked.

"Gosh, let me think. I had a Monday meeting in Phoenix, so it would have been a week ago Tuesday."

The night Sloane Winslow had been murdered. John had canceled a hot date with Susan in order to have dinner with Sloane, a woman with whom he was at odds. It didn't make sense, but at least Kali understood now why John's appointment book had listed a dinner reservation with "S." Susan, not Sloane.

"It didn't look like a business meeting," Susan added.

"What makes you say that?"

"They looked like they knew each other pretty well, if you know what I mean. I was devastated. I left as soon as I saw him, even though I'd already been shown to a table."

"He didn't see you, then?"

"I'm sure he didn't. He was totally focused on her. Whatever they were talking about, it must have been pretty intense. Then when he never called again . . . well, I assumed . . . I almost didn't call this time." Susan paused. "I hate to seem desperate, but I liked John. A lot."

Enough to kill "the other woman" in a fit of jealousy? Kali wondered.

"For what it's worth," she told Susan, "John's dinner companion was someone he worked for."

"Really?" Susan seemed to take heart in this information. "Maybe it actually was business, then." She drew in a breath. "My condolences to you and your family. Your brother was a special guy."

"Thank you." Kali felt the loss doubly. Not only for the brother she'd known, but for the one she hadn't.

When she'd disconnected, she hit the message button. Kali knew there were no new messages, but Susan's call had made her curious about other people John might have talked to in the week or so preceding his death. She mentally chastised herself for not checking before now.

She held the PLAY button down and listened to an appointment reminder from his dentist; a short message from Sabrina; and another from a man named Wayne Clark, who sounded Australian and said only that he'd "talked to Jim, who knew nothing."

Kali had no idea who Jim was, but Wayne Clark rang a bell. She frowned, trying to remember why.

Then it came to her. The date book Graciela had returned yesterday. She found it on the counter where she'd left it and flipped back through the pages.

She'd remembered correctly. John had noted a two o'clock meeting with a W. Clark on the Monday following the murders. She checked the log of incoming calls. Clark's must have been one of the numerous "private caller" listings because his name didn't show up.

Her own name and number did. Hers had been the last call John had received before he died. Kali recalled that hurried conversation where she'd hung up on him in a huff. Her eyes filled with tears and she brushed them away. God, she was such a fool sometimes. A self-righteous ass, as Sabrina would say. She'd known John had been trying hard to reach her, yet she'd been unwilling to cut him any slack. Was she so busy telling others how to live their lives that she never looked at herself? There was time still to build her relationship with Sabrina. But she'd run out of chances with John.

She took her coffee into John's office to work on her remarks for the funeral tomorrow, pushing aside boxes she and Sabrina had packed up. She wished she had access to his computer and again tried a few possible passwords before giving up. Instead, she wrote out in longhand ideas for what she'd say.

Half an hour later, she heard Sabrina shuffling about in the kitchen, and then the sound of the doorbell. Sabrina appeared a moment later.

"We got flowers."

"Who from?"

"Bryce Keating. Isn't he the detective you've been seeing?"

Kali nodded.

"Come into the kitchen and look. They're lovely."

*They* are *lovely*, Kali thought, as she looked at the bright, colorful arrangement. And thankfully not at all funereal. She recognized tulips, irises, alstroemeria, and yellow baby roses, but there were probably half a dozen other flowers she couldn't name. The note, addressed to both her and Sabrina, was short: *You are in my thoughts. Remember, I'm here for you. Love, Bryce.*

"That's so sweet," Sabrina gushed. "He must be a good man."

"Yeah, he is." In ways Kali had perhaps failed to see before.

Bryce was an attractive guy, a "stud muffin" as her friend Margot put it. Dark hair, dark eyes, a sexy smile, and a body that was lean and muscular. They'd met working a murder investigation when she'd been on special assignment with the DA's office. With an ex-wife and, as rumor had it, countless on-again-off-again girlfriends, he wasn't someone Kali had taken seriously when they'd first started going out. But somehow, without her fully realizing it, the relationship had grown. She still found him too brash at times, too hardheaded at others, and a bit of a cowboy when it came to the fine lines of law enforcement. But she'd also discovered that he could be generous and tender and kind, and that he seemed to care for her a great deal. For someone who was used to keeping her emotional distance, it was an unsettling realization.

"Guess I'd better call him," Kali said.

"Tell him thank you from me, would you?"

"Will do." Kali started to leave, then turned back. "Did John ever talk about a woman he was dating? Someone from New York named Susan Harris? She called here this morning looking for him."

"I don't know her name, but he did say he'd met someone who lived in the East. She came to town on business sometimes."

"Sounds like the same person," Kali said. "John broke a

date with her in order to have dinner with Sloane the night she was killed. I wonder why."

Sabrina shrugged. "Must have been important. Or maybe Sloane insisted. She liked to call the shots."

Kali went into the bedroom and called Bryce.

"Thanks for the flowers," she said when he picked up. "And the sweet thoughts. Sabrina says thanks, too."

"How's it going?"

"It's weird. I'd go for weeks, even months, without talking to John. I rarely thought about him. Now that he's gone, I feel this incredible sadness and loss. On some level, I feel closer to him now than I ever did. It doesn't make a lot of sense."

"Makes sense to me," Bryce said. "Family has a hold on all of us, whether we like it or not."

Kali sat on the bed and leaned against the headboard. "I think I'm just now beginning to realize that."

Growing up, she'd seen her home life as a collection of individuals—a mother who'd deserted those who loved her by taking her own life, a father who'd done the same by losing himself in a bottle. John and Sabrina, she knew now, had been battling their own demons, but at the time she'd seen only that they ignored her. In recent years, though, and especially in the few days since John's death, family had taken on new meaning to her.

"When are you coming back?" Bryce asked.

"Another week probably."

"That long?" Bryce sounded disappointed.

"Sabrina's husband and kids will be arriving any minute. The funeral is tomorrow, and then we have to finish cleaning out John's house. There are also loose ends about the murders. I guess I need some answers, even if nothing comes of it with the cops."

No matter how damning the evidence—and knowing that one of the women in the photo was Olivia Perez didn't help matters—Kali couldn't see John as a cold-blooded killer. "We may never learn what really happened, but I have to try."

"I understand, but I miss you."

"I miss you, too."


Peter and the kids arrived in a flurry of boisterous energy. Kali hadn't seen any of them in over a year, and she was surprised by how much the boys had changed. Joey, at eighteen, had grown from a gawky kid into an athletic-looking young man who towered over her. Todd, fifteen, was no longer the shy little boy she remembered. His blond hair was shoulder length, his pants baggy, and the earphone jack from his iPod appeared to be permanently attached to his ear. He greeted her with a thumbs-up and a "Yo, Aunt Kali." Even Jeremy, whom she still thought of as a baby, was very much the teenager at fourteen.

Peter gave Kali a kiss on the cheek. Sabrina, she noted, didn't get much more.

"I'm sorry about John," he told Kali. "It's a rotten shame what happened. And that stuff about Sloane . . ." Peter shook his head sadly.

He'd aged in the last year, as well. His dark hair was noticeably grayer and thinner, the lines on his face more pronounced. He'd never been what Kali considered handsome, but there'd always been an easy, blue-blood confidence about him she'd found appealing. Now he looked like a miscast actor playing the role.

With a nod toward their boys, Sabrina shot her husband a silencing look. "How was the drive down?"

"It's not much of a drive," Peter said tersely.

Sabrina gave a martyred sigh. "I was just asking."

"And I answered."

Kali winced at the tension in those few short remarks. "I've got stuff to do in the kitchen," she said, excusing herself.

Jeremy had shoved a stack of boxes out of the way and turned the television on to a football game. All four males gravitated toward it. Sabrina shot daggers in Peter's direction, then turned and followed Kali to the kitchen.

* * *

Dinner was casual. Salad and take-out pizza, with chocolate chip cookie dough ice cream for dessert. A far cry from
the formal, solemn affair Kali had been dreading. They
shared memories of John, fond remembrances as well as irksome habits, all delivered with a mixture of tears and laughter. Then the conversation moved easily to other topics, from
SATs to soccer to video games. With enough wine, the tension between Sabrina and her husband seemed to ease. Or
maybe the wine Kali had drunk only made it seem that way.

After they'd finished eating, the kids commandeered the
television and DVD player while the adults remained around
the kitchen table talking. At one point Kali went outside for
some fresh air. She was surprised when Todd followed a few
minutes later, minus the iPod.

"So, you're in high school now," she said to him. "Pretty
exciting."

"Yeah." It was about as unenthusiastic a response as Kali
could imagine, but she realized her own comment had been
pretty inane. It was the sort of meaningless banality people
had thrown at her when she was Todd's age, and she'd vowed
not to inflict it on future generations.

Todd dropped into the patio chair next to hers. "Is it true
the cops think Uncle John killed a couple of women?"

Oh, God. How was she supposed to answer? She didn't
know how much Sabrina had actually told them. "Where'd
you hear that?"

"It was on the news. Did he?"

"They were investigating the possibility," she said, tread-
ing lightly.

"What do *you* think?"

There was a reason she'd never had children, Kali decided. She clearly wasn't up to the task. Todd was looking at
her intently, his strong features pinched, his blue-gray eyes
troubled.

"I don't know," she said finally.

"My mom refuses to talk about it. She says John never
killed anyone and that's the end of it."

"She knew him better than I did."

"Why? You're his sister too. Didn't you guys get along?"

"We got along okay," Kali said. "It's just that we never . . . we never really connected, I guess."

Todd shifted in his chair. "I figure the cops wouldn't be saying he did it if they didn't have something to back it up."

Kali nodded. "But lots of times the police are wrong. Even when they go so far as to arrest someone. And they never arrested John."

"Still"— Todd wiped his palms on his cargo pants—"it's just so hard to believe. Uncle John was always good to me. I mean, he was good to all of us, but him and me, we really hit it off. We'd shoot skeet, hang out, talk about music and stuff. Both black sheep of the family, I guess."

Kali couldn't help smiling. "You're a black sheep?"

Todd shrugged. "I'm not a Goody Two-shoes like Joey or a baby like Jeremy. I kind of do my own thing."

Kali was sure Sabrina would dispute the goody-two-shoes label. She'd listened to her sister vent enough about all three boys to know they each presented challenges. But she hated that Todd, who clearly identified with his uncle, was now struggling with the possibility that John might be a killer.

"John was good to you and he cared about you," Kali told her nephew. "That's what you need to remember. The other stuff, well, maybe we'll be able to get some answers at some point."

"Find out if he really killed them, you mean?"

"Yeah. I guess in my heart I can't believe he did it either."

Todd kicked the sole of his shoe against the flagstone patio. "What about *his* death?"

"What about it?" Again, Kali wasn't sure how much Sabrina had told the kids. Did they know about the drugs and alcohol?

"Do you think he did it on purpose?"

"Committed suicide, you mean?" Kali shook her head. "No, I don't. It's not that the thought never crossed my mind, but there are better ways." Better ways to kill yourself. What a conversation to be having with a fifteen-year-old. There were pitfalls to parenting she never imagined.

Todd rocked in his chair, a sort of upper-body nod of agreement. "Yeah, I guess. It's just that it's pretty hard to drown in a backyard pool."

"It happens."

"Like if he slipped and hit his head or something?"

She nodded.

They sat in silence for a moment. The air was warm, the moon just a sliver.

"I'm going to miss him," Todd said.

"Me too."

Todd rocked forward and stood. "Well, thanks. You're easier to talk to than my mom."

"Any time." Kali looked at the slender, shaggy boy she'd first held when he was only hours old. He was taller than she was now, but his eyes held the same solemn bewilderment they had fifteen years earlier. Her heart went out to him. "I mean it," she added. "Any time."

Todd headed back inside and Kali followed not long after. Sabrina and Peter had gone off to bed. Todd had joined Joey and Jeremy in front of the television. Kali said good night and wandered off to her own room. It wasn't until she was under the covers that she remembered the porn DVDs she'd found in John's collection. Short of barging in and retrieving them, which was bound to raise questions, she could only hope the boys didn't go looking for something new to watch.

# CHAPTER 18

As strains from a recording of The Byrds' "Turn! Turn! Turn!" filled the funeral hall, Sabrina inched closer to Kali in the pew and grabbed her hand. "I'm not sure I can do this," she whispered.

"You'll be fine," Kali told her. "Just remember to breathe." Breathe and try not to think about what's happening—it was advice that had carried Kali through a lot over the years.

Kali'd had no idea what kind of turnout to expect, but as she turned and surveyed the room, she was surprised to see more than a handful of faces. She wondered how many had actually known John and how many were simply curious on-lookers or media personnel. They'd passed by news cameras coming in, and she was sure there were reporters inside as well.

The music ended and she turned her attention to the front of the room.

The service was simple and relatively brief. Peter talked of John's energy and sense of adventure. Joey spoke of his uncle's kindness and goofy sense of humor. Kali added a few words about their childhood, recounting tales of John's determination in sports; his love of all things mechanical; and his devotion to the family dog, Sierra. Sabrina had insisted she wasn't up to the task, but several of John's friends offered words of their own. A. J. Nash, the attorney from Logan Foods whom Kali had met earlier, a neighbor she'd talked to by phone, a man with whom John played tennis. Fond memories with a sprinkling of light moments, and nothing of the terrible crime of which John had been accused, nor of the unseemly manner of his death.

Kali got through her own short speech by following the advice she'd given Sabrina. It wasn't until she sat down again that the reality of John's death took hold anew. She'd lost a brother—her only brother—without ever knowing him.

Following the service, when coffee and cookies were served in an adjoining room, Kali finally had a chance to study those who'd come to pay their respects. She recognized only a smattering of faces: A. J. Nash, of course; John's secretary, Alicia; a few neighbors; and Graciela, the housekeeper, who huddled uncertainly near the door. She left before Kali had a chance to thank her for coming.

People mingled in small groups, then briefly sought out Kali and Sabrina to offer condolences and a few kind words about John, though it was clear all were uncomfortably aware that John had been a murder suspect. There were so many questions Kali wanted to ask. Had any of them known John was abusing drugs? Had he seemed depressed in the weeks before his death? Had he talked to anyone about his difficulties with Sloane? And most of all, did they know why he might have had a photo of Olivia Perez hidden inside the pages of his office dictionary?

Instead, she nodded numbly and shook the hands of strangers, many of whom seemed to have known her brother better than she had.

At one point, Nash approached, and Kali introduced him to Sabrina.

"It was good of you to come," Kali told him. Not many people from Logan Foods had. She hadn't really expected that Reed would, although a part of her had held out hope, but she had thought more of John's coworkers might have shown up.

"Were you and John close friends?" Sabrina asked Nash.

"I wouldn't say we were close, but we shared an interest in cars. Did a couple of track days together, in fact." Nash scratched the fair skin of his cheek. "We'd go out for a drink on occasion. If I needed financial advice, I'd sometimes run it by John. If he had a legal question, he'd come see me. As I told your sister the other day"—he nodded in Kali's direction—"John was well liked in the company. Dedicated and hardworking. Someone whose opinion I respected."

"Thank you. That's nice to hear considering . . ." Sabrina paused and bit her lower lip. "Considering everything."

Nash cleared his throat, pushed his glasses up the bridge of his nose. "I understand the girl's family might be pursuing legal remedies."

"How'd you hear that?" Kali's gaze had drifted to a baby-faced black man standing alone by the coffee urn, but now her attention snapped back to Nash.

"I got a call from their attorney," he said. Kali's expression must have revealed her surprise because he hastened to add, "It was a fishing expedition. I didn't tell the woman a thing, I assure you. In fact, I tried hard to discourage her."

"Fishing for what?"

He shrugged. "Whatever she can get, I imagine. She's not entitled to police records, not officially at least, so she's got to build her case from scratch."

Assuming the lawsuit went forward. Kali was hoping it didn't come to that.

Sabrina's displeasure was evident from her expression. "The attorney's got a lot of gall, if you ask me."

"I'm sorry," Nash murmured, shaking his head in apology. "I shouldn't have said anything. Not today. But I wanted you to know that we, Logan Foods, that is, aren't involved in this in any way. I can't speak for Reed personally, but the company isn't taking sides."

"We appreciate that," Kali told him.

"I'm available if there's any way I can help." Nash's hazel eyes met hers warmly. "John was someone I considered a friend."

When he'd gone, Sabrina fanned herself with her hand. "Nice man, but I wish he hadn't brought up that stupid lawsuit."

"I think he was trying to be helpful." Kali appreciated the fact that Nash had come to the funeral while most of John's coworkers hadn't. And he'd gone out of his way to be friendly.

The hall was thinning out. Kali saw Peter glance at his watch a couple of times. He and the boys were heading back to Scottsdale that afternoon, and Kali knew they were eager to get going.

She turned to Sabrina. "Why don't you go on back to John's with Peter? I'll finish up here."

"You sure you don't mind?"

"There's hardly anyone left but staff. I won't be long."

When Sabrina had gone, Kali wandered over to the refreshment table, suddenly feeling drained. She wasn't hungry, but she picked up an oatmeal cookie and nibbled on it anyway. It was sugary and tasteless. She wrapped what was left in a napkin and dumped it in the trash.

The baby-faced black man she'd noticed earlier joined her and held out a hand. "Doug Simon," he said. "You're John's sister?"

She nodded and shook his hand. "Kali O'Brien. Were you a friend of my brother?"

He shifted uncomfortably. "Not exactly."

"Why are you here, then?" She wondered if Simon might be a reporter, though he was hardly the most inconspicuous person the newspaper could have sent.

"I'm afraid that came out wrong. I didn't mean we *weren't* friends." He smiled to put her at ease. It was a warm smile, accompanied by a twinkle of his eyes. "Can we talk privately?"

"Now?"

"It won't take long." Simon took her elbow and led her

aside where their conversation wouldn't be overheard. "I actually never met your brother, but I did talk to him by phone." He paused. "I'm a private investigator."

"A . . . PI?" It was the last thing she'd expected. Her mind set off in a spin. "John hired you?" Then another, more worrisome thought struck her. "Or was he the subject of your investigation?"

That smile again. "No, he hired me."

"What for?"

Simon rubbed his palm against his pant leg. "First I want to apologize for crashing a funeral like this. I didn't mean to be disrespectful. I just wanted to get the lay of the land before talking to you."

Kali shook her head in confusion. "You've lost me."

"John asked me to run a background check on a couple from Oregon. Ray and Martha Adams."

Now she was really lost. "Adams? Did he say why?"

"We were working in stages," Simon explained. "John was going to tell me more. In fact, he had something else he wanted me to check. But he died before we had a chance to discuss it."

"When did he hire you?"

"A little over a week ago."

Right around the time of the murders. The bite of cookie Kali had just eaten felt like lead in her stomach. Were the Adams couple involved somehow?

Simon frowned. "So the name means nothing to you?"

Kali shook her head. "My sister might know, though. Did you find these people?"

"I was able to get some of the information for him. And since he paid for it, I'd like to pass it along. That's why I wanted to get the lay of the land first. If you and your brother were in a pissing contest—" Simon held up his hands. "Sorry, that just slipped out. What I mean is, if there was a lot of hostility in the family, well, I didn't want to give out information that might cause more problems."

"How do you know there's not? Hostility, I mean?"

"Well, it's something of a gamble, I admit. But usually

I'm a pretty good judge of people." He looked at her intently, but with that same twinkle in his eye. "You're not going to prove me wrong, are you?"

She shook her head. "No hostility." As for causing problems, a lot depended on what John's interest was in Ray and Martha Adams, and who they were. She fervently hoped it wasn't going to lead to problems.

"What makes you think he was interested in the information for himself," Kali asked, "and not acting on behalf of his employer?"

"He was clear about that."

Kali knotted her fingers. "So what did you find out?"

"I've got a report I'll send you. The short of it is the couple divorced eleven years ago after seven years of marriage. Martha Adams died eight years later in an auto accident. Ray remarried not long after the divorce and has two kids by his second wife. He manages a Chevy dealership in San Diego."

"How old is Ray?" Kali asked. Maybe he was someone John knew from college.

"Forty-eight. Martha was a year younger."

That made them both older than John. "Did they have any children together?"

"One daughter. Martha got custody in the divorce, but I believe the girl went to live with her father and his new family after her mother's death." Simon squinted at her. "None of this rings a bell with you?"

"Not at all."

"I was sure hoping it would. Your brother was eager to get the information. He paid a premium for expedited service."

Fragmented thoughts and questions whirred in Kali's brain until she thought her head might explode.

"I don't suppose you want me to continue with the investigation?" Simon asked.

"I . . . I don't know. Let me talk to my sister." With luck, Sabrina would put an end to the mystery. "Do you have a card?"

Simon reached into his wallet and handed her his card. "Where shall I send the report?"

"We're staying at John's. You can send it there. I assume you have the address?"

Simon nodded.

"What information did John give you besides the names?" Kali asked.

"Only that they were living in Portland, Oregon, in 1991."

Portland. John had moved around quite a bit, but Kali didn't recall him ever living anywhere in Oregon. "And what was it he wanted to know about the couple?"

"Present whereabouts, general background, family. Pretty much what I've told you."

Kali fingered Doug Simon's card, then tucked it into her pocket. "Do you think you can get me the report soon?"

"It will probably be a couple of days, at this point, before I can get it written up."

"I'll be looking for it."


The house was quiet when Kali got back to John's. Peter's car was gone, and so were the Game Boys and iPods and assorted boys' shoes that had only that morning been strewn about. She wondered for a moment if Sabrina had gone back to Scottsdale as well, then remembered she'd seen her car in the driveway.

Kali checked the living room and bedrooms, then called out Sabrina's name.

"In here," she answered.

Kali followed the sound and turned on the light in the darkened den when she entered. Sabrina was curled on the leather couch holding a tall glass of clear liquid in her hand. Water or vodka and tonic, and Kali was willing to bet it was the latter.

"It's only two o'clock," Kali said.

"So?"

"So, it's a wee bit early, wouldn't you say?"

"Who appointed you master of the universe?" Sabrina giggled and started to get up. She listed to the left, grabbing the arm of the sofa to steady herself. "Guess I'm a bit tipsy."

"Honey, you're more than tipsy. How much have you had to drink, anyway?"

"Not that much, really." Her words were slurred. "This is only the second one, I think."

"You think?"

"It's not the booze," Sabrina said. "I took some of John's Valium. One before the service, and another when I got home." Tears sprang to her eyes. "Then one more when Peter left. Don't lecture me, okay? It's just that I can't face my life. Not today. I needed a little break, is all."

"Well, looks like you've got it. I just hope you don't feel like crap tomorrow."

"I don't want to deal with tomorrows. Any of them. Ever."

Kali sank onto the couch beside her.

"You want something?" Sabrina asked, wiping at her eyes. "Take your pick. Vodka or Valium, though mixing them probably wasn't such a great idea."

"Probably not."

That didn't stop Sabrina from taking another sip before offering the glass to Kali.

"No, thanks."

"You know what my shrink would say about this, don't you? That I'm doing it as some sort of homage to John. Pretty ironic that I drink and pop pills to deal with his doing the very same thing."

Kali frowned as Sabrina's earlier remark finally sank in. "What do you mean, you took John's Valium? The cops said it was Xanax, and they confiscated what was left."

"I know the difference," Sabrina said indignantly. "What I took was Valium. It was in John's medicine cabinet. Practically a full bottle."

Kali got up and went to check. The medicine cabinet in John's bathroom held the usual array of over-the-counter medications—aspirin, cough drops, Sudafed—as well as pre-scription bottles of Valium, Vicodin, and Lopressor. Kali poured the Valium into her hand and counted. Twenty-five pills.

Sabrina watched over her shoulder.

"What? You think I was lying? Jesus, Kali."

She shook her head. "It's not about you."

"What are you doing, then?"

Kali returned the pills to the bottle but kept hold of it. Better not to tempt Sabrina by leaving it within easy access. "Why would John have gone and bought an unmarked baggie of Xanax on the street when he had plenty of Valium from a legitimate pharmacy? They do pretty much the same thing."

"Beats me."

Kali felt the tickle of something that didn't add up. She looked up the prescribing doctor in the phone book. An internist. She called his office and left a message, though she wasn't sure he'd tell her anything. Wasn't sure he'd even call her back.

"By the way," Sabrina said, "someone named Graciela called for you a while ago."

"Did she leave a number?"

"It's by the phone. Who is she?"

"John's housekeeper. She was the one who found him in the pool. She was at the service today."

Sabrina's face clouded again. "Oh shit, the service. For a moment there I'd forgotten what was so rotten about today."


Kali didn't want to tie up the land line in case the doctor called back, so she used her cell phone to call Graciela.

"It was kind of you to come to the service," Kali told her.

"I pay my respects to Mr. John. He treat me good." She paused before continuing. "You ask me about the morning when your brother die."

"Yes."

"Today I remember, but maybe it nothing."

"Remember what?"

"When I arrive, the kitchen is messy, like Mr. John make a sandwich."

"Right," Kali said. "I remember you said that."

"The jars," Graciela continued. "Mustard and pickles and mayonnaise."

A little bell went off in the back of Kali's head at the same time Graciela explained.

"Your brother not eat mayonnaise. I fix him sandwich sometimes. Mustard, yes, no mayonnaise."

It was one of John's strong food dislikes. Why would he have had the mayonnaise out?

He wouldn't have unless it was for someone else.

She remembered the voice she'd heard in the background when she'd called John the night he died. Not the television, after all.

Kali could feel her heart racing. She wasn't sure what it all meant. Maybe nothing. But at the very minimum, whoever had been with John might be able to help them figure out what had happened that night. Beyond that . . . Kali shook her head to clear it. In light of what she'd just learned about John's almost full bottle of prescription Valium, the presence of another person raised disturbing questions.

"Graciela, do you remember if the lights were on inside the house when you arrived Wednesday morning?"

"I . . . I think no. The sun is out. It's day."

But according to the medical examiner, it had been night when John had died. Had he stumbled around in the dark before falling into the pool, or had someone else turned the lights off on the way out?

# CHAPTER 19

K ali could have sworn she remained awake all night, tossing and turning, her mind racing in twenty directions at once. But when the brilliant morning sun streamed through the bedroom window and jolted her from the torment of a dream, she realized she must have eventually fallen asleep. Not that it mattered. Her sleep had been as fitful as the hours preceding it.

Even now that she was awake, the suffocating grief and guilt that had peppered her dream continued to haunt her. She pulled the sheet up under her chin and turned onto her side, away from the memory, but she couldn't shut it out.

A youthful John, laughing and joking with his friends. Kali, a part of that circle the way she never had been in life. In her dream world, she'd experienced a wonderful sense of serenity and belonging, of being loved and accepted by those around her. Then, out of the corner of her eye, she'd caught sight of John unwittingly backing toward a steep cliff while several of his faceless friends munched on ham sandwiches with mayonnaise, oblivious of the danger. Couldn't they see what was going to happen?

Kali knew she should warn John, but she was too engrossed in flirting with a boy, whom she recognized now as Doug Simon, the private investigator. Bryce was there too, though Kali was ignoring him. Yet the whole time she was flirting with Simon, she was wishing he were Bryce. Suddenly John was in the ocean below the cliff, thrashing madly in the surf, struggling to stay afloat. He looked pleadingly into Kali's eyes, called out to her with words she couldn't decipher, and then, as Kali watched silently, he slipped under the surface. Kali ached with remorse, yet she made no move to save him. How could she have let John fall to his death and done nothing?

Fully awake, Kali ached still. It was a raw, gnawing pain that pervaded every fiber of her body. She couldn't have saved him, she told herself now. Not literally, not in real life. But she wasn't so sure that was true. At the very least, she could have tried.

And Doug Simon, what was he doing in her dream? She couldn't imagine why she'd been flirting with him. Maybe it was what he'd told her that she'd been flirting with rather than the man himself. The strangers her brother had been looking for—Ray and Martha Adams. Had they been part of the faceless crowd? Kali couldn't remember.

She rolled to her other side and tried shutting her eyes. By now her brain had kicked into overdrive again. Had someone been at John's the night he died? Was that where the Xanax had come from? Several scenarios presented themselves. A small party. A buddy dropping by and a late-night snack. A drug dealer, though Kali doubted a drug like Xanax would command home delivery.

And the terrible possibility that had vaulted into her thoughts as she crawled into bed last night: that John's death had not been an accident at all. That his visitor had had a hand in it.

Kali was now beyond sleep. She got out of bed, showered, and went into the kitchen to make herself a cup of strong coffee. No sign yet of Sabrina. Kali poked her head into her bedroom to make sure her sister was still breathing. It was the damn dream, she told herself. Now she was responsible for everyone.

She took her mug into the den and settled down at John's

desk. She and Sabrina had a meeting with John's estate-planning attorney later that morning, and she wanted to have a handle on her brother's finances before then.

An hour and a half later, after Kali had worked her way through two cups of coffee and most of the bank records and bills, Sabrina appeared, sleepy eyed, at the door. She was still in her yellow cotton nightgown and her face was creased from sleep.

"I'm sorry about what happened yesterday," Sabrina said.

She sounded genuinely contrite, Kali thought, but it might just have been a hangover. "How are you feeling?"

"Like shit." Sabrina leaned against the wall. "Thanks for not lecturing me, by the way. I know what I did was stupid. I promise to be better in the future."

"It's your life."

Sabrina laughed, a mirthless bark. "That, unfortunately, is the crux of the problem."

"Sitting around feeling sorry for yourself isn't going to help."

"If only I were more like you," Sabrina said, leaning against the doorjamb. "Strong, steady, controlled." Another forced laugh. "Thin."

"That's me, a paragon of virtue and fitness." Kali stood up. It was hard to imagine Sabrina envious of her when for as long as she could remember it had been the other way around.

"Come on," Kali said. "I'll make you a cup of coffee."

Sabrina padded into the kitchen after Kali. "You think it's genetic? This tendency to escape through liquor and drugs, I mean. Dad was like that. And then John. And me."

"Could be."

"But not you," Sabrina said. It wasn't a question and it wasn't, as far as Kali could tell, the least bit sarcastic.

"Oh, for God's sake, I drink too much sometimes. Don't go making me into someone I'm not." And Kali escaped in other ways, by keeping her distance and shutting out feelings. She'd had that thrown in her face often enough.

"Besides," she added, putting the kettle on to boil, "I'm not so sure John *was* escaping with booze and pills."

"What do you mean?"

Kali wasn't sure how much of yesterday afternoon Sabrina was able to recall. She'd been pretty out of it. "The Valium in John's medicine cabinet, remember? And the jar of mayonnaise Graciela found on the kitchen counter."

"Right. You were getting worked up about John's having had company or something."

Kali nodded. "Graciela thinks she remembers the lights being off when she arrived here that morning."

Sabrina stretched, elbows out to her side. "That's important?"

"Would John have turned off the lights himself while he was still up and wandering around?"

"Probably not. Not all of them, anyway. You think his friend . . . you think that . . ." The expression on Sabrina's face shifted. "What are you saying? That whoever was here . . ." She took a breath. "Are you saying John's death wasn't an accident?"

"It raises questions, doesn't it?"

Sabrina stared at her silently, then nodded. She collapsed onto one of the kitchen chairs, her bare legs and feet spread out in front of her. "Oh, God."

"There's something else." Kali told her about the PI John had hired. "Do the names Ray and Martha Adams mean anything to you?"

"Never heard of them."

"What about Portland, Oregon? Did John have ties there?"

"Not that I know of. I'm certain he never lived there."

The phone rang and Sabrina picked it up. She listened for a moment, then said, "I think you need to talk to my sister. She's the attorney." She put her hand over the mouthpiece and whispered, "It's Carmen Escobar, representing Olivia Perez's family."

Kali took the phone. "What can I do for you, Ms. Escobar?"

"I just wanted to make contact." The voice was high-pitched, clipped, and strident. "As I understand it, you and your sister are John O'Brien's next of kin."

"That's right."

"I represent the parents of one of his victims, Olivia Perez. It's our intention to file suit for damages." Ms. Escobar raced on as if she were reading from a script. "Because of your brother's heinous act, the Perez family has lost their only daughter, their pride and joy. Murdered in cold blood."

Kali bristled at the tone and innuendo. "My brother was never even arrested for the crime, much less convicted. And that's because there's scant evidence that he had anything to do with it. You'll have a hard time proving he was responsible."

"Not as hard a time," she replied smugly and much more slowly, "as you'll have trying to convince a jury he wasn't."

That was unfortunately all too true. Innocent until proven guilty was a laudable concept, but verdicts often sprang from emotion. And Olivia Perez was a highly sympathetic victim—young, beautiful, hardworking. Someone who'd overcome tremendous odds and was on her way to achieving great things.

"Do her parents understand they might lose?" Kali asked. "They'll have squandered money bringing suit for nothing."

"That's not an issue."

A contingency fee, in other words. "You're in a position to gamble like that?" Kali asked. "It's likely to be an expensive trial."

"Unless it settles first," Carmen Escobar observed pointedly. "These cases almost always settle. Sooner or later."

Outrage bubbled in Kali's chest. What the attorney was suggesting was nothing short of extortion, though it happened often enough. Sue and chances were you'd wind up with something. Defendants tended to shy away from costly courtroom battles.

"We're not interested in settling," Kali told her.

"Just something to think about. The Perez family is willing to be reasonable." Carmen Escobar paused just long enough to punctuate her remark. "Oops, I've got a call on another line. Speak to you later."

Kali slammed the phone into its cradle.

"What was that all about?" Sabrina asked.

"Sounds like the Perez family has hired themselves a piranha. She's hoping we'll settle out of court. Mr. and Mrs. Perez, and their lovely attorney, will walk away with money in their pocket merely for stamping their feet a few times and waving their arms."

"Why would we settle?"

Kali handed Sabrina a cup of coffee. "We might lose if we go to trial."

"But if John's death wasn't an accident—"

"Even if we had proof of that, it doesn't let him off the hook for the murders of Sloane and Olivia. But I agree, it certainly changes things."

Kali and Sabrina spent over an hour in the luxuriously furnished office of Albert Geddes, the attorney who'd drafted John's trust and will. He was a quiet, balding man with a pinched face and a no-nonsense manner. Although lacking in charisma, he seemed to know his business.

"It's not a complicated estate plan," he told them. "The bulk of the assets is in trust. There's a bequest to each of his nephews, but in the main, the assets will flow directly to the two of you. Because of the trust, there's no need for formal probate, but there will still be a fair amount of paperwork, particularly with regard to date-of-death valuation and estate tax. I'm happy to work with you in whatever capacity you wish. I can handle it all, or only what you don't want to do yourselves."

"Thank you," Kali said. She could easily manage the transfer of assets, but she had no desire to immerse herself in the minutiae of tax matters.

"I've got some inventory forms here that will help you get organized." Geddes pulled a packet of papers from a file cabinet behind his polished walnut desk. Then he folded his hands. "To the best of my knowledge John hadn't amended the trust. But he did set up an appointment for next week to discuss some possible changes."

Kali looked at Sabrina, who shrugged and said, "News to me."

"Do you have any idea what changes he had in mind?" Kali asked.

"No. I never spoke with him directly. He talked to my secretary. Not that it would make a difference if I had. The document stands as written."

Still, Kali wanted to try to honor John's wishes. "Did my brother ever mention the names Ray and Martha Adams?"

Geddes shook his head. "Doesn't sound familiar. Aside from the estate plan, I only talked to your brother now and then about tax issues. I'm afraid I don't know much about his personal life."

Outside, Sabrina asked, "Do you think John was going to change his will because of the Adams couple?"

"Got me. There are a lot of odd pieces here. I'm just trying to see if any of them fit." Kali pulled her dark glasses and car keys from her purse. "I'm off to see if I can track down Olivia's brother. You're okay with going alone to see John's doctor?"

"Sure. You think the brother will be able to tell us something about Olivia and John?"

"Probably not or he'd have spoken up before now. But there's a lot we don't know and I have to start somewhere."

Tony Perez worked at a Logan Foods store near the university campus. He was bagging groceries at a checkout counter when the clerk at customer service pointed him out to Kali.

"He's got a break coming in about five minutes," the clerk said. "Might be best if you waited until then to talk to him."

Kali stood by a magazine rack and watched Tony work. He looked to be in his early to mid twenties, three or four years older than Olivia. He was lean but muscular, with wavy dark hair trimmed short and a full mouth set off with dimples. He wouldn't have been her type even when she was younger, but he had the kind of brooding good looks that had undoubtedly broken a few hearts over the years. His movements were methodical and his face expressionless, but she noticed a quick smile whenever a customer engaged him in conversation.

She waited until he moved off, presumably for his break, then approached and introduced herself. "My name's Kali. I'm an attorney involved with your sister's death," she said. Not altogether untrue. "I'd like your input on a few things. Can I buy you lunch, or coffee? I don't want to impinge on your break time."

Tony snorted. "It's not like there's a lot I can do in a grocery mall anyway. And half an hour's too short to go anywhere else."

"So what do you usually do on your breaks?" She fell into step beside him as they moved outside.

He shrugged. "Have a smoke. Think. Listen to music."

"You hungry?"

"Nah. Coffee's fine."

They settled on a Starbucks next door to the grocery. At home, Kali was loyal to Peets, which she far preferred on both principle and taste, but the one good thing to be said about Starbucks was that it was everywhere.

She had an iced coffee, black, and Tony ordered a Caramel Chocolate Frappuccino Blended Creme with extra whipped cream and cocoa sprinkles. More milkshake than coffee. The girl behind the counter greeted him by name and they exchanged banter while Kali paid for the coffees.

"You working with that bitch my parents hired?" Tony asked when he and Kali were seated at a small round table near the window.

The bluntness of his words caught her by surprise. "Not exactly," Kali said, again stretching the truth. "But our work overlaps. You don't like her?"

"She's pushy, is all. I don't like bossy women, even if they *are* lawyers." He gave Kali a punk version of a flirty smile, then settled back and focused on his Frappuccino.

"How do you like working at Logan's?" she asked, easing into the conversation.

"Bagging groceries isn't exactly my life's ambition."

Probably better than being unemployed or in jail, which, in light of what Linette Logan had said, were the options he'd left behind. "How long have you worked there?"

"Got the job a few months back. They made me start as a bagger but promised I could work up to checker. Not that being a checker is my life's ambition either."

"What is?"

He shrugged again, gave her another smile. "I'm still finding my way."

"Tell me about Olivia."

Tony spooned a scoop of whipped cream into his mouth. "She was okay."

*Okay?* His sister had been murdered and all he could come up with was *okay?* "Were there just the two of you?" Kali asked.

"Yeah. She was my half sister, really. Same mother, different fathers."

"Where's your father?"

"Gone. I never knew him. Not sure my mother did, either," Tony added snidely. "Olivia is the success of the family. But you know that, right? She was always good in school, good at being what people wanted her to be. Like that lizard—what's it called? The one that changes colors to blend in."

"Chameleon?"

"Yeah, like that. If she had to be purple with green spots to get what she wanted, she'd do it. She knew to work the system."

"What did she want?"

"Money, clothes, excitement. Mostly she wanted to get out of Dodge." Tony laughed without humor. "You know my parents, right?"

"I've met your father. Your stepfather, I mean."

That laugh again. "Then you know what I'm talking about."

*I loved my daughter, no matter what people say.* "What were things like between your dad and Olivia?" Kali asked.

"Better than between him and me. That's not saying much, though. He's got a mean streak and he doesn't much care who he picks on. He never liked me. Or Olivia, for that matter, and she was his own kid."

"He doesn't like children?" Kali asked.

"Doesn't like anyone." Tony took a long slurp of his Frappucino.

"Even your mom?"

Tony's mouth curled in contempt. "He likes that she earns a paycheck."

Not exactly a warm and loving family. "It must have been hard having a sister who was a superachiever," Kali said.

"Being a superachiever isn't everything." Tony poked his straw around the bottom of the plastic cup. "I'm alive. She's dead. Like Icarus flying too close to the sun. Look what putting on airs got her."

Kali regarded him with surprise. "You know mythology."

He looked up. "Just because I didn't get into U of A on some fancy scholarship doesn't mean I'm illiterate."

"I wasn't implying that." Though on some level, she realized, she was. She'd made assumptions about Tony that might not be warranted.

"You asked my life's ambition. I'll tell you what it is." Tony leaned across the table. His dark eyes narrowed with intensity. "It's to be a writer. Writers are like gods. They're in charge of the worlds they create. And they get inside readers' hearts and minds. The good ones anyway." He sat back and drilled into her with his eyes. "That's power."

Tony spoke with a passion that was both impressive and a bit scary. "Good for you," Kali said. "What do you write?"

"Poetry," Tony replied. "Stories. I started a novel but I haven't done much with it." He ran his hands along the edge of the table, clearly uncomfortable with having revealed so much of himself. "Probably nothing will come of it."

"Or it might." Feeling guilt at having perhaps judged him too harshly, Kali now sought to sound encouraging.

He shrugged, gazed through the window at cars in the parking lot.

"Do you know many of Olivia's friends?"

"A few, not many. We weren't close."

A lot like Kali and John.

She showed Tony the photograph she'd found in John's office. "Do you recognize either of the other two girls?"

Tony glanced at the photo, then shook his head, but not before recognition, if that's what it was, had flickered across his face. "Never seen them," he said flatly.

"Are you sure? It looked to me like you reacted there for a moment."

Tony licked his lips. "It must have been seeing my sister alive. All happy and smiling."

Kali hoped he was better at writing than at lying. "How did Olivia feel about working for Sloane Winslow?"

"You kidding? She thought it was really cool that she got to live in a fancy house and run around like she was someone important. I told her, 'You're a fucking house cleaner, not lady of the manor.'"

"What about John O'Brien? Did she ever mention him?"

Tony's expression darkened. "The guy who killed them?"

"He was a police suspect, but he was never arrested. Did she know him?"

"Was?"

Kali swallowed. "He died."

"Well, I never heard of him except what the cops said. Besides, I thought he worked with Sloane Winslow or something. Why would Olivia know him?"

That's what Kali wanted to know, too.

# CHAPTER 20

Kali had a two o'clock appointment with detectives Shafer and Parker. She was sure they'd agreed to meet with her again only because the sheriff's department valued community relations. Shafer's tepid response to her earlier phone call told Kali that Sloane Winslow's murder was no longer a priority.

Michelle Parker was in the entryway of the sheriff's station, talking to a male officer, when Kali arrived. She raised a hand in greeting and appeared glad to grab the chance to extricate herself from the conversation.

"Men," Michelle said, with a shake of her head. "They can be so stubborn sometimes."

"How true."

She laughed. "But it would be a pretty dull world without them."

"That's true also." Kali chuckled in female comradery.

"You married?"

"No. How about you?"

"Not anymore. First time was such a disaster I'm not sure I have the courage to try again." Michelle nodded to another officer as they took the stairs to the second floor. "Don't ever marry a cop," she told Kali. "They want to call all the shots."

Although she and Bryce had never spoken of marriage,

sometimes determinedly steering the conversation in the opposite direction, it was something Kali thought about now and then. Whether or not it was something she wanted, she hadn't decided, but Michelle's warning resonated with her own well of doubts.

Michelle took her through the double doors to the violent crimes unit. Shafer was on the phone at his desk, but he held up a finger to indicate he'd just be a minute. There was a tightness to his expression Kali hadn't seen before. She hoped it wasn't because he was irritated with her.

But when he hung up the phone, he greeted her pleasantly and gestured to a chair. "I understand you have information you think we might be interested in hearing."

"Right. There are actually a couple of things I thought you should be aware of."

The detectives sat opposite her and gave her their full attention. Shafer seemed eager to hear what she had to say.

"First," Kali said, "John had a doctor's prescription for Valium and a practically full bottle of the stuff in his medicine chest. If he wanted pills to help him deal with the stress of being a suspect, why would he go to the trouble of buying a baggie of Xanax on the street?"

"We don't know that he bought it recently," Michelle pointed out.

Kali ticked off a second item on her fingers. "Another thing, John seemed distracted when I talked to him the night he died."

"That's not surprising, given that he was high at the time." Shafer hooked his thumbs over the edge of his desk and drummed first one thumb, then the other. "Besides, if I remember correctly, you said it wasn't much of a conversation."

"Enough that I formed an impression of what was going on," Kali said. "I heard a voice in the background. At the time, I assumed it was the television. Now I think someone was there."

Shafer stopped his drumming. "Why's that?"

"John didn't like mayonnaise. He couldn't stand it, in fact. But the housekeeper said when she got there the next morning she cleaned up the kitchen. This was before she discovered John was dead. There were sandwich makings on the counter, including a jar of mayonnaise."

Shafer rocked back in his chair, arms crossed over his chest. "This is the important new information you wanted to see us about? Mayonnaise?"

"And the prescription for Valium. Also, the housekeeper said the inside lights were off when she arrived. She didn't think anything of it at the time because it was morning. But John died during the night. The lights would have been on."

Michelle frowned, a nice blending of irony and skepticism. "What are you suggesting? That your brother's death wasn't an accident? That someone killed him?"

Kali took a breath. "Yes. And that bears on the question of John's guilt."

The muscles in Detective Shafer's jaw twitched. "None of what you've told us changes the evidence we have tying your brother to those murders."

"But there could be—"

"And nothing you've said sheds any light on why this phantom killer might target your brother."

"I admit there's a lot we don't know—"

"*We?*" Shafer's palms came down hard on the desktop. His hawk-brown eyes turned cool. "I'll tell you what we know, Ms. O'Brien. Those of us actually authorized to investigate murder know that the evidence points overwhelmingly to your brother, and that we've been unable to turn up a single other viable suspect. This poppycock about mayonnaise and lights makes as much sense as a Ouija board."

Shafer pushed back his chair and stood. "Excuse me, I've got other matters to attend to." He turned and left the room.

With sudden clarity, Kali realized the detectives had been hoping her new information would give them further evidence of John's guilt. The exact opposite of what she'd actually delivered.

"Sorry," Michelle Parker said, looking slightly embarrassed. "I don't know what's eating him lately. He's not usually so brusque."

"But you weren't persuaded by what I had to say, either."

The detective spread her hands. "I have to be honest. I think you're grasping at straws. Even if your brother made a sandwich for someone, it doesn't mean that person drugged and killed him."

"I realize it's a bit of a leap, but it *feels* important to me. One of those little mind tickles that doesn't make sense, if you know what I mean."

"I do, but feelings are notoriously unreliable in situations like this." Michelle's voice softened. "I know you probably feel guilty for not making time to talk to your brother that night. And you don't want to believe he's capable of murder. That's only natural." She paused. "I think Detective Shafer was a bit harsh just now, but bottom line, I think he's right."

Maybe she *was* grasping at straws. If the roles were reversed and she found herself in Michelle Parker's shoes, she'd probably be skeptical too. And, in truth, Kali wasn't convinced John was innocent. He'd had Olivia Perez's photograph, after all. That compounded his link to the murders. For all she knew, his death might actually have been an accident.

Still, she couldn't let it go. She owed John that much. She owed it to herself, as well.

"It's rather convenient that your prime suspect wound up dead," Kali noted. "That alone should raise questions."

Michelle ran her tongue over her lower lip. "The coroner ruled his death accidental."

"It's not something you'll follow up on, then?"

"What's there to follow up?" The detective sounded irritated. "Do you have someone in mind we should talk to? A potential suspect or witness? An inkling of a motive?"

Kali shook her head. If John had been murdered, his killer could be the same person who'd killed Sloane Winslow and Olivia Perez. Or someone connected to that person. But she hadn't a clue as to who or why.

"I'll look over the report again," Michelle said finally. She glanced toward the door as a gray-haired clerk entered the room. "In the meantime, if you think of anything else, give me a call."

"Thank you."

"Don't thank me yet," Michelle said, with a trace of a smile. "I'm not promising results."

The clerk handed the detective a sheet of paper. "Here's the final sketch and description we're going to the public with."

"You'll get it to the media right away?"

The woman nodded. "They've already been notified it's on its way."

Kali barely heard the exchange. Her eyes were riveted on the sketch the clerk had brought in. It showed a young woman with curly, shoulder-length hair; apple cheeks; and wide-set eyes.

Kali's heart skipped a beat. "Who's that?" she asked, trying for offhand indifference and failing.

Michelle Parker seemed not to notice. "That's what we'd like to know. Her body was found a couple of weeks ago."

*Body.* "She's dead? How did she die?"

"Asphyxiation. She was dumped in a wash in East County. Looks like she's been dead a couple of weeks, maybe longer."

Kali's mouth was dry. She forced herself to swallow. "You must know *something* about her."

"Best guess is she was in her late teens or early twenties. She doesn't fit the description of any missing persons report we've got. We're hoping with the public's help we'll get an ID."

*Breathe*, Kali reminded herself. *Keep calm and don't give anything away until you've had time to think this through.*

"Sad, isn't it?" Michelle continued. "I think it's what has Detective Shafer so upset. Part of it anyway. He has a daughter about the same age."

"Terrible," Kali concurred. The sour taste in her mouth was making her ill.

Michelle picked up the sketch, her expression pained.

"So you understand why we aren't off chasing phantom killers who take mayonnaise on their sandwiches. We've got our hands full looking for real creeps like the one who did this."

Kali nodded numbly. "Sorry to have taken your time."

The deputy shook her head apologetically. "I wasn't trying to be dismissive. I just wanted to put things in perspective."

When Kali got to the main lobby, she slipped into the women's room, where she splashed cold water on her face and rinsed out her mouth. It couldn't be, she told herself. But it was. The similarity was too striking to be a coincidence. The young woman in the sketch who'd been so brutally murdered had to be Olivia's friend—the redhead on the right in John's mysterious photo.

# CHAPTER 21

Erling was in the break room pouring milk into his coffee when Michelle swept through the door, angling a sideward glance his way. She grabbed a Diet Coke from the communal fridge, then turned and leaned an elbow on the counter.

"You've certainly blown your nomination for today's Miss Manners congeniality award."

Erling grunted acquiescence. "I guess maybe I was kind of short with her." He'd known at the time he was overreacting. He couldn't help himself. Everything about Sloane Winslow's murder made him tense. "Sorry," he muttered.

"Don't apologize to me. It's no skin off *my* nose."

"I know she just lost her brother and all," Erling said. "But really . . ." He shook his head and chuckled. "Mayonnaise, of all things."

Instead of sharing in the humor, Michelle sucked on her cheek. "It's an interesting theory, though. And the point about buying Xanax off the street when he's got a prescription for Valium does make you wonder."

"Wonder what?" Erling about choked on his coffee. "You don't seriously doubt that John O'Brien was our guy, do you?"

"Hey, don't bite my head off. We're supposed to be on the same team here."

"Exactly." Erling bristled. "And you're changing horses midstream."

"I'm not changing horses and we're not midstream." Michelle set down her soda can and crossed her arms. "Besides, it's a stupid analogy. Our oath of duty doesn't say anything about naming a suspect and sticking to it no matter what. We're supposed to get at the truth. Our job is to find the bad guys and protect the good ones."

Before they started working together, Erling had assumed that Michelle would be a pushover. She was a woman, she was younger than he was and junior in rank, and she was physically petite. It hadn't taken him long to learn he'd misjudged her. Her tenacity exhausted him at times, but he respected her and he liked her. Nonetheless, her little tirade annoyed him.

"You don't have to be so literal. It was just an expression."

She regarded him silently as she picked up her soda can and rolled it between her palms.

"You know damn well I understand what our job is. I might point out that I've been doing it a lot longer than you have."

Michelle managed to appear sheepish, though Erling suspected she put on the look intentionally. "I'm sorry. I know you're a good cop. The best I've ever worked with."

He gave a resigned sigh. "But you were right." And Erling knew he'd reacted badly precisely because she'd touched a sore spot.

She took a sip of soda. "May I ask you something?"

"Sure."

"What's going on? Ever since we got the Winslow case, you've been on edge."

*Take it easy,* Erling told himself. He didn't want Michelle thinking this case was anything but routine for him. "If I've seemed a bit grumpy, I apologize. I've got a tooth that's bothering me."

"Have you been to the dentist?"

"You sound like my wife." He kept his tone light and jocular, hoping she'd drop the subject.

Michelle traced a finger around the rim of her soda can. "I thought maybe it had something to do with the fact that we're dealing with two young, female victims, both about the age of your daughter. I can imagine how that might get under your skin."

He nodded. "That too. At least the cases aren't related."

"A serial killer, you mean? Someone targeting young women?"

"Right." Erling would never forget the string of kidnappings and murders that had terrorized the Tucson area back when Mindy was eight. Five girls, all within a year or so of her in age, and all with her same fair coloring. He'd been frantic with fear that his daughter would be next. Along with every other parent for miles around, he'd breathed a tremendous sigh of relief when the guy had been caught and sentenced.

Thank God they weren't dealing with anything like that. "I'll feel better," Erling added, "once we know the victim's identity. It's almost impossible to work a case without it."

"Maybe we'll get lucky now that the sketch is going out to the public. And something may still come of the dance angle."

"I hope so." They had a couple of uniforms canvassing the nightspots, but the odds were still long. There were even more seedy bars in Tucson than tattoo studios.

Michelle started to leave, then stopped and turned back. "I'm going to take another look at the report on John O'Brien's death. If nothing else, it'll appease his sisters. And there might just be something there."

Erling hoped not, though he could hardly stop Michelle from looking. "Let me know what you find."

He poured what was left of his coffee down the drain and rinsed his cup. His stomach felt sour enough as it was. *If John O'Brien had been murdered . . .* Erling shook his head. He didn't want to start down that path. But his mind marched on regardless.

If O'Brien's death was a homicide, it would call into question everything they'd put together on the Winslow/Perez case. The thought of that unraveling now made Erling ill. He'd managed to skate through the investigation without the affair coming to light. His career and marriage remained intact. He wanted to keep them that way.

That they'd been able to name a suspect so quickly had worked in Erling's favor. But a quick solution wasn't unusual. Cases either went nowhere quickly, or the pieces fell into place right away. True, O'Brien's death had been fortuitous. It meant no eager defense attorney would be poking around Sloane's personal life in search of alternative suspects and uncovering, instead, an affair with the lead detective.

But it wasn't as if they didn't have evidence connecting O'Brien to the crime. The guy had motive. He owned a gun similar to the murder weapon. A witness had placed him at Sloane's house within the right time frame. He had no viable alibi. In fact, he'd told them an outright lie about where he was at the time of the murder. None of that had changed.

*But if John O'Brien had been murdered . . .* Erling again shook the thought from his head. No, all this talk of mayonnaise and prescription drugs was nothing more than the grieving sisters' inability to accept the truth.

# CHAPTER 22

Sabrina was doing her nails at the kitchen table when Kali arrived. A vodka and tonic rested close at hand, and the inventory form Albert Geddes, the estate lawyer, had given them was spread out in front of her.

"Hi," she said, looking up from her candy-apple-red nails. "I'm making progress here. Do you think those abstract paintings in the living room are valuable?"

Kali flopped in a chair across from her. "I haven't the foggiest idea. They look like blobs of mismatched paint to me, but I guess we should have them appraised."

"I can't say they do much for me, either." With a laugh, Sabrina added, "At least we won't have to fight over who gets them."

"Great."

"You look hot," Sabrina said. "And tired. I'd make you a drink but my nails are still drying."

*If only numbing myself with alcohol would make everything better,* Kali thought.

Sabrina blew on her nails to dry them. "I got in to talk to John's doctor, by the way. An older guy, very sweet. He prescribed the Valium. He was puzzled by the Xanax. John had apparently tried that and found it gave him a headache."

Sabrina glanced up and waited, looking just a little bit smug. "Aren't you pleased? I did good, didn't I?"

Kali nodded, but her sister's words had barely sunk in.

"Well, you might show a little gratitude," Sabrina huffed.

Kali reached for Sabrina's vodka and tonic and took a sip. "No gratitude and now you're poaching, as well."

She set the glass down and nudged it in Sabrina's direction. "Good work with the doctor."

"I thought so myself," Sabrina said, with a self-satisfied air. She uncapped the nail polish and began layering on a second coat.

"Do you have to do your nails right now?" Kali was feeling irritable. "We need to talk about John."

"You think I can't do two things at once?"

"This is important."

Sabrina gave her a withering glance. "What's eating you?"

"Remember the photo I found in John's office?"

"Geesh, you and that photo. Just because he had a picture of Olivia doesn't mean he killed her."

"Put the damn nail polish away and look at this." Kali pulled the photo from her purse. "That girl on the right, the redhead—she was also murdered."

That got Sabrina's attention. "What? How do you know?"

"I saw a forensic artist's rendering. She was strangled and dumped outside of town. The police don't know who she is but they're hoping someone will see the sketch and identify her."

"You're sure it's the same girl?"

"It looked like her."

"It might not be, though." Sabrina looked at Kali, then shuddered. "That's so creepy." She replaced the nail brush in the bottle, her left hand forgotten. "Did it just happen?"

"No. But they didn't find her body until last week. Sounds like she died before Olivia did."

Sabrina sucked in her breath. "Did you tell them you recognized her?"

Kali shook her head.

"They don't know about the photo, then?"

"Not from me." This was part of what was making Kali ill. She was keeping information from the police that might help with the investigation. "If I tell them about the photo," she told Sabrina, "they'll try to pin her murder on John."

And they might be right, the rest of what was making Kali ill. Any way you looked at it, the photo connected John to the girls. It could well be an innocent connection, but Kali couldn't at that moment imagine what it might be.

Sabrina blinked. "You told them someone was here the night John died, right?"

"They weren't impressed."

"But if he was murdered"—she looked at Kali—"it all has to be tied together somehow, doesn't it?"

"That's not the way the detectives see it." Kali got up and opened the fridge. She wasn't so much hungry as agitated, and eating was a way to take the edge off. "Anyway, they didn't seem to put much stock in John's being murdered."

"But there's *got* to be a connection."

The refrigerator was depressingly empty. Kali shut the door and got herself a glass of water instead. "Yeah, probably. But it could be that John was part of something along with Sloane or Olivia."

Sabrina's brow creased. "Part of what?"

"I don't know," Kali snapped. "What if the third girl was murdered, too?"

"So what do we do?"

"Try to identify the girls and figure out what John was doing with that photo. Then we'll go to the authorities." She locked eyes with Sabrina. "No matter what John got himself involved in."

Kali didn't really want to go out again. It had been a draining day and she was exhausted. But she was also agitated by the discovery that John had been hiding a photograph that included two young women who had been murdered. Tired as she was, there was no way Kali could twiddle her thumbs until morning.

Olivia's high school friend had given her two names: Joanna Sommers, who'd worked in the library with Olivia; and a guy named Randy, who had a great body. Joanna was the obvious place to start. At least Kali knew where to find her.

The university was a good half hour from John's house, and although it was rush hour, most of the heavy traffic was headed in the opposite direction. With classes done for the day, Kali had no trouble finding a parking spot near campus. Unfortunately, the heat was not done for the day, and by the time she had walked through the long, open quad to the library, Kali felt flushed and lightheaded. The moment she walked through the wide doors of the entrance, she headed for the drinking fountain. She was beginning to understand the appeal of air-conditioning.

Kali approached the pimply-faced young man at the information desk and asked if Joanna Sommers was working that evening.

"I don't think so," he said.

"I need to talk to her. I don't suppose you know her phone number?"

"Why would I know that?" He sounded almost offended. "Try the student directory on the U of A Web site. There's a whole bunch of computers downstairs."

Kali descended the stairs and found that the entire basement, the size of several football fields, was given over to modular workstations and glassed-in group-study areas. It was an impressive sea of well-designed technology at work. Kali looked on with envy, recalling her own college days in dark and cramped library carrels.

She found an empty machine and logged onto the university's main Web page. From there, she found the directory of faculty and students. Joanna Sommers was a sophomore with an undeclared major. No address was listed for her, but there was a phone number. Mindful of the signs warning students to turn off cell phones or set them to vibrate, Kali stepped outside to make her call. When Joanna answered, Kali introduced herself as an attorney who wanted to speak with her about Olivia Perez.

"About her murder, you mean? I don't, like, really know anything about that." Joanna's voice had a soft, almost breathless quality.

"Mostly it's just background information," Kali said.

"Well, okay, uh, sure. I guess."

"I'm on campus. Is now a good time?"

"Yeah, now's fine. I'm just heading back to the dorm. I can meet you in front in about ten minutes. I'm in La Paz. It's near the stadium."

Kali went back to the information desk and asked the pimply-faced student to point her in the right direction.

Only a handful of students milled about in front of the dorm, which wasn't surprising given the heat. They were engrossed in conversation and didn't even glance in Kali's direction, so she assumed none of them was Joanna. She pressed herself into a spot of shade to wait.

A few minutes later, a ponytailed blonde in a tank top and thigh-length skirt wandered up the walkway. She looked at Kali, hesitated, then approached.

"Joanna?" Kali asked.

"You must be the attorney."

Kali nodded. "I appreciate your meeting me on such short notice."

Joanna tucked a couple of stray hairs behind an ear. "I don't mind. I've got, like, nothing to do tonight but homework. What is it you want to know?"

"How well did you know Olivia?" Kali asked, inching back toward the shade. "I understand the two of you worked at the library together."

"I still work there," Joanna said, with a sigh. "We lived in the same dorm, too. We hung out together and stuff. We even, like, talked about rooming together this year. Then she got that job and was going to, like, live in a fancy house. I was totally jealous." Joanna's face clouded and her voice grew tight. "But if it hadda been me that got the job, I'd be dead instead of her. And that's really freaky, you know?"

Kali nodded. She was reminded again how very young nineteen was.

"I still have trouble believing she's gone. Olivia was so alive. You know what I mean?"

"I'm sorry. I know how hard it is to have someone close to you murdered."

Joanna's chin quivered and she looked at the ground without saying anything.

"I've got a photo of Olivia and a couple of friends," Kali said. "Are you up to looking at it?"

When Joanna responded with a wordless nod, Kali showed her the photo. "Do you recognize either of the girls with Olivia?"

Joanna took the photograph and studied it a moment, shielding it from the sun. "This one"—she pointed to the golden-haired girl—"it sort of looks like Crystal. She has a birthmark just like that."

A birthmark, not a bruise, as Kali had initially thought. "Crystal who?"

"I don't know her last name."

"Do you know where I can find her?"

Joanna shook her head. "I'm pretty sure she's not a U of A student."

"A high school friend?"

"No. She's someone Olivia met a couple of months ago."

"What about the other girl?"

"I don't recognize her."

"What can you tell me about Crystal?" Kali asked.

"Not much. Only time I met her was at a party. There were a lot of people there. Music, dancing, you know, but not a lot of real talking."

"Was she with anyone in particular?"

Joanna gave an exasperated sigh. "It wasn't like I was watching her."

Sensing Joanna's growing impatience, Kali moved on. "When did you last talk to Olivia?"

"A couple of days before she was killed." Joanna's eyes had been tracking the students coming and going around them. Now she turned back to Kali. "We hung out together, like all the time last year, but this year, with her living off campus and everything, it wasn't the same. We didn't even have any classes together this semester. Besides, her job kept her kind of busy."

"Her job?" Kali said. "You mean working for Sloane Winslow?"

"Well, that too. But she had another job." Joanna's face clouded again. "I really miss her. I missed her before she was killed. This year just wasn't the same."

"What other job?"

Joanna shrugged, let her gaze drift to a group of students exiting the dorm. "I don't know, but it was better pay and better hours than waiting tables at the River Inn, which is what she was doing before. She hated that."

Kali had worked as a waitress for a stint while she was in college. It was hard work and she'd hated it too. "Tell me about Olivia. What was she like?"

"Smart. She got really good grades without even trying. But she liked to have fun, too." A hint of a smile tugged at Joanna's mouth, as she relived some private memory. "She liked nice things, not that she could afford them. But that was part of her dream. With Olivia, you knew she'd get what she wanted eventually."

"Does the name Randy ring a bell with you?" Kali almost added that he supposedly had a great body, but she thought the comment might be misunderstood.

"I knew a boy named Randy in high school."

"But no one Olivia knew?"

Joanna shook her head. A couple of male students passed by on their way into the dorm and waved to Joanna, who seemed suddenly eager to be off.

"Are we done?" she asked Kali. "I've got stuff to do."

"That's it. Thanks for your help."

Joanna adjusted her ponytail and followed the men into the dorm.

# CHAPTER 23

Back in her car, Kali pulled out her cell phone and debated calling Reed. He'd been willing enough to blame John for his sister's death when all he had to go on was police theory, but things were different now. It was beginning to look as if John, too, might have been murdered. If Kali explained her growing suspicions, maybe Reed would be open to the possibility that John was innocent. And if she wanted to find out what John had been up to—what his connection was to Olivia—Reed was as likely to know as anyone.

Kali had found Reed's home number programmed into John's cell phone, but when she tried calling him now, she got the answering machine. Without leaving a message, she tried him at work. It was already 5:30, so she wasn't surprised when the receptionist told her he'd gone for the day. On impulse, Kali asked to speak to A. J. Nash instead.

"Another couple of minutes and you'd have missed me," Nash said amiably. "I was just packing up my stuff."

"Sorry, I can call back tomorrow. I don't want to keep you." Kali opened the driver's-side door to let in some air. As she did, she noticed a midsized beige sedan several spaces back with its engine running and, no doubt, its air conditioner blasting away. Definitely a better option for cooling off in ninety-degree heat than merely opening the door.

"Not a problem," Nash said. "What can I do for you?"

If only it were that simple. Kali didn't even know what questions to ask. "It's about John. I guess I'd just like to talk to someone who knew him."

"I understand. I was the same way when my dad died."

"There are things about him I don't understand," Kali said. "I know that sounds awfully vague, but you said you were a friend of his and I thought—"

"I'd be happy to talk with you, although I'm not sure I'll be much help. Are you by any chance free for a drink?"

"You mean now?"

"Right. I've got time. Are you still staying at John's? I know it's a bit of a drive into town, so if you'd rather—"

"No, now is good. I'm actually near campus at the moment. And I'd love to meet with you."


Half an hour later, Kali was sitting across from Nash in an upscale bar sipping the Cosmopolitan he'd insisted she order instead of her usual wine. He was wearing a suit, as he'd been the day she'd met him at Logan Foods, but he'd removed his jacket and tie and rolled up his shirtsleeves, revealing tanned arms and a platinum Rolex watch.

"How is it?" he asked, referring to the ruby-tinted concoction in her martini glass.

"Good." It was, in fact, a little too sweet for Kali's taste, but far more drinkable than the very dry gin martinis she'd tasted in the past. It was also strong. She'd have to remember to sip slowly. "I hope I'm not putting you in an awkward position with regard to Reed and the company," she said.

Nash shook his head. "There's been no company directive, official or otherwise. Reed, himself, has said very little, in fact."

"When I talked to him, he seemed convinced that John was responsible for Sloane's murder."

"From what I hear, the police had fairly convincing evidence." Nash sipped his drink and regarded her appraisingly over the rim of the glass. "But you're a defense attorney, if I recall correctly. You're probably a bit more skeptical than the rest of us."

A hint of a smile flickered in his eyes. He was, Kali decided, a good-looking man in an urbane and refined sort of way. Not the kind of guy she usually found attractive—she preferred a less polished look—but with his lean build and hazel eyes, he cut an impressive figure. She hadn't appreciated that until now.

"Defense isn't all I do," Kali told him. "It wasn't even what I set out to do initially."

"Which was what?"

Kali laughed. "Make a lot of money. Well, I did work for the DA's office for a few years right out of school—no money there. But then I joined one of the hot boutique San Francisco firms and worked my tail off for five years. I was on the brink of making partner when the place went belly up."

"So you jumped into criminal defense?"

"It's more like I stumbled and fell into it," Kali said.

"How's that?"

"The short of it is, a friend of mine was a suspect in her husband's death and I got involved with the case. My personal life was tanking right about then, too. One thing led to another, and before I knew it, I ended up in Silver Creek, where I grew up, with a criminal defense practice."

"But you're back in the Bay Area now."

Kali nodded. "But there's no short version to that switch."

Nash leaned forward. The amber flecks in his eyes glimmered in the light from the tabletop candle. "Some day I'd love to hear the longer version of both."

She shrugged. "It's not very interesting."

Nash caught the waitress's eye and ordered another round of drinks and a plate of nachos.

Kali protested. "I shouldn't really—"

"We haven't even begun to discuss whatever it was you wanted to see me about."

And somehow she'd finished the entire Cosmopolitan. "What the heck?" She settled back in her chair. "What about you? How'd you end up working for Logan Foods?"

"I didn't have a lot of options, I'm afraid. I went to law school at night—you know the kind of place, accredited but not exactly a *name* school. It's worked out well, though. I can't say that my job's exciting, but I like what I do and I like the people I work with."

"That's what counts."

Nash nodded. "You wanted to talk about John?"

The noise level in the bar had increased as it had filled with patrons shouting to be heard over one another. The big-screen television over the bar, broadcasting a baseball game, didn't help.

Kali, too, raised her voice. "I'm not convinced John's death was accidental," she told Nash. "I think someone may have been at the house the night he died."

The waitress brought their order. Nash waited until she'd left before responding. "Have you told the police?"

"They weren't interested." Kali scooped a nacho into her mouth, catching the dripping cheese with her free hand. Then she leaned back and sipped her drink. "It's not like I have hard evidence. But I called John the night he died and I heard a voice in the background. I'm thinking they had a snack. The cleaning woman found sandwich makings on the counter the next morning—and drinks. That could be how John got the drugs into his system."

Nash frowned. "Could you make out what this other person was saying?"

"No. It could have been the television, even. That's what I assumed at the time. But the thing is, one of the items on the counter was a jar of mayonnaise. John hated the stuff, never ate it. So he clearly made a sandwich for someone besides himself."

"Who do you think it was?"

Kali's phone rang and she quickly checked the screen. Bryce. With a twinge of guilt, she turned off the ringer and slipped the phone back into her purse. "I was hoping you might have some ideas."

Nash shook his head. "I can't imagine who would want to kill John."

Kali hated to even *think* the words she was about to say next. "I know he and Sloane were having a disagreement about the future of Logan Foods. John might have lost his job if Sloane had had her way. But he couldn't have been the only one who'd benefit from having her out of the picture."

Confusion, and then disbelief, clouded Nash's face. "Reed?"

"It's possible, isn't it? And there might be others. Some of the directors, maybe. I'm not really familiar with the structure of the company." And because it wasn't publicly held, there was no way for her to find out.

But Nash wasn't buying any of it. "I can understand it's hard for you to believe John was responsible, but the police were on top of this. I assume they know what they're doing. I don't want to speak out of turn here, but maybe you should let it go."

"Let's put Reed aside for the moment, then," Kali said. "Are you aware of anything John was involved in that might . . . might put him in a position to be killed?"

Again, Nash shook his head. Kali thought he was probably beginning to regret suggesting they meet for drinks.

"I'm not sure what you're getting at," he said after a moment.

"What about women? Sex? That sort of thing."

She'd thought Nash might be offended, but instead he seemed amused. "I can see I'd never make it as a defense attorney. I'm not nearly creative enough. John was dating a woman who lived back East. I met her once but I'm afraid I can't remember her name."

"Susan Harris?"

"Yes, that's it. She seemed like a nice woman. As for sex"—here Nash actually grinned—"I never asked John about that aspect of their relationship."

"Did you ever see him with other women? Much younger women?"

"Can't say that I did. Why do you ask?"

Clearly Nash was not in a position to be of help. The evening had been pleasant, but not especially useful. "Just curious," Kali said lightly.

"You must have had a reason to ask."

What the hell? Maybe something would trigger a memory in Nash's mind. "I'm exploring the possibility that Sloane wasn't the target victim after all," Kali explained.

Nash stroked his chin. "Corporate law is looking better and better. At least there's logic to it." His tone was light, good-natured. It was obvious he didn't buy her concerns but, at the same time, didn't want to appear dismissive. In fact, he seemed more interested in her than in what she had to say.

She'd been hoping Nash would take her concerns seriously. Now she could see he didn't. "I need to be going," Kali told him.

"You haven't finished your drink."

"Good thing, too. Or I might never find my way home."

"I can give you a ride." His eyes met hers.

She smiled. "Thanks, but I'm fine."

Nash seemed reluctant to have her leave. "Have you ever been to the Desert Museum?" he asked.

"I've heard of it, but I haven't been there."

"Would you like to go sometime? I'm a member, supporting member actually. I've got an annual pass and I'd love to take you."

Kali remembered the call from Bryce she'd ignored. She felt a little uncomfortable, almost as if he were watching, but that was silly. And Nash's offer to show her one of the town's attractions was hardly a date.

"I'm not sure how much longer I'll be around," she told him. "But if it works out, I'd love to go."

Commute traffic had thinned out, but cars still crawled along at well below the speed limit. It sometimes took Kali two light cycles to get through an intersection. Which was why, as she neared John's, she sped up instead of braking when the light turned yellow twenty feet in front of her. She was chiding herself for pushing it, especially after two Cosmopolitans, when she noticed the beige sedan behind her had sped through as well. He'd *really* pushed it, she thought. Then it struck her that the car was similar to the one parked behind her at the university.

That was crazy. It couldn't be the same car. Hadn't Nash teased her about having a creative imagination? Besides, beige sedans were common. Still, she felt better when the car turned right at the next corner as she continued straight.

She pulled into the driveway and headed inside.

"I'm in here," Sabrina called out as Kali closed the front door.

Kali followed the sound of her voice to John's office, where she found her sister seated at the computer.

"John sure got a heck of a lot of spam," Sabrina said, scrolling down the screen. "Other than that it's mostly car stuff, except for the e-mails from me and the kids."

Kali peered over Sabrina's shoulder, momentarily speechless. "How did you log on?" she asked finally. "Onto the computer, I mean. It's password protected."

"Well, you know what they say, that people aren't very inventive. They use their birth date or phone number or pet's name. It only took me half a dozen guesses."

Kali had tried those same things herself, with no luck. "So what was it?"

"Nippercles."

"What?" No wonder she hadn't gotten it.

"John's pet hamster," Sabrina said.

"John has a hamster?"

"Not now. When we were growing up. Don't you remember Nipper?"

Now that she'd been prompted, Kali did recall the soft, furry ball of brown fuzz that had been John's constant companion during junior high. Hercules he wasn't, except maybe in John's imagination, but Nipper had morphed into Nippercles and the name had somehow seemed to fit. At the moment, though, Kali was most astounded by her sister's resourcefulness.

"I'm impressed," she said. "How did you think to try that?"

Sabrina gave her a long look. "Maybe if you'd spent a little time getting to know John, you'd have figured it out too."

"No need to get snippy."

"I wasn't. I was merely making an observation." Sabrina pushed the keyboard away and stood up.

"Come on," she said, "let's eat. I made us a Cobb salad."

"Out of what? The fridge was empty."

"What do you think grocery stores are for?"

Sabrina wasn't someone who willingly spent a lot of time in the kitchen, but when she set her mind to it, she could put together a five-star meal. The salad was an artful arrangement of poached chicken, hard-boiled egg, avocado, and cherry tomatoes on top of a bed of mixed greens. Despite the nachos Kali had had earlier, she was suddenly famished.

"So what else was on the computer?" Kali asked over dinner. After two Cosmopolitans, she'd decided to stick to water, but Sabrina had her usual vodka and tonic.

Sabrina brushed the air with her hand. "Music files, correspondence about some car repairs, a spreadsheet of investments, a bunch of photos. John got himself a good digital camera a while back and he was getting into photo editing. He's got some really great shots."

"Photos?" Kali felt a prickle of interest. "What kind of photos?"

"Nature stuff mostly. Nothing with those girls in it, if that's what you're wondering. Or any girls."

That was precisely what Kali had been thinking.

Sabrina took a bite of chicken. "Did you find Olivia's friend?"

Kali nodded. "She didn't recognize the girl who looks like the dead Jane Doe, but the other girl is apparently someone named Crystal."

"Well, Crystal ought to be able to identify the dead girl."

"But we don't know how to find Crystal. In fact, we don't have anything but a first name."

"Maybe the cops will be able to find her."

Kali bit her lower lip. "That would mean telling them about the photo. And it would bring John's name in."

Sabrina sighed. "You really think there's a link between Olivia's murder and that other girl's?"

"It's odd that two of the girls in the photo were murdered, and within weeks of each other."

"It could be a coincidence," Sabrina argued halfheartedly.

"You believe that?"

"Jesus," Sabrina muttered, "I sure hope Crystal's not dead, too."

# CHAPTER 24

Kali spent a restless night, struggling with her decision about the photo when she was awake, and dreaming about terrified girls in peril during those rare occasions when she managed to drift off to sleep.

After breakfast, she left Sabrina to finish cleaning out closets and filling boxes for Goodwill, while she drove to the four-star hotel downtown where Olivia's mother worked as a maid.

Kali started to approach one of the clerks at the front desk, then thought better of it. Even if they knew the names of the housekeeping staff, which they might not, they weren't going to summon the woman downstairs at Kali's request. Instead, Kali walked past the reception area and pressed the elevator button.

She started at the top. Luckily, there were only twelve floors, rather than twenty or thirty, like some of the larger hotels. A housekeeping cart was parked outside a room at the end of the hallway to the right. Inside the room, two women were making beds and conversing in Spanish. Both were too young to be Olivia's mother, but Kali knocked lightly on the open door and asked if they knew where she could find Angeles Perez.

They exchanged a few words in rapid Spanish, then, looking embarrassed, shook their heads.

Kali repeated the exercise on floors eleven and ten. On nine, she found someone who directed her to four. There she waited near the housekeeping cart until a middle-aged woman in a maid's uniform returned to the cart for fresh towels.

"Mrs. Perez?" Kali asked.

The woman looked startled. Her dark eyes were alert. "Yes?"

"I'm sorry to bother you, but I wanted to talk to you about your daughter."

The woman pressed her lips tight and lowered her gaze.

"I'm truly sorry for your loss. I can only imagine how terrible it must be for you."

Angeles Perez nodded softly without speaking. She was a pleasantly plump woman with dark, wavy hair and remarkably unlined skin. She looked to be in her early forties, probably only five or ten years older than Kali, but her shoulders were rounded, her posture that of a woman much older.

"You're a reporter?"

Kali shook her head. "I'm an attorney involved in an investigation of your daughter's death," she said and waited for a lightning bolt to strike her dead. It wasn't really a lie, she reminded herself, and since she'd not actually been served with papers in the wrongful death lawsuit, there was technically nothing wrong with talking to the woman directly. Still, Kali knew she was pushing the limits of what was ethically correct.

It didn't stop her.

Angeles pressed a knuckle to her mouth. "She was my baby. My little girl." Her eyes welled up. "I thought it was a *good* job, my Olivia working for Mrs. Winslow. I was so happy for her. And now . . . because she was there . . . my baby's dead."

Another one of the housekeeping staff stepped up to the cart. She was younger, Anglo, with bleached hair and thin lips. She addressed Kali. "Is there a problem?"

"No, I just needed to speak to Mrs. Perez. It's a personal matter."

"It's okay," Angeles said to the woman. "It's about my daughter."

"Still?" The woman tapped her foot. "Well, don't take all day. I'm not doing more than my share."

"I know you're busy," Kali told Angeles. "Maybe if you've got a break coming up, we could talk then."

"Lunch is in two hours."

"I'll wait," Kali said.

Angeles Perez nodded. "Across the street by the art museum. I'll meet you in front."

Lacking the patience for an art museum right then, Kali used the time to browse the museum store and the shops of Old Town a block away. By the time she met Angeles Perez, she'd purchased a pair of silver earrings, a pack of desert-flower note cards, and a lovely hammered-copper vase she was having shipped back to California. It had been an interesting, but costly, two hours.

"Can I buy you lunch?" Kali asked after she'd greeted Angeles.

The woman held up a paper sack. "We'll talk, and then I will eat."

They sat on the sculpted metal bench in the shade in front of the museum. A hot, dry breeze sent a candy wrapper dancing at their feet.

"You must have been proud of Olivia," Kali said.

"Yes, very. Such a girl—smart, pretty, sensible." Angeles smiled wanly. "And headstrong, like a bull. My husband, he didn't understand. He didn't like it that she talked back. I tried to tell him it was good. The fire inside her is what made her work so hard."

"You obviously did a fine job raising her."

"Olivia was a good daughter. She told me, 'Mama, I'm going to be rich someday, and buy you anything you want.'

She told me to start making a list." Angeles looked down at her hands. "I miss her so much."

"Did you know many of her friends?"

"In high school. Not now."

"Does the name Crystal mean anything to you?"

She shook her head. "No. Sorry."

"I have a photo of your daughter," Kali said, "with two of her friends. I'd like you to look at it and tell me if you recognize either of them. Will that be too painful for you?"

"I have pictures of her in my house," Angeles said gently. "Many pictures. I look at them every day. But a mother doesn't need pictures to remember, and the pain never goes away."

She took the photo from Kali and studied it with a frown. "I'm not sure, but the girl at the end, the redhead, she might be the girl who buys lottery tickets."

"Lottery tickets?" Kali asked.

"Every Friday she buys. Five tickets."

"You know her name?"

Angeles shook her head. "Olivia was with me when we bought gas at the Circle K. The girl was there. They talked, you know, girl talk. Then back in the car, Olivia told me about the lottery. Every Friday. The same Circle K."

"Which one?" Kali asked. "Where's it located?"

"On Oracle, near Grant."

"Was she someone Olivia knew from school?"

"I think she met her during the summer. It might not even be the same girl, but it looks like her."

"When was this? Do you recall?"

"Early August, I think. She'd been living at Mrs. Winslow's a while."

Olivia had met Crystal recently, too. At her job? "Your daughter worked at the River Inn for part of the summer, didn't she?" Kali asked. "What about after that?"

Angeles fiddled with her lunch sack. "She wasn't happy waiting tables, but I told her, 'You think I'm happy cleaning people's rooms? You do what you have to do to support yourself and, God willing, your family.' It was only a summer job. Then she was going back to the university. 'Three months,' I told her, 'it's not so hard.'"

Kali hesitated, then prodded gently. "So she stuck it out?"

Angeles nodded. "No more complaining."

*I bet,* Kali thought. No more complaints because, if Joanna was right, she'd quit and gotten a different job.

But she hadn't told her mother. Why was that?

# CHAPTER 25

The River Inn was located, not surprisingly, on River Road.

When Kali had first looked at maps of Tucson, she'd seen River Road marked as a broad boulevard paralleling a blue river that snaked along the northern section of the city, stretches of it bordered in green, designating parkland. Having crossed River Road regularly on her way to and from John's, however, she knew the bucolic lushness she'd envisioned didn't exist. In the rainy season, she'd been told, the river did, indeed, have water in it—rushing torrents of muddy brown runoff from the flash floods that followed heavy rain. The rest of the year it was a wide, rocky wash. And the only thing remotely green about the park was some peeling benches that had once been painted that color.

So Kali knew better than to expect a posh waterfront resort, despite the French impressionist images the restaurant's name conjured up in her mind. Still, she was expecting something a bit nicer than the square, pink stucco building sandwiched between a gas station and an all-you-can-eat Chinese buffet. The interior, with its dark wood walls and white linen tablecloths, was only a slight improvement.

Kali spoke to the manager, who confirmed that Olivia had quit her job after two weeks. He hadn't been particularly sad to see her go, because she had, in his words, "something of an attitude." He'd never seen the redhead in the photo, and neither had any of the other employees to whom Kali showed the picture. If the redhead and Olivia had worked together over the summer, it was at whatever other job Olivia had taken when she quit the River Inn.

Kali almost didn't try the Circle K, because it seemed such a long shot. There had to be scores of people who bought lottery tickets there. But her options were limited, and she needed answers.

Inside the store, two clerks were on duty. Both male. Both young. That was a plus, Kali decided. Maybe they'd remember an attractive young woman who was a regular customer.

Kali bought a packet of peanut butter crackers and a Coke and showed the photo of the three girls to the clerk with the buzz cut at the front register.

"Yeah, I've seen her around," he said. "She comes in here pretty regular."

"Do you know her name?"

He shook his head. "Sorry."

Kali tried the second clerk, who was counting bills from an adjacent register, and got a similar response.

"Is there anyone who might know?" she asked.

Buzz Cut shrugged. "Maybe Dougal. He's always hitting on the chicks."

"Where can I find Dougal?"

"He comes on in about an hour."

More time to kill and no museum or Old Town nearby, probably best for her bank account, given what she'd spent that morning. Kali drove to a bookstore she'd noticed earlier, vowing to browse, not buy.

She was back at the Circle K in just under an hour. Dougal sauntered into the convenience store about ten minutes later. He was slender and wiry with short, sand-colored hair and a goatee so sparse Kali wondered what the purpose was.

"Hey, man," said one of the original clerks, "this lady wants to ask you about a chick who comes in here."

Kali showed him the photo.

"Yeah," he said, stroking the scraggly beard, "that's Hayley."

Eureka, a name. "Hayley what? Do you know?"

He shook his head. "Is she in trouble?"

Big trouble if she was actually the murdered Jane Doe. "She didn't do anything wrong," Kali said, "if that's what you mean. Have you seen her around lately?"

"Nah, not for the last month or so. I figured she moved or something."

"She lived nearby?" Was it too much to hope Dougal knew the address?

"Probably," he said. "Most of our regulars do. Either that or they work in the area."

"So she might have worked around here," Kali noted.

"No. She worked at the Crazy Coyote."

"What's that?"

"A club over on Grant." Dougal exchanged places with the clerk behind the counter and punched a code into the cash register.

"How do you know where she worked?"

He gave Kali a withering glance. "She told me."

"What else did she say? What can you tell me about her?"

Dougal threw up his hands. "Look, lady, she came in and bought lottery tickets. Sometimes a pack of smokes. That's it. I try to be friendly but it's not like I was interested in her life story."

*I'm making progress,* Kali told herself as she climbed back into the hot car. Not fast progress, but she'd learned the first names of both girls in the photo. This was a step in the right direction, even if it was a baby step.

She only hoped the direction she was headed wasn't going to bring her face-to-face with a side of her brother she didn't want to know.

Kali thought the Crazy Coyote might not be open, given that it was only midafternoon, but the flashing neon sign said that it was.

"Club" was putting a good spin on it, Kali thought as she pulled into the gravel parking area. "Seedy bar" was a more apt description. The building was a single-story stucco building with a flat roof and no visible windows. There was no walkway or formal entrance, just a narrow door that opened onto the parking lot, empty now except for a handful of pickups and motorcycles. Kali guessed business picked up later in the evening.

As she stepped inside, she was hit first by the darkness and then by a clammy blanket of smoke, sweat, and booze. After several seconds her eyes adjusted to the point where she could make out dim shapes. She was still getting oriented when she became aware that all eyes in the place were on her. And then the pieces fell into place.

The Crazy Coyote was a strip joint.

A woman clad only in a G-string was gyrating onstage. A little too skinny, a little too saggy, definitely bored, she was arching and sliding around a metal pole while scratchy music from a tape pounded in the background. Off to Kali's left, another dancer wearing a tiny Stars and Stripes bikini and mesh tank top straddled a man's lap.

The music and dancing continued, but conversation had stopped.

*Okay*, Kali said to herself, *you can leave now and forget about Hayley, or tough it out.* Before she could give in to the temptation to flee, a scar-faced man appeared.

"You looking for a job?" He spoke with an accent, maybe Russian. An unlit cigar hung from his loose lips as he looked her up and down.

Kali felt the urge to go home and shower. She couldn't begin to imagine herself onstage writhing around a pole. "No," she said, swallowing her distaste. "I'm looking for Hayley."

"Haven't seen her for a while." And didn't care one way or the other, if Kali was reading his expression correctly.

"What's 'a while'?"

"A month, maybe more. Girls come and go." He pulled the cigar from his mouth and examined the tip, wet with saliva. "They get ideas, you know what I mean?"

Gone a month, the same timing Dougal had reported about her trips to the Circle K. Kali wondered if that jibed with what the cops knew of the dead woman. "What's her last name?" Kali asked.

"I don't recall." The man's eyelids dropped to half-mast as his eyes fixed on Kali's chest.

"Do you know where she lived?"

"Nope."

"It's not in your employment records?"

He shrugged. "Maybe."

Or maybe not. In a place like this, an employment record might be little more than a phone number scratched on a slip of paper. In any case, the man wasn't interested in pursuing it.

Kali took a stab in the dark. "How about Crystal? Is she around?"

"Who?" He lifted his gaze.

At least she had an answer of sorts. Crystal didn't work here. "Or Olivia?" Kali asked.

"What is this? Twenty questions? I got a business to run. You want to stay, buy a drink and sit down. Otherwise, it's time to move on."

She didn't have the stomach for staying. "Thanks for the help," she muttered sarcastically and left.

She'd just started her car's engine when she noticed one of the men from inside wobbling across the lot toward her car. He was bowlegged and skinny with a big gut hanging over the waistband of his jeans. She locked the door and rolled her window down partway as he approached.

When he bent down to talk to her, Kali was hit with the sour stench of whiskey breath.

"What's it worth to you to know her last name?" he asked, squinting in the bright light of the afternoon.

She hadn't a clue about the going rate for information, except this was not a high-living clientele. "Ten dollars."

The man turned away in disgust.

"Twenty?"

"Make it fifty and I'll throw in an address."

Kali pulled the bills from her wallet and warily slid them halfway through the open window.

"Hendrix," the man said, snatching the bills from Kali's hand. "Hayley Hendrix. She lives on Tyndall, a couple of blocks south of Fort Lowell. It's a two-story apartment with 'heights' or 'hills' or something stupid like that in its name."

It wasn't exactly an address, but Kali wasn't going to quibble with a drunk, even if it was broad daylight. "How well do you know her?"

"Not hardly at all. I gave her a ride once when she was having car trouble." He gave Kali a bleary-eyed grin punctuated with a burp. "I'm a married man. No touching the merchandise or my ol' woman will cut my balls off."

"Thanks."

He gave her an unsteady salute. "Don't mention it."


Kali made a quick sweep of Tyndall in the general vicinity of Fort Lowell and found nothing that sounded right. She was driving back down the road in the opposite direction when Sabrina called.

"When are you coming home?" she asked. "I'm tired of dealing with the packing by myself. Besides, we need to talk about what to keep and what to toss."

Finding the right apartment could take hours, Kali realized. Assuming she was successful at all. "I'm on my way," she told Sabrina. She'd try again tomorrow, when she could devote more time to the task.

Back at John's, she found Sabrina knee deep in boxes.

"I moved most of them into the garage for pickup," she said. "We're going to have to sell the car, too, I guess. I'll take it down to the dealer in the morning. It's probably not worth the hassle to sell it on our own."

"I agree."

"I cleaned out the inside. Stuff's on the table."

Kali glanced at the pile. Maps, coins, parking receipts, a pair of sunglasses, and a hardback thriller whose title Kali recognized from browsing the best-seller rack at the bookstore that afternoon.

"Before I forget," Sabrina added, "Nash's secretary at Logan Foods called. They finished cleaning out John's office and have some stuff for us. I said one of us would swing by in the morning to get it." She picked up the box she'd been working on, then nudged another with her foot. "Can you grab this one? We'll add these to the collection in the garage. Then I'm about done for the day."

"Sure." Kali lifted the box and followed Sabrina into the garage.

"Did you manage to talk to Olivia's mother?" Sabrina asked.

"Yes. And I know the name of the third girl in the photo. Hayley Hendrix. She's a stripper."

"You mean like in a nightclub?"

"Calling the dive she works a nightclub is like calling the No Tell Motel a resort."

Sabrina made a face. "Why would she work at a place like that?"

"Money would be my guess. Though probably not a lot, given the looks of the place."

"Are you going to tell the cops? I mean, they need to know who she is, don't they?"

Kali nodded. "But not just yet. I hate to bring John's name into it until we have a better idea of what was going on."

The girl was dead, she reasoned. It didn't much matter whether the cops learned her name today or tomorrow. For that matter, they might have already learned it on their own.

But all the reasoning in the world couldn't quiet the misgivings Kali felt at being less than forthcoming with what she'd learned.

# CHAPTER 26

Erling rubbed his thumb over the bristly spot on his neck he'd missed while shaving that morning. He doubted the spot was noticeable to the casual observer, but once he'd found the small patch of stubble, he hadn't been able to keep his hand away. It was a petty annoyance that made it difficult for him to concentrate on anything else.

*Enough.* He forced his hand away from his neck and back to the reports on his desk. A series of recent assaults, as well as a he-said/she-said rape case involving a Hollywood producer and an employee at the resort where he'd been staying. He said the sex was consensual; she said it wasn't. Erling and Michelle had interviewed the staff on duty at the time and now had as many versions of the evening as people they'd talked to. Erling was glad the final call on whether to prosecute would fall on the DA's office and not on him.

Especially now, when he was beginning to doubt his own judgment.

For the last twenty-four hours—since John O'Brien's sister had come to them with her suspicions of foul play—Erling had been feeling uneasy. Michelle had noticed, and last night at dinner, Deena had commented on his irritability, as well. He was fairly sure neither of them had bought his story of a toothache.

What weighed on him was the possibility that O'Brien *had* been killed, and that his death was somehow linked to Sloane's. The possibility that because of Erling's prior involvement with the victim, he'd missed some major angle in his investigation.

The irony was that he'd moved on emotionally. Truly. In the months since Sloane had broken it off, he'd come to see that ending it was for the best. The affair had been wrong. A quick tonic for the building loneliness inside him, but not a lasting cure. He was sure Sloane felt the same way. Her murder, though, had stirred emotions and memories he'd managed to relegate to the safe harbors of his psyche. She'd been on his mind constantly. Along with uncomfortable misgivings about himself.

Erling prayed silently that John O'Brien's death was the tragic accident they'd assumed it was.

He looked over at Michelle, who'd just hung up the phone.

"Good news," she said. "Tucson PD passed along the name of a woman who thinks she might recognize our Jane Doe. Someone who used to come into the beauty supply shop where the woman works."

At last, something positive. Erling felt the mantle of gloom lift. "Let's talk to her."

Michelle dialed the number, then mouthed "answering machine" to Erling. She left a message and hung up.

"No address?" he asked.

"Just the name and number."

He sank back down in his chair and tapped his fingers on the desktop. Casually, he turned again to address Michelle. "Have you found anything new on John O'Brien's death?"

"Not exactly." She reached into her desk for an Altoid, then offered Erling the box. He shook his head.

"I haven't had a lot of time to give it," she continued. "But if what the sister says is true about the mayonnaise . . . and that he'd gone through rehab and stayed clean for all those years . . ."

"He wouldn't have been the first person to backslide. Especially given the situation. Being a prime murder suspect has got to ratchet up the stress levels."

"True. But it's also a good cover-up for murder. And the murder of a prime suspect raises all kinds of questions." Michelle stood, brushed her trouser legs straight, then sat back down. "I think it might be helpful to re-examine our work in the Sloane Winslow case."

This was what Erling had been dreading. "You're assuming they're related."

She nodded. "I did have a chance to glance over our interviews with people who knew Winslow. It probably wouldn't hurt to talk to Reed Logan and A. J. Nash again. They might be able to point us in some new directions. And maybe a couple of individuals at the charities she was involved with."

"We did that."

Michelle squinted at him. "So what? Aren't you the one who's always telling me it pays to ask the same questions a couple of different times? There's *always* something new that comes out."

Erling nodded. She was right. It was just that in this case he was afraid of what that new information might be.

"The only thing that's jumped out at me so far," Michelle said, "is a comment by Winslow's neighbor Janet Fisher—the one who found the bodies. She mentioned she thought Winslow had been seeing someone last spring."

Erling's nerves were suddenly taut. "Do we know who?" he asked hoarsely.

"Nope. Mrs. Fisher could be wrong, of course. She was a royal pain, if you recall. Trying to claim her fifteen minutes of fame by piggybacking onto the tragedy. I talked to her again yesterday afternoon. She said she thought the guy might have been someone well known because Winslow was so circumspect about the whole thing. Personally, I suspect Winslow just wanted to distance herself from the woman."

"Right." Erling hoped he didn't sound too eager to agree.

"Anyway, the dead girl is top priority right now."

"Right," he said again, grateful for the reprieve.

* * *

An hour later, the woman who thought she might recognize their Jane Doe called back. No, she didn't really know the girl. And no, she couldn't recall her name, except that it might be Harley or Hayley or Heidi or something similar. Michelle took down the woman's address and asked if they could come by and speak to her in person.

"What do you think?" Michelle asked Erling.

"Definitely worth a follow-up interview, but I'm not holding my breath."

They were just out the door when Erling's cell phone jangled and he recognized Mindy's number.

"Hi, honey."

"Dad, I forgot the disk that has my paper on it! It's due in two hours."

"What paper?"

"The one that's due today. In Soc. 101."

How had she managed to leave the thing at home knowing it was due? The carelessness of the young sometimes astounded him. "You've got time to get it, don't you?"

"I've got class in five minutes. And the teacher always gives us a quiz on the reading. Can you go home and get it for me? *Please*." She drew out the last word for an entire breath. "I hate to ask, but I'm really stuck."

"What about your mom?"

"She's got a classroom full of kids," Mindy explained as though he were dense not to have known.

*And I've got a homicide,* Erling thought. But Michelle could handle the interview alone, and it was likely to be a bust anyway.

He sighed. "Sure. Tell me where it is."

"Thanks, Dad. You're the greatest. Really, I owe you big time."

Erling felt a glow all the way to the marrow of his bones. It wasn't often anymore that he got that kind of gushing admiration from his daughter.

* * *

Erling retrieved the disk, taking a moment to wonder at the hollow quietness of the house at midday. Rarely was he the only one home, and while Deena claimed to love having the house to herself, Erling found it oppressively empty. He got back into the car, drove to campus, and pulled up to the spot on Euclid where he and Mindy had arranged to meet.

Mindy was already there, nervously checking her watch and bouncing on one leg and then the other. When she saw him, she rushed to the curb and reached through the open window for the disk.

"Thank you sooo much. You're a lifesaver."

"Guess you've learned a lesson, right?"

"Do you always have to lecture?" She turned away in a huff, then stepped back again and leaned into the car to kiss Erling on the cheek. "Thanks. I love you."

Good thing he was wearing his seat belt, Erling thought, or he'd be floating so high he'd be right out of the car.

He'd gone only a couple of blocks when Michelle phoned him. "You don't have plans for this evening, do you?"

"Why? You've got something?"

"I think so."

"The shop clerk remembered more?"

"No, that was a washout. I mean she tried, but it wasn't like she actually knew the girl. But get this. I checked with the Tucson PD to see if names like Harley or Heidi or Hayley had come up recently in any of their cases."

"Had they?"

"Not exactly. But a couple of weeks ago a Good Samaritan found a purse in the parking lot of a Burger King on Oracle. No credit cards or driver's license inside, but it did contain a City of Tucson library card for someone named Hayley Hendrix."

Adrenaline pumped through Erling's veins. If she was their girl, they'd cleared the hurdle of identifying her. "Anything else in the purse?" he asked.

"Sunglasses, make-up, the usual. I checked with the

phone company, and there's no listing for anyone by that name. But with so many kids using cell phones these days, that doesn't mean much. Let's see if we can get the library to release her address and phone number. If not, we can try for a cell phone listing."

Erling grunted. "You know how libraries are about patron privacy these days. We'll probably need a warrant."

"We shouldn't have trouble getting one." Michelle sounded exhilarated. "I think we may have finally caught a break."

Erling looked back down at the sketch on his desk. "God willing," he told the girl silently, "we're going to find out who did this to you and bring him in."

# CHAPTER 27

When Kali picked up the box of John's personal effects from Logan Foods the next morning, she was curiously disappointed to find A. J. Nash wasn't in.

That brought her up short. Why should she care whether Nash was there or not?

*Screw it*, she told herself as she headed back to the parking lot. She didn't need complications like that in her life right now. She set the box in the backseat and climbed into her car, then thought that as long as she was there, she should try to see Reed.

Rather than trudge back through the heat unnecessarily, she called on her cell phone and after giving her name was put through to Reed's voice mail. There was at least a fifty-fifty chance he'd refused to take her call.

Screw him, too. Pushing the annoyances from her mind, Kali headed off to try to find Hayley's apartment. As she'd been doing for the last two days, she kept a watch out for beige sedans. She spotted a surprising number, though none appeared especially suspicious. Most likely, the whole idea that she'd been followed was nothing but a product of her overactive imagination.

She drove down Tyndall, keeping an eye on traffic while scanning the rows of apartment buildings on either side. Ten minutes later and one street over, she pulled up in front of a squat, two-story cinder-block structure bearing a sign that read VISTA HEIGHTS. There was no vista that Kali could see, unless you counted the auto repair shop across the street, and given the flatland location, "heights" wasn't particularly apt either.

The building was U-shaped, with an outside stairway and no main entrance. There was no landscaping, just hard-packed dirt and asphalt, but a pool was centered in what might euphemistically be termed a courtyard. A plastic lawn chair had fallen, or been tossed, into the deep end of the pool, and the water's surface was covered with an oily green film. Leisure living was apparently not the selling point of Vista Heights.

Kali found the row of mail slots and scanned the residents' names. There was a Hendrix listed for #11. With a little exploration, Kali found the unit on the first floor, in a dark corner near the laundry room and Dumpster.

She knocked on the door, hoping for a roommate or, better yet, Hayley herself, although she didn't hold out much possibility of that. Kali was sure Hayley was the girl in the police sketch.

Her knock went unanswered. A door opened down the hallway and a scruffy-looking young man emerged, heading for the parking area.

"Excuse me," Kali called after him. "Do you know the woman who lives here?"

"Nope."

"Has she been home recently?"

He ignored her and kept on walking.

Kali headed back toward the mailboxes. Next to them she'd seen a unit marked MANAGER. She knocked on the door. She could hear a television going inside, a program with laughter and lots of clapping. Another knock, and finally the door opened. An older woman with thinning hair peered out at Kali with obvious displeasure. She was wearing a shapeless housedress and smelled heavily of cigarette smoke.

The woman scowled. "You want something?"

"I was hoping I could talk to you about Hayley Hendrix. Unit eleven."

The manager's eyes showed interest. "You going to pay her rent?"

"She hasn't paid?"

"Not this month. Far as I can tell, she's up and left." The manager crossed her arms over her scrawny chest. "Doesn't surprise me. Kids these days, they sign a lease but it don't mean nothing. Now I got to get it cleaned up and go to all the trouble of filing an eviction notice and finding another tenant. That is, unless you're here to pay up."

Kali shook her head. "Was she usually prompt with the rent?"

The woman muttered something under her breath. Her lips were full and loose. "That's the kind of tenant we get nowadays. Can't trust a one of 'em. Half of 'em don't even speak the language." She eyed Kali. "What do *you* want with her?"

"My name's Kali O'Brien. I'm an attorney working on a case she's involved in."

"Trouble, huh? Doesn't surprise me none."

"Why's that?"

The manager shrugged. "That girl don't exactly keep regular hours, if you know what I mean."

"You think she was into something criminal?"

The manager bristled. "I didn't say that."

"What, then?" Hayley worked at a strip club. Maybe she'd taken "private clients" on the side. "Were there men coming and going?" Kali asked.

The woman's mouth grew pinched. "I wouldn't allow that. This here's an up-and-up apartment house. Nothing illegal. I'd be the first to call the cops." She craned her neck forward, angled her head toward Kali. "She kept to herself mostly. 'Cept for stiffing me on the rent, she was an okay tenant, I guess."

The visit had been a waste, Kali decided, except that she was now more certain than ever that Hayley Hendrix was the dead woman the police were trying to identify. She hadn't skipped out or stiffed the management; she'd been murdered.

Kali took a step back, ready to leave, then on impulse asked, "Do you think I could have a look inside?"

"The girl's apartment? I don't think—"

Kali took out a twenty-dollar bill and handed it to the woman. "You've checked to make sure she's not injured, haven't you?"

"She's not there. I looked."

"It wouldn't hurt to check again. Make sure she hasn't been back. I'll just tag along."

The manager eyed the twenty, and Kali pulled out a second one. She'd spent more on bribery in the last two days than she normally did on food for a whole week. Not that she minded, especially if it helped her prove John innocent.

"Well, I guess it wouldn't hurt to take another look," the woman said. "We'll have to clean it out before we can show it anyway. You wouldn't be interested in renting, by any chance?"

Anything to get in. "You never know," Kali told the manager. "I might be."

"Let me get the key." The woman retreated into her apartment and returned a moment later with a large key ring. They proceeded to unit 11, where she inserted the key and opened the door.

The interior was dark, musty, and very hot.

"No sense wasting money on air-conditioning when no one's here," the manager explained, turning on a light. "It comes furnished."

*That's stretching it,* Kali thought, as she eyed the stained plaid couch and yellow laminate kitchen table. Basic, ugly, and probably encrusted with years of grime. But Hayley had clearly tried to spruce things up. She'd taped posters on the walls. One of the Arc de Triomphe in Paris and another of a sun-drenched tropical beach with a hammock stretched between two palm trees. Diagonally across from the sofa was a fiberboard bookcase topped with an array of candles and a basket of potpourri. A vase of colorful paper poppies sat at the center of the yellow table.

Kali peered into the single bedroom, which contained a bed with a sateen patchwork quilt and matching shams, and a rickety dresser. She started to turn away when a pile of magazines on the floor caught her attention. Not the magazines, really, which were the sort of thing you'd expect to find a young woman reading—*Glamour, Cosmopolitan, Elle*—but a slim book with a familiar hand-tooled cover. It looked like the volume of poetry she'd found on Olivia Perez's desk.

With the manager occupied in the main area, Kali slid into the bed-room, lifted the book from the floor, and opened to the flyleaf.

> *Hayley,*
> *There are hundreds of languages in the world,*
> *but a smile speaks them all. And yours speaks*
> *to me. Because of your smile, you make life*
> *more beautiful.*

The signature was the same indecipherable scrawl she'd seen in Olivia's book, with the same smiley face in the loop of the final letter.

Kali's heart thumped in her chest.

Two friends with identical books inscribed by the same person.

Both of them dead.

She was relieved to note that the handwriting and signature weren't John's.

"Looks like her friend's gone, too," the manager said.

"Friend? What friend?" Kali was only half listening.

"The girl who was staying here," she said, poking at the pillow and blanket heap on the couch. "I told Hayley, 'This is a single unit. You can't go renting a single and then try to save on rent by doubling up.'"

"Who was the friend?"

The manager shook her head. "Young girl with a big red

birthmark on her neck. I seen her here a week, maybe two. Boyfriend trouble was what Hayley said. Still, that's no excuse for doubling up."

Kali reached into her purse for the photo of the three girls and showed it to the woman. "Is this the friend?" she asked, pointing to Crystal.

"Looks like her." She looked around the apartment and sighed. "This is why we ask for the last month's rent up front. Still, it's a pain in the behind, if you'll pardon the expression. It costs money to get the place rented again."

Kali offered a murmur of sympathy, but her mind was on what she'd learned. She needed to think, but she knew, too, that it was time to go to the cops with what she knew.

# CHAPTER 28

Kali's cell phone rang as she was pulling out of the parking space in front of Vista Heights.

"Thank God I reached you," Sabrina said, sounding breathless. "You have to come home right now."

"Why? What's wrong?"

Sabrina sucked in air. "Someone threw a rock through the big picture window in the living room. Totally shattered it."

"A rock? Were you hurt?"

"No. I wasn't even in the room. But I'm spooked. Who'd do that?"

"Did you see anyone?" Kali asked. "Hear anything?"

"I heard the crash, but I didn't see anyone."

"Call the cops and report it. I'm on my way."

Kali's heart was pounding. Sabrina was there alone and the house was isolated. What if something happened to her, too? She'd never forgive herself.

Thankfully the midday traffic was light. Kali made it back to John's in less than half an hour. Sabrina rushed outside to greet her in the driveway.

"I'm glad you're here," she said. "I've been scared to death."

"Anything more happened?"

Sabrina shook her head. "The police weren't interested," she said, spitting out the words as though the blame were somehow Kali's. "They'll send someone out 'at the first opportunity,' but it might be a day or two." She folded her arms and rested her weight on one hip. "They suggested I take a photo and call the insurance company."

"Figures," Kali muttered. "If they aren't interested in investigating a possible homicide, it's not surprising a broken window falls off their radar."

Inside, Kali surveyed the damage. The rock had come through one of the wide windows facing the deck and pool in back. The floor of the living room glistened with broken glass—a few jagged shards and thousands of tiny, diamond-like fragments.

"They said it was probably kids," Sabrina explained.

"Maybe." But Kali hadn't forgotten the beige sedan that might or might not have been tailing her.

She stepped gingerly through the mess and picked up the errant rock. It was about the size of a softball, plain and brown like every other rock she'd seen around Tucson. No note or threatening message was attached. That was a small consolation.

She sighed. "I guess we'd better get this mess cleaned up. Did you call the insurance company?"

Sabrina nodded. "They're sending someone out to board it up until they can get it replaced."

"Good."

By the time they'd swept and vacuumed and mopped to the point they felt confident they'd picked up most of the glass, the repairman sent by the insurance company had come and gone. Ugly brown plywood had replaced the expansive view of mountains to the east, and the once light and airy living area now resembled the inside of a packing crate.

Sabrina brushed dust from her slacks. "I'm going to take a shower and then maybe lie down for a bit if that's okay."

"Yeah, that's fine."

Kali poured herself a Diet Coke and took it into John's study, where she booted up the computer and typed in the password that Sabrina had so cleverly plucked from the ether.

John's computer desktop was relatively uncluttered, with icons for only the basic programs. She went into Explorer and scanned the contents of the hard drive. Again, standard fare. She clicked on "My Photos."

Sabrina was right. The images John had stored there were mostly nature shots with a few of Sabrina's family interspersed. Often there were two or three versions of the same photo with different light or color adjustments. John playing around with his camera and photo-editing software. Nothing of interest in "My Documents," either, except financial records, and they already had a hard copy of most of the files.

Like Kali, John used Firefox as his browser and Thunderbird for e-mail. She logged on and downloaded recent e-mail. Mostly spam, as Sabrina had noted, with a few auto club digests thrown in.

Kali scanned previous e-mails, as well. Several short, chatty messages from Sabrina. A couple from Sabrina's son Joey, far more heartfelt than his mother's. John had apparently offered his nephew a sympathetic ear and an occasional word of advice. One brief e-mail from Kali back in early July. But none that shed light on John's death or the murders he was accused of.

She checked the browser history next. A number of Yahoo! searches, a string of Porsche discussion forum hits, and page after page of X-rated sites with full-screen photos of bare female flesh.

Diet Coke, along with disgust and anger, rose up in Kali's throat. The photo subjects were adult women, she reminded herself, not children, although in some instances that distinction was questionable. She remembered Graciela telling her that John had been spending a lot of time at his desk in the weeks before his death. Kali had naively assumed he was working. Instead, it looked like he'd been getting his kicks online. And on the television screen, she thought, remembering the porn DVDs she'd found in John's collection.

She turned off the computer and pushed back from the desk. She'd wanted to get to know her brother, hadn't she? Well, she was getting her wish. Too bad she didn't like what she saw.

Kali was savoring a fresh cup of coffee the next morning when Detectives Shafer and Parker showed up at the front door.

"First the department brushes us off like it's nothing," Kali clucked, standing back to invite them in, "and now they're sending out the big guns." Then something in her mind clicked and she felt a tingle of dread. "You must have learned something, right? It wasn't a simple act of vandalism, after all?"

Shafer frowned, his bushy brows pulling to a straight line, but it was Michelle Parker who responded. "What are you talking about?"

"The window." Kali pointed across the living room to the bulky sheet of plywood. "Someone tossed a rock through it."

They glanced briefly at the damage, then back to her. With a fresh rush of dread, Kali realized the window wasn't what had brought them there.

Arms crossed, Detective Shafer looked ready to bite. "What's your interest in Hayley Hendrix?" he asked curtly.

Kali felt herself pale. "What makes you—"

"You were at her apartment asking questions. You want to tell us why?"

"The manager called you?"

"Other way around," Shafer said. "We contacted her. Now, once again, what is your interest in Hayley Hendrix?"

Kali's throat was tight. She didn't like finding herself under the microscope. "I was actually on my way to tell you when my sister called me yesterday about the rock through the window." That wasn't entirely true, Kali conceded. She wouldn't have gone straight to the station; she'd have come up with a story and a game plan first. And now she had neither.

"Tell us what?" Michelle Parker asked, her tone far more conciliatory than Shafer's.

Kali leaned against the wall. "Well, that sketch I saw in your office the other day, the one of the missing girl. The Jane Doe. I think it might be Hayley Hendrix."

They didn't seem surprised. But then they were here, weren't they? And they'd already contacted the apartment manager. They must have learned the girl's identity themselves.

"How do you know her?" Shafer asked, stepping closer and pinning Kali with a narrowed gaze.

"I don't. She was a friend of Olivia Perez's."

The two detectives exchanged glances. "Your brother tell you that?" Shafer asked.

"John?" Kali shook her head, perplexed. She didn't like where their questions were heading. Why would they assume John knew either girl?

"What makes you think the two girls were friends?" Shafer asked.

"I've been doing some investigating," Kali explained, hedging while she tried to figure out what the detectives were really asking. "In conjunction with the wrongful death suit Olivia's parents are threatening. In talking to people who knew Olivia . . . Hayley's name came up."

Shafer rolled his shoulders and moved toward the window. "Came up how?"

"That she was a friend."

"That doesn't explain how you'd know what she looks like," Michelle said amiably.

Kali's mouth felt dry. "I saw a photo."

"Who showed it to you?"

This was exactly why she hadn't rushed to tell them her suspicions about Hayley Hendrix being their Jane Doe. Kali couldn't explain how she'd come to see the photo of Hayley and Olivia without implicating John further.

"That's part of my legal investigation," she said. "I don't have to tell you."

"I can't see why you wouldn't, though," Michelle remarked.

When Kali didn't respond, Shafer spoke up again. "What's your brother's relationship to her?"

"Hayley? As far as I know, there wasn't one."

"But he knew her?"

Kali shrugged. "What makes you think he did?"

Shafer gave another little shoulder roll. "Would it interest you to know your brother was at the Crazy Coyote a few days before he died?"

Her pulse quickened. The news did interest Kali, but she wasn't going to share that with the detectives. "So?"

"Hayley worked there. In fact, John mentioned Hayley by name. He was asking about her."

"That would have been after she was killed," Kali said, as much to herself as the detectives. "If he'd had something to do with her death, which appears to be what you're implying, do you really think he'd show up at her workplace and ask about her?"

Shafer pulled at an earlobe. "Thing is, he wasn't asking about Hayley so much as another girl, Crystal Adams."

As though it had been zapped by an electric shock, Kali's heart turned choppy. Adams. So Crystal's last name was Adams. John had hired a private investigator to search for Ray and Martha Adams. It couldn't be a coincidence.

Kali tried to appear nonchalant. "I'm not sure I follow you."

"Who is Crystal Adams?"

"I don't know."

He eyed her skeptically, hands on his belt.

"It's true, I don't."

"But you recognized the name."

Kali nodded. "Crystal was another name that came up when I talked to Olivia's friends."

"In what context?" Michelle's dark eyes were wide and friendly.

Were they playing good cop, bad cop? Probably. But Kali sensed there was also a genuine difference in personalities. She needed to keep her guard up against both detectives.

"Just that she was someone Olivia met over the summer," Kali said.

"Why would your brother inquire about her?"

"I don't know." She tried to put the X-rated Web sites she'd found on John's computer out of her mind, but it wasn't easy. "Is she okay?"

"You have reason to think she might not be?"

"With Olivia and Hayley both murdered . . ." Kali twisted her hands together. "It's just worrisome."

Shafer's gaze narrowed. "You going to tell us what's going on? What your brother's connection was?"

"I don't know how he knew them. Truly."

"Your brother is dead," Michelle said. "You don't need to protect him anymore."

Anymore. As if she'd ever been there for him when he needed her. "My brother wasn't a murderer," Kali protested. "He was a victim himself. Why are *you* so intent on refusing to see that?"

Shafer threw up his hands in disgust and turned toward the door.

"Do you know how to get in touch with Hayley's family?" Michelle asked Kali.

"I'm sorry, I don't. I honestly don't know anything more about her than what I've told you."

"What about Olivia's friend, the one who told you about Hayley? Do you think she'd know?"

The problem with deceit, as Kali had learned many times over, was that it eventually circled back on itself and caught you in a snare. On the other hand, coming clean about the photo wasn't a viable option. Not until she had a better idea of what was going on.

"I doubt it," she replied.

Michelle shot Kali a look infused with disbelief and rebuke. "We can find Olivia's friends, you know. But it would save time if you helped us."

"I can't recall who it was."

That look again. "If you think of anything, let us know."

Misgiving formed a knot in Kali's gut. She realized how it looked to the cops. They knew next to nothing about Hayley Hendrix except that she'd been brutally murdered. They'd finally gotten an ID on her, only to learn that Kali had been asking questions, and that there was an apparent connection between their victim and John. And now they'd learned that Olivia Perez, another victim, was a friend of Hayley's. It made sense they'd be suspicious of John. And of Kali, for that matter.

Kali wanted answers herself. Real answers, not a whitewash that pinned the crimes on John because he was convenient. On the other hand, she hated to sit on information that might be significant.

As she walked Michelle Parker to the door, she asked, "Have you searched Hayley's apartment?"

"Not yet. We're waiting for the warrant to come through."

There was nothing veiled about the comment. The manager had obviously not told them everything. "When you do," Kali offered, "you might keep your eyes out for a volume of love poems inscribed with a smiley face. Olivia had one just like it."

Michelle looked at her, puzzled. "How would you know that?"

"One of her friends mentioned it."

"Do you know who the books were from?" Michelle's curiosity was clearly piqued.

Kali shook her head. "But two friends, both murdered . . ." She left the thought unfinished.

"I hope you're not playing games with us." Michelle was no longer the amiable good cop. Her jaw was set and her eyes steely. She let herself out the front door and closed it with a thump.

Kali didn't breathe normally again until the sheriff's car had pulled away from the front of the house. Even then, her heart continued to pound. She barged into Sabrina's room without knocking.

Sabrina lifted her head off the pillow and braced herself on an elbow. It was clear she'd been awake. "What was that all about?"

Kali dropped down onto the edge of the bed. "The detectives wanted to know about Hayley Hendrix." She recounted what they'd told her about John's visit to the Crazy Coyote.

"He knew Hayley?" Sabrina asked.

"Looks like he might have known all three girls. The police case against John is totally off the wall. He didn't kill Sloane over some perceived threat to his job."

"I've been telling you that from the beginning. John wasn't a murderer."

"But two of the girls in that photo are dead," Kali pointed out. "Maybe Crystal as well."

"Are you saying you think *John* killed them?"

"We don't know that he didn't."

"How can you think that?"

"Because it might be true, Sabrina. It's looking like Olivia was the target and Sloane was the collateral victim."

"So the girls got messed up in something. What's that have to do with John?"

"Aside from the fact that there's evidence against him?" Kali sighed. "John also spent a lot of hours in the last week surfing porn sites on the Web."

"I don't believe it." Sabrina fluffed the pillow behind her and sat upright.

"Check the computer for yourself, then." Kali shut her eyes, pressed the palms of her hands against them. "Maybe John didn't kill anyone, but he sure as hell was up to his eyeballs in something."

And Carmen Escobar, the Perez's lawyer, would be thrilled to get wind of it.

# CHAPTER 29

While Sabrina showered and dressed, Kali dumped the contents of her handbag on the kitchen table and dug through the mess, looking for the number for Doug Simon, the private investigator John had hired. She found his card, called, and reached an answering machine. She started to leave a message but Simon picked up before she'd done much more than give her name.

"I haven't forgotten the report," he said. "I was just about to mail it out."

"It's done?"

"Pretty much. I'm sorry about the delay. There were a couple of crises with another investigation that got in the way."

"Could I come pick it up instead?" Kali asked, aware of how eager she sounded. "I'm kind of in a hurry to read it."

"Sure. Not a problem."

"As I recall, you said Ray and Martha Adams had divorced years ago, and that Ray remarried and has a second family. Martha died two or three years ago. Am I remembering right?"

"In a nutshell, yeah."

Kali took a breath. "You said there was a daughter, too. How old is she now?"

"She'd be about sixteen or seventeen. Lived with her mom until Martha's death, then went to live with Ray and his new family."

Roughly the same age as Crystal. Kali could feel her heart pounding as she asked, "Do you know the daughter's name by any chance?"

There was the sound of papers being shuffled on Simon's end. "Raelene," he said after a moment.

Not Crystal. But then it was likely the girl wasn't using her real name. "Named after her father?" Kali asked.

Simon chuckled. "Probably. I hadn't thought about that angle."

"What about Ray's kids by his second wife?" Kali asked. "Anyone named Crystal?"

"Doesn't ring a bell."

"You asked earlier if we wanted you to pursue this matter further. I think we might."

"I have time in the next couple of days, but if it will take longer, I'm afraid I won't be able to get to it for a week or so. What kind of information are you looking for?"

"Mostly about the daughter," Kali told him.

"Kids are tough. Not a lot of public information. I'd probably have to fly out to San Diego. That gets more expensive."

"Let me look over the report first," Kali told him. "I'll be by to pick it up in about an hour. Does that work for you?"

"I'll have it ready."

"Thanks." Kali hung up the phone and turned to Sabrina, who'd finished dressing and was filling the coffeemaker with water. "If I go pick up the report from that private investigator, can you stick around to handle the window guy?"

Sabrina nodded. "I was thinking," she said as she measured coffee into the filter, "Olivia and Hayley were so different. I wonder how they knew one another."

Kali remembered what Mrs. Perez had told her. *A friend she met during the summer.* During the summer when she'd quit a waitressing job for something better. Stripping?

"Maybe they weren't as different as it appears," Kali told her.

\* \* \*

Kali drove to Doug Simon's office, which turned out to be an airy second-floor room furnished with a laminate desk, metal file cabinets, and two straight-back chairs for clients. A collection of desert wildflower photographs hung on the wall opposite Simon's desk. The room was decidedly more functional than elegant, but, like the man himself, it radiated a down-to-earth quality that appealed to Kali.

Simon greeted her warmly, his large brown hand engulfing hers in a companionable handshake. "Sorry I was late with the report," he told her. "It didn't sound like you were in any hurry."

"It's okay. It's just that a few questions have come up recently. Let me read this over, and then I'll be in touch."

She took the report on Ray and Martha Adams, then proceeded to a donut shop down the street to sit and read it. She ordered a cup of coffee and, at the last minute, gave in to temptation and got herself a donut, as well. Then she settled in at one of the small tables toward the back.

The report was only half a dozen pages long, and most of what it covered Simon had already told her. But the report contained dates and addresses and copies of official documents. It was the death certificate for Martha Adams that caught Kali's interest. Not the cause of death, which was, as Simon had told her, an auto accident, but Martha's maiden name. Crystal. Could Raelene Adams be the elusive Crystal, after all?

She found the phone number for Ray Adams, took one last sip of coffee, and stepped outside to make her call.

A woman answered. "Adams residence." Crisp and formal.

"Is Raelene around?" Kali asked.

There was a moment's hesitation. "Perhaps you should speak to Mrs. Adams."

Kali heard a click, like she'd been put on hold. Then another voice came on. "This is Pat Adams."

"I'm trying to reach Raelene," Kali said.

A moment's hesitation. "She isn't living here anymore."

"Do you know how I can get in touch with her?"

"No, I don't." Pat Adams spoke with the finality of some-one starting to hang up.

"When did she leave?" Kali asked, hoping for even a glimmer of information about the girl.

"Who did you say you were?"

"My name is Kali. I'm a . . . friend of a friend of hers."

"You mean that creep Clayton?"

*Who was Clayton?* "No," Kali said, blindly tossing out bait in hopes of snaring something. "I know Olivia and Hay-ley."

"Never heard of them. I'm afraid I can't help you."

"Who is Clayton?" Kali asked. But Pat Adams had al-ready hung up the phone.

Kali made copies of the photo she'd been carrying and circled back to Simon's office. Luckily, he hadn't gone out.

"How soon can you get to San Diego?" she asked.

"Tomorrow or the next day. You've decided to go ahead?"

Kali nodded. She handed him the photo of the three girls, pointing to Crystal. "I want to know if this is Raelene Adams. If it is, find out whatever you can about her back-ground. Mostly, I want to know where she is now. She's using the name Crystal, at least some of the time. I think she was living in Tucson a month or so ago, staying with this young woman"—Kali pointed to the photo again—"Hayley Hendrix. She was murdered not long ago."

"Who's the third girl?"

"Olivia Perez. Also murdered. John was a suspect in that murder."

"Oh, man." Simon frowned. "Was this what he wanted, to find the Adams girl?"

"He didn't give you any indication?"

"No, just the names Ray and Martha Adams. But like I told you, we were working in stages."

"I'm not sure if finding her was his goal," Kali said, an-swering Simon's earlier question. "I think so, but I have no idea why."

Simon rubbed at his chin. "Are you sure you want to know?"

Wanting had nothing to do with it at this point. She *had* to know.


Kali's cell phone rang as she was leaving Simon's office. She could see from the readout that it was Carmen Escobar, lawyer for the Perez family. As she answered, Kali looked around in vain for a spot of shade. The day's heat was already building.

"I think it might be helpful if we sat down and talked," Carmen said, lawyer-style chummy.

"Helpful how?" Kali was certain there was nothing she could say that would dissuade the woman from filing suit.

"The trial is bound to garner attention. Do you really want to see your brother's name dragged through the mud?"

Kali had reached her car. She opened the door to a fresh blast of heat. "You've got this all wrong. If we go to trial, John will be vindicated."

Carmen laughed. "I doubt it. In fact, the intrigue grows."

"What do you mean?"

"We need to talk."

"Isn't that what we're doing?" Kali slid into the car and turned on the engine to get the air-conditioning going.

"In person."

Kali sighed. "Okay, when?"

They agreed on one o'clock that afternoon.


The single-story stucco bungalow that housed Carmen Escobar's office was in need of a paint job and, to Kali's taste, a little landscaping. In the dirt patch between the building and the sidewalk, nothing was planted except a sun-bleached wooden sign that read LAW OFFICE. CARMEN ESCOBAR, ESQ.

Kali stepped into the reception area and shivered in the sudden chill of the air-conditioning. She gave her name to the secretary, a pudgy Hispanic woman, who called over her shoulder through the open doorway to the back of the house.

"Hey, Carmen, your one o'clock is here. Want me to send her in?"

A voice called, "Yeah, I'm ready."

The secretary pointed Kali to what must originally have been the living room of the house. It was now partially closed off from the entrance with a three-panel screen.

Carmen Escobar was a tiny woman who looked to be in her early forties. She had a sharp nose; full mouth; and wiry, shoulder-length hair that was clipped at the nape of her neck with a leather barrette.

When Carmen held out a hand, her dark eyes flashed with intensity. "Glad you could meet with me."

"I think it's probably a waste of our time," Kali told her, looking around. The office was pleasantly furnished with rustic Mexican- style pieces and bright, deep colors. While the attorney might not have shown much interest in the exterior of the building, she'd clearly paid attention to details in the space around her.

"I hope it's not a waste," Carmen replied. She showed Kali to a round antique-pine conference table near her desk. The show of equal footing was no doubt part of the attorney's strategy. "As you know, I represent Olivia Perez's parents. They are devastated by the loss of their daughter."

"I'm sure they are." Kali sat down in one of the heavy wooden chairs.

"And it's only right they should be compensated for their loss." She waited for Kali to jump in and frowned when Kali remained silent. "It would be in both of our interests to settle this matter, you know."

"Settle what? You've accused my brother of murder. And now you're asking to be paid off *not* to forge ahead with those accusations."

Carmen's smile was controlled. "I don't see it that way at all. I'm trying to save both sides—the Perez family as well as yours—the aggravation and expense of a trial. If we don't work something out now, between ourselves, you know

damn well the court is going to try to herd us into a settlement down the line. Only by then we'll both have invested a
lot of time and energy."

True, the judge would order a pretrial settlement conference. That was standard procedure. And by then, Carmen Escobar would have logged in countless hours of trial
preparation. Better for her that she get her cut now, with relatively little expended effort.

In all fairness, an early settlement would be easier for
Kali, too. But she didn't intend to settle. Certainly not until
she knew more about what had really happened when Sloane
and Olivia were murdered.

"They lost their child," Carmen said. "Their only daughter. She was the light of their life. Do you have children of
your own, Kali?"

"I don't see what that has to do with anything."

"The loss of a child, no matter what the child's age, is a
blow like no other."

"I'm not without sympathy," Kali said. "I can understand
that Mr. and Mrs. Perez must be grief-stricken. But my
brother had nothing to do with their daughter's death."

"It's not simply the emotional loss," Carmen continued,
"as unspeakable as that is. There's the very real financial loss
to consider, as well. These are poor people. Olivia was the
first in her family to go to college. They were counting on
her being there to help them in the years ahead."

"We don't know that she would have," Kali pointed out.
"She certainly wouldn't have been obligated to."

Carmen's smile widened, revealing sharp incisors. "I
think you'll find that most jurors are not sympathetic to that
position."

She was probably right. Emotional arguments often had
more sway with jurors than reasoned ones. Jury trials were a
crapshoot anyway. In Kali's experience you could never tell
what the outcome would be.

Still, Kali wasn't going to be railroaded into an early settlement. "I'm truly sorry for the Perez family's loss," she

said. "But paying them is out of the question. My brother didn't kill Olivia Perez or Sloane Winslow."

"Keep in mind," Carmen said, "that in a civil trial the jurors don't have to be convinced beyond a reasonable doubt." She smoothed a hand over the surface of the small conference table. "And since John is no longer around . . . well, they're likely to think helping the Perez family is, to put it bluntly, no skin off his nose."

"That's a disgusting thing to say."

"It's the truth." Carmen leaned her forearms on the table. Her eyes were fiery. "I have no doubt I'd prevail at trial. And if we go that route, we're going to ask for a lot of money, believe me." She sat back. "I grant you, a trial will take a toll on everyone. I'm particularly concerned about putting Olivia's parents through that. So we're ready to compromise. I think they'd be willing to look at a lowball offer. Maybe in the ballpark of, say, a quarter of a million."

"Absolutely not." Kali pushed back from the table. She was seething inside. She'd settled cases in the past, but she'd never felt manipulated as she did now. "And you'd better look at the evidence again before you get so cocky about winning."

Carmen raised an eyebrow and smiled smugly.

"Do you really think my brother would kill his best friend's sister over a silly job?"

Carmen looked her in the eye. "Actually, I'm thinking maybe there's more to it."

"What do you mean?"

"It seems a friend of Olivia's was killed a couple of weeks earlier. A young woman by the name of Hayley."

Kali felt sick. How had Carmen learned about Hayley? "Nothing ties John to that murder," Kali said.

"Well, not directly. But Hayley's wallet was found in a Dumpster several weeks ago. It wasn't until after they had an ID on the body that they put it all together, of course."

"So?"

"There was a slip of paper in her wallet with the phone

number for Logan Foods. I think we need to look at the possibility that it was Olivia your brother was after."

The thought had been lurking in the muddy depths of Kali's mind ever since she'd learned Olivia was one of the girls in the photo. But to hear it spoken aloud, especially by Carmen Escobar, sent ice water through her veins.

"Perhaps your brother was somehow involved with both young women. In fact, I've already got someone looking into it." Carmen smiled again. "It's a story that would certainly get media attention."

Kali was on her feet without realizing she'd actually stood. "You're way out of line."

"I'm trying to be fair and share information with you," Carmen responded. "In the hopes we can reach an amicable agreement."

Whatever happened, it wouldn't be amicable.

"I told you this meeting would be a waste." Kali grabbed her purse and headed for the door.

# CHAPTER 30

There was no sign of activity around Sloane Winslow's house when Kali pulled up in front. She would have loved to get inside again, but she was afraid to push her luck. Instead, she headed next door to Janet Fisher's.

Despite the late afternoon heat, a slender boy in his mid-teens was shooting baskets in the driveway.

"Is your mom home?" Kali asked.

"She won't be back until later."

Kali stepped to the side so the sun wasn't in her eyes. "You on the team?"

The boy laughed with good-natured humor. "Do I look like a player to you?"

He had a point. He was only a couple of inches taller than Kali, and his gait was awkward.

"You never know," she said.

He dribbled the ball in a zigzag, then tried a shot at the basket. It circled the rim before rolling off. He gave her a cockeyed grin. "See what I mean?"

"No one's a hundred percent all the time."

He laughed again. "I'd settle for half the time."

The sun was relentless. She gave him credit for being out there practicing. "My name is Kali," she said. "I'm a friend of Sloane Winslow's brother." It was easier to give the boy the same story she'd told his mother. And it wasn't exactly untrue.

"I'm Mitch."

"It must have been kind of upsetting having a double murder next door," she said, sidestepping into the questions she really wanted to ask.

He dribbled again, without looking at her. "Freaky as hell."

"I understand you knew Olivia Perez."

"Who told you that?"

"Your mom."

"Figures." He went for a drop shot and missed.

"Did you?"

"Know her?" He shrugged. "Some."

"I got the impression from your mom that Olivia wasn't very friendly."

"My mother has her own perspective on life. People are supposed to behave the way she thinks they should."

"Sounds like a lot of mothers."

"Yeah, I guess. We had this party here over the summer. It was my mom's idea really. Like something out of the seventies. She invited Olivia, then got all bent out of shape when she didn't come. Can you blame Olivia? Jeesh. Why would she want to hang out with a bunch of dweebie high school kids?"

"Because it might be fun?"

"It wasn't that kind of party, trust me." He shot another basket and this time it went in. "Besides, she had better things to do."

"It sounds like you *did* know her."

Another shrug. "Not really. I went over there a couple of times. We talked about movies and stuff. No biggie."

"Did you ever meet any of her friends?" Kali asked.

"A couple of them. It's not like I was over there that much."

Kali showed him the photo. "Do you recognize these other girls?"

"Yeah. Well, one of them. Her." He pointed to the photo.

"Crystal?"

"Yeah, I think that's her name."

"What can you tell me about her?"

"Not much." Mitch spun the ball between his hands. "She's my age, sixteen. Only she dropped out of school."

"Doesn't seem like someone as smart and focused as Olivia would have much in common with a younger high school dropout."

Mitch looked faintly amused. "There was another side to Olivia," he said knowingly.

"What do you mean?"

"She got around." Mitch looked over his shoulder at Kali, then sank another basket. "Like the party thing. She told me about some big shindig she was at—waiters walking around with free drinks and plates of fancy crap like stuffed mushrooms and skewered shrimp. That's what I meant about her not wanting to come to our stupid party."

"How'd she get invited to parties like that?" Kali asked. She'd considered the possibility that Olivia was stripping and that's how she'd met Hayley. But maybe she was doing more than stripping. Maybe all the girls were.

Mitch shrugged. "That wasn't anything I'd ask her."

"What about Crystal? Did she go to those parties, too?"

"Probably. They were both, you know—" Mitch reddened, but Kali couldn't tell if it was the heat or a blush—"kind of out there."

"Do you know how I might find Crystal?"

"Nope. Except, like I told Mrs. Winslow, I think she'd sometimes grab a free meal at that youth shelter downtown, Sunshine House."

"Like you told . . ." Kali wasn't sure she understood. "Sloane Winslow was asking about Crystal?"

"Yeah. I guess Crystal and Olivia had a falling-out or something. Crystal stopped coming around. Seemed weird that Mrs. Winslow would care, but she was really worried."

"When was this?"

"I don't know, maybe a week before the murders."

Sloane and John, both. Why the interest in Crystal? "Thanks," Kali said. "Take care out here in the heat."

Mitch rolled his eyes at her. "I think I know that."

* * *

When Kali arrived back at John's with supplies for dinner, she found Sabrina sitting woodenly on the sofa in the living room, staring at the wall. A half-empty glass, which Kali instinctively knew held gin and tonic, rested on the coffee table in front of her.

"You realize you're making a habit of this?" Kali asked.

"A habit of what?"

"Hitting the bottle early."

Sabrina looked up and Kali saw that she'd been crying.

"What's wrong?" Kali asked.

"You were right about the porn on John's computer. It's like that's all he did on the Internet recently."

Kali nodded, recalling the disgust she'd felt when she'd discovered the Web sites. On the other hand, Sabrina's distress seemed a bit over the top. "I know you don't want to think badly of him," Kali told her, "but John was an adult. It's not like he did anything really wrong."

"It's not just that." Sabrina stood, steadier on her feet than Kali would have predicted. "Follow me. I want to show you something."

She was no longer tearful. As she sat down at the computer, Sabrina seemed more frightened than anything. Her hand shook as she clicked the mouse. Whereas Kali had seen just enough flesh to get the gist of John's activities, her sister had apparently watched some of the downloaded videos.

"It takes a minute or so to load," she said.

"Sabrina, I'm not interested in watching this stuff."

"Just wait. You will be."

The video started. There was no sound aside from background music, but the picture quality was better than Kali expected.

The scene opened with two girls in a bedroom, or maybe a dorm room. The redhead was lying on a bed, leafing through a magazine, which hid her face, and listening to music on her MP3 player. The other, a slender blonde, was at a desk, writing. Kali thought at first that they hadn't known they were being filmed, but it soon became apparent that the action was staged. The blonde stood and stretched provocatively, removing her sweater to reveal a black, low-cut lace bra. More stretching and arching for the viewfinder, and then she sauntered over and sat on the edge of her friend's bed, gesturing to her shoulders as though she needed them rubbed.

"Can't you fast-forward?" Kali asked.

"Hold on."

Kali crossed her arms. At least she wasn't watching closeups of hideously large male organs being worked on by naked women—the type of porn that sometimes made it past her spam filter and showed up in her in-box. Still, she wished Sabrina would just tell her what she'd seen that was so upsetting.

Ignored by her friend, the blonde pouted for a moment, then gently poked the other girl in the ribs to get her attention, causing the girl's robe to fall open. Kali's eyes were immediately drawn to the bare flesh and very full breasts, so it took her a moment to see that the girl had dropped the magazine, revealing her face. And another moment before she recognized who it was.

"That's her, isn't it?" Sabrina asked. "That's Olivia's dead friend, Hayley."

A horrible burning sensation was building in Kali's chest. "Can you pause it?"

"I don't think so. But it's her, I'm sure."

The two women on screen were now busily undressing and caressing one another. The camera zoomed in closer.

"Look," Sabrina said, "there's a shot of her face again."

"It does look like her." Kali had seen enough. "Close it down."

"Not yet." Sabrina tapped her finger, as the action on the screen progressed. Both women were naked now, and they turned to look as a third girl entered the room.

Kali recognized her immediately.

Olivia Perez.

Now she understood why Sabrina had reacted as she had. It wasn't that John sometimes looked at pornography. It was that he'd been watching the naked sex antics of two women he was suspected of murdering.

# CHAPTER 31

"Looks like they're from the same person," Michelle said, opening the cover of the book of poetry she'd found near Hayley's bed. "Same quote, same handwriting and signature. Of course, if the girls were friends, I guess it's not so odd." She dropped the little book into an evidence bag and handed it to Erling to label. "Maybe they were dating the same two-timing guy or they have a mutual friend who's short on gift ideas."

Erling looked around the tiny bedroom. The warrant had come through, but so far they'd learned nothing useful from their search. Hayley Hendrix had a thing for eye shadow and nail polish—she had enough tubes and brushes and bottles to open her own beauty shop. She liked blueberry yogurt, rocky road ice cream, and Honey Nut Cheerios. She had $400 in a checking account and $3,300 in a savings account. No sign of drugs or other illegal activities. No computer, letters, or address book.

He stretched his neck. "I'd sure like to know where the O'Brien sisters fit into this."

"You think there's a connection over and above their brother's involvement?"

"Seems reasonable. Kali knew about Hayley, was at her

apartment even. She knew about Crystal Adams, whoever she is." They'd run the name and come up empty-handed. But John O'Brien had inquired about Crystal at the Crazy Coyote, so if they asked around at enough strip joints maybe they'd finally get lucky and find someone who recognized the name. "And the thing with the rock through the window. I'm not convinced they didn't throw it themselves."

Michelle cocked her head. "You're getting pretty far out on this, don't you think?"

"Maybe. Or maybe they're the ones who've gone to extremes to misdirect us."

Michelle pulled off her latex gloves and dropped them into her pocket. "I grant you that John O'Brien's name keeps coming up, and that his sister Kali seems to know more than she's sharing with us. But the truth is, we don't really have anything that connects him to Olivia or Hayley."

"Don't forget the phone number in Hayley's wallet. Why else would a girl like her be carrying around the number for Logan Foods' corporate headquarters?"

Erling's gut told him that the murders of Olivia Perez and Hayley Hendrix were connected, and that John O'Brien was very much a part of the mix. It didn't do much for his original hypothesis that Sloane had been the primary target, but at least O'Brien still figured into the picture. And Erling was breathing easier now that the focus of the investigation was no longer on Sloane.

"I wish we had contact information," Erling noted. "It was probably all stored in her cell phone."

"We'll get the records eventually," Michelle said. "Maybe they'll point in the direction of her killer, as well."

Erling nodded. At least they'd been able to pin down a possible time for the murder. Hayley's mail had been piling up since the end of August. She'd been a no-show at the Crazy Coyote about the same time, but since she'd talked of leaving, no one thought to report her missing. That jibed with the coroner's estimate of time of death.

Michelle's phone rang, and she stepped closer to the window for better reception. "Parker here. Yeah. No kidding? You're sure? Right, call for forensics but we'll head there too."

She disconnected and turned to Erling. "They found Hayley's car. It's been in impound for three weeks. It was towed from the Home Depot lot on Broadway when an employee there noticed it hadn't been moved for several days."

The Home Depot store was nowhere near the wash where Hayley's body had been found. Had she been abducted from the parking lot, or had she been grabbed somewhere else and her car driven to the lot after the fact? Erling suspected the latter, simply because he had trouble imagining what Hayley would be doing at a Home Depot. But he was determined to keep an open mind.

The employee on duty at the impound lot walked them to the car, a white 1994 Saturn with a wide scrape on the passenger-side door. The scrape looked like an old one.

Erling peered inside. A clutter of personal odds and ends was strewn about on the backseat: a sun hat, a water bottle, a packet of Kleenex, and an open bag of pretzels. There was a hairbrush on the front passenger seat and loose change in the cup holder.

"Anyone been inside?" Erling asked.

"Not since it's been in our facility. But it was unlocked when we found it, so who knows?"

Erling donned a pair of gloves and opened the front passenger door. The air was stale but heavily perfumed from the floral-scented air freshener that hung from the dash. No obvious signs of a struggle, although that didn't mean much. He opened the glove box—nothing but the car's registration and owner's manual. Under the front seats he found a ball-point pen and a comb. The trunk was empty except for the jack and some flares.

"Maybe forensics will turn up something," Michelle said.

"You think our killer conveniently left a set of prints for us?" Erling laughed. "Not likely."

"True. He might not have been anywhere near the car." She opened the back door of the car and a folded map fell to the ground. "This must have slipped down next to the seat," Michelle said. She tossed it back into the car, then stopped and reached for it again.

"What is it?" Erling asked.

"A map of Tucson. Might be nothing, but it's folded open and there's an address written off to the side."

"What's the address?"

She read it to him and Erling wrote the number and street down in his notebook. "Leave the map for forensics. The location is all we need for now."

"You think she was meeting someone the night she was killed?"

"Possibly. Or the thing could have been down there for months. Maybe we'll have a better idea once we check the place out."

It was too much to expect that the address somehow related to John O'Brien, but that's what Erling found himself secretly hoping for.

# CHAPTER 32

"Sorry to be leaving again," Sabrina said, tossing her small suitcase onto the backseat. "I promise to be back early next week."

"Don't worry. I know you've got your family to think about." Sabrina claimed she was feeling guilty about spending time away from her kids. But Kali wondered if her sister's dismay over John's Web-surfing habits wasn't what had prompted her hasty decision to head home.

Not that Kali begrudged Sabrina the time. In the ten days since Kali had arrived, they'd accomplished most of what needed doing in terms of cleaning out John's house. Sabrina had set aside what items she wanted, and Kali had packed a box for herself. They would donate the bulk of the furniture and clothing to charity when they were ready to put the house on the market. And they'd already spoken with a real estate agent who assured them the place would go quickly.

Kali could have headed home herself, but she had too many questions, even without the looming threat of a lawsuit. She'd decided to stick around for a bit longer and see what she could learn.

"You're sure you don't mind my leaving?" Sabrina asked.

"I'm sure." Kali hugged her sister. "Give the boys my love. And drive safely."

*  *  *

Kali was cleaning up the coffee mugs from breakfast when Bryce called.

"Do you have plans for tonight?" he asked.

"Plans?" His question was so unexpected she was sure she'd misunderstood.

"Yeah." He sounded like the cat who'd swallowed the canary. "Want to get together for dinner?"

She dried her hands on a kitchen towel. "Where are you?"

"At the airport."

"In Tucson?"

"L.A. I had to come down for a meeting, but I don't have to be back at work until Monday morning."

She still didn't understand. "You've lost me."

"I'm standing here at the big Southwest board, and I realized I'm halfway to Tucson. I figured I could stop in and see you on the way back to Oakland. That is, if you'd like."

"It's not exactly on the way, you know." In fact, it wasn't on the way at all. Bryce's offer, coming out of the blue, caught Kali by surprise. But she was aware of a giddy excitement building inside her.

"Says right here on the display that Tucson's only ninety minutes away."

Kali laughed. "You're nuts."

"Nuts about you."

"And corny, too. But I'd love it. I am so in need of some fun."

He sounded relieved. "I'm an expert at fun."

"What time will you be here?"

"About two, assuming I can get on the next flight out."

"I'll pick you up at the airport."


Kali had almost three hours before she'd have to leave for the airport, but she felt she was racing against the clock as she frantically cleaned up the house, did a load of laundry—two loads actually, including the sheets and towels—and then showered and washed her hair.

Even with all that, she arrived at the airport early, awaiting Bryce's arrival with the anticipation of a kid on Christmas Eve. Had it really been only two weeks ago they'd camped out under the star-studded Sierra sky? It felt like a lifetime.

As she watched Bryce emerge from behind the security barrier, Kali felt the familiar flutter of joy. He greeted her with an eager hug and kiss.

"I can't believe you really came all this way for twenty-four hours on the ground."

He looked at his feet. "Am I on the ground? Feels like I'm in the clouds. It's so good to see you."

He'd set his carry-on down to hug her. Now he again hoisted it, slung the strap over his shoulder, and followed her outside to the parking lot.

"Do you want to see some of the sights of Tucson," Kali asked, "or head straight to John's?"

"I didn't come for the sights. Besides, I'm eager to meet the infamous Sabrina."

"She just left for home this morning."

"Not because of me, I hope."

"No, she was gone by the time you called. She wanted to get back to her family. She was a bit upset too, I think." Kali knew she'd have to do it eventually, so she brought Bryce up to date on what she'd learned about John, his interest in porn, and his ties to the three girls. Bryce asked questions now and then for clarification, but mostly he just listened.

"That's about it," Kali said when she'd finished. "And now I don't want to talk about it. I want a break."

He grinned. "And to have fun."

"Right."


And fun is what she got. A lovely mix of sex and margaritas and grilled filet mignon and a twilight swim followed by more sex. The perfect antidote for the trials of the last ten days. That night she slept soundly and peacefully for the first time since she'd learned of John's death.

After a morning swim and a sudsy wash-off in John's over-sized, double-nozzled shower, they faced the empty fridge. In their eager shopping for a delectable evening meal, they'd neglected to think about breakfast. Kali had thought maybe they'd have Sunday brunch at one of the fancy resorts in the hills, but the only flight Bryce had been able to get out left at ten that morning, so they settled for cold cereal and coffee.

"I still can't believe you flew here just for dinner," Kali told him. "But I'm glad you did."

"I hope you don't think dinner was the big draw. Admittedly, it was a first-rate steak and all, but . . ." He turned suddenly serious. "I've really missed you."

Kali had missed Bryce, too. She hadn't fully realized how much. "I won't be staying much longer. It's just that I don't know what John did or how he died. I can't live not knowing whether he was a murderer."

Bryce rolled his empty mug between his palms. "Defense attorney syndrome?"

"He was my brother, for God's sake. And I want to *understand,* not to whitewash whatever he's done."

"You seem to care more about him now than when he was alive." Bryce paused. "Is that what it takes to get your attention?"

"What do you mean?"

He touched her hand. "Forget it. I guess I just feel that you sometimes shut me out."

"I'm sorry. I don't mean to." But she did mean to, Kali realized. It was more that she didn't understand why.

She got up to pour more coffee. When the phone rang, she said to Bryce, "You want to get that? My hands are full. It's got to be Sabrina. You won't get to meet her this trip, but you can talk to her."

He picked up the phone. "Kali's up to her elbows in coffee. I'm Bryce." There was a moment of silence; then he said, "Just a moment," and handed Kali the phone. "It's not your sister," he whispered.

"Hello," she said, then felt the heat rise on her face as she recognized A. J. Nash's voice.

"I was hoping you might be free to take in the Desert Museum today."

"Uh, afraid not."

"I know it's kind of last minute, but I—"

"It's not that. I have a friend visiting from home."

"The man who answered the phone? Bryce?"

Kali cupped the receiver closer to her mouth. "Right." If he was waiting for a fuller explanation, he wasn't going to get one.

"I see. Maybe another time, then."

"Okay, that sounds good."

By the time Kali hung up the phone, her palms were sweating. *Get a grip,* she told herself. *You haven't done anything wrong.* But she felt as though she'd been caught with her hand in the cookie jar.

"Doesn't take you long to make new friends," Bryce observed when she returned to the table.

"He's a friend of John's. Someone John worked with, in fact."

"Calling you on a Sunday morning." It wasn't a question, but the inflection in Bryce's voice made it sound like one.

"He has an annual pass to the Desert Museum. He offered to take me sometime. That's all."

Bryce nodded and let the subject drop. But the mood of the morning had changed as surely as if ominous gray clouds had rolled across the open expanse of brilliant blue sky.

# CHAPTER 33

Kali was of the last generation whose formative years had been spent in the precomputer era. She was comfortable with modern technology now—in fact, she depended on it—but her brain was wired the old way. When she wanted to think, she resorted to pen and paper. Which was why, after returning from the airport, she was sitting at the kitchen table scribbling her thoughts down on paper and trying to make sense of them with the help of squiggly lines and arrows.

The making-sense part wasn't coming easily.

She allowed herself a gratifying, if fleeting, reflection on the weekend and the sensation of Bryce's touch against her skin. The house felt surprisingly empty without him. Once again Kali savored the memory of his departing kiss—the tension generated by Nash's call seemingly forgotten—then reluctantly forced herself back to the task at hand.

For the moment, she was operating under the assumption that John had been murdered and that his death was most likely connected to the deaths of Sloane Winslow and Olivia Perez. While she was less clear about Hayley Hendrix's murder, logic told her it must also be relevant. What were the odds that two friends, both involved in porn, would randomly meet a violent death within weeks of one another?

Kali worried about Crystal's safety, but she also wondered about the girls' complicity in the crimes. Why had both John and Sloane been interested in finding her?

Kali drew a triangle and labeled the three points. The girls—Olivia, Hayley, and Crystal—at one apex, Sloane at another, and John at the third. They were all pieces of a puzzle, but she couldn't see how they fit.

She shouldn't assume the girls were an entity, she decided. Kali took out a fresh piece of paper and drew five circles, one for each of the players. Then she added a sixth circle with a question mark inside. Were John and the girls together in something, and Sloane the odd person out? Maybe Sloane and the girls were in on something, and John was the odd one. Or was it John and Sloane facing off against the girls? Or Crystal against them all? Or all five players united against a common, outside enemy?

Kali traced over the question mark inside the last circle. There was clearly a lot she was missing.

John had been asking about Crystal at the Crazy Coyote. Sloane had asked the neighbor boy about her. Crystal had been living with Hayley before Hayley was murdered. It was obvious to Kali that Crystal would have answers. How to find Crystal was anything but obvious.

Mitch Fisher, the neighbor's son, had said she sometimes grabbed a free meal at Sunshine House. Kali's chances of actually running across Crystal there were slim, but with luck she might find someone who'd have an idea where the girl could be found.

She looked the address up in the phone book and headed out.

Sunshine House was located a couple of blocks off a main thoroughfare in a neighborhood that had seen better days. It was a single-story structure that might at one time have been part of a church or a school. As she stepped inside, Kali heard the muffled drone of activity, although the hallway was empty. To her right, another hallway led to what looked like offices and meeting rooms. Farther down and to the left, through partially opened doors, Kali caught a glimpse of a large room that seemed to be the hub of activity.

The walls were decorated with bold, urban-themed murals, which Kali guessed had been painted by the kids themselves. Mismatched area rugs dotted the floor, surrounded by overstuffed couches and puffy floor pillows. Bookshelves stood in one corner, a television set in another, and a Ping-Pong table at the far end. Music from a radio played in the background.

As she stepped into the room, Kali saw maybe a dozen kids sprawled about inside—several of them dozing on the couches, a handful watching television, and others staring blankly into space. Near the library corner, two girls appeared to be deep in quiet conversation.

Off to Kali's right, a muscular man with heavily tattooed arms was loading canned soda into an ice chest. He wore cargo pants, a dark blue T-shirt, and a single ear stud. He looked to be in his late thirties. When he caught sight of Kali, he set the soda aside and came over.

"Can I help you?" he asked.

"I'm looking for whoever is in charge."

"You've found him. Well, it's my wife who's in charge of this end of things, but we operate as a team." He offered a hand. "Gary Ellis. Sorry if my hand is cold. I've been digging around in the ice."

"Kali O'Brien. You and your wife run the center?"

He grinned. "With a whole lot of help. But, yeah, we're central casting. Are you law enforcement, Social Services, a pastor, or a reporter?"

"I'm an attorney," Kali said.

Ellis raised an eyebrow. "Can't say we've seen a lot of them around here."

She wasn't sure if he was implying that was a good thing or bad. "I'm trying to find a girl who might have had some contact with Sunshine House."

He gave her a questioning look. "She do something wrong?"

"No. She's missing and I'm worried about her."

Ellis rubbed the back of his neck with his hand. "Our mission is helping kids, but we stay on the right side of the law. We've got a good working relationship with the cops and Social Services."

"I've got no problem with that," Kali told Ellis. "In fact, I think it's great."

A woman appeared in the doorway. "Gary, where are the chips?"

"Still in the trunk, I think." He turned to Kali. "Come meet my wife. This is Mara," he said, making the introduction.

"Hi." Mara was trim and athletic with honey-blond hair pulled into a ponytail. She had an apron on over a sleeveless blouse and shorts.

"Kali wants to talk to us about one of the kids."

"We're kind of busy right now," Mara explained to Kali. "Sunday is always hectic because we encourage kids to come by for a hot meal. Today we're shorthanded, though. There was a mix-up about which group was sponsoring the meal."

"Maybe I can help," Kali offered.

"Great. Come with me." Mara led Kali into a kitchen area at the end of the hallway. "Different organizations—churches mostly, but some schools and women's auxiliary groups, too—usually take responsibility for Sunday meals. Today fell through the cracks, so Gary and I made a quick trip to the grocery. It won't be the full-fledged hot meal we usually offer, but it's food." She put Kali to work making cheese sandwiches.

"You don't offer food at other times?"

"Yeah, we do, but not one big meal. There're always snacks and soda, and when we get a kid in need of a real meal, we usually order takeout. We're more of a community center and referral service than a real shelter, though we'd love to have the funding to do that, too." Mara pulled a large plastic platter from the cupboard. "A lot of what we do is outreach work, trying to hook up with the kids who need our help. It's a slow process."

Kali had a friend in the Bay Area who volunteered with a similar group there. "Are you like Covenant House?" she asked.

"Don't I wish? They are much bigger and much better funded. They've got centers in six or seven cities and can offer so much more than we can. But we're it for Tucson, so we do what we can."

"And what's that, exactly?" Kali peeled the cellophane wrappers from packages of presliced cheese.

"We offer a safe place for kids to hang out, study, or meet with friends. We do have counselors and a basic medical clinic twice a week. We can get kids into shelters when need be, or a drug treatment program, or what have you. All of that is done one to one, as needed. Crisis by crisis, so to speak. The kids here today aren't the hard-core cases." Mara emptied containers of deli coleslaw into a bowl. "Oh, some Sundays one of the really needy ones ends up here. Mostly these Sunday kids just need a friendly face. It's a way to get the word out, though."

"Where do they come from, the kids?"

Mara shrugged. "It runs the gamut. Some come from homes where there's abuse and neglect. Some are runaways. There are kids who've been bounced out of the foster care system, or outgrown it. Kids whose parents are drugged out, dead, or just don't care. Throwaway kids. Every one is a sad story, and every one is different."

Mara looked at the tray of sandwiches. "That's enough for now. Why don't you get the cookies and put them out on a plate?" She washed bunches of grapes and laid them in a bowl. "Who's the girl you're interested in?"

"Crystal Adams."

Mara's forehead scrunched in thought. "We get so many kids. You think she's been here recently?"

"Maybe, but earlier too, back in the summer."

Kali had started to reach for the photograph in her purse

when Mara's face lit up with recognition. "Slender girl, right? With a birthmark on one side of her neck?"

"Right."

"I do remember her. She was a drifter."

"A drifter?"

"She wasn't a regular, and she wasn't a kid in crisis. At least not that she let on to us. She'd show up now and then. Never was interested in any counseling or referrals or any kind of help. I haven't seen her lately." Mara picked up the bowl of slaw and a handful of napkins. "Grab the sandwiches, will you?"

They headed back toward the assembly hall. "That's one of the toughest aspects of this work," Mara continued. "You bond with some of these kids, whether you want to or not, and then they disappear. You never know what's happened to them. The only hope is that you've planted a seed. That you've shown them life can be better, that they deserve better."

"What can you tell me about Crystal?"

Mara tilted her head. "What's your interest again?"

Kali gave the same explanation she'd given Mara's husband: "She's missing."

"We get a lot of runaways. Sometimes, I can't say I blame them. Let's set the food down and get the rest." Mara turned to a pudgy, freckle-faced boy who was standing eagerly by the food table. "Think you can keep everyone at bay until it's all out? We'll be right back."

The boy grinned. "No one's going to get past me."

"Thanks." On their way back to the kitchen, Mara greeted a few of the other kids

"About Crystal," Kali prompted, following after Mara.

"She's bright. Seemed like she was always in our library corner reading. And she borrowed books. She's articulate." Mara smiled. "She has a bit of a foul mouth, but she doesn't have"—Mara made quotation marks in the air with her fingers—"an attitude, like some of the girls."

"Do you know anything about her background?"

"No. She was very closed, very private. I suspected she

was living on the street at least part of the time. I tried to get her to open up, but she was like a feral cat. She kept her distance."

Kali showed Mara the photo. "What about the other two girls? Do you recognize them?"

Mara studied the picture, her green eyes sad. "I'm afraid I don't." She pointed to Olivia. "I'd remember a girl like that. She seems to have a presence and vivaciousness we don't see here. Our kids either cower or they're totally in your face. The other girl"—here she tapped Hayley—"looks a lot like a sketch the sheriff's department showed us. A body they found not long ago."

"It is," Kali said. "They've identified her as Hayley Hendrix." She watched Mara to see if the name rang a bell. Apparently it didn't.

"She was a friend of Crystal's?"

"Right."

"How awful. And now Crystal is missing? You think . . . Oh, God, I hope not."

"If she comes here again, will you let me know?"

Mara looked Kali in the eye. "Only with her permission."

"Tell her I want to help. She can call me anytime. Day or night." Kali wrote her cell number and John's local number on a piece of paper and handed it to Mara. Better than a business card. Sometimes "attorney-at-law" could be a barrier.

She gestured toward the auditorium. "Do you mind if I talk to the kids?"

"Go ahead. I should warn you, they might not be willing, and even if they are, they won't always give you a straight story."

Gary Ellis came into the kitchen just then with two large bags of chips. He poured them into a bowl. "Is everything ready?"

Mara nodded, and the three of them carted the remaining food into the hall, where the number of kids milling about had almost doubled since Kali first arrived. Gary gave a high-five to a scrawny boy with pants so baggy Kali wondered that he could walk in them. Mara handed out paper plates. A few kids raced to the table; most hung back or nonchalantly moseyed over. Kali wended her way through the group, photo in hand, asking about Crystal. In response, she got a lot of shrugs, a few wary glares, and a flash or two of hostility.

But one heavyset girl with yellowed teeth looked at the photo and tossed her head. "Her, she's such a snob."

"You know her?" Kali asked, barely containing her excitement.

"Not like we're friends or anything, but, yeah, I seen her around."

"Recently?"

"A week or two ago. She looked right through me, like she don't want nothing to do with me. Cut her hair real short, and bleached it. Totally fake blond. Like she's hot shit or something."

"Where did you see her?"

"Over by campus."

Kali wondered if she might have walked right by Crystal when she was on campus. Wouldn't that be ironic?

"She's in trouble, isn't she?" The girl's chin jutted forward.

"What makes you say that?"

"Well, you asking about her. Isn't no one ever comes here asking about any of us unless it's trouble."


The first thing Kali did when she walked back into John's house was check the window. Nothing broken, nothing amiss. Still, she wandered through the whole house, just to be sure. It was untouched, but depressingly empty without Bryce.

She took a quick shower, her second of the day, but she was hot and feeling at loose ends. The cool water refreshed her. A psychic cleansing as well as a physical one.

About four o'clock, her phone rang. She figured it might

be Bryce, who would be back home by now, or Sabrina, though, of course, she hoped it was Crystal.

Wrong on all counts. Her caller was Robert Winslow, Sloane's ex-husband. When Kali had called him initially she'd been thinking he might be able to give her insight into people with motives for killing Sloane. At this stage, she was less sure he'd be able to offer anything helpful.

"Sorry I didn't return your call before now," he said. "I've been out of the country."

"Thanks for getting back to me."

"I know I've met Sabrina, but I don't believe you and I have met, have we?"

"I don't think so. I never even met Sloane."

"I still have trouble believing she's dead." He paused to clear his throat. "Reed hasn't kept me in the loop. He never liked me much. Barely spoke to me at her funeral. Have they arrested anyone yet?"

"No arrests."

"Really?" Robert hesitated. "I know they were looking at your brother early on. I guess maybe they finally saw the light."

"The light?"

"John killing her. It didn't make a lot of sense to me."

"Why's that?" Kali asked, intrigued.

"He and Sloane were old friends," Robert told her. "Good friends despite their differences. There was a time I was actually jealous. The two of them were simpatico, even when they argued."

Kali took a breath. "Do you know John's dead, too?"

"What? No, I didn't know. How did it happen?"

"He drowned. The cops think it was an accident. He was . . . inebriated."

"Jesus." Robert sounded genuinely surprised. And genuinely confused. "So who do they think killed Sloane?"

"They still think it was John. They were close to arresting him when he died. They figure that's why he got loaded. Because he was worried. Or feeling guilty. Or something."

"How terrible. You have my sympathy."

The police had supposedly cleared Robert as a suspect, and there was nothing in talking to him that made Kali wary, but she was hesitant to share her suspicions about John's death with anyone who might conceivably have been part of it. "Yes," she said, "it was terrible."

"How can I help?"

She fell back on the original reason for her call. "You and Sloane kept in touch after your divorce?"

"Yeah. We got along better after than when we were married."

"Do you have any idea what might have gotten her killed? Anyone she was at odds with?"

Robert's laugh was empty of humor. "Sloane could be irritating, no doubt about it. But she never mentioned anything to me about a big blowup or anyone who had it in for her."

"Did she talk about John? About wanting him fired?"

"I tried to stay clear of the whole Logan dynasty. What went on in the company was her business, not mine."

"What about the young college student who was living with her? Did Sloane talk about her?"

"Only in passing. Sloane was in her element with that girl. She always wanted children. Maybe if we'd had them our marriage would have worked out." He sounded wistful. "This young woman was someone Sloane could *save*. A hardworking, deserving youngster who'd fought the odds to get ahead. Sloane had a soft spot for that sort of thing."

There was none of the bitterness Kali was used to hearing when people talked about an ex-spouse. "Why did the two of you divorce, if you don't mind my asking?"

Another short laugh. "Years of rubbing each other the wrong way, I guess. One day we just looked at each other and said, 'This is silly.' The spark was gone. We were moving in different directions. No kids, so there wasn't any real reason to stay married." Robert paused. "The cops cleared me of her murder, if that's what you're thinking. Besides, if I was going to get upset it would have been when I learned she was involved with some other guy, right? Not months later."

Janet Fisher had also said that Sloane had been seeing someone. Had the cops questioned him? "Do you know who it was?" Kali asked.

"A married man, which is pretty ironic since it was my fooling around on her that finally pushed us over the edge. He was local. In Tucson, I mean."

"Do you know his name?"

"Something unusual. Emory. Ennis. Erskine. Something along those lines. He had a kid. A girl about seventeen or eighteen. That bothered her. Sloane didn't talk about it much but she did slip up and tell me she felt bad about the kid."

Kali flashed on the nameplate she'd seen on Detective Shafer's desk. Her heart thudded into her throat. "Could it have been Erling?"

"Yeah, could be. You know him? Is he a suspect?"

"You said the cops cleared you," Kali noted, her pulse racing in her ears. "Who was it who questioned you?"

"A cop here in L.A. A Hispanic guy. And I talked over the phone with someone in the Tucson Sheriff's Department. A woman."

"Michelle Parker?"

"Could be. I don't remember."

Was Erling Shafer, the lead detective on the case, the man with whom Sloane had been having an affair? No wonder he'd been in such a hurry to pin the crime on John.

# CHAPTER 34

Monday morning Kali picked up the phone to call Michelle Parker. She punched in the first three numbers, then put the phone down again. She'd spent a good part of the night wrestling with the best way to handle her suspicions about Detective Shafer. Talk to Shafer directly? He'd most likely deny everything and that would be the end of it. Go to the top? Kali had no idea what the personalities and internal politics of the sheriff's department were. If they were so inclined, the big brass could circle the wagons so fast she'd be trampled. The press? Better as a last resort.

In the end, she picked up the phone and again punched in Michelle's number. It wasn't a perfect solution, but it was the best she could come up with.

"I'd like to talk to you," Kali said when Michelle answered. "Alone."

"Is this about Hayley Hendrix?"

"I don't know. It could be." Kali hadn't yet sorted through the repercussions of what she'd learned from Sloane Winslow's ex-husband, and she wasn't ready to rule out anything.

"I can meet you here at the station any time before noon," Michelle told her.

Kali hesitated. "Is there someplace else?"

"What were you thinking?"

"Somewhere we could get a cup of coffee maybe?" Jeez, she made it sound like she was suggesting a social meeting. "It's just that I'd rather not run into Detective Shafer."

Silence. Michelle must have been weighing her response.

"I'll explain why when we get together," Kali told her.

"Okay." Michelle's tone was wary, but at least she'd agreed. "There's a Java Joe's a couple of blocks from here." She gave Kali the location. "In an hour?"

"I'll be there."

Kali arrived first. Java Joe's was a small space, sandwiched between a UPS Store and a pet supply outlet. Inside, a handful of tables and easy chairs gave the place a homey ambiance, and the air was filled with the welcoming aroma of fresh coffee. Kali was in line to place her order when her cell phone rang. She fumbled around in her purse before retrieving it and picking up. The private investigator Doug Simon was calling.

"I'm in San Diego and wanted to give you a quick status report," he said.

"You've talked to Ray Adams?"

"I have. The girl in the photo is definitely his daughter."

Kali noticed a man with a newspaper two tables away giving her the evil eye. He pointed to a sign showing a red circle with a slash superimposed on the graphic of a cell phone. She stepped outside, where the heat rising off the asphalt parking lot hit her full force. She almost turned around and went back inside. Nasty glares be damned.

"Does he know where she is?" Kali asked.

"No, and he didn't seem interested in finding out. He and his new wife haven't talked to the girl in about ten months."

Kali pressed herself into the small spot of shade under the overhang at Java Joe's. Not that it helped much. "So she's a runaway?"

"More like a mutual parting of the ways from what I gather, except, of course, the girl's a minor child. I have to be honest with you, parents like that really stick in my craw."

"Their letting her go, you mean?"

"That, and everything that led up to it," Simon said. "Best I can tell, after Ray walked out on Martha and the child, he never looked back. Maybe he sent birthday cards, though I wouldn't bet on it. He had virtually no contact with his daughter until Martha died, and then he only took her in because there wasn't anyone else. He and the second wife have two little kids of their own. Wifey wasn't at all happy about having the girl 'horn in'—that's the way she put it—on their family."

"Crystal's mother had just died, for God's sake. Does the woman have no compassion?"

"Very little, I gather. But Ray's not much better. His own daughter, and he doesn't care." Simon's disgust was evident in his tone. It was a sentiment Kali shared.

"How long did Crystal live with them?" she asked.

"Almost two years. According to them, she was difficult from the get-go. Mouthy, causing trouble. They finally got fed up and kicked her out."

Kali had been roughly the same age as Crystal when her own mother had died. She knew firsthand how teenage pain often disguised itself as anger. Especially when no one was there for you. The girl needed love and comfort, not a boot out the door.

"What kind of trouble did she get into?" Kali asked.

"Nothing so terrible. I managed to talk to one of her teachers, who said the girl wasn't a problem at school. Maybe not the most diligent student, but she attended classes, did her work, followed the rules. She did fall in with a bad crowd—parties, drugs, probably sex. But we're talking about an upper-middle-class area here, not gang-banger territory. No trouble with the law, either."

"When she left home, her parents didn't want to know where she went?"

"She was seeing some boy, which I gather was part of the problem—"

"Clayton?"

Simon sounded surprised. "How'd you know about him?"

"I don't know anything but the name. The wife mentioned it when I called there looking for Raelene."

"Well, the girl and this Clayton went off together. Supposedly to Arizona, where he had a grandmother. The Adamses more or less figured Crystal was no longer their problem."

The man who'd glared at Kali earlier exited the shop and glared at her again. She turned her back. "Do you have any information on the boy's grandmother?" Kali asked. "Name? Address?"

"I'm working on it. That is, if you want me to."

"Absolutely. Thanks."

She returned the phone to her purse and headed back inside, where she got herself a cup of coffee and a biscotti. She'd just sat down at a table near the window when she spotted Michelle Parker crossing the parking lot. The detective had a brisk, sure stride and an easy manner that Kali liked. Under different circumstances she could imagine they might have been friends. But Michelle was a cop, with all of a cop's biases, suspicions, and predispositions. This was something Kali couldn't afford to forget.

Michelle nodded a greeting as she came through the door. She went to the counter and got her own cup of coffee, then joined Kali at the table.

"No trouble finding the place, I see." Michelle shook a packet of artificial sweetener into the cup. "The place is a little funky but I prefer to patronize local establishments rather than Starbucks."

"Me too. On principle, and it's usually better coffee." Kali broke off a piece of biscotti. "Any progress on the Hendrix investigation?"

"Nothing I can talk about."

"But you're looking at connections between her murder and Olivia Perez's?"

Michelle fixed Kali with a penetrating look, then nodded.

Kali took some comfort in the fact that the detective had actually listened to her.

"We're also looking at your brother's connection to both women," Michelle added, then took a sip from her mug.

"What makes you think there is one?"

She gave Kali a look that said, "Let's not play around

here." "We've established his connection to the Winslow/ Perez murders," she said. "And we know he asked about Hayley Hendrix at the Crazy Coyote. I think it's pretty clear there's a link of some sort."

"And now you've found Hayley's wallet with the Logan Foods number in it."

Michelle looked up. "How'd you know that?"

"I heard it from Carmen Escobar. She's the attorney representing Olivia's parents in the civil suit against my brother." Kali chewed on her cheek for a moment. "A better question might be, how'd Escobar hear about it?"

Michelle shook her head. "It wasn't from me."

"What about Detective Shafer?"

"No way. That's not how he operates." The detective leaned forward, both forearms on the table. "It would be helpful if you'd level with us."

"I've already told you what I know," Kali said. She silently carved out an exception for the video she'd seen on John's computer and for Crystal Adams, but she wasn't ready to share that information just yet. Besides, the cops had Crystal's name too. Maybe they'd even located the girl.

Kali wrapped both hands around her mug. "When you were first working Sloane Winslow's murder, did you look into her love life?"

"You must know as well as I do that that's always an avenue of investigation."

"Did you find anything?"

Michelle gave her an amused smile. "What makes you think you're privy to any of this?"

"Just give me a general idea. I may have information for you."

A heavy sigh. "Winslow had a few dates with a man she met through a friend who lives in L.A., but it went nowhere. We did talk to him. Also to the ex-husband. We cleared both of them." Michelle ran a hand through her short, dark hair, feathering the sides away from her face. "So what was it you wanted to see me about?"

Kali leaned back. "Tell me about Detective Shafer."

"What about him?"

"Is he a good cop? Do you trust him?"

"Yes on both counts. I also admire him. He truly cares about his cases and about serving the community."

"What about his personal life?"

The detective shook her head with growing impatience. "What's this about?"

"He's married, right? Does he have a teenage daughter?"

"Yes." The response was wary, hesitant.

"Whose idea was it that you be the one to interview Sloane Winslow's ex-husband?"

Michelle eyed her quizzically. "How'd you know it was me?"

"He told me."

"You've been getting around, haven't you?" She took a sip of coffee, then shrugged. "We often divide up the interviews. I can't recall who decided I'd make the call, but as lead detective, Shafer would have the final word." She checked her watch. "Unless you've got something real to tell me, I need to get going."

Kali took a breath. "Sloane Winslow's ex-husband told me that Sloane had been romantically involved with a married man named Erling. And that the man had a daughter about seventeen or eighteen years old."

Michelle's expression grew tight. "What are you insinuating?"

"You didn't know about it, did you? At the very least, it's a conflict. He should never have been assigned to this case. It raises questions about the whole investigation."

The detective recoiled. "Why are you telling me this?"

"It was either you or the higher-ups. I'm not saying I won't go to the top at some point, but I'm not out to cause trouble. People's private lives are their own. I'm not even positive the man she was seeing was Detective Shafer, but I'm guessing it was."

"I'm not—"

"My only interest in this is my brother. There's a strong probability he was murdered"—Kali help up a hand to ward off protest—"which is something you and Shafer have refused to take seriously. I don't think he killed Sloane Winslow, either. Shafer had his own personal reasons for wanting the case wrapped up and John was a handy suspect."

Michelle leaned back, crossed her arms. "Erling Shafer isn't that kind of cop. He wouldn't railroad a case against an innocent man."

"No matter what was at stake?"

"No matter what," Michelle said firmly.

"Maybe he didn't do it intentionally," Kali conceded. "But he didn't come clean about his affair with Sloane Winslow, either. He didn't remove himself from an investigation he had no business being part of. His hands aren't exactly squeaky clean."

"Assuming you're even right about this supposed affair."

Kali conceded the point with a nod but argued her position. "Erling is not a common name."

"Your brother had motive, means, and opportunity. There were reasons he was our prime suspect," Michelle said. "And now a tie-in with Hayley. His hands aren't squeaky clean, either."

The whir of a blender whipping up an iced coffee concoction momentarily filled the air. Kali waited until the noise abated. "Now that you have this new information, don't you think you should reexamine those reasons?"

Michelle pushed back her chair, leaving her half-full cup of coffee on the table. "Why didn't you go directly to Shafer with this?"

"I want to make sure the information doesn't get buried."

"How do you know I won't bury it?"

"Because then you'd be a party to the same charade. You wouldn't do that." Kali hoped she was reading Michelle correctly.

The detective held her gaze for a moment, then rose from the table. "Think about your own charade, pretending you know nothing about John's involvement with Hayley. People in glass houses should be careful about throwing out accusations."

Kali thought of the shattered window at John's. She wondered if the detective's choice of words was deliberate.

# CHAPTER 35

Erling was leaving the courtroom where he'd spent the morning testifying in an armed robbery case when Michelle Parker caught up with him. She fell into step as he headed for the elevator.

"Hey, Michelle. What are you doing here?" He hadn't expected her, but he was ready for some good news. "A break on the Hendrix case?"

The address on the map they'd found in Hayley's car had turned out to be a vacant rental unit. A lot pricier than what he assumed Hayley could afford, but she might have had a sugar daddy in the wings somewhere, or even a potential roommate. It was an angle they were pursuing, but getting through to the investment company that owned the place was proving difficult.

Michelle wasn't smiling. "Hoping to catch you."

The elevator was jammed. Erling waited until they were outside, without extraneous ears to listen in, before he asked the obvious next question.

"What's up, then?"

"Let's take a walk." Michelle pushed through the courthouse doors without looking back to see if he was following.

Alarm bells sounded in Erling's head. Michelle was a straight shooter. She didn't play games and she didn't go in for dramatics. Yet she was clearly upset. Had something happened to Deena or Mindy? His heart pounded like a sledgehammer in his chest before he convinced himself it wasn't that. Michelle's manner was too brusque. Maybe something in her own life? A serious illness? A job offer elsewhere too good to ignore?

He hustled after her. "What is it?"

She stopped in a shady spot at the edge of the plaza and turned to face him. "Were you involved with Sloane Winslow?"

For a moment Erling was too stunned to speak. "Was . . . I . . . involved?"

She crossed her arms. "Involved. Romantically involved. Sexually involved. Personally involved. Whatever."

So there it was. The bullet he thought he'd dodged. Erling considered denying it. What proof could she have? But a lie would only dig him in deeper.

Michelle waited for him to speak, her eyes boring into him.

He could simply refuse to respond. Take affront that she'd even ask such a question. But Michelle was perceptive. And a lie was a lie, no matter how it was disguised.

"At one time," he said at last. His mouth was so dry he had trouble speaking. "It was over by the time she was killed."

"Jesus." Michelle feathered her hands through her hair, turned away from him and then back again. "Why didn't you speak up? Ask for the case to be reassigned?" She hit her head with an open palm in the sort of dramatic play he'd just told himself she wasn't capable of. "Because then you'd have to admit to the affair, right? Better just to sweep it under the rug and hope no one ever found out."

"It wasn't something I was proud of."

"What, the affair or lying about it?"

"Both."

"What if it had come out at trial? This could have blown our case against John O'Brien right out of the water." She gave an exasperated sigh, then looked at him with an expression he'd never seen before. "You didn't have anything to do with *O'Brien's* death, did you?"

Erling was appalled. "I hope that's not a serious question."

But it must have been, because she was waiting for an answer.

"You can't honestly think I'm a murderer."

"I don't know what to think anymore. You were quick to latch on to O'Brien as a suspect. As I recall, you were the one champing at the bit to arrest him. If the DA hadn't raised some issues . . ."

"They weren't issues, Michelle. It was more a matter of making sure we'd crossed all the t's and dotted all the i's."

"That's called making sure you've got probable cause for an arrest." Her voice snapped with anger. "Shit, Erling. This throws the whole investigation wide open. Maybe O'Brien's sister is right. Maybe he didn't do it. It's something to think about, especially in light of evidence that he may have been murdered. We don't even know that Sloane Winslow was the intended victim. Not with Olivia Perez being a friend of Hayley Hendrix's."

"If anything," Erling said, trying to make his words sound reasonable, "we've got more on John O'Brien now than we did earlier."

Michelle shook her head, not so much in disagreement as confusion and dismay. "I don't know. It's a mess. We've got to take a fresh look at everything. Rather, *I* have to take a fresh look at everything. You need to take yourself off this investigation."

"If this gets assigned to a different team," Erling protested, "it will take them weeks to get up to speed."

"What, you think I'm not up to speed?"

"I didn't—"

"And you know one of the first names that's going to come up as a possible suspect, don't you?" She pointed a finger at him. "Yours."

He took a breath. "I know I messed up not coming clean about my relationship with Sloane. Believe me, I've agonized over that. But for personal reasons—"

"Like screwing around on your wife."

He hadn't expected sympathy from Michelle, but neither had he expected quite so much anger. It brought him up short and made him realize anew what a mess he'd made of things.

He nodded. "You're right. I . . . I wasn't sure my marriage could take it if Deena found out. But I haven't compromised the investigation. I swear to that."

"I was so happy to be partnered with you," Michelle lamented. "I admired and respected you. I wanted to learn from you. I never thought you were someone who—"

"Could be human too?"

"That's a lame excuse."

Erling spread his hands. "I've admitted I was wrong. What more do you want? I can't undo what's done."

She'd been glaring at him but now she looked away. "It's a disappointment is all. I had you pegged for a better man."

Her words cut to the quick. There wasn't much he could say in response.

Michelle turned on her heel, back toward the station. "I'm going to be spending the rest of the day going over the file. Let me know when you've spoken to the lieutenant."

Erling felt beads of perspiration forming on his forehead. Talking to the lieutenant would be tough, but not half as tough as admitting to Deena what he'd done.

As Erling watched Michelle's retreating form, his stomach knotted with shame and regret, and with dread about what would follow.

# CHAPTER 36

As she was leaving Java Joe's, Kali called Sabrina, but her sister didn't call back until Kali was in line at the grocery, where she'd stopped to pick up lunch from the salad bar. A morning of coffee and biscotti had left her feeling queasy, and she was hoping a dose of healthy greens might be a remedy. She suspected, though, that her discomfort had more to do with recent discoveries than with what was in her stomach.

"You think she'll follow through?" Sabrina asked after Kali had reported on her conversation with Michelle Parker.

"The odds are better than if I'd gone straight to the top. The big guns usually have their sights trained on public image and putting the right spin on things. I was afraid they'd stonewall the entire incident."

Kali had reached the cashier. She tucked the phone against her shoulder and paid for the salad, then headed for her car. "How are you doing?"

"Okay. And Peter's being very sweet. For all his flaws he's a decent man and a good father."

"That's nice. What about the gambling?"

"He's getting help. And we've set up a meeting with a financial adviser about paying off the debts." Sabrina sounded more upbeat than she had in days. "I think it's going to work out."

"I'm so glad."

"I've been thinking about the kids at Sunshine House," Sabrina said. "It's so sad. Our boys coming first is one thing Peter and I have always agreed on."

"And it shows. They're great kids." As Kali neared the car, the signal began to break up. "The connection's fading," she said. "I'll talk to you later."

The message light on John's answering machine was blinking when Kali arrived home. Five calls, all of them hang-ups, and all identified as "private" on the caller ID log. Telemarketers, Kali concluded. Anyone who knew her would have left a message.

Kali poured Pellegrino water over ice, added a wedge of lime, and had just popped the top of the plastic salad container when the phone rang again. She answered it, feeling mildly irritated.

"Hello."

The sound of breathing greeted her on the other end.

"Hello?" she said again.

"Too bad about the window." The voice was male and throaty. Not one she recognized.

Kali's skin prickled. "Who's this?"

"Guess you're having something of a *rocky* stay here in Tucson." His laugh was a mirthless bark.

"What do you want?"

"Face facts, dear. Your brother isn't the upstanding guy you thought he was. Why not cut your losses and go back home?"

"Who are you?" Kali's heart was racing. She glanced through the window, half expecting to see a masked figure watching from outside. The yard was as placid and peaceful as always. Still, she felt like a bug under a microscope.

"I'm simply looking out for you," the caller said. "I'd hate for something . . . unfortunate to happen."

"Is that a threat?"

"I'm trying to help. There are so many dangers out there."

Kali dropped the phone into its cradle and rubbed her hand against her pant leg, as if she could wipe away the slime of the call. Her heart was pounding. She waited, thinking he might call back. When he didn't, she checked caller ID again—another "private"—then took a deep breath and punched in star sixty-nine.

A recorded message informed her the return-call service was unavailable for the number she was trying to reach.

Kali hung up. She realized she was shaking. The rock thrown through the window had not been a simple act of vandalism. Someone was trying to scare her off. Someone didn't want her digging into . . .

Into what? That was the key.

She remembered the beige sedan she'd seen earlier. Maybe she hadn't been imagining that it was following her.

Her pulse fluttering wildly, she backed away from the phone. She was being silly, she knew, but she couldn't bring herself to turn her back on the suddenly sinister instrument. She checked all the doors and windows in the house and looked out to the street. Nothing.

She wasn't in imminent danger, she decided. The caller wanted her to drop her investigation and go home. If he'd wanted to harm her, he'd have done so. Just as he hadn't harmed Sabrina the day he'd tossed the rock.

But if Kali didn't back off, all that could change.

She thought of contacting Michelle, but she had no proof of the threatening call. And Kali felt she'd laid enough on the detective already. Though she was no longer hungry, she made herself swallow a few bites of the salad. Her nerves weren't being helped by the fact she'd eaten nothing so far today but caffeine and sugar.

The CDs and book Sabrina had pulled from John's Porsche were on the kitchen counter. While she nibbled, Kali reached for the book and read the blurb on the back. Political intrigue and international machinations—not the sort of book that generally appealed to her. When she opened the cover to read the inside jacket, the business card John had been using to mark his place fell to the floor. As Kali leaned over to pick it up, the name on the card caught her eye.

Wayne Clark.

One of the names she'd found in John's datebook. The man with the Australian accent who'd left a phone message on John's machine.

What caused her breath to catch were Clark's job title and company: *Wayne Clark, Executive Producer, Nice'n'Naughty Productions.* A post office box and phone number, both in Tucson, were listed. On the back of the card, someone had scribbled a couple of names and phone numbers.

Nice'n'Naughty Productions had a . . . well, a *naughty* sound to it. Kali was reminded of the porn sites John had visited. The DVDs in his cupboard and the videos he'd downloaded. She went into his study to look the company name up on the Web. Maybe she was wrong. Maybe Nice'n'Naughty had to do with manners instead of sex. Or with dog training. But once she saw the Web site, she knew her initial instinct had been correct.

Kali's knowledge of the porn industry was limited. True, she'd watched a couple of videos with a former boyfriend, though she'd been more turned off than titillated. And sometimes she'd inadvertently click on an e-mail that slipped past her spam filter and wind up with a screen of X-rated images. What little she knew beyond that she'd picked up here and there from reading or from news coverage. Porn was widely available and more mainstream than it used to be, but for most people it was still part of a seamy underworld they tried to avoid.

With trepidation, she reached for the phone and punched in Wayne Clark's number. Just when she expected voice mail to click in, a man picked up. She recognized the cadence of Clark's accent right away.

"This is Kali O'Brien," she said, "John's sister."

If Clark was surprised to hear from her, he didn't show it. "Such terrible news about John's death. My condolences to the whole family. I know I should have dropped a note or something. Sorry to be such a bludger."

Kali could hear conversation in the background, and over that, a female voice sounding impatient. Clark must have put his hand over the mouthpiece briefly because there was a muffled "Give me a minute" before he came back to the phone.

"If you're calling about whatever money your brother had coming," Clark continued, "you need to talk to our accounting people. Or better yet, have the attorney handling the probate get in touch."

"Money?" Kali wondered if Clark had confused John with someone else.

"Payouts are made on a semiannual basis."

"What payouts?"

"Return on investment. John was one of our backers. Isn't that what you're calling about?"

John in the pornography business? "Not really," Kali answered, confusion overriding dismay. "I was calling because my brother met with you a few days before he died."

"Ah, that." Clark didn't seem inclined to elaborate.

It was a conversation better handled face-to-face, she decided. "Is there a time when we can get together?"

"We're in production right now, so the days are pretty busy."

"How about after work?"

Clark seemed to hesitate, then finally acquiesced. "This evening, around seven? We should be winding down by then."

"That's fine."

He gave Kali an address and directions for finding the door and buzzer once she was there. "It sounds more complicated than it is," he explained.

"I'll figure it out. See you at seven."

The agitation over the ominous phone call was overshadowed now by uneasiness. And, yes, curiosity over John's ties to the porn industry.

\* \* \*

Kali had taken the tourist tour of Universal Studios in Los Angeles, and she'd been on a small company's set where a friend of hers once worked as a production assistant, but when it came to porn films she didn't have any idea what to expect. She'd sort of assumed they were shot in the back bedroom of a run-down bungalow in some seedy neighborhood where every house had bars on the windows.

Nice'n'Naughty Productions, however, was housed in a sleek and modern warehouse-like building out by the airport. The entrance was on the east side, off the paved and striped parking lot. Kali rang the bell and a buzzer sounded, signaling her to open the door. She stepped into a small, carpeted reception area that resembled the waiting room at her dentist's, right down to the artificial, and slightly dusty, ficus tree in the corner.

A moment later, one of the two interior doors opened and a man emerged.

"You must be John's sister," he said, offering his hand. "I'm Wayne Clark."

He was in his early thirties, of medium height and build, though he had a bit of a bulge around his middle. He was wearing blue Bermuda shorts and a yellow polo shirt. She could more easily picture him teeing off on a golf course than filming hot and heavy sex.

Wayne ran a hand through his hair. It was golden and wavy, curling around his ears. "Like I said, I'm sorry about John. I didn't know him all that well—I try to leave the business end of things to others—but he seemed like a nice guy."

As he talked, Wayne led her past several offices, a sound booth, an editing room, and a couple of production studios. Through the glass panel of one of the studios, Kali could see a cameraman on rails positioning a shot on the set of an empty living room. A pretty high-class living room, Kali thought. Oriental rug, overstuffed couch, mock fireplace, and big-screen televison.

Clark's gaze followed hers. "Fun's over for today. He's

just setting up for tomorrow's shoot. We've got the girl-girl in the morning, and a girl-girl-boy after that."

"A what?"

"The scenes. Most of our productions incorporate the standard variations. It's pretty formulaic, but you've got to have them because customers expect it."

A young woman in workout pants and a T-shirt emerged from an area to Kali's right. "The shower sucks," she said to Wayne. "Still no water pressure. I thought you were going to get that fixed."

"I thought it was fixed, love."

"Yeah, sure."

"I'll get the guy back out tomorrow."

"*Before* I go on." She tossed her canvas tote over one shoulder and strode out the door.

Wayne turned to Kali. "That's Amber Lane. She's a pain in the ass sometimes, but she's dynamite in action."

Kali tried not to imagine the action but failed. She could feel herself blush.

"You want a soda or something?" Wayne asked her.

"No thanks."

He grabbed one for himself from the fridge in an alcove off the hallway, then pointed her to an office with a wide wooden desk, a couple of comfortable-looking chairs, a walnut bookcase, and a credenza. As classy as the typical law office, but in place of the customary diplomas and awards of recognition hanging on the wall, Clark's office offered framed blowups of graphic sex scenes.

Kali studied them while trying to appear that she was looking elsewhere.

"Have a seat," Clark said, pointing to a chair. He ignored the desk and sat opposite her.

She pulled her gaze from the photos on the wall. "So you make porn films?"

Clark winced. "We prefer the term 'adult content' or 'X-rated.' It's all strictly legal."

"For Web sites?"

"No, except for what we put out as teasers. The Web stuff is generally trash. Our stuff comes out on DVDs and cable. Hotels are a huge market. Insatiable, if you'll excuse the term." He grinned and popped the tab on his soda. "But the home consumer market is a gangbuster, too. Americans spend over ten billion a year on adult entertainment. Did you know that? It's a huge and profitable business."

In spite of herself, Kali was impressed by the numbers. "You make feature films, then?"

Clark nodded. "Everything from artsy, soft core to really hard core, though my personal preference is for stuff in the middle. Some of the schlock out there, especially on the Web, you get no story at all, clunky dialogue, amateur filming, sometimes just a single handheld camera. We try to be a step above." He paused to down a gulp of soda. "Well, we try to be several steps above, but I can't say we always get there. Trouble is, too many people don't give a rat's ass about quality. The market gets flooded with crappy product, and then consumers, they start to think that's the norm."

"Sounds like an uphill battle," Kali offered lamely. She wasn't sure that *quality* and *porn* belonged in the same sentence.

"Isn't that the truth," Wayne said. "We want to be known for quality. Good sets, good plots, attractive people—actors who can actually remember their lines. Everything you'd expect in a mainstream movie. We don't do the extreme stuff—no shots of women getting beaten, raped, suffocated, or strangled. No slasher films and no sadoerotic stuff."

"How commendable." She couldn't conceal the sarcasm.

Clark gave her an amused smile. "I take it you're not a fan."

"Not really, no."

He leaned back and held up his hands as if fending off attack. "Not one of those righteous crusaders who wants to dictate how others live, I hope."

"No, not that either. So what's your role in the company?"

"I started out as a director but I've gotten more into the production end. A good script and the right talent make all the difference. I try to make sure we've got both. Not the big-name stars, obviously. We can't afford them. But folks starting out, fresh talent, there's a lot to be said for that too. We're not in the same league as the major studios, but we're doing well and growing."

"Major studios?"

"VCA, Vivid, Wicked Pictures. They're known for big-budget films. Most of the biggies are in the Valley, near L.A. It's the epicenter of the adult film industry. But smaller studios are springing up around the country."

"And my brother," Kali asked reluctantly, "what was his role?"

"Strictly financial. Small time, in fact. He wasn't one of the major players." Wayne took another long swig of soda. "The bigger studios, they have corporate backing. Some are even publicly traded. We rely on private investors."

"So that's what you and John met about recently?"

Wayne shook his head. "No. Like I said, I don't handle the financial stuff. That was the first time I'd met your brother, in fact. I got a call from our financial guy saying John wanted to meet with me. About a girl."

"A girl?" Kali's mouth felt dry.

"That's what he said. I assumed your brother had a friend who was trying to get into the business and he wanted to use his contacts to find a role for her. But that wasn't it. He had a photograph of three young women. Wanted to know if I recognized any of them."

Kali swallowed. "Did you?"

"One of them. Dark hair, exotic looking. A real beauty, which is rarer than you'd think in this business. She'd been murdered a couple of days earlier and John seemed to think he was a suspect."

"Olivia Perez," Kali said, as much to herself as Wayne. "She'd worked for you?"

"Only a couple of films. Minor roles. To look at her, a hot babe like that, you'd think she'd be a natural. But she had no charisma on the set. I mean zip. She did a scene with Randy Gibbons, who's like our leading male, and she could barely manage to look interested. Her only enthusiasm was for collecting the paycheck at the end of the day."

Randy. The good-looking guy with the great body Joanna Sommers had told her about seeing at the mall. Not a boyfriend, but a porn star coworker.

Clark tossed his empty can. "Happens way too often. Girls come to the industry because they think it's an easy road to good money. They all think they're going to be the next Jenna Jameson. Most of them bail pretty quick."

"Jenna's a big name?"

He laughed. "Guess you're really *not* a fan, are you? Yeah, she's probably the most successful porn star ever. She still makes films but she's also CEO of her own company and brings in as much money as any mainstream celebrity. Maybe more."

Kali had never considered herself a prude, but she was beginning to realize she was more buttoned-down than she imagined. "When did Olivia start working for you?"

"Last spring. But it was the other girls in the photo John was most interested in. I didn't recognize either of them. I gave him the names of other folks in the industry who might have worked with them. And that was it."

Kali remembered the names and numbers written on the back of Wayne Clark's business card. She showed them to him. "Were these the contacts you gave John?"

"Yeah. I never talked to him after that, so I don't know if he had any luck."

"Did he by any chance tell you *why* he was looking for the girls?"

Wayne shook his head. "I didn't ask and he didn't offer. Sometimes it's best not to know."

So true, Kali thought. Unfortunately, not knowing was a luxury she couldn't afford just now.

# CHAPTER 37

Erling stared at the reports on his desk. It was impossible to concentrate. Rather than working on his open cases, he'd spent the afternoon trapped in his mind, watching his marriage and his career crumble.

Why hadn't he asked to be taken off the case the moment he recognized Sloane was one of the victims? It would have been embarrassing, but it wouldn't have permanently impacted his job. And Deena might never have heard.

Except, as Sloane's ex-lover, Erling would have come under suspicion himself. His job and his marriage *would* have been affected. Just as they were now.

He hadn't avoided anything. He'd only postponed, and compounded, his problem.

Erling shuffled the reports. He read the words, but nothing sank in. He squirmed in his seat, wiped the dampness from the back of his neck. What had possessed him to get involved with Sloane in the first place?

He'd known it was wrong, but even now he couldn't honestly say he regretted it. Sloane had been so alive. Vibrant and sexy in a way Deena had never been. Sloane tapped into feelings he'd thought were long dead. Maybe it was simply the novelty of the relationship, the rush of feeling desired, the excitement of breaking the rules. Or maybe it was the electric charge that had sparked between them the moment they'd met. Her blue-gray eyes had grazed his skin, taking stock, causing his flesh to tingle.

It wasn't that Erling loved Sloane more than Deena, or in place of Deena. He wasn't sure he'd even loved her at all. Rather, she was an addiction. He'd craved her and the dizzying pleasure of the here and now. Like a glutton in a candy shop, he'd been focused only on the next bite. It had been about him and how Sloane made him feel, not about Deena or their marriage.

But no longer. Tonight his two worlds would collide.

And Deena would be caught in the crush. Erling felt the weight of his wrongdoing like shackles on his soul. He couldn't bear to think of the ways he'd harmed her.

They'd married right out of college. Deena was only the second woman he'd been with, and the first had been little more than a drunken one-night stand. He was taken by her warmth, her laughter, the fact that she wanted him. *Him.* It was a heady feeling.

In retrospect, Erling realized that he'd loved the idea of Deena as much as the woman herself. But over the years of their marriage, he'd grown to care about her more deeply than he'd ever imagined. She was a warm and selfless woman, maybe a little controlling at times, but also someone who propped him up when he needed it, taught him to laugh at petty annoyances and not to take himself too seriously. But after Danny's death, she'd retreated into a place where Erling wasn't invited. Maybe he hadn't tried as hard as he should have. He realized that now, but after all, he'd been hurting, too.

The unbearable loss of their son was something neither of them would ever get over. But instead of holding tight to each other in their grief, they'd pulled apart. On the surface, nothing changed. They didn't argue or pout. Deena kissed him good-bye each morning, made his dinners, and inquired about his day. Erling checked the tires on her car, opened the jars with tight lids, chuckled at the stories she told about her students. They made love, comfortably if not passionately, but Erling sensed that the tiniest puff of ill wind would rip the fragile fabric of their marriage to shreds.

And now he'd opened the door to that wind.

Erling again rubbed his neck. He got up and walked to the men's room, where he washed his hands and splashed water on his face. He dried himself off with a rough paper towel from the dispenser and tossed it into the trash. A uniformed deputy entered the restroom and greeted Erling with a friendly nod.

"Must be nice to have that Winslow murder wrapped up." The deputy headed for the urinal.

"Yeah," Erling replied, aware of the strain in his own voice.

"You and Michelle did good."

"Thanks." Erling blotted his face again and headed back to his desk.

His family and his job. He'd made a mess of both. Not only hadn't he removed himself from the case, protests to Michelle aside, but he couldn't be certain he'd been totally objective in the investigation.

John O'Brien was clearly a person of interest. His name had surfaced right away. There was evidence linking him to the crime. But Erling wondered if, in his own self-interest, he hadn't taken the easy way out. He'd wanted the murders cleared and put away before anyone started asking questions. Before his connection to Sloane surfaced.

Erling looked around the congested and cluttered squad room that had been his home away from home for more than ten years now. He was a good cop. He knew that. Took pride in it. He didn't want to become anything less.

Swallowing the fear and remorse crowding his throat, Erling pulled the file on the Winslow/Perez murders and went through it again, detail by detail. Nothing jumped out at him.

At five-thirty he put it all away and went home to face Deena.

* * *

Deena was at the kitchen table, scissors in hand, cutting shapes out of multicolored construction paper. He surprised her by announcing he was taking her out to dinner.

"Right now?"

"Whenever you want."

Her eyes sparkled. "Half an hour? I need to get cleaned up."

Erling called and made reservations at one of their favorites, a restaurant that was a bit upscale without being pretentious.

"Are we celebrating something?" Deena asked when they were seated. Their table was by the window, away from the main artery of activity and noise.

"We don't have to have an occasion to go out to dinner, do we?"

"No, but you have to admit this spur-of-the-moment stuff is a bit unusual."

That was true. Maybe going out had been a mistake. "I guess I realized I don't tell you often enough how important you are to me and how much I love you."

She angled her head and smiled at him. "I sense there's a bit more to it than that, but maybe I should just shut up while I'm ahead."

Deena ordered scallops and Erling had prime rib. They both had wine. The food was delicious, but Erling could barely swallow. How did one begin to broach the subject of infidelity? Confession might be good for the soul, but it was hell on the digestive system.

"Anything more about Mindy's new boyfriend?" he asked, poking at his mashed potatoes.

"Only that there's definitely someone she's interested in. I overheard her talking on the phone in her room. I couldn't hear what she said, but the tone was a dead giveaway. Very different from the way she talks to her girlfriends. And I've noticed she's been paying more attention to what she wears."

Subtleties. It made Erling wonder what Deena had noticed about his own behavior. "Have you asked Mindy about him?"

"Not in so many words. We agreed to respect her independence, remember?"

"Easier said than done."

"That's true." Deena paused. "After Danny, I worry so much about her. I know you do, too." She touched Erling's hand. "But it's important that we don't burden her with our fears. She deserves her own life."

Erling nodded.

Deena gave him a secretive smile. "I noticed a new book of poetry on her bookshelf the other day. Looks like something a guy would give a girlfriend—soft leather cover, velvet ribbon marker. Not the sort of book that's assigned for English class."

"Maybe you should have a talk with her. She may think she's all grown up, but we both know what it's like to be young." Erling had taken so many risks at her age that the mere memory made him cringe still.

Deena patted his hand. "She's entitled to her life, honey. You worry too much. Your day is filled with bad guys, but for the rest of us, bad guys are a rarity."

"The *guy* part is enough of a worry."

Deena smiled. "Better get used to it."

She'd raised the subject of work. It was an ideal segue into the topic Erling wanted to discuss. He cleared his throat, but he couldn't bring himself to say the words.

"Speaking of which," Deena continued after a moment. "I saw in the paper that you finally identified that poor young woman whose body was found in the wash a couple of weeks ago. Do you have any idea who killed her?"

Erling shook his head. "We don't even have much of an identity. Just basic stuff—name and address. No next of kin, but we do have a lead on someone who may be a relative. A woman in Minnesota."

"Have you contacted her?"

"Not yet."

Deena grew quiet and Erling knew they were both remembering the call from the hospital following Danny's accident. It had come out of the blue—he'd been spending the afternoon at a buddy's house—and that one simple call had knocked their world off its foundation.

Now Erling was about to wield another hammer blow.

Deena speared a scallop. "You think her killer might be someone she knew?"

"Possibly. But she was apparently a friend of Olivia Perez's, the girl who was killed in that double homicide not long ago." *That double homicide where one of the victims was a woman I slept with.* His tongue itched with the words.

"You caught that killer, didn't you? An employee with a grudge against the older woman."

*Older woman.* Sensual, passionate Sloane. Erling felt a wracking hollowness in his gut. "We were pretty sure he was the guy. We were building a case when he died."

"But you don't know for sure?"

Erling shook his head, took a sip of water. He could feel his pulse racing. Here was another opening where he might move from the case to his own misconduct. He took a couple of breaths, but again the words wouldn't come.

"Two young women," Deena said slowly. She sounded worried. "You don't think there's a serial killer on the loose, do you?"

"The two murders don't fit the same pattern, but we can't rule out anything at this point."

She sighed and put her hand on his. "Not good dinner conversation, is it? How's your prime rib?"


When they arrived home, Erling pulled the car into the garage and turned off the engine. Then he turned to Deena before she could get out of the car.

"There's something I need to tell you, honey." Despite the dim interior light, he was able to make out the expression on her face. He watched as confusion gave way to alarm.

"What is it?" Deena asked, her voice husky with concern. "Are you sick?"

Erling shook his head, ashamed that her first thought had

been concern about him. "I meant what I said earlier about loving you."

"What's wrong? Has something . . . Oh, God." She covered her face with her hands. "I think I know where this is going. There's someone else, isn't there? Another woman."

"Not now. Not anymore. But we . . . I . . ." Erling's heart was in his throat. This was the hardest thing he'd ever done. "I was involved with someone last spring. It didn't last long."

Deena removed her hands from her eyes, but she didn't look at him. Nor did she say anything.

"I don't really know why I did it," Erling continued. "I'm ashamed. Deeply ashamed, and so sorry. You don't deserve this."

"No, I don't," she whispered. She bit her knuckle.

"I'm sorry," he said again. Never had words been so inadequate.

"Who was it?" Deena asked finally. Her voice was thin and ragged. "Anyone I know?"

Erling shook his head, but Deena wasn't looking at him. "It was the woman who was murdered," he said. "Sloane Winslow."

"The Logan Foods heiress?"

The description didn't fit Sloane any better than "older woman" had. "It's a family business," he said lamely.

"How did you meet her?"

"At a civic event."

Deena was crying now and trying not to, which only made her sobbing more plaintive. "When?"

"Last fall. It was a luncheon honoring community contributions of local businesses. I was one of the speakers. Sloane attended on behalf of Logan Foods."

"Someone introduced you?"

Erling shook his head. He could recall that afternoon as clearly as though it was yesterday. "We were seated next to one another at the head table."

"And you just somehow ended up sleeping with her?"

"More or less." Not that afternoon, but Erling had no doubt that the seed had been planted in both of their minds by then.

"*Why?*" It was a pathetic sound, like the meow of a hungry kitten.

Erling spread his hands, reaching for words that wouldn't hurt her further. How could he explain his behavior to Deena when he didn't really understand it himself?

"Never mind," she said. "I'm not sure I want to know." She reached for a tissue from her purse. "Why did it end? Because she died?"

"No, it was over before that. It was never anything serious."

"It's serious to me," Deena shot back.

"I never stopped loving you. You have to believe that."

"But screwing the heiress was more fun, right?" The tears had given way to outrage. "She was thinner, prettier, sexier, better in bed."

"It wasn't like that."

"Like hell." Deena's face contorted with anger. "Damn you!" She threw open the door and stormed out of the car.

Erling followed on her heels. He reached for her arm and she spun around, pushing him against the garage wall.

"Stay away from me."

"Deena, please."

"Please what?"

He didn't have an answer. He'd agonized so much about telling her, he hadn't thought how she'd react. It had been about him again, he realized, not her. With sudden clarity, Erling understood that Deena had been right all those times she'd accused him of being insensitive.

"Why are you telling me this, anyway?" she asked.

"I'm tired of keeping secrets."

"Great, unburden yourself so you feel better. How do you think I feel now?"

"Terrible," he said. "You must feel hurt, and angry, and humiliated. Totally devastated."

His words seemed to calm her some. She took a deep breath. "Right."

"I shouldn't have been involved in the investigation of her murder," Erling added. "I'm going to recommend that we take another look at the evidence."

"Fine. Whatever." Deena turned to go inside.

Erling cleared his throat. "I saw on our caller ID readout that Sloane called here. It was a few days before she was killed." He paused. "Did you talk to her?"

"That woman called you at home?" Deena asked shrilly. "I thought you said it was over by then."

"It was. I have no idea why she called. But I'm wondering if . . . maybe the call was important. Relevant to her death, I mean. You didn't speak with her?"

"No, thank God. She'd have gotten a kick out of that, I bet. The mistress playing coy with the unsuspecting wife."

Erling wanted to tell her that Sloane wasn't like that. But he knew he'd lost the right to say any such thing.

Deena headed straight for their bedroom and locked the door. Erling was sure she was allowing herself the tears she'd fought in the car. When she emerged twenty minutes later, her eyes were puffy and her face red. She handed him a folded set of sheets and a blanket. "You can come get your toothbrush and whatever else you need from the bathroom."

Another consequence he hadn't foreseen. "Where am I supposed to sleep?"

"The den or the living room—take your pick."

"You have every right to be angry, but shouldn't we—" He took one look at her expression and shut up.

When he'd retrieved his gear from their bathroom, Deena brushed past him into the bedroom and again locked the door. A few minutes later he heard her running a bath.

Mindy was in her room. She'd poked her head out long enough to say hello when they'd first come home, but she'd apparently picked up on the tension between them and had quicky retreated to her room. A good thing, really. Neither he nor Deena could have kept up a pretense of normalcy.

He prowled around the kitchen, though he wasn't hungry. The house seemed bleak and lifeless, like a place abandoned. But it was Erling who'd been abandoned. He hadn't realized how much he depended on the vitalizing energy of his family for comfort.

Finally, he poured himself a tumbler of scotch. What if Deena left him? Would he ever feel whole again? And how could he explain to Mindy what he'd done? He'd never be able to look her in the eye.

He already felt the pang of missing them.

He turned on the television and flipped through the channels. Nothing held his interest. Finally, he tiptoed down the hall. He could see from the crack under the door that the lights in the master bedroom were out. Later, Mindy's lights went out as well.

Erling chose the living room sofa because it was roomier than the one in the den. He remembered shopping for a replacement sofa with Deena. It was only last week but seemed a lifetime ago.

He spread the sheets and crawled between them, pulling the blanket over the top. He turned from side to side but he couldn't get comfortable. At a little after two, he got up to get a glass of water and stopped at Mindy's door. He opened it softly and stared at his sleeping daughter. Moonlight glimmered on her golden hair and fair skin. She had a tiny, rosebud mouth. He remembered how, as a baby, she'd suckled at her mother's breast while he'd watched with a contentment he'd never thought possible.

Mindy breathed evenly, the sleep of innocence. At times like this, she seemed still a child. *His* child. Erling loved his family. He didn't want to lose them.

Erling couldn't sleep. The lumpy couch was uncomfortable—too narrow to position himself any way but facing out, and too short to fully extend his legs. But it was the internal discomfort that kept him awake. Would Deena ever forgive him?

Finally abandoning the idea of sleep, he rose, left Deena a note telling her he loved her, and drove to work.

He was at his desk by seven. Michelle arrived half an hour later.

"Did you spend the night here?" she asked, joking.

He shook his head. "On the living room couch."

She stuck her purse in the bottom desk drawer and popped the lid on a cup of coffee. "Not by choice, I take it."

"I told Deena about Sloane Winslow."

Michelle nodded and sipped her coffee. Erling was grateful she didn't push for details.

"I told the lieutenant, too," Erling said.

"What did he say?"

"The case is going to be reassigned." Erling hadn't been canned or sent up for formal reprimand, but the lieutenant's seething displeasure had burned to Erling's core. "Until then," he said, "I want to wrap up what we can."

"Am I off it, as well?"

"I'm not sure." Erling knew Michelle would have to be a fool not to suspect him, but he pushed ahead anyway. It was either that or wallow in shame. "I've been going through the file on the murders," he said. "John O'Brien still looks good for them. We assumed Sloane was the primary target and found motive. Now, with the Hayley Hendrix connection . . . it does raise questions. I don't know what his motive might have been in targeting Olivia, but the witness report, the shoe print, the gun—they all point to O'Brien."

"But they don't directly link him to the crime."

Erling leaned back in his chair. "We know John O'Brien was at the Crazy Coyote. And his sister showed up at Hayley's apartment. There's also that slip of paper with the Logan Foods phone number in her wallet. Seems like O'Brien's an even better bet now than before."

"We're missing something," she said. "It hangs together but it doesn't make sense."

"Maybe O'Brien killed Hayley," Erling speculated. "Then Olivia found out and threatened to turn him in. Or blackmailed him."

Michelle shook her head. "Why kill Olivia when Sloane was around? Besides, he was asking about Hayley at the Crazy Coyote *after* she had been killed."

"Covering his tracks, maybe. If he killed her, it's only smart to act like he doesn't know where she is." Erling was clicking the end of his pen, a nervous habit that drove Michelle nuts. He stopped as soon as he caught her looking at him. "Could be Olivia shared her suspicions about John with Sloane, and that's what she and John were arguing about at dinner that night."

"So he killed them both." Michelle seemed to be trying the theory on for size. From her expression, it wasn't going well. "What about the other girl? Crystal Adams. John was asking about her at the Crazy Coyote, too. And the sister, Kali, recognized the name."

"Too bad she's not sharing." Erling stood up. "We need to talk to people who knew Olivia. Friends, family, people she worked with."

"We should have done that a long time ago. We would have, in fact, if you hadn't been so eager to blame it all on John O'Brien."

Erling looked down at his hands, then raised his eyes to hers. "I fucked up, okay? I'm trying to make it better."

Michelle nodded slowly. "Okay."

Not a resounding show of support, but it was better than nothing. "What say we start with that inn where she worked over the summer? You think they serve breakfast? I haven't eaten since last night and I'm starved."

Erling drove while Michelle pulled together a list of contacts for Olivia's friends. They had only a couple of names, but he knew the list would grow. Focusing on Sloane had been a mistake. A misstep that occurred because he'd been personally involved. That was why he should have stepped away from the case at the start.

"What about O'Brien's murder?" Michelle asked, closing her notebook. "How does that play in all this?"

"Are you thinking that's what happened? That he was murdered?"

Michelle frowned. "I know we wrote it off as the sister having trouble accepting the truth about her brother. But her points are valid. The housekeeper confirmed that John never ate mayonnaise and that the lights in the house were off when she came to work that morning. And he did have a doctor's prescription for Valium. Wouldn't he just take that instead of something he'd picked up illegally?"

"The housekeeper didn't see signs that anyone else had been there, did she? Aside from the jar of mayonnaise."

Michelle shook her head. "No, she was clear there was only one plate and one glass on the counter. She put them in the dishwasher when she cleaned up. But if his killer wanted to cover his tracks—"

"Our best bet is going at this through the victims we're sure about—Hayley, Olivia, and Sloane." Erling slowed for a dip in the road. Tucson was full of them. Every winter when it rained, some fool got stranded in three feet of water because he ignored the sign warning about entering when flooded. "Any word on Hayley's family?"

"Minneapolis police are going to show our sketch to the woman we think might be her mother. She's apparently an alcoholic with a taste for abusive men. The daughter was placed in foster care."

"When's the officer going to get out there?"

"Today." Michelle gazed out the car window. "I talked to Hayley's coworkers again. She wasn't much of a party animal and she wasn't into drugs. A couple of guys at the club apparently came on to her, so that's something we need to follow up on."

"Was John one of them?"

"I don't think so. Too bad the Crazy Coyote isn't the sort of place that asks for a resume. Then maybe we'd know more."

Erling tapped his fingers against the steering wheel. "Ditto with the apartment." The rental application Hayley had filled out hadn't been of any use aside from listing a Minnesota driver's license, which had put them on the track of the woman they were hoping turned out to be Hayley's mother.

"She and Olivia seem like a strange pair," Erling noted. Olivia's mother had confirmed the girls knew each other. "I wonder if they met through the friend who gave them the poetry books."

"The handwriting isn't John's," Michelle pointed out. "At least not according to his friend Reed Logan. And it *was* Kali who told us to check for the books."

Kali, again. Bad enough the woman was a thorn in his side; she could also be involved in some way. But Erling couldn't fathom how, and that made her meddling all the more irksome.

"I was thinking," Michelle said, "that maybe the books come into play as more than showing the girls had a common friend."

"Why would—"

"A guy who's stalking them, maybe. Someone who doesn't take rejection. A jealous lover. It's a long shot, but it's unusual for friends to have identical volumes of poetry from the same guy."

"We don't know it's a guy."

"Friends don't write inscriptions like that." Michelle consulted her notes. "The books are unusual. The hand tooling on the cover, the velvet ribbon page marker—it's got to be a small-press specialty item. If they were purchased locally, maybe we can find out where."

Erling's heart stopped. Hand tooling. Velvet ribbon. What was it Deena had said about the poetry book she'd discovered in Mindy's room?

"I think it's worth looking into," Michelle said, slipping her notes back into her pocket. "What is it? What are you thinking?"

Erling shook his head. *Don't start imagining the worst*, he told himself. *Lots of girls read poetry.*

"Nothing," he told Michelle.

But he couldn't forget Deena saying that Mindy had a new poetry book.

And a new guy.

# CHAPTER 38

"Kali O'Brien?"

"Yes," Kali answered warily. She'd assumed when she opened the door that the leather-skinned man on John's doorstep was a salesman or a neighbor who'd only recently learned of John's death—not someone who knew her name.

The man thrust a large envelope into her hands. "Have a good day." He turned and headed to his car.

Kali ripped open the envelope and skimmed the contents. A formal complaint, filed by Carmen Escobar on behalf of the Perez family.

With a trembling hand and growing agitation, she read the words of the complaint in greater detail. She'd been hoping the talk of a civil suit had been just that—talk. Idle grumbling borne of grief. Not so.

Kali's blood was boiling. She was certain it was the attorney, Carmen Escobar, who'd planted the seed for the lawsuit in the first place, and she'd done it purely for financial gain.

Her own financial gain.

*These cases almost always settle . . . It would be in both of our interests to settle this matter . . . The Perez family is willing to be reasonable.* The smug tone had infected the attorney's voice in every conversation. She'd been less interested in alleging John's guilt than in making veiled extortion demands.

Well, Carmen Escobar had a surprise or two coming.

Kali and Sabrina had reluctantly agreed that a reasonable out-of-court settlement would be preferable to a protracted and public trial, despite their belief in John's innocence. But that was when it appeared as though Olivia was an unintended victim, and a sympathetic victim at that. Before Kali learned about her X-rated extracurricular activities. Before she discovered that Olivia hung out with a stripper and fellow porn actress who'd also been murdered. Rightly or not, those revelations were bound to color the jury's perceptions.

Kali wasn't happy about springing any of this on Olivia's mother. In spite of the lawsuit, Kali felt nothing but sympathy for Mrs. Perez. She hoped that sharing the information with Carmen Escobar would be enough to convince the attorney to back off. She wasn't counting on it, though. Kali's sense was that Carmen didn't care whose name got dragged through the mud, or whose nose got rubbed in the filth, as long as Carmen herself came out ahead.

Kali tossed the notice onto the table and stomped around the kitchen for a few minutes before calling Sabrina.

"I thought Carmen Escobar was urging a settlement," Sabrina said after Kali had filled her in.

"She was. Still is, I imagine." Kali wondered if Carmen could have been behind the broken window and the threatening phone call. She wouldn't put it past her. "Filing suit is Carmen's attempt to push us in that direction. But her victim isn't going to play for the jury as the innocent, hardworking student she's imagining."

Sabrina laughed. "That's for sure."

"I learned something else interesting," Kali said and then told Sabrina about Erling's involvement with Sloane Winslow.

"Holy moly. You've been busy. So what's next?"

"I'll file a response to the complaint and hope Carmen Escobar sees the light. We have bargaining chips we didn't have before."

"I hope it's enough."

"Me too. I've got some names of people in the porn business, names Wayne Clark gave to John. I'm talking with one of them later today. I'm hoping to find out why John was interested in Hayley and Crystal. I'd also like to talk to Olivia's brother again. When I showed him the photo, he claimed not to recognize either girl, but I think he was lying. If I press him about Olivia's acting career, he may open up. I'm sure he wasn't telling the whole story."

"Anything I can do to help? I'll be back down there later this week."

"Everything's under control for the moment. How are things at home?"

"From the mom perspective, pretty good. All three boys seem to be handling John's death fairly well. They miss him, but they aren't dwelling on it."

"That's good." Kali waited for Sabrina to continue. When she didn't, Kali took a deep breath and prodded, "And from the wife perspective?"

"This thing with Peter has really turned my life upside down. Sometimes I'm so angry I find it hard to be civil. But I love him, too. And that makes me even madder. What kind of pathetic person am I to love such a louse?"

"You told me the other day that he was a decent guy."

Sabrina sighed. "He is. That's what makes it so hard. He's a really good guy and a great dad."

"And you said he was getting help."

"Yeah, he is. He's really trying to make it up to me, too. But I'm having trouble overlooking what he's done."

Kali was in no position to give advice on matters of the heart. She wasn't sure she'd ever truly been in love. Maybe this was what love was—enduring the peaks and valleys of disappointment, but caring anyway.

She thought of Bryce and the trip he'd made to Tucson just to see her. The look in his eyes when he'd answered her phone and heard a man's voice. The way the hurt had been tempered by tenderness when they'd kissed good-bye at the airport.

Human relationships were messy, no way around it.

"I imagine kids complicate things," Kali offered.

"Yeah, it's not like I can just walk away, even if I wanted to. Peter will always be a part of our lives. And the boys deserve a dad." Sabrina was silent a moment. "About the lawsuit—if we agree to settle, we'll get whatever's left over sooner than if there's a trial, right?"

"Assuming there's anything left in John's estate after the settlement."

"But they'll ask for more if we go to trial, won't they?"

"Probably. Why?"

"No reason really. It's just . . . Peter was asking."

"Hold on, Sabrina. Whatever you inherit is yours, not Peter's. An inheritance is separate property."

"Whatever."

"No, not whatever." Kali reminded herself not to yell. "This is one of the times you need to use your brain."

"There you go again acting like you know what's right for everybody."

"Sabrina, please—"

"I don't want to argue with you, Kali. Let's just drop it."

"Fine." *For now,* Kali added silently. But she wasn't about to let Sabrina do something foolish.


Of the names Wayne Clark had given John, only one was a woman—Larissa LaRue—a director who'd started out on the other end of the camera. She'd agreed to meet with Kali as a favor to Wayne, but only if they could do it the next morning at the shop where she was getting new tires put on her car.

"It always takes at least an hour," she'd explained. "And I get so bored just waiting there."

Even ex–porn stars needed new tires, Kali supposed. The incongruity amused her.

Two women were seated in the tiny waiting area of the tire shop when Kali arrived: a pudgy woman who looked to be in her midforties, and a young mother reading a storybook to the toddler nestled in her lap. Kali wondered if Larissa had been delayed.

The older woman looked up. "Kali?" When Kali nodded, she said. "I'm Larissa LaRue."

Kali tried to keep her surprise from showing. Larissa was attractive, but far from stunning. The skin on her face was taut, almost too taut, except around her eyes, where it was puffy. Her lackluster blond hair was puffy too. An aging Farrah Fawcett. Her turquoise crop pants and short-sleeved pink shirt were snug on a frame that carried an extra twenty pounds. But she stood and shook Kali's hand with a genuine smile and down-to-earth manner that belied the image of aging porn star.

"I appreciate your taking the time to meet with me," Kali said.

"Not a problem. Wayne's been good to me. Besides, I'm happy for the company. We're leaving on a trip tomorrow morning, so I had to get new tires today."

As Kali took a seat on the hard plastic chair next to Larissa, she noticed the toddler watching them. Larissa smiled at him, and the boy hid behind his hands. He opened them long enough for Larissa to wave at him, then giggled and again hid his face.

"Cute kid," Larissa said. "You have kids?"

"Nope. How about you?"

"A daughter. She's eight now. It's funny how kids change your whole perspective. She's one of the reasons I think about getting into a different line of work. I have no qualms about having been in the business. I know there are people who feel differently, who think women are exploited and only stay out of desperation. And maybe that's true in some cases."

"But not in yours?"

Larissa shook her head. "I got into it by accident, but overall it's been a positive experience. I was able to earn a living, to grow and learn to stand up for myself." She grinned. "And it's how I met my husband."

"He's a . . ." Kali glanced at the young mother sitting across from them. "He's in the business?"

"A cameraman. One of the best. He always made me look hotter than I was."

That had to be weird, Kali thought.

"If we'd stayed in L.A. he'd be at the top of the profession by now."

"But you moved to Tucson?"

Larissa nodded. "After our daughter was born. We both wanted a change. The porn industry is megamillion huge. Some big, mainstream corporations are involved, but it's virtually impossible to cross over into straight films once you've been associated with adult. That goes for cameramen as well as actors and directors. Kiz tried, but it was like hitting his head against a brick wall. The irony is that in a lot of ways adult films are among the most challenging to shoot."

"Really?" Kali had caught the young mother glancing their way at Larissa's mention of *porn*. She'd stopped reading to her son.

"Think about it. The action's not rehearsed. I mean, there's a basic storyline, but you can't choreograph sex scenes—they just happen. You miss a climax, you're done. It's not like you've got the option of half a dozen takes."

"No, I guess not," Kali said. It wasn't something she'd considered before. From the look on the young mother's face, she hadn't either.

"The angles are tough, too," Larissa explained. "Viewers want to see more than thighs and butts. So the cameraman has got to get up close and personal without interrupting the action. Not easy, believe me. But Hollywood snubs its nose at us, even though half the sex scenes they shoot nowadays come close to being X-rated."

"Doesn't sound fair," Kali murmured.

"But it's all worked out because Kiz and I love Tucson. He's an EMT now, and we've got a nicer house than we'd ever have if we'd stayed in L.A. It's better for our daughter, too."

Over the loudspeaker, the service manager announced the

white Camry was ready. The young mother packed up her son, his box of crackers, and his books and scurried out of the room with a backward glance toward Larissa.

"But you're still in the business?" Kali asked. "As a director?"

"Strictly small-time. I'm not under contract with any studio. I work independently and make only the films that interest me. So what can I do for you? You're a friend of Wayne's?"

"Not exactly. I only met him yesterday. Because of my brother, John O'Brien. Did John by any chance contact you?"

Larissa shook her head. "Should he have?"

"He was looking for some girls, and you were one of the people Wayne suggested he get in touch with."

"He's in the business?"

"No. I mean, he was an investor, but that's all. He died a couple of weeks ago."

"I'm sorry." Larissa seemed unsure what was expected of her.

Kali handed her the photograph. "Do you recognize these girls?"

Larissa studied it. "So many young women look the same to me these days, but this one"—she pointed to Olivia—"I talked to her at the industry open-call party this summer. She's only done a couple of films, but she's a beauty. Dark, exotic, definitely not the norm. I didn't have a project going right then, so I introduced her to Larry."

"Larry Stanton?"

Larissa's face registered surprise. "You know him?"

"He's another name Wayne gave me."

"Larry's an agent. Out of L.A. but he works with talent from all over the country. I don't know what came of it, but they talked for a while after I left them alone."

"Where was this open call?" Kali asked.

"It wasn't officially an open call. Not in the sense of a production company opening the doors to anyone who wants to audition. It was just a big party with a lot of the movers and shakers in the business. Directors, agents, actors and actresses, even make-up and camera folks. A chance to meet and mingle. Mostly local talent, but Larry was there and some other folks from L.A."

"And it was open to anyone?"

"Technically you needed to know someone to get an invite, but they weren't hard to come by. Especially for actresses."

"How about investors?" Kali wondered if John had been there. Maybe that's where he'd met the girls. "Were investors there, as well?"

"Not the big, established ones. But some of the others." Larissa shot Kali a conspiratorial grin. "Supposedly they go for business reasons, but mostly they're there because they think they'll get laid."

"Do they?"

Larissa's grin broadened. "Depends. The ones who are good-looking, wealthy, or have clout usually do okay." She turned back to the photo. "I don't recall these other two girls, but that doesn't mean they weren't there. What's your interest in them?"

"The girl you talked to and this one," Kali said, pointing to Hayley, "they were both murdered. I'm hoping the third girl will be able to shed some light on what happened."

Larissa's eyes widened. "How awful. Was it someone associated with the industry? As if we don't get enough bad press."

Kali hadn't considered that angle—a killer with a vendetta against women and porn. "Do you know of any others in the porn industry who've died recently?"

Larissa shook her head. "No, but I didn't know about these two, either. None of the major names, though. I'm sure I'd have heard about that."

Kali took the photo and tucked it into her purse. "May I ask you something?"

"Sure."

"Didn't, uh . . . performing in front of the camera, in front of people . . . weren't you self-conscious?" Embarrassed was what she was thinking, but that seemed too much like criticism.

"It's funny," Larissa said, "but I wasn't. I had a great body and I liked sex. I'd kind of get into it and forget anyone else was around."

The service manager announced that a green Ford Explorer was ready. "That's me," Larissa said, standing. "You should talk to Ron Silverman. He was one of the organizers of the event I was telling you about. He might have a list of those who attended."

"Thanks."

Larissa checked her cell phone for his number and jotted it down for Kali. "Pleasure talking to you. It made waiting for the tires much easier."

# CHAPTER 39

Kali caught up with Tony Perez just as his shift at the Logan Foods market was ending. Ten minutes later and she'd have missed him.

"Getting up at five in the morning is a pisser," he told her as they crossed the blazing asphalt of the store parking lot, "but getting off work at three in the afternoon almost makes up for it."

"I can see how that would be nice." Kali treasured found hours in the afternoon more than extra time in the morning. "What do you do with the free time?"

Tony shrugged. "Some days I go to the university and sit in on classes that interest me. Other days I go to the gym or hang out with friends. I try to get in a couple hours of writing every day, but it doesn't always happen."

The first time they'd talked, he'd told her his dream was to be a writer, but Kali had assumed that was mostly bravado. Maybe she'd been wrong. He'd at least kept his story straight. "How's the novel coming?" she asked.

"It's not, but I finished a short story this week." They'd reached his car, an older Taurus with a dented fender. He opened the door and tossed his apron inside. "What do you want? I'm kind of in a hurry."

"I was hoping to ask you a couple more questions."

Tony gave her a dimpled smile and waited for her to continue.

"What do you know about your sister's . . ." Kali paused to search for the right words. "About her work as an actress?"

"Actress! Olivia? Not hardly. Unless you mean her whole life was an act. That I'd buy. Like I told you before, she played whatever role it took to get ahead."

"You told me she was ambitious. Sometimes it's beneficial to adapt to the situation." Kali was stalling for time, trying to think how to rephrase the question without asking him point-blank if he knew his sister made porn films.

"I guess you could call it ambition," Tony said, with a thinly disguised sneer. "The only person she really cared about was herself, but I'll give her credit for going after what she wanted. She didn't let anything get in her way."

Sour grapes, Kali wondered, or an honest appraisal? She broached her original question from a different angle. "I understand Olivia had a summer job that paid very well."

"At the River Inn? I don't think the pay's anything to write home about, but, yeah, it was more than she made working in the school library."

"She quit the job at the inn," Kali told him.

Tony shook his head. "No way. She needed the money for school."

"That's not what Joanna Sommers says. Do you know her?"

"I know who she is. She and Olivia were in the same dorm last year."

"How about other friends? Do you know Crystal Adams?"

Tony shook his head, looked at his watch. "Look, I really need to get going. Here, let me give you my cell phone number." He reached into the car, pulled out an old gas receipt, and wrote out his name and phone number. "Call me if you want, but Olivia and I weren't all that close."

Kali folded the slip of paper and stuck it in her purse. "How about Hayley Hendrix?" she asked as he was sliding into the driver's seat.

It was just the faintest break in motion, like a film that had been poorly spliced. But Kali was sure Tony not only had recognized Hayley's name but had had a visceral reaction to it.

"You knew Hayley, didn't you?" Kali said as Tony closed the door. "Why did you tell me you didn't recognize her photo?"

Tony glared at her for a moment through the rolled-up window, his dark eyes narrowed, his face flushed. Then he gunned the engine and drove off with a squeal of rubber.

Hayley was his sister's friend, Kali reminded herself. There was nothing odd about Tony's knowing her. But that wasn't the point. The point was that he'd denied it.

As Kali crossed the pavement toward her own car, her cell phone rang. The caller was Doug Simon.

"I'm back in Tucson," he told her. "I've been following up on Crystal Adams like you asked."

Kali's breath caught. "Did you find her?"

"Afraid not. I just spoke with the boy's grandmother, though. First off, she's in a nursing home, so there's no way Crystal and Clayton were living with her. They did go visit her one time, to ask for money. She gave Clayton forty dollars, all the cash she had. He threw a fit. The staff supervisor threatened to call the cops if he didn't leave."

"When was this?"

"Early January."

Not long after Crystal had left home. "The grandmother doesn't have any idea where they are?"

"Clayton's incarcerated. He was arrested on a drug charge over Memorial Day weekend. The grandmother's heartbroken that she didn't have the funds to hire an attorney for him. I can try to visit him, but I'm not sure they'll let me."

So Crystal had come to Tucson with Clayton and then been stranded when he got sent off to jail. Piecing together what she'd picked up from other sources, Kali put together a scenario of Crystal's movements. She'd lived on the streets for a while, stopping in at Sunshine House for an occasional meal and shower. At some point she'd hooked up with Olivia and Hayley and ultimately begun crashing on Hayley's couch. Unfortunately, none of that brought Kali any closer to knowing where the girl was now.

Except that one of the other kids at Sunshine House claimed to have seen Crystal near the campus. At the very least, the odds were she was still alive.


The University of Arizona campus was only a stone's throw from where Kali now stood. Her chances of running into Crystal Adams were no better than those of winning the lottery, but Kali occasionally bought a lottery ticket. She could also afford to gamble an hour of her afternoon.

If not for the heat, she'd have left her car in the Logan Foods parking lot and walked to campus. But she'd learned that as much as she sometimes complained about the fog and cool breezes of the Bay Area they were far preferable to brutal hundred-degree temperatures. She drove the six blocks instead. The car's air conditioner had barely kicked in by the time she parked in the structure on the north end of campus.

Kali walked up Euclid to the quad and found a bench in the partial shade of a building near the student union. The bench was made of metal and Kali could feel it burning her skin through her pant legs. For the next forty minutes she sat there sweltering as she watched students parade past. None of them was Crystal Adams.

What had she been thinking? It was a huge campus. She'd never find Crystal by waiting to run into her. The heat and the frustration finally got to her. Kali crossed over to the library on the chance that Joanna Sommers was working that afternoon.

She was in luck. Seated behind the checkout counter, Joanna looked up when Kali approached. Blankly at first, then a flicker of recognition, but it was clear she couldn't place Kali.

"Hi, Joanna. I'm the attorney who spoke with you last

week about Olivia. You recognized one of the girls in the photo. You said her name was Crystal."

"Right. Sorry I didn't place you right away."

"Don't worry about it. I was just wondering if you'd seen her around campus lately."

"No. I'm pretty sure she's not a student." Joanna scooted her chair sideways to scan a book for a student.

"I'd like to talk to her, so if you run into her would you let me know? See if you can get her phone number or something. From what I hear, she may have cut her hair and bleached it, so she probably looks different."

"Is she, like, a suspect or a witness or something?"

"Not that I know of. But it's important I talk to her." Kali gave Joanna her cell number, then reluctantly left the air-conditioned cool of the library for the walk back to her car in the blistering afternoon heat.

The day had been a waste of time. She was spinning her wheels, getting nowhere. If it weren't for the damn lawsuit, she'd pack up and go home.

*I'm sorry, John. Sorry I wasn't there when you needed me. Sorry I'm failing you once again.*


On her way to the house, Kali stopped at an office supply store to pick up folders and paper, and then she spent the remainder of the afternoon getting organized and drafting a response to the wrongful death complaint.

When she was done, she wandered into the kitchen and fixed herself a cheese sandwich, which she ate in front of a home makeover show on television. But she couldn't keep her mind on the program. Finally, she turned it off, got a clean sheet of paper, and drew a grid. Once again, she was back to thinking with pen and paper.

John and the three young women—Olivia, Hayley, and Crystal. There was clearly a connection. Kali had started out assuming the bridge was Olivia because John had been accused of her murder. But it was no longer that simple.

She entered into the grid the various bits of information

that tied one of the four to another. John had hired Doug Simon to gather information on Crystal's parents. Hayley's wallet had contained the phone number for Logan Foods, and John had gone to the Crazy Coyote to ask about her, so he knew where she worked. Olivia and Hayley were both involved in the adult entertainment field. Another link. Kali drew a line between the names, then put a question mark next to Crystal's name. Crystal had moved in with Hayley, at least temporarily. Kali drew a dotted line between those two names. And the photo, of course. Whatever the connections, the three girls had known one another.

Hayley and Olivia had been murdered. Kali tapped her pen against the paper. John had hired Doug Simon two days after Olivia's death. That couldn't be a coincidence. Had he suspected Crystal's parents of the crime? Or Crystal herself?

There *was* evidence suggesting John's having been at Sloane's the night of the murders. Why was he there? Might he have gone to see Olivia rather than Sloane?

Even with the benefit of pen and paper, Kali's mind was spinning. It was like trying to grab hold of smoke. Every time she tried to pin down a thought, it drifted out of reach.

She leaned back on the couch and rested her feet on the coffee table. How did Crystal figure into things? Potential victim, killer, or simply the only person on Kali's grid who might still be alive? Any way you looked at it, Crystal was the key to understanding what had happened.

Tony claimed not to have recognized Crystal, but Kali felt certain he'd known Hayley, even though he denied it. He might not be telling the truth about Crystal, either. At the very least, he'd known two of Crystal's friends.

Kali pawed around in her purse until she found the gas receipt on which Tony had written his name and phone number. She stared at it for a minute while she sorted out what was familiar about the loose round lettering and the loopy *y* with eyes and a mouth.

Then it came to her: Tony's was the handwriting she'd seen in the inscription of Olivia's and Hayley's books of poetry.

# CHAPTER 40

Deena gave Erling the cold shoulder when he arrived home from work. Walked right past him as if he weren't there. He'd brought flowers, but when he handed them to her, she set them on the kitchen counter, not even placing them in water. She opened the cupboard and reached for the package of chocolate chip cookies.

"Can we talk about this, Deena?"

"What's to talk about?" She took out a cookie, resealed the package, and put it back.

"Us. Me. How sorry I am."

She regarded him coolly for a moment. "Truthfully, I don't know. But definitely not yet. I'm not ready for it."

"So what are we going to do—walk around like zombies passing in the night?"

"You could move out."

She'd said it so calmly it took a moment before the words registered. When they did, Erling's heart thudded to a stop. "Is that what you want?"

Deena turned her back on him. She closed the cupboard door.

"It's not what I want," Erling said emphatically. His arms hung awkwardly at his sides, but he was afraid that if he touched her, it would only make her angrier. "What I want is for you to give me a chance to show you how much I love you. I want to make our marriage work."

Her back was still to him but he could see her wipe away a tear with the back of her hand. "Fine, suit yourself." Her tone was sharp, but underneath, Erling heard the cottony timbre of choked tears. "You usually do anyway."

With that, she left the room.

*Give it time,* Erling told himself. *She's hurt and angry. With good reason.* He unwrapped the flowers and put them in a jar of water to keep them from wilting.

Then he wandered down the hall and knocked on the door to Mindy's room. He wasn't sure what, if anything, Deena had told her, and he wanted to offer his own regrets and assurances to the mix. Maybe he was even looking for a little reassurance in return. Erling was beginning to realize just how much of a mess he'd made of everything. He couldn't bear the thought of his daughter's rejection on top of everything else.

Mindy wasn't home yet. As he stood at the doorway, it struck him that his daughter's room was no longer that of a little girl. He knew the changes had come gradually. He'd even helped make many of them—painting over the Disney border on the wall, assembling the new double bed with its maple headboard, hanging the metal-framed full-length mirror. But he'd never really stepped back and thought about what it all meant. As Deena occasionally reminded him, Mindy was no longer a child, but a young woman. Her parents weren't the center of her world anymore.

Moving inside, Erling caught a whiff of vanilla from the scented candles atop the bookshelf. He marveled at the clutter of cosmetics in an acrylic tray on the dresser. Did Mindy really wear all that stuff? Next to the tray was a framed family photo—one he knew well. It had been taken only months before Danny's death. A wave of emotion rolled over him, causing his throat to grow tight and his eyes to sting. It wasn't just Danny. It was everything. What had he done? Was he going to lose everything he held dear?

The book of love poems Deena had told him about was

on the table near Mindy's bed. Erling picked it up. He crossed the room to the light and opened the flap. And felt as though the air had been sucked from his lungs.

*Mindy,*
*There are hundreds of languages in the world, but a smile speaks them all. And yours speaks to me. Because of your smile, you make life more beautiful.*

The signature under the inscription was illegible but penned with a flourish. The last letter had a sweeping bottom loop embellished with two eyes and a smile.

The same quote and the same handwriting he'd seen in the other books.

Hayley. Olivia. And now his daughter.

All three about the same age. All with identical books inscribed in an identical manner.

And two of the girls had been murdered.

Erling tore through the house looking for Deena. He found her in the den reading, the wireless earphones she'd given him for Christmas two years earlier insulating her from the disruption he'd created in the ordered rhythm of her life. She looked up briefly, then went back to her book.

"Deena, I need to talk to you. It's important."

She ignored him.

"It's about Mindy."

Deena slid the earphones back behind her ears. "She's out with friends."

"This book"—Erling thrust the volume in front of Deena's face—"where'd she get it?"

"What are you doing going through her room?" Deena's words were sharp.

"Who gave it to her?"

"I don't think that's any of our business. And you have no right—"

"That *guy* you said she was seeing. Did he give it to her?"

Deena rolled her eyes. "She's nineteen years old, for

God's sake. She's entitled to have boyfriends. Besides, the protective daddy's-little-girl act is a bit dated."

Erling sat down next to Deena. "Honey, listen to me. This isn't about her having a boyfriend." Though the very thought of his daughter with this boy—the same boy Olivia and Hayley had known—turned his blood to ice. "It's that this book of poems, inscribed the same way . . . each of the two murdered girls had one just like it."

Deena stared at him. The color drained from her face. She ripped the earphones from her head. "Is this some sick joke of yours to get back at me for being angry?"

"You think I'd do that?" Erling was appalled.

"I never thought you'd cheat on me, either."

"It's not a joke. Now tell me what you know about this guy of hers."

"Nothing."

"Nothing?"

Deena hugged her chest. "You must be mistaken."

"I hope I am."

"You think the boy who gave Mindy this book . . . you think he killed those other girls?"

"It's possible." Erling had to remind himself to breathe. "Is that who she's with tonight?"

"Friends is all she said. Oh, God, what are we going to do?"

"I'm going to call her cell phone."

He went to the desk, picked up the phone, and punched in Mindy's number. It rang five times, then went to voice mail. He left a message: "Hi, it's Dad. Call me as soon as you get this. It's urgent."

He paced back and forth across the room until it became clear that Mindy wasn't going to call right back. Then he expanded his pacing route to include the entire house. He tried to settle into one spot, to finish the newspaper, to make himself a bite to eat, but whenever he stopped moving, the pressure inside him built until he thought he might explode.

Deena stayed frozen on the couch in the den. She was so

still Erling checked now and then to make sure she was still breathing.

At ten past eleven, Mindy's car pulled up in front of the house, and a few minutes later she burst through the door. She looked startled to see both parents hovering in the entry-way.

"What are you guys doing up? Aren't you usually in bed by now?"

"Who were you with tonight?" Erling demanded.

Mindy pulled back. "A friend."

"A boy?"

"What's this, the Inquisition?" She looked to Deena. "I told you I'd be late."

"It's not that you're late, sweetie. Your dad is worried—we're both worried—about this boy you've taken an interest in."

"You're what? I can't fucking believe this. What are you doing—spying on me?"

"Watch your language," Deena said.

Erling showed his daughter the book. "Did he give this to you?"

Mindy snatched it from his hands. "What were you doing in my room? Why are you snooping through my personal stuff?"

Erling's approach was all wrong. He knew that, but he couldn't help himself. He sounded angry and accusatory when what he really felt was the icy hand of fear mixed with relief that Mindy was home safe. He took a breath. "I wasn't snooping," he said. "The book was in plain view."

"In *my* room."

He stopped himself from responding: "In *my* house." "I looked in to say hello when I got home from work."

Rather than smooth the waters, he'd made things worse. "You looked in . . . and then went right to my bedside table?" Her voice rose. "Or did you go through my drawers, too? The closet? Did you look under the mattress?"

He gave up. "We've had two homicides in the last couple of weeks," he told her, trying to stay calm. "Both girls about your age. They had copies of this same book with the same inscription and the same signature."

"So?" Mindy clutched the book to her chest. She was in defiant mode now. She was hardly going to give her parents the satisfaction of knowing they'd gotten to her.

"So who gave it to you?" Erling asked.

"A boy I know." Mindy's mouth quivered. It was hard to tell which upset her more: learning her boyfriend made a habit of giving girls love poems, or her father's warning that the boy might be a killer.

"What's his name?"

"I can't believe you're doing this."

Deena spoke softly. "What's his name, honey? It's important."

She hesitated. "Tony."

"What about his last name?"

"I don't know."

"You don't know?" Deena looked aghast.

"You're dating a boy," Erling asked, "and you don't know his last name?"

"I'm not dating him. We're just friends."

"Where can I find him?"

"You wouldn't!" Mindy looked mortified. "Next time I see him I'll ask him, okay? I'll ask him about your dead . . . victims." She stormed into her room and slammed the door.

# CHAPTER 41

K ali hated to be a pest. It had been only forty-eight hours since she'd talked to Michelle Parker, but she wanted to find out what had happened with Detective Shafer and to pass on her discovery about the smiley face signature. Since she'd raised the issue of the poetry books to begin with, it seemed only fair to let the detectives know she'd been on the wrong track. She should tell Michelle about Hayley's and Olivia's involvement in the adult entertainment business too, but she was still hoping to figure out John's role first.

She finally made the call, bracing herself for a cool reception, even a straightforward "Bug off." So she was surprised when Michelle Parker greeted her pleasantly.

"You will be happy to know," Michelle said, "that we're taking a fresh look at the Winslow and Perez murders."

"There's new information?"

"Well, no . . . not specifically. Your brother remains our only real suspect, but there are a number of things we're looking into."

*Like the fact that the lead detective had been sleeping with the victim,* Kali thought to herself. And now they were covering their tails by taking a "fresh look." She wondered how much effort they were actually putting into it. Maybe she should have gone over their heads in the first place.

"Did you talk to Detective Shafer? What did he say?"

"That's not something I can discuss with you. But I assure you the matter is being dealt with." Michelle hesitated. "That's part of the reason we're taking another look."

"So he *was* involved with Sloane Winslow."

"One of the avenues we're exploring," Michelle continued, ignoring Kali's comment, "is the possible connection between the murders of Olivia Perez and Hayley Hendrix. Don't you think it's odd that your brother knew one of Olivia's friends?"

"He knew where Hayley worked," Kali pointed out. "That doesn't mean he knew *her*." Though silently she concurred that the connection between John and the girl was troublesome.

"His phone number was in her wallet."

"It was the corporate number," Kali said. "Hayley could have been in touch with Sloane Winslow."

"Your brother knew another friend, too," Michelle noted. "Crystal Adams. He asked about her at the Crazy Coyote."

That wasn't the half of it, Kali thought. "Of course he'd talk to people who knew Olivia," she protested. "John knew you suspected him of murder. He was hoping one of her friends might have some idea who killed her."

"Why would he assume Olivia was the target, and not Sloane?"

"We don't know he assumed that," Kali shot back. "Maybe he talked to Sloane's friends, too." Her duplicity was making her testy.

How much easier it would be if she could simply tell the detectives what she knew. But she was afraid that if she did she might be putting a noose around John's neck, so to speak. Carmen Escobar would love it. And Sabrina would never forgive her. Kali wasn't sure she could forgive herself.

"You're missing the point," Michelle said. "It's not surprising John would know Sloane's friends. They worked together, and he was a longtime friend of her brother Reed's. In fact, John and Sloane dated at one time, didn't they?"

"Years ago." Kali wondered briefly if the old flame had

been rekindled. Sloane's murder could have been the fallout of a current romance with John. Her ex-husband maybe, except the cops had cleared him. Or Susan Harris, the woman John had been dating.

Or even Detective Erling Shafer.

But Kali had seen no evidence of a renewed romance between John and Sloane. If anything, there were bad feelings between them.

"Anyway," Michelle added, "we've found nothing to indicate that John talked to Sloane's friends after the murders."

"What about the murder of Hayley Hendrix? You must have some leads there."

"I'm not at liberty to discuss that."

Unless there was something in it for the police. Kali sighed. "That's why I called. It's about the poetry books. I know who inscribed them. At least I think I do. Olivia's brother."

For a moment the detective was speechless. Then she demanded, "How do you know that?"

"He wrote down his name and phone number for me. The handwriting's the same, and his signature has the same smiley face in the loop of the *y*."

"Her brother, huh."

"So the books probably aren't significant after all. He gave one to his sister and one to her friend. It's not unusual that he'd know his sister's friends. The only odd part is that when I asked him if he knew Hayley, he denied it."

"You asked him about her? Why?" Michelle's interest was clearly piqued.

"I told you, I'm dealing with a wrongful death suit."

Silence stretched between them. Finally, the detective asked, "Is there anything else you'd like to tell us?"

Even though she was alone in John's study, Kali felt the detective's eyes on her, sharp and suspicious. Deceit was damn uncomfortable. "Like what?" she croaked.

"You knew about Hayley. You knew she and Olivia had similar books of poetry. You know something about another of Olivia's friends, Crystal Adams. At a minimum, you recognized her name. Seems to me you know a lot for someone who supposedly knows nothing."

"I've told you what I know," Kali insisted.

"Then why don't you tell us about your brother's connection to these girls?"

"Because I don't know what it was."

That at least was the truth.

Erling felt like shit. He'd spent a second sleepless night on the living room sofa. After his confrontation with Mindy, Deena had spoken to him only in monosyllables, and Mindy not at all. And then this morning, he'd really done it. Now neither one was speaking to him.

He'd waited until Mindy had arrived at the breakfast table, then tried to reason with her. Just tell him how to get in touch with the boy, that was all. Erling had promised he wouldn't make a scene. The more he'd pleaded, the more adamant Mindy had become that it was none of his business.

Finally, Erling had lost his temper. "It is too my business," he'd thundered, hammering the tabletop with his palm and sloshing his cornflakes. "You're living in my house, eating my food, taking my money."

"That doesn't mean you own me."

"You want to be in charge of your own life or not? You can't have it both ways."

"We love you, honey," Deena had interjected with a warning glance at Erling. "We're worried. We just want to know about the boy. I'm sure it's all a big mistake, but—"

"If you're sure it's a mistake, then why the inquisition?"

"Inquisition?" Erling had barked. "If we're supporting you, you're going to follow our rules, understand? Now tell me how to find this so-called friend of yours, or else."

Deena had thrown up her hands. "Erling, you're being a jerk."

"Fine," Mindy had yelled. "I'll move out if that's what you want." She had pushed away from the table and run to her room.

Eyes shooting daggers in his direction, Deena had run after their daughter. Erling's apology, shouted through the closed bedroom door, had gone unacknowledged.

Finally, he'd left the house and come to work.

But not before he'd called Norm Giff, who'd been his partner before Michelle. He had explained the situation and asked Norm to keep an eye on Mindy.

Now he headed to the break room for an aspirin, and that's where he ran into Michelle.

"Another rough night?" she inquired, giving him the once-over.

"Rough night. Rougher morning." He filled his cup with water from the cooler and popped two aspirin. "You know the poetry books inscribed to Olivia Perez and Hayley Hendrix?"

"Yeah, I need to talk to you about—"

"Mindy's got one just like it."

Michelle's face registered surprise, and something else Erling had trouble reading. Worry, maybe. "What?" she asked. "Are you sure?"

"Same inscription. Same signature. She's met some new guy but she won't tell me who he is."

"Tony Perez," Michelle said, rocking back on her heels. "Olivia's brother. That's his signature. At least according to the oddly knowledgeable Kali O'Brien."

Erling's mind was racing almost as fast as his heart. He wasn't sure which name caused him the most aggravation, Kali or Tony. But Tony was the immediate problem.

"Remind me," Erling said. "Was there anything that sparked suspicion when we interviewed him?" He had a vague recollection of a slender, dark-haired man in his twenties. But Erling's mind had been on other things. Yet another example of how easily he'd let himself become distracted during the investigation.

"He was present when we spoke with the girl's parents," Michelle said. "His statement's in the file. He's a couple of years older than Olivia. Not the high achiever she was. In fact, he had some trouble with the law when he was younger."

"What kind of trouble?"

"Petty stuff, as I recall. Shoplifting, vandalism. None of it recent."

Recent or not, that wasn't the sort of guy Erling envisioned for his daughter.

Michelle was biting her lower lip, a habit Erling had noticed she fell into when she was thinking. "I figured Olivia and her friend, no big deal. So what if Tony gave them books. But Mindy—that changes things."

Damn right it did. "She won't tell me anything about him," Erling muttered. "She won't even talk to me."

"Something else Kali said." Michelle kicked her heel back against the wall. "She said Tony denied knowing Hayley Hendrix."

How had they missed this guy? Because Erling had messed up, that's how. Focused on Sloane and John and didn't run the full and open investigation he should have. And now his own daughter was in danger.

As he dumped his paper cup in the trash, Erling gestured to Michelle and they headed back toward the squad room. "Where can we find him?"

"The case has been reassigned, remember? We should let Bob Morgan handle it."

"The case may be Morgan's, but Mindy is *my* daughter."

Michelle nodded. "Where is she? Is she safe?"

"Norm Giff is keeping an eye on her. But I'm going to call and alert him, just in case."

Five minutes later, Michelle was leaning over Erling's desk. "Tony Perez works at a Logan Foods store near campus," she said. "But he called in sick today."

Erling's heart froze. He picked up the phone and punched in Giff's cell number.

"I lost her," Giff told him. "She went into the women's locker room at the gym and that's the last I saw of her. I was just getting ready to call you."

Erling's jaw clenched. Michelle gave him a stricken look. "What's wrong?" she asked.

He covered the mouthpiece. "Giff lost her." He told her about the locker room.

"Maybe she's still there."

Erling shook his head. In his gut, he knew she wasn't. "How long ago was this?" he asked Norm.

"About half an hour ago, maybe a bit longer. I'm sorry. I swear, I was watching the door the entire time."

And realizing that she was being watched, Mindy had no doubt sneaked out a side entrance.

Erling hung up and tried Mindy's cell. It was turned off. He turned to Michelle. "Find out what kind of car Tony drives and put out a BOLO on him. I'll try to reach his parents."

Erling made the call. Tony's father was home and sounded sloshed, though it wasn't yet noon. Hadn't seen his son all day, he said. Erling did get a description of the car, which he handed to Michelle at the very moment she was printing out the license number from the Arizona MVD.

"Don't assume the worst," Michelle said, trying to reassure him.

"Easy for you to say." It was clear she wasn't a parent. Parents had trouble not assuming the worst. "Why was Kali O'Brien talking with Tony anyway?"

"I assume it was about his sister."

Erling muttered to himself. The O'Brien woman was up to her eyeballs in this. She could be the key to the whole thing. They should have put the pressure on her before this.

"I'm going to run Tony's name through the system," Erling said. "Can you monitor the phones? Let me know when they locate the car."

He prayed they wouldn't be too late.

# CHAPTER 42

Kali nursed a cup of coffee as she studied the pages spread out on John's dining room table. She'd spent the morning polishing the legal proceedings she'd drafted yesterday. She was feeling frustrated. If only she could figure out what was going on between John and the three girls.

She decided to take one more shot at getting Reed Logan to talk to her. If anyone would know about John's extracurricular activities, it would be Reed. Rather than call, giving him yet another chance to dodge her, this time she'd go and confront him in his office. As she was grabbing her purse, the phone rang.

"This is Ron Silverman," the caller announced.

It took Kali a moment to place the name—the producer whose number she'd gotten from Larissa LaRue. Kali had left a message for him yesterday.

"Sorry it took me so long to return your call," he said. "I've been so busy I've already forgotten the details of your message. Something about our industry event last spring?" Silverman's tone was imbued with the breezy, self-important air of someone who fancied himself a Hollywood mogul.

"Right," Kali told him. "I'm interested in a couple of girls. Larissa LaRue suggested you might be able to tell me if they were at the event and whether they have agents or contracts."

"Hell, Larissa knows everyone in the business, but, yeah, I'd be glad to help. Which studio are you with? Or are you independent?"

Kali realized he'd misunderstood the purpose of her call. She didn't see a lot of advantage in setting him straight. "Uh, pretty much independent."

"Tell you what. I'm on the road right now and all the paperwork from the event is at the office. I usually swing by La Cantina after work. Why don't you meet me there, say, six o'clock?"

"Great." Kali felt heartened. Between Reed Logan and Ron Silverman, maybe today she'd finally get some answers.


It wasn't until Kali pushed through the wide doors of the Logan Food headquarters that she stopped to wonder: Had she subconsciously planned the trip as a pretext for running into Nash? No, she told herself. Not true. But she wasn't entirely convinced.

She turned determinedly from the hallway that led to the legal counsel's office and asked the receptionist for Reed Logan. After a muffled call to Reed's secretary, the receptionist directed Kali to go on back.

John's former secretary, Alicia, was seated at the desk outside Reed's office. She greeted Kali like an old friend.

"I'm just filling in while Mr. Logan's secretary is on vacation," she explained. "Did you have an appointment? I didn't see it listed."

"No appointment. I was hoping I could just get a few minutes of his time."

"He's got someone with him right now, but I don't think they'll be long. Why don't you have a seat and I'll see what I can do?" She ran a thumb over one of her long, scarlet nails. "I miss working for your brother, you know. It's hard to believe he's gone."

Kali nodded. "I appreciate that you came to the funeral."

"Well, yeah, of course."

Kali sat in one of the sage-green side chairs against the wall. "Did you know John well? Outside of work, I mean."

Alicia gave a little wisp of a laugh. Embarrassed, and maybe a bit flattered, too, that Kali could even ask the question. "No, it wasn't like that at all. Believe me."

But Alicia would have liked it to be, Kali realized.

The door to Reed's office opened just then and he emerged, followed by A. J. Nash. They both appeared surprised to see Kali, but while Nash grinned with obvious pleasure, Reed scowled at her.

"You're persistent," he growled.

Nash raised his eyebrows, shot Kali a sympathetic look, then wisely excused himself to head back to his office.

"Please, Reed," Kali pleaded, "just give me five minutes."

"What for?"

"Doesn't your friendship with John mean anything?"

He sighed. "Okay, five minutes max." He stood back and let Kali enter his office.

"You want to convince me John is innocent, right?" Reed seated himself behind the wide walnut desk. He rested his forearms on the surface, pressed his fingertips together, and regarded her with a mixture of belligerence and quiet resignation.

Kali took a seat in one of the visitor's chairs. "Not really," she replied. Now that Reed had agreed to talk to her, she was at a loss how to begin. Finally, she decided to get the worst of it over first. "There's evidence suggesting John's death wasn't accidental," she said, watching Reed's reaction. "Evidence that he was murdered."

Reed recoiled slightly. "What do you mean, murdered? He went on a bender and drowned."

"But there was someone else at the house that night," Kali said.

"Do you know who?"

Kali shook her head.

Rubbing his jaw, Reed stood and walked to the window. "And you think this . . . this person is responsible for John's death?"

"It's possible." Kali paused. "I was hoping you'd have an idea who might have been there."

"Me?" Reed's expression was puzzled. He looked down at his flat, blunt fingers. Then suddenly he laughed. "What you're really wondering is, was it me?"

Kali didn't return the laugh. "Was it?"

He stared at her a moment. "Unbelievable."

"What is?"

"You are. You have a hell of a lot of nerve." A vein in Reed's temple throbbed. He jingled some change in one of his trouser pockets, then returned to his desk. "But I guess that explains why the cops have been back asking questions."

So Michelle Parker had been telling the truth about taking a fresh look. "What kind of questions?" Kali asked.

"About the company. About John." Reed ran a hand across his high forehead and over his scalp. "How could you even consider the possibility that I'd do something like that? I'm insulted."

"*You're* insulted?" Kali leaned forward in her chair. "You've been ready to blame John for your sister's death from the start. You weren't open to other ideas at all. If you don't think better of John, why should I think better of you?"

For a moment Kali thought he was going to throw her out of his office. Instead, he folded his hands and looked her in the eye. "I assure you, I had nothing to do with John's death. Of course, if you think me capable of murder, you're hardly going to take my word for it."

Reed got up again and poured himself a glass of water from the pitcher on the credenza. "Are you suggesting that whoever killed John, assuming someone did, is the person who also killed Sloane?"

"If it wasn't the same person, there's at least some connection. Doesn't that seem obvious?"

Reed drummed his fingers on the side of the glass. "Interesting theory."

"Do you have any idea what the connection might be? You were closer to both John and Sloane than just about anybody else."

He took a sip of water. "Not a clue."

"What about the girl who was living with Sloane? Did John know her?"

"Olivia?" He drained the glass. "I doubt it."

Kali took a breath. "Did you know John was involved in pornography?"

Reed set the glass down and returned to his chair. "He mentioned it. He was kind of embarrassed about the whole thing, but he was raking in the money. After some of his earlier setbacks, he was determined to build another nest egg."

Alicia's voice came through the intercom. "Sorry to bother you, Mr. Logan, but your two o'clock is here."

"I'll be there in a minute." Reed addressed Kali: "I don't like thinking John was a murderer any more than you do. I'd be thrilled if the police came up with a different suspect. But I don't have any information that's going to help them do that."

Kali nodded and rose, feeling far from satisfied. "Thanks for seeing me."

Back in the parking lot, Kali started the engine and flicked the air conditioner up to high. As she started to back out of the parking space, the car pulled to the left and rolled awkwardly. Her stomach sank.

When she got out to take a look, her fears were confirmed. A flat rear tire. Damn. Just what she didn't need.

Muttering under her breath, she pulled out the rental agreement and her cell phone, then punched in the number for Hertz. While she was waiting to be connected, she examined the tire more closely. The valve cap was missing. How had that happened?

Then she noticed a brown, softball-sized rock under the chassis near the rear wheel. It was similar in size and color to the one that had been thrown through John's picture window.

Tucson was full of rocks, but there were no others here in the paved lot of Logan Foods' corporate headquarters. The message was clear: *Get out.*

And clever, too, because there was no way Kali could prove the flat was meant to be a warning.

But she knew that it was.

# CHAPTER 43

Damn computer. Cursing it was about as useful as shooting the proverbial messenger, but it made Erling feel better. Tony Perez had a clean record. Whatever trouble he'd had with the law, it had happened while he was still a juvenile. He'd managed to keep his nose clean in the four years since he'd turned eighteen.

Michelle motioned to Erling and then pointed to the receiver pressed to her ear. "Tucson PD has located Tony's Taurus," she said. "Your daughter's with him. She's fine."

Erling's body went soft with relief. "Get the location and tell the uniforms to hold them until we get there."

Minutes later they were on their way. Michelle had insisted on driving.

"I can't wait to nail this piece of shit," Erling grumbled.

"Better find out if he's our killer, first."

"He's got Mindy, doesn't he?"

Michelle gave him a sidelong glance. "Remind me, is giving someone a ride a felony or a misdemeanor?"

"I'm in no mood for humor."

"I wasn't trying to be funny," she said pointedly. "At the moment we don't know squat about this guy and what he's done. It was personal involvement that tripped you up on this case in the first place. You'd better watch out it doesn't happen again."

Eyes straight ahead, Erling grumbled, "It won't."

They pulled up behind two police cruisers on an open stretch of four-lane road. In front was the dented Ford Taurus. Erling got out, spoke briefly with one of the officers, then opened the Taurus's passenger door.

Mindy looked up at him, her face contorted with rage. "I knew you'd pull something like this. I just knew it. How could you?"

"Why aren't you in class?" he asked.

"Class is over. We were going out to a movie."

"In the middle of the day? When you could be studying?"

"I can't study *all* the time."

Erling looked across the seat to the young man seated behind the wheel. He was leaning back, his eyes half closed, as though he hadn't a care in the world. Erling would have preferred some sign of nervousness or annoyance.

He turned back to Mindy. "What are you doing with a loser like this, anyway? Especially after what I told you about those other girls being killed."

"He's not a loser," Mindy protested. "Tony works hard. He's had to struggle for everything he's got."

"Spare me the sob story. Please."

Mindy turned to Tony. "I'm really, really sorry. My dad's such a jerk." Her pleading tone made Erling sick.

A thin smile graced Tony's mouth. "It's okay. Don't sweat it."

Erling took Mindy by the arm and pulled her from the car. "Take her home," he told the officer.

She jutted her chin at him. "My car's at school."

"Take her to her car, then, and follow her home." He gestured to Tony. "You come with me."

"What? What did I do?" Tony emerged from his cocoon of self-absorption and gaped at Erling. "She's not a minor, is she?"

"We've got some questions for you."

"About what?"

"Murder. Now get out of the car."

"*Murder?*" Tony's voice rose.

"I said get out. And keep your hands where I can see them." Erling half hoped the punk would resist; then he could pummel the guy.

Reluctantly Tony obliged, easing himself from the car. "What are you talking about? I don't know about any murder."

"What about your sister?"

Tony shook his head. "I didn't have anything to do with that."

"Because of your smile," Michelle said, "you make life more beautiful."

"What?"

"You recognize that line?"

"Yeah, it's a quote by Hanh, a Vietnamese monk."

"Literate, aren't we?" Erling chided. "You ever inscribe a book of poetry that way?"

Tony gave an elaborate sigh. "So I gave your precious daughter a book and told her she had a nice smile. Big deal. It's not like I gave her edible panties or anything."

Erling wanted to slap the guy, but Michelle's light touch on his forearm reminded him to keep his cool.

"Who else did you inscribe books to?" Michelle asked.

"What business is that of yours?"

"Your sister?"

Tony shoved his hands into his pockets. "Yeah, not that she cared. If it wasn't made of gold or diamonds, she had no use for it."

"Anyone else?" Erling asked.

Tony hesitated, then shook his head.

"You sure about that?" Erling took a step closer. "Come on, Tony. Tell us."

"A girl. Someone I was sort of dating."

"She have a name?"

"She was someone my sister knew."

"Hayley Hendrix?"

Tony's head jerked up in surprise. "Jesus, I can't believe this."

"So what happened? You date her long?"

He shrugged. "A couple of months. Here and there."

"When was this?"

"June, maybe. It wasn't any big thing."

"Who broke it off?"

"What's it matter? It's over."

Erling grabbed Tony's shirt. "She did, in other words."

"That must have made you angry," Michelle said.

"I treated her nice. Turns out all she wanted was a meal ticket." He looked at them. "She's a stripper, for Christ's sake. It's not like she's living in a nunnery."

"She wouldn't put out for you," Erling said. "Is that what you mean?"

Tony looked embarrassed.

"She humiliated you, didn't she?" Erling pressed. "That made you angry. So angry you killed her."

Tony's eyes widened. "She's dead?"

"As if you didn't know."

"I didn't! How'd she die?"

"You tell us."

Tony shook his head, breathing hard now. "You've got this all wrong. I had nothing to do with it."

"What about your sister? You kill her too?"

"Are you nuts?"

"Far from it."

"What about the other one?" Tony asked. "Crystal. You going to tell me she's dead too?"

Michelle cocked her head. "You know Crystal?"

"No, but some woman's been pestering me, asking me about them. She's got a photo of my sister with Hayley and the other girl."

"Some woman. You mean Kali O'Brien?"

"Yeah, that's her."

Erling exchanged glances with Michelle. "Come on, Tony. We're taking you in."

"I want a lawyer," Tony yelled as Erling prodded him into the car. "I'm not saying another word until I talk to my lawyer."

# CHAPTER 44

The rental agency insisted on giving Kali a replacement car. It was white, rather than silver, which made Kali feel less nervous about being followed. Unless whoever was behind the threats had tailed the tow truck to the Hertz agency, he or she wasn't likely to recognize the new car. Still, she checked the rearview mirror frequently, and she parked in a highly visible spot in front of La Cantina.

Her first thought when she walked through the door was that this was a happening place. The bar was standing room only and the entry was jammed with people waiting to be seated. Her second thought was that she'd never find Ron Silverman in the crowd.

But she was spared the need. The maitre d' approached her, asking, "Are you here to see Mr. Silverman?"

When she nodded, he showed her to a table in the center of the dining room.

Ron Silverman was on his cell phone. He nodded at Kali and gestured to the empty chair across the table. He was probably in his late forties, with a full mouth, thinning hair, and skin rendered soft by an underlayer of fat. His white silk shirt was open at the neck, revealing a gold chain and way too much chest hair.

After a moment, he snapped his phone shut and held out

a hand weighted by a diamond pinky ring. "Ron Silverman," he said. "Sorry about the call. Nobody's willing to take the ball and run with it anymore. They all gotta pass it by me first. Cover their asses if there's a screwup."

If Silverman was upset with the arrangement, he was hiding it well. More likely, he thrived on being indispensable.

"Kali O'Brien," she replied.

"What are you drinking?" He waved a waitress over.

"I'll have a glass of Chardonnay."

He repeated the order for the waitress. "And another vodka gimlet." Then he turned to Kali. "So, how's Larissa? What's she up to these days?"

"I really only just met her."

His phone sounded again, the theme from *Mission: Impossible*. Silverman checked the number, then silenced the ring. "Never a moment's peace. You looking for work?"

In a porn film? She almost laughed. "No, I'm trying to locate someone. Did you get a chance to check the party guest list?"

"Yeah, I brought it with me, in fact. What were the names?"

"Hayley Hendrix and Crystal Adams."

Silverman pulled a folder from his soft-leather briefcase and flipped through the sheets of paper inside. He shook his head. "No one by either name on the list. Course they could have come in on someone else's invite, or with a date. Hot babe shows up, we don't always insist on an actual admit card."

Their drinks arrived. Silverman finished off his other one first and handed the empty glass to the waitress. "Put them on my tab," he told her.

Kali pulled the photograph from her purse and handed it to him.

"This them?" Silverman asked.

"The girls on either end."

"Nope, they don't look familiar. I do remember the one in the middle. She was at the party. Spent time with one of the local investors."

Kali's heart skipped a beat. "John O'Brien?"

"You know John? Wait"—Silverman held up an index finger—"O'Brien. I should have made the connection sooner. So what are you, the wife?"

"I'm his sister."

"I seem to recall some trouble. He passed away recently, didn't he?"

She nodded. "A couple of weeks ago."

"Sorry to hear it. But no, it wasn't John. He didn't mingle much with people in the business. His interest was strictly financial." Silverman angled sideways in his chair so that his eyes could take in a broader sweep of the room. "Some folks view their investment as a way to live vicariously. Adult entertainment groupies, know what I mean? John wasn't like that."

Good for John. "What is it you do?" Kali asked. "Are you a director?"

"Producer. I've put together, oh, hundreds of films by now. And I'll admit it"—he grinned at her—"I'm a groupie with the best of them. I mean, where else is an old, soft-around-the-middle guy like me going to find himself surrounded by gorgeous female flesh?"

Silverman was clearly fishing for a compliment, but Kali wasn't about to lie just to oblige him. "Not many people can be so objective about themselves and their limitations." She sweetened the jab with a smile.

He choked on his gimlet, then laughed. "Good comeback."

She sipped her wine.

"Wit," Silverman added pointedly, "is an asset in a woman. Not as useful as a great body or real beauty, but at least it's something to fall back on when the other two are lacking."

Tit for tat. Kali laughed, too. She had no illusions about her body or her beauty, though she'd never heard complaints about either.

"How long have you been doing this . . . production work?" Kali asked.

"Probably too long, if truth be told. With VCRs, DVDs, the Internet, guys like me are getting squeezed. On one side, every Tom, Dick, and Harry is coming out with product. On the other, the conglomerates have moved in big-time."

"Change is pretty much the norm in every industry."

"Some more than others. Excuse me. I see someone I want to say hello to." He rose from the table. "I'll be just a minute."

Kali watched as he crossed the room and greeted another man, taller and younger than Silverman, who was just sitting down at a table of women, all of whom displayed even white teeth and ample cleavage.

While he was busy talking to his friend and ogling the women, Kali reached for the guest list he'd left by his drink. She scanned it quickly, hoping she'd find a name she recognized. The list was several pages long, in small print, and nothing jumped out at her as familiar. Except an Angus Nash. Angus. A.J.?

She saw Silverman returning to their table and slid the list back to his side.

"Sorry about that," Silverman said. He remained on his feet. "I haven't seen Randy for a while. Last I heard, he was in L.A. Signed on with the big guys."

Was this the porn star Olivia had worked with? "Randy Gibbons the actor?"

Silverman gave her a smarmy grin. "You're familiar with Randy's work?"

Kali shook her head. "No, I've just heard the name recently."

Silverman gathered his belongings and drink. "There's plenty of room at the table. Care to join us?"

She glanced at the half dozen twenty-somethings swooning over Randy, and decided she definitely wouldn't fit in. "I need to be going, but thanks." She reached for her purse. "My brother had a friend, another executive at Logan Foods, A. J. Nash. Was he by any chance at the event?"

"Yeah," Silverman said. "That's who I was telling you about. The guy that Hispanic girl in your photo was talking to."

# CHAPTER 45

Erling drummed his fingers on the gouged metal table of the interrogation room. The two hours spent waiting for the arrival of Tony Perez's attorney, a sharp-featured terrier of a woman named Carmen Escobar, had put his nerves on edge.

Michelle handed Tony a can of Coke, and Escobar a glass of water. Then she sat down next to Erling.

Tony pulled himself up in his chair and popped the tab on the soda. "Don't suppose I can get a glass and some ice for this?"

"Afraid not," Michelle replied, with what looked like a smile.

Erling fought to keep himself from backhanding the creep. "Tell us about Hayley Hendrix," he said.

"What's to tell?"

"Your relationship. Your breakup."

Tony took a long gulp of soda. "There was nothing to break up. We went out a few times. That was it."

"But you stopped going out. She must have said something to put an end to it."

Escobar's dark eyes narrowed, shooting venom in Erling's direction. "You don't know that's what happened. Maybe it was my client who lost interest."

Erling leaned forward. "Is that the way it was, Tony? You decided she was beneath you?"

"Don't answer," Carmen instructed sharply. When she looked at the detectives, her expression softened. "We're trying to cooperate here, but I'm not going to allow these scattershot questions. You've got no evidence tying Tony to Ms. Hendrix's murder. The fact that he had a few dates with her is irrelevant."

"It is her refusal to continue seeing him that pushed him over the edge and drove him to kill her."

"Oh, please." Escobar rolled her eyes. "Kids date. Kids move on."

"Two of the women he gave books of poetry to were murdered," Michelle added. "It's a pattern."

Carmen laughed harshly. "There have got to be a lot of people the girls knew in common. They were friends, for heaven's sake."

"Why did you give a book of love poems to someone you only dated a few times?" Michelle asked Tony.

Tony shrugged. "Girls like stuff like that. They like poetry. They like guys who like poetry. And they like to think they're special. It's a no-brainer."

Erling's skin crawled at the thought of Tony with his daughter. "Why your sister, then? Or were you trying to get into her pants, too?"

"That's disgusting," Tony said.

"And entirely out of line," Carmen Escobar added. "Tony didn't come here to be insulted."

*He didn't come here at all,* Erling thought. *We hauled his ass in.* "Where were you the night your sister was killed?" he barked.

Tony shrugged. "I worked until midnight. Then I went out for a few beers with some friends." Another slug of his soda. "Talk to them if you want. They'll vouch for me."

Michelle slid a notebook over the table to Tony. "Give us their names and contact information."

He looked to Carmen Escobar, who nodded. Tony started writing.

"What about Crystal Adams?" Erling asked. "Do you know her?"

"Nope. Never even saw her except for that photograph Kali O'Brien showed me."

Michelle leaned on the table. "Did Olivia ever talk about Crystal?"

"Olivia didn't talk about anyone but Olivia."

Erling scooted his chair away from the table and rose to lean against the wall. His nerves were as taut as steel. "What about Mindy? What's your interest there?"

Tony held up his palms, mocking the question. "My intentions were honorable. Your little girl is safe."

"What's your interest in her?"

"Why not?" Tony looked genuinely puzzled. His eyes softened. "She's cute. She's bright. She's fun."

"How'd you meet her?"

"She's taking this contemporary fiction class I sit in on sometimes." Tony's expression grew animated. "We discovered we like a lot of the same stuff."

Erling couldn't imagine that Mindy would have anything in common with this creep.

Carmen Escobar gathered the papers she'd pulled out at the start of the interview. "This is a waste of everyone's time. You've got nothing on my client. I assume he's free to go?"

In the heat of Erling's fear for his daughter, Tony had seemed a maniacal threat. Now Erling wasn't so sure. The kid was a punk, but bottom line was, they didn't have enough to hold him. "He's free to go for now," Erling said.

Tony pulled himself to his feet, a smirk distorting the earlier softness Erling had noted. "Thanks for the Coke," he muttered.

"We'll have our eyes on you," Erling warned. "We'll be watching your every move."

Tony laughed. "You're in for some boring days."

Carmen Escobar ushered her client out, stopping at the door to glare at the detectives. "You have your killer—John O'Brien. I don't understand why you're hassling the victim's brother. The family has been through enough."

"We're not hassling him," Erling said. "We're looking at all viable possibilities."

"Does that mean you've cleared O'Brien?"

"No," Erling said emphatically.

Michelle nodded in agreement. "It's still an open investigation. We're looking at several different angles."

When they were alone again, Michelle tapped the notebook where Tony had written the contact information for the friends he was with the night of his sister's murder. "We can check his alibi pretty easily," she pointed out, "but I suspect it will hold up."

"Then why did he originally lie about knowing Hayley?"

"A stripper who thinks she's too good for him. He probably didn't want to get into the whole seamy story with us."

"Maybe." Erling shoved his hands into his pockets. "I'll feel better when I know he has a solid alibi for the time when she was killed."

Michelle rolled a pen between her palms. "For myself, I'd feel better if I knew what Kali O'Brien is keeping from us."

Erling nodded. "I think it may be time to push her a little."

"You're off the case, remember?"

"Right. But it wouldn't hurt to talk to her. Sort of a follow-up on our little conversation with Tony."

He was afraid Michelle would refuse. She regarded him for a moment, then tossed her pen on the desk. "Let's go."

# CHAPTER 46

Kali hadn't eaten since breakfast, and the half glass of Chardonnay she'd had with Silverman had gone straight to her head. The smart thing would be to go home. Sabrina would be arriving soon from Scottsdale. They could eat something healthy and call it a night. But after seeing Nash's name on the guest list, the questions buzzing in her brain wouldn't leave her alone.

As soon as she got back into her car, she pulled out her cell phone and called him. If he wasn't home or if he sounded annoyed at being bothered, she'd forget it and try to reach him at work the next day.

Instead, he sounded pleased to hear from her.

"I was just going out to grab a bite," he said. "You want to come along? Nothing fancy, I'm afraid. But I'm starved."

"Sure. Where are you going?"

"I was thinking pizza or Chinese. What's your preference?"

"They both sound good."

"Let's do Chinese. There's a great place near St. Phillips Plaza. It's called Hunan Village." He gave her the address.

"Great. I'll meet you there in twenty minutes."

* * *

Nash had already ordered when Kali arrived at Hunan Village, a cozy place with a large plastic fern near the entrance and red upholstered booths along the walls.

"We can add to it," he explained, "but I thought food sooner was better than food later."

Kali slid into the booth across from him. "Sooner is definitely better." She hadn't realized how hungry she was until she smelled the spicy aromas of vinegar, hot peppers, and soy sauce.

The waitress brought spring rolls and fried wontons, followed by hot and sour soup. While they were working their way through those, they ordered two more dishes along with steamed rice.

It wasn't until the Schezwan prawns and Mongolian beef arrived that Nash asked the obvious.

"To what do I owe this pleasure?" He nudged the prawns closer to Kali. "Something about John? Or was it my personal charisma that prompted your call?"

"A little of both." It had seemed so straightforward earlier, but now she wasn't sure how to approach the subject. Finally, she just blurted it out. "Why didn't you say anything about knowing Olivia Perez?"

Nash blinked, looking stunned, then recovered and shot her a grin. "What makes you think I knew her?"

"You were at a party earlier in the summer. Some kind of adult entertainment event. You and Olivia spent time talking."

He regarded her thoughtfully as he poked at his food with his chopsticks.

"I know my brother was a financial backer," she said, "so if you're worried about keeping his name out of it, don't be."

Nash nodded. "John turned me on to the opportunities. It can be a profitable business. We both made out pretty well. John put the bug in Reed's ear, too."

"Was Reed at the party? Did he know Olivia?"

Nash sipped his beer. "He wasn't at the event, but he must have known Olivia through Sloane."

"So tell me about her."

"There's not much to tell. I talked to her at the party. I talked to a number of women there. That was the fun of going. As you can imagine, I nearly keeled over when I heard about the murders and learned she was the young woman Sloane had taken in."

"Why didn't you say something?" Kali asked again.

"What was there to say? That I invested money in X-rated enterprises? That she'd acted in a few films? None of it seemed relevant." He paused. "Is it?"

Kali leaned back. "I don't know. But don't you think it's odd that John would wind up accused of her murder?"

"It was Sloane's murder he was actually accused of. I got the impression Olivia just happened to be there."

"That was the original theory," Kali said. "But the police may have been wrong about that."

Nash raised an eyebrow. "Why would he kill Olivia? He wasn't at the party. I doubt he'd ever met her."

Nash's words were reassuring. He and John had been friends, after all. And they both had financial ties to the porn industry. If John had been involved in something illicit, wouldn't Nash have known about it?

"It wasn't just Olivia." Kali told him about Hayley and Crystal, and the photo she'd found tucked inside John's dictionary. "John never said anything about these girls?"

Nash shook his head. "It was strictly about the money as far as he was concerned."

Kali was about to press him further when her phone rang.

"Ms. O'Brien? It's Joanna Sommers, Olivia's friend. I see that girl you were asking about."

Kali's heart jumped. "Crystal? Where?"

"Outside a liquor store. It's on Sixth near Speedway. She's just standing around, like she's panhandling or something."

"Thanks, Joanna. I appreciate you calling me." Kali flipped off her phone and turned to Nash. "I hate to run off, but someone just saw one of the girls I told you about. I need to talk to her. I may be getting close to having some answers."

"You have to go right away? Don't you want to finish your dinner first?"

"I don't know how long she'll be there." Kali pulled out some money to put on the table, but Nash stopped her.

"My treat," he said.

"Thank you."

He signaled the waitress for the check. "If you insist on leaving, why don't I come with you?"

"That's not necessary."

He smiled. "Necessary has nothing to do with it. I was looking forward to your company for a bit longer."

Kali was tempted. But two of them might scare Crystal off. Better to do this alone. "We'll do dinner again," she said. "My treat next time."

"You sure you don't want me to come along? What if there's trouble?"

"Nothing's going to happen. I just want to talk to her."

Kali grabbed her purse. As she rushed for the exit, she saw Nash reach for his billfold, his gaze following her out the door. She would definitely have to make it up to him.

# CHAPTER 47

Kali found the liquor store near a busy intersection and pulled over to the curb half a block away. From where she sat, she might not have recognized Crystal if it hadn't been for the burgundy-hued birthmark on her jaw and neck. The hair that had been shoulder length in the photo was now short and spiky, and platinum instead of honey brown. The face in the photo appeared fresh and animated. Not so the one now trying to catch the eyes of passing strangers. Crystal's expression was wary, her posture lifeless as she slouched against the building. Despite the warm night, she wore a sweatshirt, which fell over her jeans to midthigh.

As Kali watched, an occasional passerby dipped into his pocket for spare change or a single bill, but most people walked past without acknowledging the girl's presence.

After maybe five minutes, Kali got out of the car. As she locked the door, she glanced across the street and recognized Nash's silver BMW parked at the curb. She checked traffic, then crossed over. He rolled down the window when she approached.

"What are you doing here?" she asked. "Did you follow me?"

He gave a sheepish smile and held up his hands in mock surrender. "I wanted to make sure you were okay."

"I said I would be, didn't I?" Kali supposed she should be flattered that he cared about her safety. She wasn't one of those women who took affront at male chivalry. But at the same time, she didn't like others micromanaging her life. Or ignoring her wishes.

"I was also hoping we could go out for a drink or something when you were done," Nash added.

"Not tonight. I'm sorry."

"You're not mad that I'm here, are you?"

She allowed a hint of a smile. "A little. But I won't hold it against you."

He nodded. "Be careful, okay?"

Kali crossed the street again. As she neared the liquor store, Crystal mumbled, "Spare change, ma'am?"

Kali reached for her wallet and handed over a dollar. Crystal tucked the money into the front pocket of her sweatshirt. "Thanks."

"There's more if you'll talk to me," Kali told her.

"What do you mean, 'talk'?"

"A conversation."

Crystal eyed Kali skeptically. "That's all?"

Kali nodded and took out a five-dollar bill. "I'm John O'Brien's sister."

"Who?"

"John O'Brien."

Crystal looked away. "Whatever."

"I know you were a friend of Olivia Perez's and Hayley Hendrix's, too."

Crystal's gaze bounced back to Kali, her expression sparked with alarm. "I don't know what you're talk . . ." Her breathing quickened. "I haven't said a word. I swear."

"About what, Crystal?"

She shook her head, nervously scanning the sidewalk to either side of her.

"How do you know John?" Kali asked.

But the girl was no longer listening. Lightning quick, she grabbed the five dollars from Kali and bolted up the street. Kali sprinted after her, hobbled by open-back sandals and the awkward weight of her shoulder bag. She pushed past a sauntering pair of baggy-pant teens and grabbed Crystal's sleeve.

"Please," Kali urged. "Talk to me. I want to help you."

Crystal yanked her arm free, spilling the bills and coins from her sweatshirt pocket onto the pavement. For an instant, she hesitated, glancing with anguish at the lost treasure, then took off again, zigzagging past pedestrians and into traffic.

"Watch out!" Kali screamed, just as a taxi swerved to avoid the fleeing girl. There was a sound of ripping metal as the taxi sideswiped a sedan parked at the curb.

Kali raced after Crystal, ignoring the angry words and gestures spewing from the taxi driver.

Half a block farther, she caught up with Crystal again. But just as she got hold of the girl's wrist, a wiry guy in a bicycle helmet tackled Kali, knocking her to the ground. Crystal pulled free and slipped away.

"Listen, lady, I saw it all."

Kali gasped for air. The wind had been knocked from her lungs, her left leg felt as if it were on fire, and her palms stung from scraping the pavement where she'd caught herself. She sat on one hip, holding the knee that had gotten the worst of it. The pain was intense but already ebbing by the time she caught her breath.

Crystal was nowhere in sight.

She glowered at the bicyclist. "What do you think you're doing?"

"Holding you until the cops get here. What gives you the right to hassle that poor girl? She wasn't hurting anyone. You caused an accident, lady. And you about got me killed."

Kali shut her eyes. "That's not what happened."

"The hell it isn't. I saw it."

"I wasn't hassling her," Kali argued. "We have a mutual friend. I merely wanted to talk to her."

"Well, she obviously didn't want to talk to you."

On that point the young bicyclist was dead-on.

The driver who belonged to the parked car emerged from

the liquor store and started yelling at the cab driver. A deep gouge ran the length of the sedan, and the cab's bumper was still crumpled against its fender. A cop car pulled up moments later and the shouting intensified. Kali limped over to explain as best she could.

When she looked for Nash, he was gone. Not that he could have helped right then, but despite her earlier protests of independence, she'd have welcomed a little moral support.

An hour later, following a stern lecture and a ticket for impeding traffic, Kali pulled into the driveway at John's. She wanted a hot shower and a stiff drink, not necessarily in that order, but when she saw the now familiar black sheriff's sedan in the driveway, she knew she wasn't going to get them. Not right away.

"My God. What happened?" Sabrina asked, rushing to greet Kali at the door.

"I'll explain later." She gestured toward the car in the driveway. "Is that who I think it is?"

Sabrina nodded. "They just got here."

"What do they want?"

"They have some questions for you."

Could they have heard about her encounter with Crystal already? Did they have new information about John? Or maybe it was simply a follow-up to the information she'd passed along about the poetry book.

Kali limped into the living room, where her sister had settled the detectives in with coffee. Shafer looked ready to snap her head off, but Michelle Parker had that same soft-eyed, swallowing-a-smile look she always did.

"What can I do for you?" Kali asked, without a trace of diplomacy. "Is this about Tony Perez?"

"Indirectly," Michelle said.

Shafer interrupted before his partner could continue. "He tells us you showed him a photograph of Olivia with two other girls—Hayley Hendrix and a third girl he assumed from your questions was Crystal Adams."

Kali nodded. No use denying it. She wasn't sure she wanted to anyway.

"What are you doing with a photograph of two, possibly three, murdered girls? What's your interest?"

"Only two," Kali said. "Only two of them are dead. Crystal is still alive. I just saw her." That was the silver lining in today's disaster. Crystal was alive and Kali wanted to keep her that way, so she was going to tell the detectives everything. Even if it cast John in a bad light.

"That doesn't answer the question," Shafer said.

Kali dropped into an empty chair. "I found the photo. John had it."

Sabrina shot her a dirty look. "Kali, be careful."

"Your brother John?" Michelle asked.

"Right. I have no idea where he got it or why he had it. At first, I didn't think much about it. Then I saw a news picture of Olivia Perez and recognized that she was one of the girls in John's photo." She turned to Michelle. "When I was in your office and saw the artist's sketch of Hayley Hendrix, I realized she was one of the other girls."

"But you didn't speak up?"

"Do you blame me?" Kali could feel anger beginning to churn inside her. "You were so sure John was a murderer. You wouldn't even seriously consider the notion that he might have been murdered himself. You"—she pointed to Shafer—"all you cared about was covering your own ass."

"That's not true!"

"Why are you still involved in this, anyway?"

Michelle Parker put a hand out. "Let's not spin our wheels on what's in the past. Your brother clearly had ties to the three girls. Any idea what these ties were?"

Kali ignored Sabrina's stony glare and told the detectives about Hayley's and Olivia's involvement in porn. And John's. "From what I can determine, his interest was purely financial, though."

Shafer got up and paced the room. "You've been sitting on vital information," he snapped. "We should haul you in for obstruction of justice."

"Maybe if you'd actually done your job," Kali shot back, "you'd have learned what I did."

Michelle leaned forward. "What else can you tell us?" Her voice was soft.

Kali handed over the photograph. "That's Crystal Adams," she said. "Only her hair is short now and bleached. Her real name is Raelene. Her mom's dead and her dad lives in San Diego."

"Does she make porn movies, too?"

"I don't know. My brother hired a private investigator to locate her parents, but I have no idea why. She was outside a liquor store on Sixth near Speedway earlier this evening. She ran off when I tried to talk to her." Kali closed her eyes. She needed some Motrin and a drink. Not a good combination, but right then, a necessary one. "That's everything. Now please leave."

Shafer grumbled. Michelle handed her card. "I wrote my cell number on the back," she said.

While Sabrina showed them out, Kali mentally relived her encounter with Crystal. She'd handled it badly. The girl was clearly scared, and Kali had managed to spook her further. She could only hope the detectives would succeed where she'd failed.

# CHAPTER 48

"What do you think?" Erling asked Michelle once they were outside the house.

"I don't know. None of it fits as nicely as I'd like."

"No matter what Kali says, John O'Brien has to have been involved somehow."

"Involved in what, though?" Michelle asked. "And with whom?"

Erling opened the car door, slid behind the wheel, and waited for Michelle to buckle up before starting the engine.

"Anyway," she added in a tone just short of accusatory, "it's not your case now. I'll fill Bob Morgan in on today's events and we'll take it from there."

Erling knew he'd brought his troubles on himself, but this being shunted aside still rankled. Besides which, Morgan was a lightweight who cared more about seeing his name in print than nose-to-the-ground investigation.

He said, "Sounds like this girl, Crystal Adams, might be the key."

"Yeah. We'll talk to the Tucson PD beat cops and ask around. Trouble is, sounds like she doesn't want to be found. And now that Kali has scared her off, she'll be doubly skittish." Michelle checked her watch. "You want to grab a bite to eat before calling it quits?"

"Sorry, I've got some fences to mend at home. Assuming they let me anywhere near the ranch."

"I have a spare bedroom," Michelle offered. "You know, if you need a place to stay for a few days."

"Thanks, but I'll manage." He pulled into the station lot. "You were married once, right?" Erling didn't really know much about Michelle's personal life. Wasn't interested, either. But she was the only woman besides Deena he knew well, and he respected her.

"If you can call it that."

"Who left, you or him?"

"Physically, I kicked him out. Emotionally, he was never there. But you're really asking about you and Deena, right? Your situation is different. The two of you have been married a long time. You have a daughter." She hesitated. "And a son who died. I'm not saying what you did doesn't matter, because it does, or that Deena will forgive you for it. Just that your situation is different. There are bonds that are not easily broken."

"I seem to be making a mess of my entire life," Erling said, with a sigh. "Now I'm on the outs with Mindy, as well."

Michelle made a face. "That I can't help you with at all. I know nothing about kids."

"Except that you were one yourself, a lot more recently than I was."

"And I was a holy terror. I know I gave my parents a shitload of grief. But I also loved them, though I didn't realize it at the time. Mindy will be pissed at you, but I bet she'll get over it eventually. You overreacted because you care about her."

He nodded. Too bad he couldn't defend as easily what he'd done to Deena.

"By the way," Michelle said, "I was going over the list of people who called in after we announced finding Hayley's body—back when she was still unidentified. Sloane Winslow was one of them."

"Why didn't she come forward with the girl's identity, I wonder?"

"We didn't have the sketch yet," Michelle reminded him.

"And from the notes, it looks like she was thinking the body might be someone else."

"Crystal?" Erling remembered Sloane's phone call to his own machine. Had she tried to reach him for more information?

"That's what I was thinking," Michelle said. "The sooner we find this girl, the better."


Erling was expecting the firing squad at home. What he got instead was isolation.

Mindy acted as though he didn't exist. She ignored anything he said, walked right past him, and talked to her mother as if he weren't standing right there. She refused to eat dinner with them. Instead, she made a tuna sandwich and ate it in her room.

Deena lambasted him for overacting and making a scene by having the cops pull Mindy over, then fell into a hostile silence. She recognized his presence at the dinner table only long enough to ask him to pass the salad. The fact that she'd even served dinner should have made him hopeful, but her indifference cut through him like a knife. He was incapable of feeling anything but pain and yearning and deep regret.

"Let me do the dishes," he said when they'd finished their silent meal.

"Why, so you can tell yourself you're trying, you're being a good guy and I'm such a bitch to be mad?" Deena pushed back her chair and started to clear the dishes.

"No, of course not."

"So you can tell yourself you've been an attentive husband and I'm ungrateful?"

He followed her into the kitchen. "Deena, that's not the way it is. Believe me. I know I made a mistake—"

"*Mistake*?" She turned to face him. Cheating on your wife is not a mistake—it's a conscious betrayal."

"Maybe mistake was the wrong word. What I meant is, I know what I did was wrong. And I'm terribly, terribly sorry. It's just that I don't know what else to do at this point."

"Maybe there's nothing you *can* do."

Her words caused Erling's blood to run cold. "Are you saying you can't forgive me?"

Deena turned back to the sink. "This isn't something I can just tell myself to get over, you know."

"I understand that." Although part of him, he realized, did want her to simply get over it. It wasn't like he'd run off with Sloane, or even seriously contemplated it. And it was over now anyway. Had been over even before Sloane was killed. Whatever happened to "Let bygones be bygones"?

Erling tentatively touched Deena's shoulder. She brushed him away. "Fine, do the dishes. I'm going to take a bath." She left the room.

Remorse gnawed at him like some vicious animal chewing on his gut. He'd destroyed everything. Everything he'd held dear. How could he have been so stupid? So thoughtless? He promised himself that whatever it took, he was going to make it up to Deena. He was going to earn her forgiveness. And Mindy's, too.

When he'd loaded the dishwasher and wiped the counters, Erling faced the long night. A pariah in his own home.

He knocked on Mindy's door, then opened it without waiting for an invitation.

"I'm studying," she said. Though she lay on her bed with a magazine rather than school books.

"I want to tell you I'm sorry about what happened today. It wasn't my intention to embarrass you." Erling sat down beside her and she didn't protest. "I was so worried," he said.

"Tony will probably never speak to me again."

"If he's a decent person he'll understand."

"Yeah, sure. You are so clueless sometimes." Mindy's eyes were on the magazine, but Erling could tell she wasn't reading. "Is he in trouble?" she asked after a moment.

"No. At least not based on what we know now. His sister was murdered, and another girl he knew. But there's nothing that links him to those crimes."

"You sure came on charging like there was."

Erling leaned back against the headboard, exhausted. "I

thought there might have been. He knew both victims, and then he gave you a book of love poems like he'd given them. If he was involved . . . and anything happened to you . . ." Erling's voice broke. He put his head in his hands.

What a mess he'd made of everything. Mindy. His marriage. His job. It all washed over him, sucking the air from his lungs. His shoulders convulsed. "I couldn't bear it if anything bad happened to you. I love you so much."

Erling felt the bed shift as Mindy swung her legs over the side. He thought she was leaving, flaunting her disdain for him. Instead, she scooted next to him and hugged him.

"I know you do, Daddy." She paused. "And I love you, too, even though I'm still mad at you."

Erling gave up trying to choke back the tears. He cradled his daughter in his arms and she let him hold her.

He felt his cell phone vibrate on his belt. He wanted to ignore it, but he knew it had to be work. "Sorry, honey," he said, reluctantly releasing his hold on her. "I need to take this call."

"It's okay, Dad." She actually patted him on the knee.

"Yeah," Erling said into the phone as he eased himself from the bed. He stopped at the door to Mindy's room and blew his daughter a kiss.

"I know you're off the case," Michelle said, "but I think you're going to be interested in this."

# CHAPTER 49

Kali was exhausted but she couldn't sleep, despite a couple of glasses of wine and a heavy dose of Motrin. Her body ached and her nerves were jumpy.

Finally, a little after midnight, she got out of bed, limped into the kitchen, and made herself a cup of lemon herb tea. She took it into John's study to check her e-mail. When she set the cup down on the desk, her elbow knocked over one of the boxes Sabrina had packed up to take home, spilling a loose collection of old family snapshots onto the floor.

Kali picked up the photos one by one. She worked slowly, taking time to savor each one before putting it back into the box. Her parents on their wedding day. John as a baby in their mother's lap. The three of them as kids in front of the Christmas tree. John had been about ten, squared shoulders and cocky grin even then. She was reminded once again of all they'd lost by years of estrangement.

There were photos taken at birthday parties and soccer games and summers spent on the beach down by the river. John's high school graduation photo, just like the one her parents had displayed in a frame on the mantel back in Silver Creek. A picture taken at John's college graduation. He was in his cap and gown standing beside their beaming dad. Another showed him with a younger, thinner Reed, also in cap and gown. With them was a girl a few years younger. She had Reed's pale coloring, broad-set eyes, and square jaw.

Even though it was one in the morning, Kali went into Sabrina's room and turned on the light.

"What's happening?" Sabrina shielded her eyes from the brightness with her hand. "Is something the matter?"

"I couldn't sleep."

"So you had to wake me up, too? It's the middle of the night, Kali."

"I know what time it is." Kali showed her the photo. "Who's this?"

Sabrina grumbled and reached for her glasses. "It's John." She gave Kali an accusatory look. "You had to wake me to ask that?"

"Who's with him?"

"The guy is Reed. The girl is Sloane."

"Reed and Sloane. Don't they look a bit like Crystal in that picture of John's?"

Sabrina looked at the photo again. "Yeah, sort of, since you mention it." She set her glasses back on the bedside table. "Can I go back to sleep now?"


Kali never did go back to sleep. But she waited until seven in the morning to call Doug Simon and ask him to look into the family histories of Ray and Martha Adams.

"Are you looking for something in particular?" he asked.

"See if either of them is related in some way to the Logan family."

"The murdered woman's family?"

"Right. Her brother, Reed, is still in Tucson running the family business started by their grandfather. As far as I know, Sloane was his only sibling, but they probably have cousins and other extended family."

"Sure, I can do that," Simon replied. "It shouldn't be too difficult."

\*   \*   \*

Despite the lack of sleep, Kali was keyed up and antsy. She wanted desperately to find Crystal—although she had no idea how she'd convince the girl to talk to her when Crystal had already run from her once.

Sabrina focused less on the running and more on Crystal's plight.

"I feel so bad for that child," she told Kali. "We know what it's like to lose your mother when you're young. Dad may not have been the rock of Gibraltar, but he loved us. He did the best he could."

For years, Kali had assumed their mother's death had barely touched Sabrina. That she, Kali, had been the only one to suffer. But as she and Sabrina had gradually mended their differences, she'd learned that wasn't so. Each of them, and John, too, had borne the weight of grief. They'd simply grieved differently.

"She must feel so alone," Kali agreed.

"She *is* alone." Sabrina shook her head sadly. "It breaks my heart. Imagine living on the streets, reduced to begging. No youngster deserves that, no matter what she's done."

They had planned to devote the day to filling out the reams of paper sent by the bank and brokerage house John used. But like an elusive gnat near one's ear, thoughts of Crystal nagged them both. Finally, Sabrina went to ask Reed about cousins named Adams, and Kali went off in search of Crystal.

First stop was Sunshine House. No one had seen Crystal, of course. That would have been too easy.

She went back to the liquor store, where the clerk shook his head. "Some guy was by here earlier asking the same thing."

"A police detective?"

"Musta been."

She walked around the campus, drove by Hayley's old apartment, then finally gave up and went back to John's, feeling discouraged by her fruitless afternoon. Sabrina hadn't returned yet.

The phone started ringing the minute Kali stepped through the door. She picked up. "Hello."

Silence, though she could hear breathing on the other end. Then a girlish voice, high-pitched and thin. "This is Crystal. Are you the woman who wanted to talk to me yesterday?"

Kali's pulse quickened. "Where are you?"

"You still want to talk?"

"Tell me where you are. I'll come right away."

Crystal's voice quavered when she gave Kali the address. "It's off Gate's Pass Road."

"I'll leave the minute we hang up."

Kali scribbled a quick note to Sabrina and was on her way.

# CHAPTER 50

It wasn't until she was on the road that Kali wondered how Crystal had known how to reach her. Then she remembered she'd said she was John O'Brien's sister. John was listed in the phone book. It wouldn't have been difficult for Crystal to get the number, assuming she didn't already know it.

The directions took Kali south and west, out of town to an area where she'd never been before. It was more open and rural than the city proper, an uneven mix of newer homes and ramshackle structures on lots strewn with old appliances and cars on blocks. The farther she drove, the fewer and more widely spaced the houses.

What was Crystal doing way out here? Kali wondered. Was she staying with a friend? And how had she gotten here?

Or was Crystal not the innocent Kali and Sabrina imagined?

At the end of a rutted, single-lane road, Kali found the address she was looking for—a newly constructed house that looked to be not quite completed. The exterior siding hadn't been painted and blue tape still lined the glass panes of the windows. No vehicles were around, and no sign of work in progress. Kali guessed the owners had gotten this far and run out of money, or there'd been a construction dispute.

She started to knock on the front door, but it swung open with her first touch, and she stepped into the dim interior. Concrete subflooring and Sheetrocked walls. Loose nails and scraps of molding were strewn about, but no tools.

"Crystal?"

She heard a muffled whimpering from off to her right, followed by what sounded like a peacock clearing its throat. Kali moved forward cautiously. She noticed signs of squatters: food wrappers, blankets, empty soda cans.

"Crystal?"

The sounds seemed to be coming from a room in what she guessed was the bedroom wing. She passed an open doorway and felt her heart stop at the flicker of a human form until she realized it was her own image reflected in the bathroom mirror.

Kali pulled out her cell phone and set autodial to the sheriff's number she'd programmed in weeks ago. If there was trouble, all she'd have to do was hit SEND.

"Crystal?" she called again.

The whimpering was louder now, coming from the room at the end of the hall. Kali peered inside—a large master bedroom suite from the looks of it.

Crystal lay on the floor, bound and gagged, but squealing frantically. Her eyes were wild and darting.

"My God, what happened?"

As Kali rushed to the girl, she felt the movement of air behind her, the splitting pain of something hard coming down on the back of her head. She staggered forward and crumpled to the floor.


A sharp pain in her right shin pulled Kali from the inky blackness.

She opened an eye and the room began to spin. She closed her eye again.

Another kick in the shin. Groaning, she tried to prop herself up on an elbow. Only then did she realize that her hands and feet were tied. Her mouth was gagged.

And her cell phone was nowhere in sight.

Confusion gave way to panic when she remembered what had happened.

A sour taste rose in her throat. No, she couldn't be sick. Not gagged like this. She'd choke on her own vomit.

Just as Hayley Hendrix had.

The flush of fear grabbed her. *Breathe slowly,* she told herself. *Stay calm.*

She swallowed hard several times, pulled air in through her nostrils. Gradually her mind focused and she saw that Crystal, still bound and gagged, had managed to scoot close enough to kick her. The girl's eyes locked on Kali's with fear and pleading.

A thousand questions skittered through Kali's brain, but she could manage to make only unintelligible sounds. Finally, she nodded toward the door and raised a questioning eyebrow. Crystal shrugged and responded with her own garbled attempts to speak.

Kali didn't know where their abductor had gone or how long it would be until he returned, but she was certain he would come back. They had to get free somehow.

She squirmed, trying to maneuver her body along the floor to get closer to Crystal. Her hands were bound behind her, as were the girl's. If they could get back to back, maybe they could work the ropes free.

The cement floor scraped Kali's sore body as she inched herself around. Her head throbbed, and as she moved a little too fast the world started spinning again. But she kept going.

Crystal's eyes were wide with fright. Suddenly she seemed to understand what Kali was trying to do. She maneuvered her own body to a position where their backs were almost touching.

Working blindly, Kali felt for the girl's wrists. At the same time, Crystal was frantically scrambling for Kali's. They'd never get themselves freed this way. Finally, Kali took hold of Crystal's hands and held them firmly for a moment, then squeezed them to signal that Crystal should remain still.

Then she went to work on the knots. They were tight and hard to get at. And she had to work backward, by feel, without being able to see what she was doing. After what seemed like forever, she managed to loosen one knot, allowing some slack in the tie. But there were so many remaining knots and twists, Kali almost gave in to a wave of defeat.

Instead, she slid her body higher and worked the knots of Crystal's gag. After a minute or so, she was rewarded with a deep gasping of air and a grateful "Thank you."

"I'll get yours now," Crystal said, as she inched her body into place. "He made me call you," she hiccuped. "I'm so sorry I got you into this."

Crystal began working Kali's gag. "Oh, God, I'm sorry it's taking me so long. I'm so clumsy." Her voice was quick and breathless. Kali could feel Crystal's hands trembling. Her whole body.

She willed the girl to work faster. Finally, the gag loosened and Kali rubbed her cheek on the floor to pull it free.

"I thought you were with him," Crystal said.

"With whom?"

"The man. I don't know his name. Hayley arranged it."

Kali slid back to where she could work on Crystal's hands. "Arranged what?"

"Our gig at the party. Some movie guy. Hayley really wanted to get into the business, so it seemed like a good thing to do. Only it wasn't a party. And—"

"Shh. I hear a car outside." Kali froze and Crystal whimpered.

Footsteps in the house.

He'd come back for them already.

They were trapped like animals about to be slaughtered.

Kali's eyes were riveted on the doorway to the bedroom. As the footsteps grew closer, her heart kicked into overdrive, beating so furiously she could feel it in her toes. When a shadowy figure appeared, panic choked her.

Then she saw who it was and relief washed over her.

A. J. Nash.

She'd been angry when he'd followed her the other day. But not now.

"Thank God, it's you. How did you find us? Quick, untie us. Call for help."

Crystal shrieked. "What are you talking about? That's him!"

As Crystal's words registered, Kali realized Nash was holding a gun. And it was pointed at her.

Her stomach roiled. "Why?" she whispered.

Nash laughed, a humorless guttural sound like the bark of a seal. "What is it with women, always wanting to know *why*? Always butting into things that are none of their business. You should have let well enough alone. I tried to warn you."

"What do you mean?"

"You didn't think the rock was an accident, did you?"

"It was you who broke John's window? You let the air out of my tire?"

"I made sure it got done. Why couldn't you have just cleaned out John's house and gone back to la-la land?"

"That's L.A." she said. "I live in the North."

"I don't give a fuck where you live. You won't live anywhere pretty soon."

Kali's throat closed. Her pulse rang in her ears. She looked at Nash with disbelief. Did he really plan to kill her?

With an awful, knifelike clarity, she realized what was happening. "You killed Sloane and Olivia," Kali whispered.

"That's what happens when you stick your nose where it doesn't belong."

"And John." Her breath caught at her brother's name. "He was your friend."

"He was trouble," Nash muttered. "Asking questions and stirring things up just like Sloane. His being the cops' chief suspect was an added bonus. Getting rid of him meant an end to their investigation. Until you came along, that is."

"What about Hayley?" Crystal shouted. "That was his fault."

"My fault?" Nash looked at Crystal with fury and contempt. "You're the one who got hysterical. You're the one who was the problem." He turned back to Kali. "Hayley was nothing. Girls like her are a dime a dozen. No one would have cared one way or another except that Sloane got on her high horse about finding Crystal."

"What did she want with me?" Crystal squeaked.

"She was a know-it-all who couldn't keep her nose out of other people's business," Nash shot back angrily.

Kali recoiled at the venom in his voice. He was nothing like the quiet man with the droll sense of humor she'd had drinks with.

"What about Olivia?" Kali whispered. "Whatever your problem with Sloane, why kill an innocent bystander?"

"Olivia's dead?" The pitch of Crystal's voice rose.

Another seal-like bark. "The cunt tried to blackmail me. She was too good to work for me but she was happy enough to squeeze me for money. I don't know how much she told Sloane, but Sloane was looking high and low for Crystal. It was only a matter of time until my name came up. Seemed easiest to get rid of them both at once."

Crystal was breathing hard now. "You can't get away with this, you know. You can't just keep killing people."

"I don't have to keep killing people," Nash scoffed. "You two are going to wrap it up nice and neat. Crystal is going to shoot Kali—"

"No, I'm not!"

"You don't have to pull the trigger, sweetheart. I'm going to do that. But I'll make it look like you did it. Then you're going to shoot yourself."

"No!"

"I'll help—don't worry. Simple and tidy."

Kali thrashed against the ropes that bound her. "You think the cops are going to believe that?"

"Sure. Especially when I tell them how you figured out it was Crystal who killed Hayley and Olivia."

"But I didn't," Crystal sobbed. "Hayley was my friend. I tried to save her. I didn't even want to do the bondage stuff, but *he*"—Crystal spat the words in Nash's direction—"he made us."

"I hardly think I forced you."

Crystal shook her head. "Hayley didn't do drugs. You kept pushing them on her. She told you the collar and mask were too tight. She was gagging and choking and you wouldn't let go!"

"Shut up." Nash raised the gun.

"They'll know it wasn't Crystal," Kali told him. "They'll be able to tell by the angle of the bullet."

Nash laughed. "I watch *CSI*, too. They'll know the killer was standing, but that's all. Besides, I've just been out establishing an alibi. There's nothing that connects me to any of this."

"Besides six murders, you mean."

He smirked. "You never learn, do you?"

The gun fired.

Kali rolled to her left just as the first bullet sailed past. A scream locked in her throat. She couldn't breathe. Nash stepped closer and fired again as she rolled the other way. Pain exploded in her shoulder.

Out of the corner of her eyes, Kali saw Crystal kick her bound legs, quick and straight, catching Nash in the knees. He staggered and the gun went off a third time, shattering a window.

Crystal had managed to work one hand free. She grabbed Nash's leg and sank her teeth into his ankle. He howled and the gun went skittering.

Nash kicked Crystal in the face with his other foot, breaking her hold on him. She yelped in pain and he scrambled after the gun.

Kali's shoulder felt as though it had been drilled through with a red hot poker. The pain radiated and pulsed through her entire torso. She felt herself growing light-headed and faint.

When a familiar female voice yelled, "Drop it!" Kali was sure she was hallucinating.

# CHAPTER 51

Kali remembered only snippets of what followed. The ambulance ride to the hospital with the dark-haired paramedic holding her hand urging her to "stay with us." The bright lights of the operating room. The nurse calling her "honey" as she inserted the IV apparatus and injected painkilling drugs, bringing blessed relief. Her parched throat and sweat-soaked bedding.

And then Sabrina standing by the side of the hospital bed spooning ice chips into her mouth.

"What day is it?" Kali mumbled. Her mouth felt as though it were filled with cotton.

"Saturday. You've been here two nights. And you're going to be fine." Sabrina's voice choked, and Kali knew her sister must have had her doubts over the last forty-eight hours.

"Your tennis serve might suffer a little," Sabrina added, trying for levity, "but the doctor thinks that with physical therapy you'll have pretty much full use of your arm and shoulder."

Kali felt as though she never wanted to move that part of her body again, anyway. The painkillers were helping, but the shoulder still burned and throbbed. "Was it Detective Parker who showed up in the nick of time or am I imagining that?"

"As usual, you're as sharp as a tack." Sabrina grinned.

"Why was she there?"

"I called her."

"You what?"

Sabrina held a cup of water with a straw for Kali to drink. "You left me a cryptic note about going off alone to some godforsaken place. You don't think clearly sometimes."

Coming from Sabrina, the last remark was almost laughable. Except that Kali was in no laughing mood and Sabrina was right. Her sister's phone call had saved Kali's life.

"Thank you," Kali whispered. "If you hadn't alerted them—"

"Don't even think like that! I lost my brother—I wasn't about to lose you, too. And I knew the detectives were interested in talking to Crystal."

"Even if it implicated John?"

"John is dead. You were alive. I wanted to make sure you stayed that way." She set the water back on the bedside table. "He didn't do anything wrong, you know."

"He didn't kill Sloane and Olivia. But he *was* trying to find Crystal. And he had that photograph. And all that . . . pornography."

Sabrina hesitated, smoothing the bedsheets. "As long as you're so clearheaded, I may as well tell you the rest. Think you're up to it?"

Kali nodded. Lying in bed and listening, she could handle. Just nothing that involved movement.

"I talked to Doug Simon. He couldn't reach you on your cell so he called the house. He didn't find any connection between Crystal's parents and the Logan family, but that doesn't matter. Turns out Crystal is adopted. And, get this"—Sabrina moved closer and folded her arms—"Sloane had a baby girl who was born the same day and at the same hospital as Crystal. Her baby had a red birthmark on her neck and jaw."

Kali remembered how the photo of the young Sloane and Reed had reminded her of Crystal. "Are you saying Crystal is Sloane's daughter?"

Sabrina nodded. "But that's only part of it. I think John was her father."

"Our brother John?"

"John and Sloane were definitely together then. And the last time he called me, to tell me Sloane was dead, he said something I didn't think anything about at the time. But now . . ."

"What was it?"

"He said, 'In hindsight, I should have married Sloane seventeen years ago. We'd all be better off.' I just assumed he was upset that she'd been killed and that he felt bad they'd been going at it over the stupid company. But now I think it was because of the baby." Sabrina paused. "Besides, Crystal has John's eyes, don't you think?"

"I never thought of it before, but you're right. There is a resemblance."

"That makes her our niece."

Kali felt an odd sensation, like warmth blooming inside her. "John's child," Kali said, in wonder. "Our niece."

Sabrina pulled a chair closer to the hospital bed. "I think Sloane recognized Crystal when she came around the house to be with Olivia. She must have told John she suspected Crystal was their daughter. Probably over dinner the night she was killed. Sloane must have been worried because Crystal disappeared so suddenly. Didn't that neighbor boy tell you she'd asked him where she could find Crystal?"

Kali nodded gingerly, with as little head movement as possible.

"John must have driven to Sloane's after their dinner that evening. Maybe he wanted to talk to her further. Or maybe he wanted to ask Olivia about Crystal. I'm betting Sloane asked for his help in locating her."

"Crystal's okay, isn't she?" Kali asked anxiously.

Sabrina nodded. "Physically, she's fine. She's with Children's Protective Services at the moment. She's only sixteen, you know. A child. I tried to get them to release her to me—"

"To you?"

"Just temporarily, although I'd love for it to be longer. Crystal is blood, but more than that, she's a scared kid who's been through hell several times over. I'm not 'licensed,' though, and bureaucratic wisdom prevailed." Sabrina's eyes burned with the injustice of the decision. "At least they didn't send her to juvie."

"Why would they? She didn't do anything wrong."

"Well, the cops are trying to figure all that out. They want to question her, but I said she needed an attorney to be there."

Kali nodded. "Good for you. They've appointed one?"

"Crystal wants *you.*"

The hospital released Kali the next afternoon. On Monday she met with Crystal and Detectives Parker and Morgan in a conference room at the main sheriff's department station—the same conference room where she and Sabrina had first learned that John was a murder suspect.

It was a room without windows, but there was carpeting on the floor, and photographs of historic Tucson hung on the wall. Not elegant, but a far cry from an interrogation room, and for that, Kali was grateful—for herself, but mostly for Crystal.

The girl—her niece—was surprisingly articulate. Dressed in jeans and a white T-shirt, and sipping a Dr Pepper provided by the detectives, she answered their questions clearly, without getting defensive or trying to gloss over her own questionable behaviors.

All three girls had posed for a guy who ran a porn Web site. Then Olivia got a role in a film produced by a "real" studio and decided she wasn't interested in "low-end" work anymore. She told Hayley and Crystal about a guy "in the business" who wanted a couple of girls to work a private party—dancing, stripping, flirting. Olivia had been to some parties like that in the past. She said the work was easy and the pay was good. If you wanted to give guys blow jobs, you'd earn even more.

Kali cringed for her, but Crystal treated the whole thing in a matter-of-fact manner.

Hayley liked the idea of getting into "real" films, Crystal said, and thought the contact might pay off. The party thing sounded better than straight stripping anyway. Crystal was simply interested in the money. It was that or panhandling, which, she confessed, she was never very good at. "It's embarrassing to beg for money," she told them somberly.

Kali wanted to ask if it wasn't equally embarrassing to have your body plastered on Internet porn sites, but she didn't want Crystal to think she was judging her. When you were all alone at sixteen, what kind of options did you have?

Crystal took a sip of soda. "That's what we expected when we showed up at the house that . . . that man told us to go to. But it turned out not to be a party at all. It was just him and a video camera. I was kind of pissed that it wasn't what he promised, but Hayley said it didn't matter. He was nice enough, and the house was nice, and he was paying us. He offered us booze and Ecstasy and coke. At first it was just posing for some photos. Then he took some video of the two of us just, you know, simple stuff. Dancing, undressing, stuff like that."

"So he didn't force you to do anything?" Michelle asked. "You did everything freely?"

Crystal nodded. "Except that Hayley was drinking a lot and snorting coke. I'd never seen her take drugs before, and I think if that man hadn't been pressuring her to take more and more, she wouldn't have." Crystal looked down at the table and wiped the tears from her eyes. "I told her to slow down, but she wouldn't listen."

"You can't blame yourself for the decisions she made," Michelle said kindly.

Crystal looked doubtful. "Anyway, he wanted to do some S&M stuff. At first it was just me and Hayley. Then he wanted to be part of it, too. That's when it all went bad. Hayley was face down on a mattress with this collar thing around her neck and a leash—" Crystal's voice broke, but when Detective Parker put her hand on the girl's, she pulled it away. "I'm okay." She took a breath. "He was on top of her and I was supposed to spank him. I did, but not hard enough, he said. Then Hayley started bucking. I could tell she was choking. I screamed and told him to stop, to get off, but he wouldn't. I tried to pull him off, but that seemed to make him fiercer. He kept riding her and she kept thrashing, and then suddenly she jerked violently and went limp."

"What happened then?"

"When he realized she was dead, he freaked. He slapped me hard across the face and started calling me names." Crystal was crying now, and Kali felt the urge to comfort her. "He made it sound like it was my fault, like if I hadn't messed up, everything would have been okay. He hit me and shoved me hard. I was afraid he was going to kill *me*, too."

Crystal paused to wipe her eyes with the back of her hand. "He was bundling Hayley up in the bedspread when I ran out of there. The man was totally crazy."

Kali felt sick. It would have been hard for her to imagine Nash as the man in Crystal's tale if Kali hadn't seen that same crazed Nash the day he shot her. What he'd done was despicable. That he'd tried to blame it on Crystal made it worse. She'd have hated him even if he hadn't tried to kill her.

But it was Crystal who Kali was focused on right then. She seemed so young. Innocent in a way that had nothing to do with whatever use she'd made of her body. Behind the facade of words, which were chillingly frank, Kali sensed a girl who was scared and confused and lonely.

That she was John's daughter made the ache in Kali's heart more agonizing. She understood Sabrina's desire to shelter Crystal. Kali felt the same.

When the interview ended, Kali walked outside into the hallway with the detectives. They explained that Nash was in custody, charged with the murder of Hayley Hendrix. They were hoping they'd have enough soon to charge him with Sloane's and Olivia's murders as well.

"I'm afraid we might not be able to pin your brother's death on him," Michelle told her. "Not with enough behind us to stand up at trial. But we do have evidence of an ATM transaction on Nash's account in the area of your brother's house the night of John's death. We've also got a credit card record showing an Internet purchase of Xanax. We'll see what the DA says."

"Just as long as Nash goes away," Kali said.

"Oh, he'll do that. You heard the girl."

Kali was a defense attorney. She knew how a witness could crumble under tough cross. "Attempted murder maybe, for shooting me," Kali told her, "but Crystal is young. I'm not sure how she'll stand up at trial."

"I doubt it'll come to that. The house where Hayley died is a vacant rental owned by an investment company Nash heads. We found the address written on a map in Hayley's car."

"You think he'll plead out on that?" Kali knew it would never happen.

Michelle shook her head. "Not just that. We searched Nash's house. We've got his gun, his phone records, his—"

"None of that is solid."

"No." Michelle grinned. "But we've also got the whole thing on film. Well, not film, but disk. He was recording everything that happened with Crystal and Hayley."

"And he was stupid enough to keep it?"

Michelle nodded. "I guess he couldn't bring himself to destroy it. I mean, if you're a sicko, action like that's got to be gold."

Kali remembered Nash saying the police would never think to tie the murders to him. Stupid, yes. But arrogant, as well. The double Achilles' heel of criminals.

"May I talk to Crystal alone?" Kali asked. "I'll just be a few minutes."

"Take your time. We're not holding her. We just need to wait until someone from Protective Services comes to pick her up."

"And then what?"

Michelle shrugged. "That's not up to us. My guess is they'll ship her home."

\* \* \*

Kali went back into the conference room. Crystal had moved from the chair to one of the framed photographs of old Tucson hanging on the wall. She had her back to Kali, but she turned at the sound of the door.

"How're you doing?" Kali asked.

Crystal shrugged. "Okay, I guess. How about you? You're the one who got shot."

"But thanks to you, Nash's aim was way off."

"Does it hurt?"

Kali nodded. "Some. But I'm going to be fine."

"I feel bad about tricking you, but I'm glad you showed up."

"I'm the one who inadvertently led Nash to you, remember?"

"He would have found me eventually." She pulled a tube of lip gloss from her jean's pocket and applied it. "I was scared all the time. It's good to have it over."

"Why didn't you go home?" Kali asked.

"Home? Where's that?" Crystal's laugh was clipped. "What's going to happen to me now?"

"I don't know. They'll probably send you back to your dad's."

"No way. He doesn't want me and I don't want to go. I'm not even his, you know. My parents adopted me. My mom said they chose me because I was special and they loved me, but all my dad cares about is his new family."

"Then foster care, maybe," Kali said slowly.

"Like Hayley? She was in foster care. You should have heard the stories she told."

"I think my sister would like to have you live with her. I don't know if the state would allow it, but—"

"Why would she do that?" Crystal asked skeptically.

"Well, she's a kind person. She has three kids of her own." *Because you're special.* Kali hesitated. "Do you know why Sloane Winslow was looking for you?"

"No, I hardly knew her. I only met her a couple of times. She was kinda strange. I don't mean bad strange. She was a nice lady. But she asked me a lot of questions about where I was from and my parents and stuff. And she made us all pose for photos." Crystal caught herself and looked at Kali, embarrassed. "Not those kinds of photos. Just, you know, the three of us hanging out. She said we were the same age as her daughter and she liked having young people around. But Olivia told me afterward that it was a lie. Mrs. Winslow didn't have any kids. So I figured she was just a little weird."

"She did have a daughter," Kali said. "She gave her up for adoption sixteen years ago. I'm pretty sure she thought you were that daughter."

"Oh, my God." Crystal's eyes widened. She moved back to the conference table and sat down again. "My God. You mean she was my . . . my birth mother?"

"I think so. And my brother was your father."

Crystal looked at Kali in stunned silence. "That would make me and my sister your aunts."

The color had begun to return to Crystal's face. Now a small smile pulled at her mouth.

"We could tell for sure with a DNA test," Kali said. "That is, if you wanted."

"So that your sister would take me, you mean?"

Kali shook her head. "No, I think Sabrina wants you to live with her regardless." She let the words sink in for a moment. "Would you like that?"

Crystal nodded. "I've never had an aunt."

"And now you've got two of them." Kali hesitated, remembering how Crystal had pulled her hand from Michelle's during the interview. "Can I give you a hug?" she asked.

"Sure, I guess." Crystal stood awkwardly.

"It's more like a half hug, considering my arm," Kali said, then slid her good arm around Crystal and hugged her. When Kali started to pull away, Crystal clung to her tightly, like a small, frightened child.

Kali pulled her close. She could feel Crystal's heart beating in syncopated time to her own. John was gone, but he was here, too. And maybe, just maybe, Kali would have a chance to know his child in ways she'd never known her brother.

# CHAPTER 52

Erling rarely stopped off for a beer after work, but the last few days he'd made a habit of it. Not simply to brace himself for the tension at home—he also needed time to dig himself out from under the bitter disappointment of being shunted off to the side of his own case. It was his own damn fault—he understood that—and the fact that he'd brought it on himself only made the disappointment harder to swallow. At least he hadn't been fired or permanently reassigned. All things considered, the lieutenant had been more than fair. Still, it rankled to watch his case coming together without him.

He saw Michelle come into the bar and head his way. "I thought I might find you here," she told him, sliding onto the stool next to his. The bartender set a napkin in front of her. "Whatever you've got on draft," she said to him.

"How'd it go?" Erling asked. Michelle had been good about keeping him in the loop, and he was grateful to her for that.

"Crystal was cooperative. We've got Nash dead to rights for Hayley. We've got a good case against him for Sloane Winslow and Olivia Perez, too. With both Crystal and Kali able to testify about his admission of guilt, and the evidence we found when we searched his house, I think the DA will go with charging him on those counts as well."

"Even without conclusive evidence?" Erling knew they'd found a gun and ammo at Nash's, but they couldn't definitively tie it to the murders. They'd also found traces of type-O blood, Sloane's blood type, on the floor mats of Nash's car, and a hand towel in his closet that matched those in Sloane's guest bath. A good defense attorney could blow holes through all of it.

"We're hoping that given the cumulative weight of what we've got, Nash will see the handwriting on the wall and agree to a deal. The specter of death row is usually a big motivator."

"Let's hope so in this case." Erling took a sip of his beer and grimaced. He wasn't much of a drinker, and after the first couple of sips, beer didn't have a lot of appeal for him.

"Crystal is one tough little cookie," Michelle added. "And I mean that in the best way. She'll do fine on the witness stand."

Sloane's daughter. It brought a lump to his throat imagining how Sloane must have felt when she realized the sort of life her child had been subjected to. Sloane, who devoted so much energy to rescuing people, had failed to protect her own daughter. He could understand now how desperate she must have been when the girl suddenly disappeared.

In the aftermath of Erling's apology to Mindy, she'd confessed that "some woman" had called weeks earlier about a missing girl, and that she had neglected to give him the message. That accounted for the listing of Sloane's number on the phone's caller ID readout. Sloane had called the station the next day to inquire about their Jane Doe, but she'd presumably still been waiting for Erling to return her call.

The bartender slid Michelle's glass across the bar to her. "What amazes me, as always," Michelle said, "is how a person can turn one mistake—admittedly a horrendous one in this case—into something so much worse. If Nash had come clean from the start, he'd probably be looking at manslaughter.

With the murders of Sloane Winslow and Olivia Perez, not to mention John O'Brien, he's upped the ante to multiple counts of premeditated murder."

A heaviness tugged at Erling's chest. He understood how easily even a rational, well-meaning man could compound a mistake. "It's surprisingly easy to fool yourself into thinking you can cover up a wrong," he said. "Believe me, I know."

"You corrected things, Erling. In the end, you did what was right."

Would he have come forward if Kali O'Brien hadn't found out about his affair with Sloane? Erling wanted to think so, but in truth, he didn't know. If John O'Brien were still alive, he might be in jail right now facing trial for murder. An innocent man wrongly accused all because of Erling's own self-serving weakness. He was having a hard time looking at himself in the mirror these days.

Michelle seemed ready to say more, then changed the subject. "I know you weren't the one who leaked information to Carmen Escobar, by the way," she said.

"Is this part of your renewed faith in me?"

"Well, that, but it also turns out she's dating a guy in records." Michelle traced a squiggly line in the condensation on the side of her mug. "How are things at home?"

"There are some signs of a thaw, but there's a lot of tension, too." He chewed on his lower lip. "It's Deena I worry about most. Not how she's treating me but what I did to her. The hurt and damage I caused by thinking only of myself."

"Sounds like that's a step in the right direction."

Erling nodded, though he wasn't convinced. His concern about his wife's feelings might be a case of too little too late. "That idea you had," Erling said to Michelle, "the cruise? Deena said she'd think about it." This offered him a glimmer of hope. He was trying not to hang his heart on it, but it was all he had at the moment.

"That's good." Michelle offered a smile of encouragement. "Most of us are willing to forgive a lot when we know the regret is heartfelt."

"I'm hoping that's so. I can't imagine my life without

her." Erling checked his watch. "Speaking of which . . . I need to be going." He reached for his wallet, set a twenty on the bar, then slid off his bar stool. "I know I let you down, too, Michelle. I'm sorry. Genuinely sorry."

"I know you are, Erling."

"You okay being partnered with me still?"

"I wouldn't have it any other way."

He grinned. "Good. I wouldn't have it any other way, either."

# CHAPTER 53

The sun was a bright orange ball on the horizon. As Kali sipped her champagne, she watched it slowly sink into the ocean beyond the Golden Gate. Back in her own home, nestled on the sofa next to Bryce, her dog, Loretta, snoring softly at her feet, and the tingle of champagne in her veins, she felt content for the first time in weeks.

"I talked to my sister this afternoon," Kali said, adjusting her arm in its sling. "It's only been a couple of days, but Crystal seems to be doing well. And the boys are going out of their way to make her feel welcome."

Bryce squeezed her free hand. "Good for them. I hope it lasts."

"I'm sure it won't. There'll be ups and downs, but they are basically nice kids, so I think it will be okay in the end. And Sabrina, for once in her life, seems to have a grasp on reality."

Kali knew Crystal was better off with Sabrina than here with her. Sabrina had a husband and children, and she knew how to open her heart to others. Still, there was a part of Kali that would have liked Crystal with her. "I'm going there for Christmas this year," Kali said. "And then Crystal is going to come home with me for the week until school starts again."

"I'm missing you already."

"You could come, too."

Bryce gave her a quizzical look, then smiled. "I might just do that." He sipped his champagne. "Are the DNA results in yet?"

Kali shook her head. "We don't really need them, though. Crystal's father confirmed that Sloane and John both signed the adoption release. It was a private adoption but everything was done legally."

"And he doesn't have a problem that his daughter is going to be living with Sabrina?"

Kali laughed. "Hardly. Especially when he found out it wasn't going to cost him anything."

"What a stand-up dad."

"My thoughts exactly. No wonder Sloane was so eager to find Crystal. She thought she'd done right by her baby and found her a good home. And it probably was until Ray realized he was no longer the center of attention and went off to get his jollies elsewhere. Even then, Martha seems to have been a devoted mother."

The doorbell rang and Loretta sprang to her feet, barking. Kali pulled herself off the sofa and went to answer it. Her neighbor Margot stood there with a plate in her hand.

"I won't keep you," Margot said, in a conspiratorial tone. "I see by his car in front that Stud Muffin is here. But I made some fudge and wanted to bring it to you. Sort of a welcome-home gift."

"Thanks." Kali took the plate and decided not to think about the calories. Margot's fudge was to die for. "I should be giving *you* a gift. I really appreciate you keeping Loretta for me."

"Any time. You know that." Margot craned her neck to look over Kali's shoulder and then winked at Kali. "Enjoy your evening. We'll talk later."

"Stud Muffin?" Bryce said when the door closed.

Kali handed him the plate of fudge. "That's Margot's impression."

"Wonderful. Margot's a man."

Kali made a so-so gesture with her hand. "Whatever, she makes fantastic fudge."

"What about you?"

"Me? I'm a lousy cook."

"No. I mean, do you think I'm sexy?"

Kali grinned. "You know the answer to that."

"I wouldn't mind hearing you say it."

She leaned forward and whispered in his ear, "You're the sexiest man I know."

Bryce grinned. He refilled their glasses with champagne, then returned to the sofa. "Can I ask you something?"

"Sure."

"How involved were you, really, with A. J. Nash?"

Kali turned. Her eyes found Bryce's. "We went out once for drinks and then when I had some questions, we met once for Chinese food."

"And the Desert Museum?"

"He offered to show it to me. I never took him up on it. Why? Are you jealous?"

"Should I be?"

Kali didn't hesitate. "Not at all."

"I really missed you, you know." Bryce leaned back and took her free hand in his, caressing her palm with his thumb. "Sometimes I wish I understood you better."

"That makes two of us."

He smiled wanly. "Seriously, Kali. Do you think we have a future together?"

She brought his hand to her lips. "I hope so. I really do hope so." And she did. She'd come to see a lot of things differently in these last couple of weeks. Not the least of how she tended to distance herself from those she cared about.

The phone rang and Kali groaned. "I'll let the machine get it."

A few seconds later, Jared's voice boomed through the room. "Hey, boss, you coming in tomorrow? Daryl Jensen's at it again. Says he was just trying to bring the baby a present but his ex called the cops. The hearing's at eleven." He paused. "It will be good to have you back. Things get kind of dull around here without you."

"I should let him know I'll be there," Kali said reluctantly.

"I'll bring you the phone in a minute." Bryce traced his fingers along the back of her neck. "About the future—I'm banking on it, okay?"

A warm glow that had nothing to do with the champagne filled Kali's veins. She felt her eyes tear with happiness, and when Bryce went to fetch the telephone, she brushed the tears away.

He handed her the phone. "Whether your shoulder's healed or not, I guess it's back to life as usual."

Kali nodded. But nothing was really the same as before. She was a woman who'd lost a brother, as well as the years when she might have grown closer to him. A woman with newfound appreciation for the sister she'd so often found irritating. A woman with a new niece she was looking forward to knowing better, and—she let herself acknowledge it—a man she might be falling in love with.